Second Chances

Book Two of

The Maryland Shores

Lauren Monroe

Shore Thing Publishing

Second Chances

Book Two of The Maryland Shores

ISBN-13: 978-0-9912822-2-7 (eBook)
ISBN-13: 978-0-9912822-3-4 (print)
ISBN-13: 978-0-9912822-5-8 (large print)
Copyright © 2015 by Lauren Monroe

For information about this or regarding subsidiary rights, contact Shore Thing Publishing at shorethingpublishing@gmail.com

This is a work of fiction. Apart from well-known, historical people, data and events, all names, characters, products, places, and other content are the product of the author's imagination and is used fictitiously, with no relation to anyone bearing the same name(s) and circumstances. Any resemblance to actual persons, living or dead, business establishments, organizations, events, or locales, known or unknown to the author, is entirely coincidental and is used for characterization and other elements in this fictional narrative. West Riverside Hospital Center, Better Days Therapy Associates, Benefits Plan Provider Services, Three Rivers Primary Care, Shore Landings, and Crazy Vinny's Pawn Shop have been created fictitiously for the purpose of this novel series.

Cover Photo by Shore Thing Publishing/Click Twice Design
Shore Thing Publishing: Queenstown, Maryland

www.laurenmonroenovels.com
www.facebook.com/lauren.monroe.novels

For questions, comments, or to contact the author, please email
shorethingpublishing@gmail.com

The publisher is not responsible for websites or Internet content that has not been generated by the author or Shore Thing Publishing.

First Printing: June 2015; Large Print: October 2016;
Second Printing January 2017

To Bob

My Italian guy,
who taught me to appreciate
European style,
Italian cooking and culture,
and with whom I share a lot
of nautical fun.
Ti amo!

Other Women's Fiction
by Lauren Monroe

Letting Go:
Book One of The Maryland Shores

Books available in large print also

Chapter 1

Liz Kramer sat with clients in her office. Her stomach grumbled since she had given up her lunch hour so that this couple could use theirs. To kill each other.

"How can you be such an ass?" the wife asked. "You're no help. I work part-time, have three kids, and all the responsibility."

"Kids you're suing me over," her husband barked. "Bleed me dry and blame me. While you carry on like a cougar, I have a career."

"Me? One date. He's only three years younger. You're the one who screwed the college intern right on your desk." The woman shot Liz a steely gaze. "Because your boss walked in and put you on probation isn't my problem, you..."

"Women: all bitches. I'm through with this one." The man squared his shoulders toward Liz.

"We have five minutes left to this session." Liz glanced at the red numerals flashing the time on the clock facing her. "Let's take a minute." Drawing a breath herself, she held it before visibly letting it go. Modeling good behavior she hoped for two sparring, soon-to-be ex-spouses at opposite ends of the upholstered sofa in the offices of Better Days Therapy Associates.

"If this is about Ricky and school, why are we talking about us?" Mrs. Maloney wasn't the least bit improved by the therapeutic intervention. "He's the one who got suspended."

The child with parental stress, Liz thought. This session had brought as much awareness as had the last one. None. Liz fluffed a layer of her short brown hair that normally dangled across her brow. She didn't dare glance at the small calendar she used for scheduling. This situation would take all of 2003. It was merely February.

"Mr. Maloney, your son was suspended from kindergarten, speaking out of turn from what your referral indicates." Liz left out the nice butt comment the boy had made to his teacher. And weirdo Ricky had lobbed, landing him in a sexual harassment dispute. At age six.

"Well, maybe she deserved it," the boy's father returned. "I teach my boy to stand up for himself." Now smirking, he turned to the boy's mother. "At least he said nice butt, not nice ass."

"Enough! Talk about harassment," Mrs. Maloney shouted into the small space they shared. "This is so embarrassing, Ms. Kramer. What about our son's issues?"

"I hear your concern," Liz said. "Ricky looks to you as parents for guidance. He'll join these sessions next week." She wondered how that would go the minute she said it. "I'd like you to each bring at least six values you'd like to impart to him." *Peacefully.* Would Ricky still be a client at age 25 if these sparks kept flying?

Mr. Maloney huffed on his way out. Mrs. Maloney sought refuge in the restroom before letting the door close with a thud. Liz inched open the blinds. No bloodshed in the parking lot.

Looking at her wall—with her maiden name Kramer framed on her degree and license as a clinical social worker and therapist—she recited the marketing line her employer used. *We bring calm and positivity into your world.*

Because she had to share her office, Liz kept few personal effects. Needing calm, she took a photo out of her drawer, a candid taken last summer on the Chesapeake Bay with her two kids and her husband piloting their boat. Liz picked up the phone and punched her husband's number.

"Tim Phillips here."

"Hi, worse days for me with chaos and negativity in *my* world."

"One of those, huh? Done today?" he asked.

"I earned the long weekend. Weather update?"

"Starting out as rain, turning into snow."

"Tim, I'd like to get across the bridge, beyond Annapolis traffic and settled at Maren's. Your suit is set out with my dress."

"Liz, I'm really behind. With the forecast, lucky if I show any homes this weekend."

"What are you saying, Tim?" Her reply was razor sharp much like Liz's fingernails now tapping on her desk. Eliciting information from people was her day job, made more frustrating when pressed to use the same skill with her husband. Who says *use your words* to a 37-year-old?

"About the dinner tonight, I have to work."

"We're talking about the event Mom chaired and labored over since New Year's!" Liz hoped that reality cut a bit deeper.

Dolores Kramer expected them all at this benefit. She and Bill Kramer had spent a pretty penny hosting a table, especially for Liz's brother Steve. After many adult decades as a bachelor, he had popped the question and gotten a yes. While the wedding wasn't until June, the engagement celebration would take place tonight.

"You better take Hannah and Tyler without me. We'll have Steve and Maren over for dinner. Your parents won't even notice."

Tim Phillips was married more to real estate than her older brother had been to surgery. Triangles people create, Liz thought. Some men put their hobbies between them and their relationships. Tim had a 36-foot, twin-engine powerboat, but as Liz's blood began to boil, not even a swim off their dock in the frigid Chesapeake would temper the heat she felt this February afternoon.

"Liz...you there?"

"I'm here Tim. I guess I need to get Hannah at daycare and meet Tyler's bus?" She swallowed hard. "Which means I have to run."

"My best to the happy couple; see 'ya Monday."

Liz heard the call click off in Tim's seemingly anxious return to work, without saying three words that would have gone a long way.

Saying *I love you* would have conveyed something. *Happy Valentine's Day* would have been even more appropriate.

The center lane of the Chesapeake Bay Bridge allowed Liz a clip speed to pass tourists unfamiliar with the four-mile journey. Ever since she had quit her job in hospital casework and moved from the Baltimore apartment she had reluctantly shared years ago with her brother Steve, Liz was happiest on Maryland's Eastern Shore.

"Count the boats," she reminded her kids. Every car ride promised a different view. For Liz, this one failed to relax her mind.

She had met Tim at a bar in Baltimore's Inner Harbor after work in 1994. The minute she saw that wide smile played off his perfect set of teeth, Liz knew Tim found her irresistible. What she'd give to have recent evidence of that grin, that playful demeanor he showed off on Ravens weekends when they traveled to away games. Now Tim barely reserved recreation for Tyler and Hannah. He combed the multi-list more than his sandy hair and polished his BMW that chauffeured clients more than he helped at home.

Their courtship culminated November 1995 exchanging vows in Chevy Chase, just outside Washington, DC. Real estate license in hand, they left city life for Stevensville, the first real town on Kent Island across the Chesapeake Bay.

"Isn't this the perfect place to raise a family?" That was the promise: all tucked away from traffic lights and western shore drivers who raced only to slam on their brakes. On the island, Tim and Liz found subdivisions along the rural landscape—a close-knit community if you didn't mind a major highway running through it, all too busy in the summer. But then, it was that wide expanse of blue that made this a special and tranquil place to call home especially with the waterfront property Tim had brokered for them.

Since their children came along, Liz had never enjoyed a leisurely summer with them there. If she got pregnant again, Liz would take time off to be with Tyler, Hannah and a baby. She would write a business plan, for her own private practice, and fulfill all of her dreams within her 30s.

Not bad, considering her younger brother Eric, a 25-year-old professional student, spent more time with his band than with his books or his girlfriend. Steve would turn 40 in April and walk down the aisle in June, settling the endorphins that had ruled him since he met Maren. Wasn't love the essence of this very day?

"He stole my Valentine box," Hannah squealed as Liz steered her Toyota Highlander south of Annapolis. Fifteen minutes, barring traffic.

In first-grade, Tyler Phillips both admired and tolerated his three-year-old sister Hannah. Much like herself and Steve, Liz mused.

"Give it back Tyler," Liz directed. "You know better than to grab things." If her thoughts weren't elsewhere, she would have reminded to DEBUG. The mnemonic stood for: Do ignore, Exit or move away, Be friendly, Use firm words and Get help. Not so easy to effect the first three when strapped into a car seat. Hannah had seemingly mastered the last two steps.

"One's from a boy. I thought Uncle Steve was your sweetheart?"

"I'm *his* sweetheart you goof. Give it back. Mommy said."

Tyler complied. Liz asked her children about the parties they had, and they about the one she would fancy herself for. No one dared touch the gown laid flat atop suitcases in the back.

"There's Dylan," Tyler shouted. "Stop the car!"

Liz pulled over and lowered her window with the driver's door button. "Hey, want a ride?" Liz saw Dylan Mitchell, Maren's six-year-old, stop in his tracks. He carried a decorated shoebox under one arm as he jostled his backpack higher.

"I can drive you down the street," Liz told him.

"No rides from strangers," Hannah said.

"Quiet!" Tyler corrected. "Get in, dude." Tyler scooted over when Liz unlocked the doors.

"We're almost cousins," Dylan said, hopping into the back seat. "Thanks. Hi Hannah."

In the rear mirror, Liz saw a smile. Going for the older guys, reciprocating Dylan's schoolboy crush, Hannah certainly was her daughter.

Liz pulled her gold Highlander into the driveway within minutes. After she unbuckled Hannah and popped the hatch, Liz clutched the dry cleaning bag showcasing her dress. "Tyler, not so fast. Grab a few things. You, too, Hannah."

The kids had packed a duffle and rolling case to stay the night. Maren arranged a sitter for all three children. Tomorrow, Liz would take hers to her parents' bayside home in Southern Maryland for President's Day weekend. Liz had spent most summers there as a teen, occasionally with a boyfriend, until Steve found one pawing at Liz and put the fear of God into him. That boyfriend was history; Steve's God complex remained. Pumped up surely by tonight's tony charity ball.

Timed to occur during Heart Health Month, this was the signature event of the West Riverside Hospital Foundation, founded by her late Grandfather Kramer. A heart attack had cut short his life years earlier.

Since its inception, Dolores and Bill Kramer had hosted a table. Liz would dine along with Steve, his fiancée Maren, her parents Audrey and Jack Cole, Eric and date Shelly, and believe it or not, Hilary and Brad Morgan, parents of Steve's unrequited love. Shelly's as well. Liz understood the complexities there, but as three kids bounded into Maren's house, she refocused.

"Where's Tim?" Maren extended her arm and held the front door. The kids had charged up to Dylan's room. A chill blew into the foyer.

"Not here."

Maren searched Liz's face. "I'll take that." She slung an arm under the bag. "Be right back."

The kids got away with quickly discarded jackets at home, but Liz stooped down and hung them up. Her brother would likely have revealed her disheveled habits. Thank God she and Steve had only shared his apartment for a brief stint.

Liz heard Maren trot down the stairs. She massaged the forearms through the sleeves of her chunky knit purple sweater.

"Fire's nice," Liz said. She took a seat on the stone hearth in hopes the crackling heat would melt her frosty mood. "Tim bailed on us. Says he has to work. Who the hell works the weekend when WBAL predicts a snow free-for-all?"

"He really thinks he's going to show houses?"

"Yeah," Liz replied, her attention diverted by the laughter one story up. "I'm pissed." She looked at Maren. "You watch your language, but mine's going to pieces. And on Valentine's Day."

"Cupid can go to Hell this evening, huh?" Maren held sympathy in her eyes. "How about hot cocoa? I was going to offer the kids some."

"That'd be great." A half-smile played on Liz's lips, partly because Maren swore, validating how this sucked, a word she couldn't picture Maren using at all. Stacked boxes, labeled with heavy black marker, lined a distant wall. "How's the packing?" Liz asked.

"My third job, fourth with wedding planning. I got more assembled while I worked from home today." Maren poured milk into cups fixed with cocoa. She punched the microwave to warm two at a time and called the kids down. "These have lids, but be careful not to spill," she told them. "We have to keep this place in good shape."

Thankfully, Liz thought, Maren didn't mention the new house—the one workaholic Tim brokered for her and Steve. "Your department helped with tonight's event. Bet that kept you busy."

"We just promote it," Maren replied. "Alicia brought on another marketing associate at the end of December. Gabe has helped a lot. I'll introduce you." Maren pulled their mugs out of the microwave and offered one to Liz. "Speaking of December...Paul's wife Vicki is in the hospital again. I can't believe everything they're going through. I'm afraid for them."

"What's happening with Vicki's pregnancy? Steve said she was hospitalized in Pittsburgh at Christmas, something with her autoimmune condition." Liz matched Maren's justifiable worry. "How's Paul doing through all of this?"

"Paul's obviously concerned about Vicki taking certain medications. Her lupus flared." Maren's face froze into a fretful cringe. "You can ask him yourself. Steve emailed me two words: Mission Accomplished. Colluded with Vicki to get him away from her room a few hours. Your mom added one more to our table."

"Makes sense. He's your best man." Liz had enthusiastically agreed to be the couple's other honor attendant. Paul was the friend who had lured Steve from Hopkins in order to join him at West Riverside Hospital Center, south of Annapolis, at the end of the '90s. Sharing apartments with Steve through medical school and residency, Paul was like a third brother to Liz.

She savored another sip of the steamy cocoa. "I won't feel so awkward if I'm not the only one going stag." She looked up, holding back tears. "Whatever you put in here is delicious."

"Extra chocolate shavings." Maren clutched her own mug and took a seat on the hearth. "Payback for all your encouragement last fall."

"How are your former in-laws, the Mitchell's, taking your decision to keep your current job?"

"The contempt seeps through each time they call for Dylan," Maren replied. "I was polite, but assertive. Remarriage is a sin greater than rejecting Walter's offer to work for the family firm."

"You deserve it after what life has handed you," Liz said. "Working there would grant the Mitchell's control. Happy people don't dictate."

"Agreed. They're probably upset that I have Steve, the new house. If they knew I had a sister-in-law I can actually relate to..." Maren bumped her shoulder into Liz, who washed with emotion.

Liz studied her mug. "I love the colorful crabs on this: blue, plus red and steamed. Like me." Before a tear dropped into her cocoa, Liz dug into her pants pocket for a tissue. "Such a special night, officially announcing your engagement, and here I am a sniveling mess."

"You're not sniveling. I don't know Tim well. It is Valentine's Day, and your mom put a lot of work into this. I'd be pissed too." Maren pulled Liz snug to wrap an arm over her shoulders.

"Cursing for my benefit—sign of a sister. Forget the in-law part," Liz said. "I love my brothers but Dr. Chief of Surgery Kramer will probably come down on my husband's side."

"When people work late, it never fazes Steve. Unless it's me, in marketing." When Liz cast a sideways glance, Maren rolled her eyes. "I work with Gabe, who is single, just a year older than me, and my shadow at work."

"My brother can't get you before a minister fast enough." Liz laughed that out.

Maren hesitated. "Obviously we've monopolized Tim. He's hauled us around house after house. At January's gift exchange, Tim showed properties then, too. He puts in long days."

"No one sees him." Liz pivoted to look at Maren straight on. "Don't get me wrong. The pictures of your new spread in Shore Landings look amazing. The market's strong. Tim's a top agent." Liz bit her lip and considered her words. "I cut my hours because he's done well. It has let me spend time with the kids, but it's lonely."

"Lonely I can speak to." Two years ago this May, Maren buried Mark, who died following a violent car accident leaving her a young widow. "We better get the kids fed. It's almost five. If you want to get ready, go ahead."

"No, this is your night. Wearing your hair long or pinning it up?" Liz asked.

"Up," Maren said. "Sometimes I wish I had an easy cut like yours."

"But you get to restyle, have more fun." Liz laughed. "Go. Point me to the fridge."

"You sure?" Maren caught herself. "I mean…"

"My brother told you I know nothing outside of mixers and baking," Liz interrupted. They both rose from the hearth and walked a few feet when Liz saw Maren curl her lips. "I knew it."

"Perfect kiddo meal, complete with baking sheet." Maren handed Liz the tray along with a pack of chilly crescent rolls, a bag of grated cheese and an eight-pack of hot dogs from the refrigerator. "Dylan loves these baked together. Carrots and ranch dip in there, too."

"Got it," Liz assured her. "You go. I'm not glamming." Why bother? Late-night action after the gala would not be found in the guest room.

"Come in," Paul Romano said, after he heard knuckles on his wife Vicki's hospital room door. He looked up from the easy chair where he sat as his best friend Steve Kramer walked in.

"How's it going?" Steve whispered.

"She's faking sleep so I keep quiet."

Vicki's eyes were closed. She looked peaceful, a good sign since she'd been admitted yesterday to the maternity wing at West Riverside Hospital Center to monitor her pregnancy.

"He's hovering Steve," Vicki answered. The Italian eyes Paul loved opened wide. Expressive. Endearing. Sexy, even when she wasn't well. "Forcibly remove him, will 'ya please."

"He wouldn't dare." Paul held his chin high. "I have fans in this hospital."

Paul's false bravado added what his 5'8" build did not. When people spotted his Mediterranean complexion, dark hair and eyes, they would often mistake him for Al Pacino. When asked if he was indeed the actor, Paul joked: "Do you want my autograph?"

Paul was a surgeon and an internist. The former put Paul under his best friend Steve's direction since he was chief; the latter made Paul all too aware of the risks his wife and unborn baby faced with her autoimmune disorder.

Steve, towering over Paul, walked closer. Smiled. "The patient's always right."

Palms to the sheets, Vicki straightened in her bed. No position hid her very pregnant status. "You're the guest of honor, Steve. What time is it? Shouldn't you both be going?"

"Shortly after five. Cocktails start at seven," Steve said. "I'm only the honoree at my mother's table. We'll miss you and Baby Romano."

"Maren stopped yesterday. Give her my congratulations again," Vicki told him. "I'm watching a movie, something other than Sophia Loren. Paul's favorite."

"It sucks confined to bed rest," Steve said.

"All for a good cause," Paul added.

Vicki made eye circles. "You have a good time and celebrate our friend's achievement."

"Your mom, like mine, must breathe easily now that you're settling down," Paul added. Getting their friend to an altar was a straight-up accomplishment. Looks would have landed him there at 19, but Steve Kramer had driven his surgical career to the success it was now.

"Affirmative." Steve smiled. "I miss hanging around her kitchen, smelling the oregano."

Paul furthered Steve's recollections. "A different sauce simmering every other day."

"Only Dolores Kramer hasn't had to settle quite as much," Steve added smugly, "like you…every other day." The wicked gleam in his eye wasn't lost on Paul, who knew the remark signified his own steady parade of women back in their apartment days. Steve had the stability of a live-in girlfriend. Paul's room resembled one of those revolving rides at a playground.

"Watch it," Paul replied. "I'm the good child."

"How you've deceived that poor woman," Steve shot back. "By the way, you're now at our table with Tim and Liz, Eric and Shelly, the Morgans, and Maren's parents."

"I'll dial it back. Until the best-man's toast."

"You'll keep that clean, too," Vicki chided as her hands moved to her abdomen, as if to shield the adult banter from tender ears still in utero. She grimaced. "Another soccer kick, I swear."

Paul settled a hand to feel it also. "Baby's killing your joy. You're killing mine." He brushed dark hair away from those stunning eyes and kissed her forehead. "Amoré."

Vicki kissed Paul's cheek and returned the same. She sighed happily.

Paul patted Baby Romano. "Take care of little Valentino." Raising his dark brows, he added, "Yes, Valentino Romano."

"Paul, absolutely not," Vicki said. "Both of you: Out of those white coats and into tuxedos."

Vicki Romano would have pushed her husband into the hallway. Since she couldn't, Steve yanked Paul's sleeve.

"Come on, you heard her. Goodnight, Vicki," Steve said.

Chapter 2

Paul Romano flicked a stray hair from his tuxedo. He and Steve had changed at work. Walking into the country club, they diverged from the beeline others made into the ballroom.

Paul glanced at his watch: 7:15. Time to cozy up to the betrothed. He hugged Maren. "Have to admit, I'm molto bello." A classic black tux set off by a navy blue cummerbund. "Can I keep it?"

Maren used tonight to test colors for her upcoming wedding. "Yes, you can." Her arms enveloped Paul in return. "How's Vicki?"

"Sends her love." He gave Maren the once-over. "Una bella donna."

A black, strapless gown, clung to her hips this Valentine's Day. A strand of pearls with matching earrings drew attention to her face and to her hair, the color of chocolate with auburn streaks. Before tonight, Steve had never seen it done up in a chignon, long tendrils hanging, softening everything about her, and inviting his touch.

"You look delicious." Steve kissed Maren on the lips. "If I hadn't met you here, I'd have made you late," he whispered. One set of fingers tucked a loose tendril behind her ear while the other ran over her curves.

"You *are* late." Maren met his eyes. Nudged him to notice his sister.

"Liz, where's…" A second jolt caused Steve to hush any *ouch* and see Liz's scowl.

"Not here," Liz interrupted. "Tim's working."

"Tonight?" If his sister answered his terse question, she might dissolve into tears, so instead Steve pulled Liz in tight. "That sucks," he whispered. "His loss. You look amazing."

Paul Romano knew Liz Phillips, introduced to her as Liz Kramer when she was a 20-year-old co-ed home from UNC. Her spring break began the same weekend Steve had helped Paul escape from dissections and advanced anatomy in med school. If studying Liz's torso had granted him a semester grade, Paul would have earned an accelerated A and welcomed more extra credit.

"Ditto." Paul ended the awkward silence and pecked Liz's cheek as he'd done Maren's. "I'm alone tonight. We'll make the best of it." He thrust his upturned palm for Liz to follow Steve and Maren into the ballroom.

"I feel bad. Vicki's not well and she's your Valentine," Liz confided into Paul's ear.

It made him stop and turn to Liz. "I echo Steve. All work and no play?" Paul jiggled his brows. "Tim's loss, and yeah I'd love to have Vicki here. Certainly in better colors though."

Paul smirked. "The way that purple clings making the black sheen shine forth. How convenient?" He distanced from the purple and black, Liz's NFL choice, not his. This *was* Maryland, after all. "That's so Italian though." Paul's lips curled to the chandeliers. "Gold would still look better with the black sheen."

"Bought it off the rack. Besides, gold is a holiday color," Liz shot back. "No Valentine red in my closet. Lavender, mauve, lilac…purple."

Paul clutched his chest. He would never wear the colors of his hometown's rival team.

"My brother cautioned 15 years ago to keep you 20 yards away." Liz laughed. Paul Romano then, probably now, was fussy about food, smug about his nationality, razor sharp with wit…and wild about women, until Vicki had tamed him.

"*Warned you*," Paul teased.

"With an oversized exclamation point. *Do not touch* added along the bottom."

"This is good." He tugged her arm back from the line of couples. "What else did he say?"

"Paul, you're so silly." Liz felt Paul's hand still clutch her upper arm. "Seriously, he said you had a good heart—one that would send out a gold line in an EKG." Liz paused. "And that warning sign for you. Same *do not touch*."

"My black and gold makes Pittsburgh proud." He held his head even higher as he let go and they kept walking. Converting one member of the Maryland-based Kramer family to black and gold status ranked right up there with passing two board certifications. "We know who inherited the sports genes," Paul quipped as they made their way to the Kramer table. "And who didn't."

"Steve? He's malleable." Liz laughed. "Wait, Vicki's from Baltimore. Not a Ravens fan?"

"I broke that one habit." Paul broke up. His mirth wasn't contagious enough to turn Liz's mood when her eyes traveled to the place cards. *Mr. & Mrs.* appeared beautifully scripted in calligraphy on most. And then there was hers.

16

"Mrs. K., you look stunning." Paul's lips landed on Dolores Kramer's cheek. Her white hair belied her 63 years, Paul thought. She always had such energy and affection for her brood, which included him over the years.

"How's Vicki?" Dolores leaned into Paul's open arms then pulled away to hug her daughter, now too frustrated to argue any Pittsburgh vs. Baltimore rivalry.

"She had a decent few hours today, but feels totally drained," Paul answered. "On bed rest."

"I'm so sorry," Dolores said, looking across her shoulder where fellow committee member Hilary Morgan whispered a question into her ear. "Excuse me, just one minute, Paul. Duty calls."

"Of course." Paul nodded hello to Hilary and turned to Liz. "You're still frowning."

"Last minute shuffling and obvious redesign." Liz lowered her place card. *Elizabeth Kramer Phillips.* "Only my mother calls me Elizabeth."

"It's a place card, Liz. Not a Harvard diploma." His dark eyes moved. "Hors d'oeuvres?"

"Yes, please," Liz managed. She inhaled through flared nostrils. Tried to flex her face. Otherwise, it would appear spitting-mad over Tim's absence on such a special night.

Dolores had heard Liz's complaints. After she finished committee business, she softened to Liz—the polar opposite, eye-searing Kramer-woman look she'd surely save for her son-in-law.

"Maren alerted me. I'm sorry, honey." Dolores clutched Liz's wrist. "Put it out of your mind for the weekend. Pounce on him next week."

Liz bobbed her chin. She drew in another cleansing breath determined to keep the moisture from spilling out of her brown eyes.

Dolores gave her one last squeeze, letting go so that Liz could take a plate Paul handed her. "The crab dip's fabulous," Dolores suggested.

"Thanks, Paul." Liz popped a stuffed mushroom into her mouth.

The frown on Dolores told Paul she'd taught Liz better manners than to eat it whole. Paul returned a what-am-I-to-do-with-her smile. Dolores patted Paul's tux before greeting Maren's parents who had just found the table.

Maren deposited her evening bag on her chair. She introduced Paul to both parents though Jack had become one of Paul's new patients. Then, Maren steered Liz, plate in hand, to another table.

"Gabe Furtinski, I'd like you to meet Liz, my soon-to-be sister-in-law. Liz, Gabe's new and a Godsend for this event," Maren declared.

Straining his neck, Maren's co-worker offered a hand, with energy in his strong grip. He looked younger and every bit the color coordinator. His lavender shirt met a deep purple cummerbund.

"Radiance abounds in your family." Gabe beamed broadly. His eyes shifted lower, admiring more. It mattered not that his own date, the graduate student also helping with this event, stood feet away chatting with their boss, Alicia.

"I've heard good things about you," Liz said.

"Gabe and I were graphic design classmates," Maren explained. "He's still the best flirt."

"You ladies give me good reason," Gabe defended. He flicked his blonde hair and punched up his shoulders. Leaning toward Liz, he continued, "I love your dress."

He should. He could have redesigned it, for his eyes gave the dress, and Liz, thorough study, especially her cleavage. She blushed.

Maren caught Steve motioning for her. "If you'll excuse me...more people to meet." Gabe stepped aside as Maren left them alone.

"The Morgans," Liz told Gabe. "Brad and Hilary, the parents of Shelly who dates my other brother Eric, and parents of Pam, who thankfully dumped my brother years ago."

"Not a verb frequently applied to the esteemed Dr. Steve Kramer." Gabe watched for a reaction.

"Good one, Gabe." Liz leaned into him, and in an unmistakable hush, replied, "I love my brother, but he's full of himself."

"Most surgeons are...ah, here." Gabe quickly added with Paul Romano hovering.

"Purple has met purple, I see." Paul prodded them, remembering that he had seen Gabe wear a Ravens tie at work. He noted also that Liz stood without a beverage though Mr. Baltimore kept sipping out of his glass. "Liz, what can I get you? A seven and seven?" Paul asked.

"A purple passion." Liz laughed.

Paul rolled his eyes, giving Liz the secondary gain her little dig desired. Liz captured Gabe's attention, boasting about Ed Reed's stellar season, but lamenting losses to the Steelers.

"That's OK, we'll meet 'em back at The Bank next year," Gabe bragged as Paul returned.

"Sure will," Liz doled out. Gabe cast a jeer at Paul before excusing himself.

"Drink up, Liz," Paul said. "It's as lavender as they could make it."

"You just cannot say purple," Liz teased.

"Looks like Gabe realized he has a date." Paul pulled back Liz's chair next to his.

"Oh Paul, he kept me company while you got my drink," Liz said as she took her seat. "Two men seeing after me. I love it."

"Bet you couldn't care less if Tim Phillips is stuck with competing offers and challenged appraisals the rest of the weekend."

"Hell no," Liz whispered close enough that her breath felt warm on Paul. "Cold rain could have collapsed the gutters before the client final walk-through today." Liz nodded to Maren's parents and to the Morgans, who joined their table. She leaned over Paul's shoulder to say, "And Tim can land on his butt in the ice since I didn't get to kick it." She clenched her lips.

"*A donna arrabbiata*." Paul moved his head back to assess her. "A bitter, angry woman, Liz."

"Not driving." She downed grape juice, vodka and triple sec. "I'll go home with Steve." Liz had to snap her fingers to conjure his name.

"Steve the Stud, my new name for him."

"Oh please, his head is big enough."

Their meal brightened Liz. She elbowed Paul when he offered to switch his cream of crab, calling her a cranky crab at that. She stuck with oysters on the half shell, probably delivered fresh that day from local watermen.

"Stop." Liz quirked up her lips and admonished Paul for his Roman myths. "Oysters are *not* aphrodisiacs, and you men just perpetuate that." Paul had their dinner companions laughing until the champagne shifted the mood to serious.

Bill Kramer, with a hint of gray highlighting his hair, got the attention of everyone at the table with what he called the Kramer recipe for true contentment in life. "Ten percent of luck starts out the secret. Enjoying what you work at every day is 30 percent of the mix and embracing outside interests another 10 percent," Bill said as he looked over. "I think Steve has those covered."

When Paul mumbled something about fishing in Steve's new boat, more people chuckled.

"Since love is a refuge from our hectic, hurried world, finding the right person to be by your side is honestly 50 percent of the secret. Your mother and I are so very glad you found Maren," Bill said as he and Dolores set off a series of clanging stemware. As people congratulated the betrothed, Liz escaped explaining Tim's absence.

"Only Hilary and Brad get to squirm given that toast," Paul whispered to Liz. He alluded to their daughter and his friend Pam dumping Steve, while both sets of parents remained friends.

Hilary passed candid photos of their little blonde granddaughter playing at their condo.

"She's adorable," Liz said of Chloé in a princess dress, her tiara resting on blonde hair.

"A sweet disposition," Hilary added. "This is what grandmothers do best. Brag." The Morgans knew Liz and Paul from their daughter Pam's medical school days. Brad Morgan pleased Jack Cole, Maren's father, when Brad flat-out said that Pam had missed her chance with the great guy who would become Jack's son-in-law.

"You think Steve needs a bigger scrub cap now, don't you?" Paul asked Liz. His champagne sat half-finished, and he saw Liz eye it. "Have it, since you aren't driving."

"I am happy for him. Maren's the perfect match as Vicki was for you." Liz smiled. "Look at Mom and Dad. They have that recipe down. Their children are coupled, even Eric with a steady date." Liz pointed to the dancing.

"When the night's over, Tim Phillips will see his loss," Paul assured. "Until then, lighten up."

Visibly smitten, Steve cradled his fiancée, as couples took to the dance floor. His hand slid lower and his lips braised Maren's hair.

"I can't stop lusting after you." He brushed her with evidence of his arousal. "My Valentine." Maren glimpsed the sex-starved eyes. "Let's get some air," Steve suggested, his arm encasing her waist as he distanced them from the music.

"Steve, it's awful outside."

The predicted Nor'easter started out as a steady, driving rain beyond the country club doors. The further he led Maren, the more she understood. Air was merely a cover as they ascended stairs to a small second floor lounge.

"Few people know this exists. The maître d' called me once to check a guy who passed out."

"It's private all right," she said. The room offered a sofa, desk and chair and what looked like a small powder room as she peeked inside. Steve twisted the lock behind them. "Steve!"

"It might be cold outside." He slid his hands over the black fabric outlining her figure. "But things are damn hot in here." His lips parted hers. The kiss drew steam. "Mair, I want you." Steve hiked her evening gown and was determined to turn any no into an instant yes.

"You've been drinking." Maren giggled.

"Only that glass of champagne." Steve nudged her to the sofa. "I haven't stolen as much as a kiss all week. Last weekend I was on call."

"There's tonight."

"My sister, three kids staying over?" He smiled. "No, carpe diem." Seizing opportunity, he slid black panties to the floor. "That's more like it." Their mouths met.

Maren let out a slight purr that grew more desperate. When Steve ran his hands from her black stilettos to her hip-crumpled gown, Maren threw her head back. She gave up any resistance to his persuasion. He fingered the banded top of each thigh-high stocking.

"Warm enough now?" Steve repositioned.

"Mm." She caught her breath as Steve claimed her and quickly satisfied himself. She kissed him hard. "I never know what to expect from you."

"Keep a woman guessing." He stepped into the powder room and tucked his shirt. Maren smoothed out the creases of her gown. When he reopened the door, Steve poked his head out. "It's legal to nail the woman I'm madly in love with, isn't it?" He eyed the nearly two-carat rock on her left hand and grinned.

"Very legal." Maren stood behind him to use the mirror. She tissued lipstick off Steve and puckered her own lips, needing a fresh coat. "Darn, I left my evening bag at the table."

"Let's get back before people miss us." Steve tucked tendrils back into Maren's upswept hair. Before opening the door, he stopped. "Maren, I love you. Happy Valentine's Day."

"I love you, too." She pulled him closer to savor the passion they'd just shared.

Though Liz sought refuge in the downstairs ladies room, and Gabe got her a third and final drink, she knew she couldn't escape every time the music slowed. Gabe's shuffling between her and his 25-year-old date—already blitzed two hours into the event—amused Liz. Alicia

21

must have worked the marketing department like dogs these past few months. They all came unleashed.

Liz returned to her table. She conversed a bit until Bill led Dolores to dance. Maren's parents joined in. They all swayed close as married couples did during a night out.

"You were happy, Lizzie. Let's not be the crab imperial." Paul pocketed his Blackberry.

"I'm fine. Updating Vicki again?" Liz asked. Her distant stare at the drape-covered ballroom windows halted. "Wait, you called me Lizzie?"

Paul nodded sheepishly. "Didn't Steve call you that years ago?"

"Now you're imitating my brother." Liz faked a smile. "Part of his fan club?"

"That's Maren's job." Paul sipped a soda. "Seriously, tell me what's the matter." He regarded her drooping chin that could fall onto the red linen tablecloth any minute. "It's Tim?"

"Yeah. Vicki would love to be here, but can't. Tim could be here, but won't. He didn't even notice Valentine's Day. Go figure." Liz placed an elbow on the table to cradle her head.

"I can't." Paul caused Liz to straighten. "Tim Philips is a fool, at least tonight." The added gleam in his eye shot her mood higher. As the remark settled, Liz caught the happy couple gliding past their table and rolled her eyes.

Sensing her jealousy, Paul leaned to capture her ear. "You know, they were gone a long time."

"So? Where could they go? Soon it'll spit sleet." Liz leaned back. "Good thing it held off."

"Imagine cancelling this? Your mother's reaction would melt snow. Worse than the look."

"What look?" Liz asked.

"The look you've sent off a good part of this evening. The Kramer-woman look."

"You really are a part of Steve's fan club. He invented that phrase, and it's so not true."

"Oh, trust me!" He flashed his Al Pacino eyes. "Ten to one Stud and wife-to-be were in some closet," he whispered. "They're inseparable."

Warmth invaded her ivory cheeks after hearing Paul's calculations. "You really do sexualize everything. That's why he told me...that's what he meant when he told me not to..." Liz stopped.

Feeling a cool drip fall from her glass, she plied a droplet from the gown's bodice. How long would Paul grant her that lecherous grin?

She changed the subject. "*The Baltimore Sun* predicts quite the blizzard," she said. "What if I never even get to my parents' place?"

"Steve told you not to what?"

Saved by couples returning when the music turned upbeat, Liz stood by her chair.

"That's such a lovely dress," Hilary Morgan offered. "The shade really compliments you."

"Thanks, my *favorite* color," Liz replied. "Paul was just telling me how they're painting their nursery lavender with purple accents."

"Yellow," Paul corrected. "If you'll excuse us, this woman has some serious delusions to shake out on the dance floor. Besides, Vicki instructed me to have fun."

A few women had kicked off their heels at the sound of Olivia Newton John singing "Let's Get Physical." With one gentle tug, Paul steered Liz underneath the lights that had turned the dance floor into a pulsating disco.

"Hey," Liz protested, with her elbow.

"I didn't say you had calories to burn," he shouted above the music. Laughed. "See, the look again." When Liz took Paul's extended arm, he swung her around.

Paul had analyzed every inch, even in the offending colors. Vicki had instructed him to enjoy the night. He followed orders. He'd behave, but his eyes languished a little.

Within minutes flinging her arms high above her head, Liz loosened, in body and mind both. She taught Paul, as well as Gabe, The Macarena. Gabe was the quicker study.

As the song changed, Paul demanded, "*What* did your brother tell you not to do?"

Liz bumped close enough to make Paul think she would confide in him and then backed off watching his wide smile. Liz no longer lamented loneliness. She finally allowed herself a good time. As the band ended, she toppled slightly, casting off her heels with one playful kick, falling tentatively until she righted herself.

"Sorry…" Liz laughed. "I guess three stiff ones are my limit." Instantly, she saw Paul's eyes rise. "Paul!"

He threw his head back. "My thoughts aren't always in the gutter. I just live up to people's expectations. Now, Steve said?"

Nearing their table, Liz did a 180. Her finger ever so lightly jabbed Paul. "He told me to quit being a little vamp near you. Feed *that* to your surgeon-sized ego."

Paul tugged her arm toward the dessert bar. "So you really *were* trying to lure me back in the day?" He sighed, amused. "Your loss."

She shot him a sideways glance, and he laughed at his own smugness.

"Were…was…back then. My college boyfriend bolted for a tramp, officially our homecoming queen," she granted. At age 20, Liz had fallen into an instant crush with the guy her brother dubbed the *Italian Stallion*. "You were comic relief then. Oh God, more for *your* ego."

"Steve contaminated my reputation." Paul took one bite of Tiramisu, set it on an abandoned table, and scrunched his face. "Speaking of contamination. This is not mascarpone." A scowl followed his hard swallow. He grabbed a dessert napkin to wipe remnants from his lips.

"What's in it?" Liz helped herself to a bite. "I wouldn't have used cream cheese. Must be the low-cal, less expensive version."

"Tell me your mom didn't oversee desserts." Paul ladled punch to chase any aftertaste.

"Hilary did. She's taken the heart-healthy diet a little too far," Liz said. "The lady fingers aren't firm enough. I've got a great recipe."

"You always want firm. With lady fingers." Paul parted his lips. "Do send *that* recipe." He watched for Liz's reaction, but before he could recognize one, Paul's chin dipped. Hilary Morgan summoned him, hand outstretched, with such urgency that it caused Paul to lose interest in being a clown. Walking toward Hilary, he overheard her conversation.

"How far are you?" Cell phone at her ear, Hilary Morgan lowered herself into a nearby chair, and her eyes glassed over. "What? I don't understand, Pam."

As Paul approached, he remembered that his friend Pam, Hilary Morgan's daughter, was returning to Philadelphia. Paul had taken her to lunch just yesterday as Pam took a few days during her little girl's winter break to accompany her husband Jerry on a Washington business trip. Concerned, Paul pivoted a nearby chair, plopped himself into it, and waited patiently.

"You're talking fast. With that siren, I can't hear you. Tell Paul." Hilary touched her parted lips as she pushed her cell at him in a take-this-please gesture. She gulped tears. Brad Morgan came to her side. Hilary leaned against him, and Paul heard her say, "This isn't good."

"Pam, what's going on?" Paul asked.

"There's been…a car accident. Jerry, ab… abnormal breathing," Pam gasped. "Air bags deployed. BP 98/60. Tachy at 135. But Chloé."

"Pam, where are you? What about Chloé?"

"Annapolis…no," she paused. "Solomons."

That was the opposite of her intended direction. "The road you mean. Where?" Otherwise known as Maryland Route 2, the highway spanned nearly 80 miles. "How badly is Chloé hurt?" Pam wasn't her usual answer-at-the ready self.

"Just cut her out. Hold on." He couldn't do anything but, struggling to listen above the ballroom music and chaos on the end of the line.

"No, I go with her," Pam demanded. Shrill on his ears, he heard her argue with the rescue squad. "Paul, Chloé got the worst impact. What if she bleeds out?" Before he could answer, he heard, "No please. I'm a doctor." Tears clogged Pam's voice. "You still there, Paul?"

"I'm here. What do you need?" He had renewed appreciation for dispatchers. Doors slamming and the police radio told him they were confined to the ambulance Pam had begged to be inside. Paul looked up to Steve walking to him. He'd surely seen Hilary on Brad's shoulder, his mom offering a tissue from her evening bag. Dolores pulled her son aside and captured his ear.

"We're going to West Riverside. Where's Steve?" Pam gasped. "Chloé was trapped. She has an airway, but she's unconscious. Tossed off the seat. Lacerated forehead. O neg blood type."

"Steve's right here, Pam." Paul looked over as Steve punched numbers on his hospital-issued Blackberry, listening to Paul with his other ear. "You need a surgeon for abdominal injuries, possible head trauma, O neg blood." Paul transmitted details. "Jerry cyanotic, coughing blood. Breath sounds absent on left side. And you?"

"I'm fine dammit. It's Chloé. Tell Steve Chloé needs…she is eight…no, wait…she's nine."

"He's on it." Paul heard a paramedic call to the ED charge nurse. "You're 15 minutes out. We'll be there. I'm hanging up Pam."

Returning the phone, Paul brushed Hilary's shoulder. Paul and Steve stepped aside from the small group gathered around. The news spread and so did the effort to comfort Hilary and Brad. Bill Kramer went to get their coats.

"Steve, you have to go." Maren's voice shook, and he held her.

If this sent shivers up his spine, hers had to freeze with memories of Mark's violent accident two years ago.

25

"Kramer here," Steve voiced into his cell, the second it rang. "Heading in but we need back-up. *Close* personal friends involved." Paul heard the third-hand report Steve gave. "Exactly, that kind of close." Steve shut his eyes. "Thanks, see you in there." He pocketed his phone in his trousers.

"I'm coming with you," Paul said. "Pam's a mess. Said Chloé was eight, then nine, but remembered her blood type. She's unraveling."

"She's shaken, that's all," Steve said. "I could donate O neg if they need it. Pam's injuries?"

"Wouldn't tell me, but her breathing was off. Kept diverting to Chloé; asked for you. Very insistent with the EMTs; wouldn't get in an ambo."

"Christ...."

"You're the boss, but three cases you can't touch unless you absolutely have to." Paul rolled his eyes. "Same for me; not as *personal* though."

"Tell me about it. I called in two more surgeons. I can oversee the OR staffing."

"Say goodbye to Maren," Paul told him. "I'll deal with Pam and make sure she's checked out."

Steve might be in charge, but Paul knew he had the tougher job. Pam was smarter than physicians twice her age, and stubborn, especially with Steve, in an oddly tangled way.

Having done hospital social work, Liz knew when to hold back and when to insert herself. "Anything I can do?" she finally asked.

"Offer Hail Marys." Paul gripped Liz's wrist.

Liz saw her brother knuckle a tear from Maren. She knew they had spent time with Pam's little girl at Disney at a medical conference in December. Per Maren, Chloé hung around with Dylan. Maren had tolerated Pam better than her brother. Audrey and Jack, Maren's parents, had cooed over Hilary's photos. They too stood stunned.

"Alert Eric. He's comforting Shelly," Paul told Liz. "Have them take clothes for Hilary and Brad. It's gonna be a long night."

"Paul, Shelly adores that little girl. Her niece."

"I know, Liz. I've got to run. Be careful out there." For once, Paul was glad Vicki was safely confined to the hospital. The weather setting in now was turning wicked.

"We'll huddle in at Maren's. Be safe," Liz stammered. But Paul had already left with Steve.

Chapter 3

Against the dark, bright red EMERGENCY reflected off the pavement. Paul stripped his tie as he paced through the ED doors to flee the rain. Steve had already pocketed his.

Paul stopped at the nurses' station at West Riverside. "The Carlton's, have they arrived?"

"Husband, down the hall, a possible pneumothorax. Pretty sure his lung has collapsed. Little girl: concussion, head lac and internal bleeding," stated the charge nurse. "Room two. Mom's with her, refusing treatment for herself."

The first two rooms inside the ambo bay—reserved for trauma. Paul wasn't sure if the weather thwarted transport to Shock Trauma or the EMTs triaged the injuries as less severe.

He stood at the desk, having done an about-face when Pam staggered out. Shirttails hung out from her jeans. A streak of blood staining her shoulder was evidence of the laceration above Pam's swollen eyes that filled with terror.

"How's Chloé? Jerry?" Paul's hand landed on Pam's back to stroke it. "And look at you."

"He may be in the OR after CT," Pam said. "They're working on Chloé. Where's Steve?" Pam ran out of breath. Gentle strokes to her shoulder brought a grimace. "Is there a good trauma surgeon on tonight? Steve's good with kids. No, he can't operate on her, but I want him here. Paul, where is he?" Both knew helicopter transport was not an available option.

"Sit down." Paul wheeled a chair from the desk and commanded Pam into it. "Steve's checking the OR board. Called in staff. He's got a trauma surgeon and neuro is on standby. He was on the phone the whole way here."

"What if Chloé needs someone now? She needs him. What's his number? Maybe I have it."

"Stop. Breathe." He crouched. "You need to get checked out." Pam's breath hitched. He caught her wince. Seeing her hand idle at her chest, Paul was afraid she'd be next one on a stretcher and honestly thought she ought to be.

"I'm fine," she claimed. Steve rounded the corner having swapped formalwear for scrubs, ditching his tux into his surgical locker.

Seeing him, Pam tried to catapult but quickly sat back down. Her tear-stung eyes met his and held mutual disbelief. "You're here…"

Steve heard the torture, and though they'd pulled plenty of all-nighters as interns, residents, and lovers, Steve Kramer had never seen Pam quite this disheveled and disoriented. "We're ready upstairs. Zigler will be here any minute. He's the best for Chloé, Pam."

"Steve, what if…" Pam flinched, unable to finish. She grabbed her rib cage. Face turning the shade of a lab coat, she drew another breath to get her story out. Paul now stood, a steady hand on Pam's shoulder as she continued. "We got a late start. Our car spun. Slick. Pavement. Chain reaction on Chloé's side. I was driving."

Steve lowered to his haunches at Pam's level. "We'll do everything we can. But you need to be checked. Now!" Steve cut off the protest he knew would follow. His eyes darted the length of the ED. "There's Zigler. I'll go in with him and see what's going on. I'll let you know, but you need to go with Paul."

"Come on, Pam," Paul said as Steve followed the other surgeon into Chloé's treatment room. "In here." Paul guided her. Pamela Morgan Carlton, too weary to argue, did as directed. Paul motioned to Denise Brannigan, the chief surgical resident in the ED. "She needs a workup. STAT."

"Sure, Dr. Romano," Brannigan told him. "Dr. Chen is with Mr. Carlton. He's acute. We're full up. All attendings have cases." Jade Chen had started in January as head of emergency medicine. This weekend: her indoctrination.

"I know. The Carlton daughter is in room two. Kramer and I trained with Dr. Morgan. I see her listed as Carlton. She's not gone in there willingly so if she puts up a fuss, let me know." He gave Brannigan a parting glance.

"Paul," Brad Morgan called from the elevator where he and Hilary, their daughter Shelly and Eric Kramer stepped off. Pam's parents looked panicked. Shelly held a duffle of casual clothes since Brad wore a tux. The sequins on Hilary's gown caught the fluorescent light.

"Everyone's in a treatment room. Had to force your daughter into one." Paul squeezed Hilary by the shoulders and pulled away. "There's a waiting room down the hallway. Restrooms, too. Might as well change while you have the chance."

"We'll be back." Hilary left with her husband and daughter, Shelly. Eric stood dazed.

"Gets intense around here," Eric said. "First Brad's emergency surgery in November, now this. Anything I can do?"

Paul hesitated. He remembered Eric Kramer with little appreciation for anything medical outside of Clearasil directions. Eric had become a handsome young man with Pam's hot sister hanging on his arm this past year.

"We wait," Paul finally offered. "Supply coffee and calm, emphasis on the latter." Paul clapped a hand to Eric's shoulders. "Could get worse. I've gotta run." He went to hang his tuxedo in a locker. Peeking in on Vicki would take him to another wing. She had enough worry.

Paul asked the charge nurse for the break room code. Patients left this place better off when freshly brewed java fueled its staff. Returning to the desk, he spotted Steve and Dr. Zigler convening. "How's Chloé?" Paul asked, resting his coffee on the large ED workstation.

"Ruptured spleen. I'm going to scrub," Dr. Zigler said.

Steve rubbed his temples. As chief of surgery, he had declared all hands on deck due to bad weather hitting the area as well as this multi-car accident. "Jade's getting a CT of Jerry's broken rib—only thoracic OR case. How's Pam?"

"With Brannigan. Here, you can finish this," Paul said handing Steve his still-warm coffee. "Your brother and Shelly are down the hall. Brad and Hilary just got here. I'll check on Pam."

Steve took one sip, drew in a measured breath, and downed the rest.

"Tough night," the charge nurse commented from behind her terminal. "We might have to divert cases if this keeps up, Dr. Kramer."

"Any updated forecast?" Steve asked.

"Snow into the double digits through Sunday," answered the med tech standing nearby. They all looked at one another. It was only Friday night.

Paul closed the door leaving Pam's treatment room. "Sprained radius and cracked rib, but she's moving air all right, unlike Jerry, and she wants a report on Chloé before they take her to x-ray."

"I promised one." Steve crushed the coffee cup and hurled it into the trash two feet away. "Join me if you want." Steve and Paul paced the few steps it took until Steve knocked on the door where the chief resident had just exited.

"Steve, Chloé?" Pam pleaded as he stepped in.

"Dr. Zigler will remove her spleen. She's got a concussion. I asked for a neuro consult," Steve said. "Blood bank alerted. Good triage you did."

"Jerry? Pneumothorax?" Pam winced. She swung her legs off the bed. An attendant had opened the door and had her wheelchair chariot to x-ray.

Still shaken, Pam looked unsteady. "Let me help you." Paul held her from falling. "You nailed that one, too. He's heading to the OR for a chest tube and closer look at those ribs. He signed his consent. You need to sign one for Chloé."

Steve popped his head out the door, asking the nurse for the requisite paperwork. When she brought it in, Pam struggled with the pen but managed a scribble.

"Can I see her?" Pam scanned their faces. "And Steve, you need to be in there. Please, can you scrub in, give me a report?" Pam implored. Every breath took four times the normal effort.

"Zigler's a competent surgeon, Pam, but I'll oversee things." Steve turned to the attendant primed to wheel her away. "Let's get her in to her daughter." Squatting to his heels, Steve clutched Pam's hand in his. "Take care of yourself or you're no use to Chloé."

Pam's eyes glistened. With her good hand still enveloped in Steve's, she squeezed it. "Yes, but... I can't explain. Our late start was my fault."

"Do you want one of us to brief Jerry?" Steve softened more.

"No, I have to do this head on." Pam closed her eyes. "Like the crash..."

"Pam, you can't fix everything. You need to see Chloé and get those films."

"Steve, stop. There are things here you don't understand." She let go of his hand, diverting her glassy eyes. "Guys, it means a lot to have you here, but I have to see Chloé. Please." Pam swallowed hard. The aide wheeled her away as Steve and Paul stood in the treatment room.

"She's a mess, Steve. Let it be," Paul told his friend. He understood. Only a few months ago, Pam had divulged to Paul a secret she had kept ten years—one Steve had never talked about even though he considered Paul his best friend. Pam had aborted the child conceived with Steve, shortly after she broke off their nearly nine-year relationship. Moving out of their apartment, into Jerry Carlton's life, Pam offered Jerry things Steve had counted on sharing, including a family.

The Paul-Pam-Steve trio—once called the three amigos by their med school clique—had ended abruptly. Yet the essence of it was alive tonight. Bits and pieces remained, emotionally strung out and severely challenged. Just like the three lives that had been traumatized tonight.

He heard the door bump. From the corner of his eye, Paul saw the nurse tiptoe out after loading another IV bag onto the pole. Paul scrubbed his face with his hands. The force of his legs closed the recliner. He stood to stretch.

What a night. Thankful for little pleasures, he stared at the water visible from Vicki's hospital room. *Good upgrade.* Paul had requested that Thursday. No doubt patients would fill every available alcove this weekend.

"Honey, what time is it?" Vicki asked from her pillow perch.

Paul smiled. Hardly a hair out of place, those strikingly dark eyes met his and held. "Buongiorno bella. It's 4:30." Now at her bed, he lowered the rail, toed off his shoes and crawled in next to her as she scooted over. "We've got time before the herd traipses in here."

"Behave. You were part of that herd once."

"When have you known me to behave?" Fingering her dark hair, he placed a gentle kiss on her lips, and pulled back. "How you feeling?"

"Not terrible. Not great. How was the gala?"

"Without you, not nearly as exciting. Steve and Maren couldn't keep their hands off one another." At that, Paul felt Vicki giggle. He always loved the warmth of her nestled next to him. "Liz went alone. She could have stoned Tim with one look. He stood her up."

"I hope you didn't tell her that. She was probably disappointed."

"With Liz, I can joke around. She got over it after some champagne and a dance or two." Paul shrugged. "Mexicans must have made the bruschetta and Somalis the tiramisu. The rest of the food was pretty good. Your evening?"

"I planned to watch a movie, but my parents surprised me. My sister came along. That was sweet." Vicki fingered her husband's gold necklace, the one he called his lucky chain, with the hope it would send hope and spring her free.

"You're wearing the chain I gave you yesterday. You must have snuck it on."

"*My* lucky chain. Makes me feel dressed up with this." She tugged on her hospital gown.

"As Sophia Loren would say 'Beauty is how you feel inside, and it reflects in your eyes. It isn't something physical.' And even with the necklace, I'll zone straight to yours."

"Sophia sayings! I love that you got this on our trip to Italy. Grazie." Vicki blew him a kiss.

31

Paul's eyes normally showed circles beneath, but today they ran deeper. "You knew Pam was in town. Stopped in here Thursday, right?"

Seeing her head bob, Paul continued. "Don't get upset but, on their way home, they got into an accident. Brought here, Jerry and Chloé had surgery. Pam ended up with a cracked rib, head lac and a sprained arm. Eventful night."

"Dio Mio. We thought we had problems."

"Life's precious. We learn that here every day, but hitting so close…to friends." Paul parsed kisses on Vicki. "Wait a second." He jumped off the bed and lodged a chair under the doorknob.

"Paul, you can't do that." While admonishing her husband, more giggles erupted.

"I just did." He hopped back into bed with her, with sudden energy. "Ti amo. Watch me do this." His whisper turned to a full mouth kiss.

Paul's antics never ceased to amuse Vicki, but later that evening she felt content. Everyone on the staff was trapped this first day of a long federal holiday weekend. Valentine's Day, falling on a Friday, had made it more. Snow started to stick, stalling the best-made plans.

Watching the weather channel helped time to pass. Pam, nursing her arm in a blue sling, had taken time from Chloé and Jerry to see Vicki. Vicki felt at ease with Pam though she had only met Paul's medical school friend a few months ago. They both worked with pregnant women in different roles—Pam as an OB/GYN and Vicki as a former nurse, now a childbirth educator.

As she sealed the envelope on yet another note, Vicki sat up to the knuckles she heard this time on her door. "Come in," she yelled out.

"Hi there," Steve said with a cup of coffee in one hand. "Before I finally sit down, would you like anything? Tea, coffee?"

"No thanks. The nurses have me well hydrated. And this," she said raising her elbow off the bed with the arm attached to her IV. "Busy night?"

"Understatement." Steve relaxed into the recliner facing her. "Where's Paul?"

"Jade Chen paged him. One of his patients was in the ER and they're swamped. She pulled his permanent anchor out of that chair."

Steve chuckled until he saw two bags on the IV pole. "Antibiotic."

"An infection. Like a pearl, I'm well cultured."

"Nice necklace. I see you're keeping busy."

"Valentine gift." Vicki held up sealed envelopes from atop hospital stationery on her tray table. "My makeshift cards. I missed getting to Hallmark. Here's one for you, Maren and Dylan."

"I like the sound of that." Steve smiled.

Vicki laughed, but cupped her protruding belly. "If you pushed off your wedding date because of our impending event, I'll feel guilty. I know you have a special honeymoon planned."

"No guilt allowed. Before hurricane season we're fine. You focus on you and Baby Romano."

"Speaking of Romano, Paul's mom called me earlier. She wanted to know if the hospital fed me appropriately, followed by 50... well at least 25 questions about why Paul hasn't called, how I was, the baby, what you were up to...oh, and now Pam and how she's doing."

"That's your mother-in-law." Steve finished another swig of coffee and held his cup in the air. "In the Romano household, this would go down the drain." They each shared a laugh.

Paul's mother was nothing if not thorough in her fully equipped Italian kitchen. "I owe her," Steve continued. "My love of good coffee, cappuccino, my cooking skills, recipes, so much more. Isabella is the quintessential Italian mom. She was *our* mom throughout residency."

"Well, Paul's brother Vinny would swap about now. She probably doesn't want to trouble me, but something's up. She said she'd like to come down here, but for the weather."

"Thwarts that," Steve interjected. "Another failed business of your brother-in-law?"

"I'm guessing, but I didn't go there. As the baby in the family, at 31, she bails him out. I know their dad died when he was little, but let's see, he's had a hair salon, bagel shop, the handyman business, a pawn-shop. Now sells insurance."

"And the pizza palace with Domino's and Pizza Hut down the block. Pawnshop?" Steve mocked out loud. "Well, a step up from jobs asking 'You want fries with that?'"

Steve had Vicki rolling in laughter by the time he realized he had best check the OR board on this weather-emergency weekend.

"Thanks for stopping by. I'm so happy for you and Maren. You make a standout couple."

Steve kissed Vicki's forehead. "I've been told that. You hang in there. This should knock whatever's dragging you down."

"Steve." Vicki clutched his wrist. "One last thing. I have a favor to ask you."

33

"Sure, name it."

She slipped an envelope into his hand, this one twice the size of her handmade Valentine greetings. "Keep this. We already did legal stuff. This is private, personal, for Paul. He already got his Valentine." Vicki smirked. "He's smiling." They laughed again. "But just in case… please keep it."

"Vicki…" Steve felt her firm arm squeeze. He saw those pleading beautiful eyes before he kissed her hand. "This won't be necessary, but it's safe with me. I'll take it to my office right now."

"Thank you, Steve."

The next morning, Paul scanned the cafeteria for Pam. People weren't here unless they worked night shift or stood vigil over sick family members. He flexed his finger joint.

Blackberry Thumb: a new malady that caused repetitive injury from using smartphones. Like he was doing now, retrieving the email Liz sent with a recipe for Tiramisu. Paul decided to protect himself, pressed dial, and waited.

"My mother would even approve of that recipe," he said when he heard a fairly upbeat hello. "You must have made it to Southern Maryland. Why are you up at this hour?"

"On my laptop. Couldn't sleep. I thought you'd like those ingredients," Liz admitted. "How's Vicki?"

"Fighting an infection. Snoozing," he replied. "Thanks for asking. They're evaluating treatment. I'm in the cafeteria with a spare minute."

"It's got to be stressful for you."

Paul hesitated. "Given a miscarriage months ago, another before that, I'm a little tapped out," he admitted. "Don't let that get around."

"You're human," Liz said. "Besides, I did casework during that brief stint in Baltimore living at Steve's. My torture years."

"His, too, I understand." Paul laughed.

"I'm serious," Liz insisted. "I remember being there for high-risk moms…and dads. You make such a nice couple. I'm praying this goes well."

"Thanks, Liz. Speaking of high-risk, breakfast mate heading my way," he said. "Ouch, she heard that. I just got dagger eyes."

"Who are you meeting at sunrise on Sunday?"

Paul paused. Years ago, he knew Liz felt Steve could have cast a wider net for a girlfriend.

"You're having breakfast with Pam?"

"Liz has had her Wheaties this morning," Paul quipped. "Breakfast mate having an AHF."

"With the weather, no one else would be at the hospital," Liz said. "What's an AHF?"

"Never mind...later," Paul snorted. "Stay safe."

"You, too. Give my best to Vicki."

Paul clicked off. "Liz Kramer. Phillips," Paul told Pam. "Saw her at the charity event Friday."

"You told her I had an acute hissy fit. Thanks a lot." Pam pursed her lips. "My mother had her own obsessive fit over that fundraiser." She set down her tray and plopped herself into the chair.

"Now, now...you inherited that precise nature." Paul took a swig of coffee. "We look worse than we did 15 years ago working six days in a row," he added now that she sat across from him.

"My body's in purgatory." Pam pushed scrambled eggs and hash browns before spearing a bite. "Have you been sleeping in Vicki's room?"

"Since Wednesday." Paul sighed and leveled concern. "This isn't going well. This morning Vicki spiked a fever. She's been on bed rest yet she's puffy as if she's done a 12-hour shift." Paul continued to update Pam, who when not by Chloé's bedside camped out with Jerry. Pam looked freshened from a shower and clean clothes after her father retrieved suitcases. The police had pulled them from Friday's wreckage. Today, Shelly sat with her niece. This was the farthest place Pam could escape with the storm predicted to be full force by afternoon.

Paul ran down Vicki's most recent lupus flare that precipitated a steroid cocktail.

"In remission when she conceived. No issues until December," Pam repeated. "Baby's been stable. A high-risk OB on her case."

"Affirmative, plus an infectious disease expert consulting by telephone. The damn weather." Paul's eyes looked at what the hospital cafeteria TV broadcast—the CNN weather map.

"What's nephrology say? They could be treating this as preeclampsia. Lupus nephritis could lurk. Harder to distinguish." Pam gently set her fork down as she studied Paul, who locked eyes with Pam before closing his momentarily.

"They just got onboard yesterday." Paul deadpanned. "Are we behind the eight ball here?"

"I didn't say that. If there's something to catch, they'll find it."

"But you'd have ruled this out earlier?"

Pam saw Paul's pain. He shuffled silverware and crumpled his napkin onto the tray sitting between them.

"Only by a day or so," she assured him. "If it makes you feel better, I'll walk upstairs with you. Chloé has fun with Shelly. They won't miss me."

Paul shot up and slid the metal legs of his chair, screeching it. As Pam took one last coffee sip, he nudged her. "Come on," he said.

Pacing out, they left remnants of their breakfasts behind.

Chapter 4

"You live dangerously," Steve Kramer told Liz as she helped him unload dishes from the dishwasher late Sunday morning. He quickly caught his sister's chagrin though he knew he had chanced safely returning to Maren's when the forecast called for bad weather. "My job demands I fight sleet and snow, but you chose to. How were the roads in Southern Maryland?"

"Not great. Good thing Dad reminded me to get snow tires." Liz laughed. "There's not as much for the kids in the winter at the bayside house. So we decided to come back here."

"That would be why they have it as a *summer* home," Steve added.

"I get it. Look at the fun all three kids are having." She and Steve craned their necks out the kitchen window at Maren's house. Maren held Hannah on the last run sledding down the slight grade next to Maren's backyard. Tyler and Dylan rolled in mounds of snow making angels nearby. "I hope your new house has a slope to it."

"We have a *petite* yard. Shore Landings has a great community playground and a park where kids can sled," Steve said. "Nine months out of the year we'll be at the pool, the marina or out on the boat. Why would I want grass to mow?"

"There's nothing *petite* about your desires or requirements," Liz shot back. "Like this?"

She held up a huge All-Clad griddle, which she knew was Steve's, in Maren's cabinets. He had packed up his apartment in January and finagled his way out of his lease, put furniture in storage, and brought prized essentials plus a big-screen TV to Maren's place. Steve planned to divvy his time between living aboard his boat, the hospital, and her place until they closed on their house well before their June wedding.

Steve snatched it from his sister. "*This* fed you along with my award-winning French toast." After putting the griddle in a bottom cabinet, Steve straightened. "All joking aside, it's fun to see the kids happy, getting along so well. I know you're pissed at Tim this week-end, but Mair and I can't wait to move to Shore Landings. So glad Tim found it for us. Love at second sight." Steve smirked. "Mair was love at first sight."

"I'm thrilled for you two," Liz confessed. "Jealous, but..." She put down the dishtowel. "I don't like what's happening with Tim. Please don't tell me he makes it all happen for us, or I'll take that griddle and whack you with it."

"Violence to go with that scowl," Steve said.

"Cut it out," Liz demanded. "What's wrong with this picture? Mom and Dad had the kids over MLK weekend. I made a candlelit dinner, right. Wore a skirt, stockings and high heels."

Liz had encountered high heels kicked off in his Baltimore bachelor pad years ago. Steve simpered, looking pleased. "Ones designed to rarely hit the floor?"

Liz towel-swatted him. "Of course."

"So you presented as a GLM with an LCB?"

"What?"

Steve laughed out loud. "Courtesy Paul. Good looking mama with a low-cut blouse." He raised his brow. "Always with the shoes."

"God, yes! I couldn't believe it when Tim asked 'What's the occasion?' Barely looked at me." Liz heaved hot air. "I had plans to miss dessert. No, cake came right on schedule. An hour later, I had to make moves on him."

Steve crossed his arms, leaning into the counter. Pensive until he uttered, "Low testosterone? Anything else going on in his life?"

"His usual routine. Scanning the multi-list, showing houses. He's hardly ever home."

"You seemed happy over your anniversary, through Thanksgiving. The economy is pretty strong. Busy after the first of the year. People don't buy houses heading into the holidays, Liz."

"Fair point. That doesn't account for the silent treatment or the stonewalling, and he gets defensive. Oh Lord, two out of Four Horsemen of the Apocalypse." Liz caught Steve's puzzled look. She stepped away reaching into a tote bag in Maren's family room just around the corner. "Here," she said, offering a hardcover book to her brother. *The Seven Principles for Making Marriage Work.* I got you one also as an engagement gift. I can see how well you've read it."

"You did?" Steve thumbed through it, quickly finding predictors of divorce. He set the book on the counter. "How's his health?"

"Physically, fine," Liz answered. "Emotionally? Not good for the frustrated, therapist wife to diagnose. Workaholic but why when we're doing well financially? We just celebrated our seven-year anniversary. There's a cliché."

Liz snatched back her copy. "No, we're better than that." Like germs on her hands, she washed that off the minute the thought touched her.

"You sure?" Steve left stillness between them.

"Certain. I work with squabbling marriages." Liz thought immediately of the marital strife she encountered at work, including the Maloney family and vowed never to be like them.

Steve drew Liz in for a hug. "Promise me, you'll call if you ever need anything, all right?"

"We're solid. This is a blip." Liz pulled away at the sound of Steve's Blackberry. They could hear kids downstairs stomping snow off their boots and Maren lightly treading up the stairs.

He studied the number recognizing West Riverside Hospital Center. "Kramer here," Steve answered. "Hey Paul, what's happening there?" He motioned Maren to come closer.

Her cheeks and nose flushed red, Maren still had large flecks of snow on strands of hair that weren't covered by her hood. She listened while Steve's strokes warmed her back.

"Wow, I'm sorry about that," Steve said. "Yeah, it is really coming down. Was chatting with Liz. Lost track of time."

"How's Vicki?" Maren whispered.

Steve held up his index finger. "I can call Sarge at the station. He'll send a police SUV and get me in there. See you soon."

"What's going on?" Liz asked. "He's been there all weekend."

"With Jerry and Chloé admitted, he reviewed Vicki's case with Pam since she's an OB."

"Over breakfast," Liz said. "I talked to him early this morning."

"Well, Pam doesn't have privileges so it was an informal review. There's a renal expert called in, and they moved Vicki to ICU."

"Not a good sign." Maren looked straight at Steve. "What if she loses the baby?"

Steve bit his lower lip. "Don't go back to being the what-if queen, Mair." The remark made Maren frown at him, but he was too busy scrolling his Blackberry to notice.

"What's this?" Maren picked up one of the identical books lying on top of yesterday's mail and a new credit card still glued onto the bank letter. "Were you reading what Liz got us?"

"Liz was," Steve answered. "I have to leave soon. Might not return if the storm's on track."

"Hm," Maren managed. Her lips appeared tight as she turned to Steve. "When aren't you dashing out? Here, our joint credit card came. I activated it." Maren rubbed the sticky elements from the back. "A grocery frequent shopper pass and a Care Aid Card for your wallet, too. Shore Landings has both within walking distance."

Steve reached for his wallet. "I love that community. Shops, restaurants, even a pharmacy." He pulled Maren close to hug. "You've done a great job packing, planning, taking all that off my plate. Sorry the weekend got away from us. I'll make it up on the unpacking end. Promise."

"In the garage so nothing touches your Jag," Liz kidded.

"You as our witness," Maren replied. "I'll leave him plenty of boxes. I'm not doing it all."

"I'll help," Dylan offered. "I get a bigger room for sleepovers." Dylan high fived Tyler. The boys went into the pantry and came back out with a bag of Oreos, offering one to Hannah.

"It's cold, Uncle Steve." Hannah tugged on his pant leg and managed her snack with her other hand. "Too cold. Almost-Aunt Maren made us come in."

Steve patted Hannah's head hearing Maren's newly coined name. He reached the station and secured his ride along snow-covered highways. The dispatch told him four inches had fallen the last hour. The sky had darkened to charcoal.

"I'm gonna miss you kids," he said. Always having a soft spot for his little sweetheart, Steve crouched. "Good to stay inside. Play a board game, or dive into Dylan's LEGO stockpile." He hugged Hannah tight and deposited a big lip smack on her. "No sledding injuries. This weekend's getting more complicated by the minute," he said, extending himself tall.

"Now who is *king* of the what-if's?" Liz asked. "You could have borrowed my SUV."

"He likes to call Sarge." Maren grinned at how Liz could call Steve out on his occasional double standards. "And, the what-if queen *is* worried about Vicki...and Paul. Your friends are now mine, too." Maren slid him a scowl.

"Oh, that Kramer-woman look," Steve said. "Good thing I'm making you part of the family." He tugged on Maren's waist, proud of himself. "You ladies may need Liz's SUV, but the governor declared a state of emergency. Don't go out unless you absolutely have to."

"We've got food to last five days with what I brought and Maren already has," Liz replied.

"And the delicious brunch you made us." Maren pulled Steve to kiss him.

Lip-locked long enough to be noticed, their spat quickly forgotten. That's how it was supposed to be, Liz mused as she joined the kids to set up *Washington In A Box* and vied to land on the popular high-priced properties.

Purple spaces on the playing board brought a smile; that it was about real estate unfortunately plummeted her thoughts back to Tim. Realizing she would just stew, crowning herself the next what-if queen, she pulled out her cell to call him. She clicked it shut hearing Tim's voice mail.

A blip? What if we're not OK? The crown, Liz decided, didn't just hurt. It stung.

Talking to Tim Sunday evening, Liz felt a pang of loneliness. Four seconds into the conversation, her head literally throbbed.

"I finally reached you," she said. Liz called from a cordless phone as she nestled onto the guest room bed at Maren's. She pulled an afghan over her for comfort.

"What part of working this weekend did you not understand?" Tim sighed. "Don't you have anything to *process* with your mom instead of checking up on me?"

Liz recoiled and fisted the blanket. "Married people touch base."

"Here we go: In a well-functioning family…"

"Yes," Liz cut him off. She caught Tim's mocking tone the minute it kicked in. "People serve as resources to one another." *Only this conversation isn't functioning very well.* "And, they clean up quick remarks and silly arguments."

Liz twirled a finger through a crocheted loop and continued before Tim could. "I just wanted to tell you we're now at Maren's house."

"That's why I didn't recognize the number," Tim replied. "What happened? You lecture your parents one too many times?"

"I thought you said you had to work, get records ready for taxes?" Liz asked. "What I'm hearing is criticism and insults." *Contempt if truth be told. Maybe we're not OK.*

"I'm not criticizing you. I'm glad the SUV is in one spot. Keep it there. You know how much the last repair bill was?"

Yes criticism: another horseman in the marriage manual's apocalypse. Liz closed her eyelids before she spoke.

"It doesn't appear there's much else to say. How's your weather?"

"News flash: there are Internet sites for that," Tim said. "Like weather.com. Type in our zip code. Amazing technology."

"Enough." Liz cast aside the protective afghan shield and swung her feet to the floor. "I thought maybe we could just…chat. I guess not."

"I'm fine, Liz. Really. I'll see ya."

Liz started to say goodbye, but what was the point with a dial tone blaring in her ear?

She hadn't called as much to check up as to simply connect with her husband. Criticism, defensiveness, contempt, and with so much left unsaid—not even a "how are the kids?"—Liz recognized stonewalling. All four ominous signs spelled the need for Maren's soothing hot cocoa. Liz shuffled on her slippers to head downstairs.

In the intensive care unit, cardboard cutouts of Washington, Lincoln, and Kennedy dangled from the nurses' station ceiling. Similar decorations had been hung downstairs throughout this state-of-emergency weekend. Only in the ED, someone had taken a Sharpie, adding pointy ears to certain presidents until Jade Chen, new at West Riverside, ordered them to come down.

Inside the ICU conference room Monday morning, Steve handed Pam a cup of coffee.

"Summa Cum Laude." Steve held his cup high. "The best brew around." He smiled at the only light moment since he had arrived Sunday.

"ICU nurses are tough. Coffee carries them through," Pam said as Steve sat down. "I'm sorry. That surgical resident in Chloé's room didn't realize I knew a thing or two." She placed her cup on the table. "That's the only reason I recited honors he likely didn't have."

"You pulled rank all right," Steve assured. Pam's behavior came back to him, like riding a bike. Only his 10-speed was still in storage; their 9-year relationship no longer a distant memory.

Three months ago they shared this small conference space when Pam's father Brad Morgan was an ICU patient. Steve attended to her dad, really Paul's patient, last November when he and Vicki vacationed. Good thing: Romano minds were far from relaxed right now.

"Glad you told Dr. Brannigan to turn over the chart," Pam said. "We moms get anxious."

"I so know that." Steve thought about Maren's worry when they first met—entirely different women yet both concerned for children.

42

When Steve had seen Pam months ago in this same room, she had jabbed fingers to justify actions, denied facts, and then ultimately divulged the ugly truth, finally, that she had cheated ten years before. Pam had broken off their steady, he-thought-solid relationship. She sealed a new one with the man she married who was, as they spoke, currently housed on the surgical wing.

"I'm sorry I scolded you Friday." Pam hung her head, partly from fatigue but also from being trapped inside West Riverside Hospital Center. "When I brag about my GPA, I'm kidding. You and Paul graduated Magna Cum Laude."

"Runners up. Helping you arrange your academic regalia, green hood, blue robe, honors cords." Steve sipped piping hot coffee. "The honor was all ours." He laughed. "You filled me in on Chloé. Jerry's recovering. How are you?" He looked at her arm, held by a sling.

Pam softened. "Thanks for asking. This will definitely complicate my work. I'll have to investigate my short-term disability and get my colleagues to cover for me."

"With the highest honors, you still need two hands to deliver babies and perform sections."

"Oh, shut up, Steve. Being one-handed is only half of it. Try getting around with a bruised rib."

"Did I just graduate from the old *screw you Steve?*" he asked. "This seems gentler."

"Jerry's upset because, as usual, my priorities put us behind schedule." She raised her head to meet Steve's focus. "I had two meetings, one with a Baltimore practice management firm. Stellar reputation for valuing practices up and down the East Coast."

"You're selling?"

"Possibly, to an associate. Then I had a TV interview on women's health. They got my name from the Philly paper where I write a column. It all made us late on Friday."

That explained the heavy makeup he spotted days ago. "You'd leave practice at the pinnacle of your career?" Steve sat back, curious as hell. "And be what…the next Dr. Nancy Snyderman?"

"What would be so wrong with that? Using my education in another way," she shot back. "It's not easy getting calls at all hours, missing important events, trying but never quite succeeding at being the dutiful corporate wife. Hell, just having a life…and family."

Steve pondered. Quietly. He motioned her on.

43

"Jerry reminds me that I have a master's degree in public health." Pam hesitated. "My hospital has an interim administration spot. I spent so much time in the hallway at that Disney conference fielding calls. If I hadn't promised Chloé and Jerry a Christmas getaway, I'd have bagged that whole trip."

If she had, he would have spent less on beer and Maalox, Steve mused. Her attending the same resort he took Maren and Dylan to was an unexpected bag of coal from Santa. "I'm sure your accountant put a positive spin on it once you turned over the receipts."

"He did, but I downed Tums, and not because of roller coasters and your smart-ass comments."

"Dr. Pamela Morgan, hospital administrator. You certainly juggle many things."

"I've always had a lot of balls in the air. It gives options, which are important for women."

"And you're all about options for women," Steve put between them. He realized it called her out on that one option she chose so long ago—aborting a child they conceived together.

"We put that to rest, remember?" Pam shifted her chair. "Keep up the sarcasm, I'm leaving."

"I'm sorry," Steve interrupted. "I'm sure balancing work and family isn't easy. Liz cut back her schedule with two kids. Maren works at home some. I'm about to find that all out."

"Thank you. It's *not*. One reason I haven't added to our family. Another bone of contention."

"Speaking of children," he said. "I saw Chloé in recovery early Saturday. One of the nurses said—and I quote—'She's got such brilliant blue eyes. Just like yours, Dr. Kramer.'"

As soon as he repeated the story, Steve slid his chair, still sitting in it, essentially blocking any pathway out. "Furthermore, Chloé's birthday is October 16, 1993. A little close for comfort, Pam." He looked straight at her. "I'd always been told she was a year younger."

"What is it about this room?" Pam huffed. "Chloé was a preemie."

"Confessional effect of enclosed spaces, Pam. Alternative scenario: you got pregnant earlier, went beyond your due date, and made up an abortion story so that I wouldn't complicate things."

"I tried to leave us on a good note in November with that quick kiss." She stared at him. "I could straight up slap you right now."

There was nothing quick about that kiss, he thought. "Pam, nurses around here like me. We're in a glass-enclosed room. Level with me."

44

Before she could respond to that self-aggrandizing comment, Pam's phone vibrated from the sweater in which she had pocketed it. Pulling it out, she studied her Blackberry. "Text from Paul: Vicki's in renal failure. Baby's in distress. Rushing in for a section."

"Oh God." Steve's mouth formed a perfect O.

Pam reached for his wrist. "This baby is 14 weeks early. Where's the highest level NICU?"

"Baltimore. We're only a Level Two." Steve pulled the door open and bolted to the elevator, slamming his hand onto the button.

"That's for feeders and growers," Pam spit out.

"I can't walk that fast. Slow down. What if this baby doesn't make it?"

"Don't say that," Steve said as they boarded together to catch Paul. For all of their collective training, much of it achieved together, answers weren't coming as quickly as they needed them.

The President's Day Blizzard of 2003 effectively dumped 26 inches of snow during the extended weekend, crippling Chesapeake communities. Nurses slept on cots and sofas in staff lounges, and patients slated for discharge remained, meaning West Riverside Hospital burst at its seams. New patient admits and surgeries abated. Ambulances could barely navigate spitting snow and icy roads.

Paul tried to refocus as Pam sat with him on a waiting room sofa, soothing away stress in his neck. "You can stop to save your only good arm." His turning forced that decision. "How long will they be? Cristo Mio," Paul muttered. "I should be in there. I'm a surgeon."

"At least 15 more minutes," Pam answered. They had sat down 30 minutes ago. "You're a husband and father right now." Pam cast caring eyes. "If this was my case, you'd sit right here, too. This isn't your average section."

How true! Paul reached into his pocket, pulling out his Blackberry to the classical ring tone of *The Godfather*. "My mother. Must have heard me swear. She'll ask 50 questions."

Pam put out the palm of her right hand, the only one she could use. "I'll field them."

Without thinking twice, Paul handed it over, glad that Pam's sister Shelly was with Chloé so that Pam could be with him.

"Mrs. Romano, this is Pam, remember me?" Pam indicated by eye exchange that Isabella Romano's voice was thick with worry. "Paul is…unable to come to the phone, but I saw it was you." Pam lied.

45

Paul's phone was passcode protected. "They took Vicki in about 40 minutes ago. No news yet…well, we're not sure. Usually. What? You and Vinny are trying to get here."

Paul's head shook sideways. "Too dangerous," he mouthed. Pam held up a silencing finger.

"I promise, Mrs. Romano. One of us will call you. Paul, me, or Steve," Pam said into the phone. "Thank you, you're so sweet, but I'll be fine. You stay safe. Yes, I'm sure Paul appreciates that. I will." Pam darkened the screen. "Only about five or six questions."

"She is *not* coming here. Pittsburgh's getting pounded, too," Paul said as Pam handed the phone back. Steve had just encased Paul between them on the waiting room sofa.

"DeNardo Weather—wow, he's still the meteorologist—declares at least 13 inches at the Pittsburgh airport, two feet in the mountains. Since Pittsburgh's better equipped to deal with snow, she and Vinny booked a Tuesday flight."

"Tomorrow? BWI has 28 inches of snow."

"I'm only the messenger. She might have said Reagan." As soon as Pam saw this new line of worry invade Paul's brow, she continued. "Said she lit candles and she's praying the Rosary for all of us with your grandmother's beads."

Paul rested his head in his two hands, elbows planted on his knees.

"She cares, Paul," Steve interjected. The sofa was tight for three as he nudged Paul over. "Hey, Vinny isn't trying to drive it."

Pam eyed them. "How could I forget Vinny?"

"Not easily," Paul said. "He finally owns a vehicle without visible rust. Flying reflects a cognitive step up."

"You once forbade me to be in a room alone with Vinny." Pam leaned forward to remind Steve, recollecting their residency days in Pittsburgh. "What's Vinny up to? Settled down?"

"Not really," Paul replied. "Probably got coupons. No one would attempt this otherwise."

"Dr. Romano," a nurse approached, her surgical mask pulled down. "You have a little girl. One pound, eight ounces, 14.2 inches," she said, before quickly giving the metric equivalents. "You should come with me. They're closing. You can't see your wife just yet."

Paul propelled off the sofa. "Steve, can you go to recovery when she's out? Pam, come with me." Desperation clung to each request.

Steve looked at them cautiously. "Sure. Go."

They followed the nurse. Paul and Pam had scrubbed thousands of times donning surgical gowns and gloves but never like this in a neo-natal intensive care unit, stepping into what seemed like Mission Control for Preemies. Could the tile floor accommodate Paul's heart when it sank there?

The Romano infant, born a little over three months shy of her due date, resembled a fetus. Only this wasn't textbook but very real as he glimpsed the glowing red probe taped to his baby's foot that measured oxygen saturation.

Paul stood back and surveyed the ventilator that did the work the infant's immature lungs could not do to sustain life. Leads were attached to monitor heart rate. An intravenous line looked purely pain-ful inserted into a tiny hand, but no worse than the one entering the baby's head.

Approaching the radiant warmer where the neonatologist and nurse cared for the newborn, Paul uttered "Madonna" softly.

Pam heard and placed her only available arm around Paul's waist. "It's OK," she whispered.

The attending physician ran the APGAR numbers. Quickly real-izing Paul was on staff with a baseline of knowledge, he offered, "This little girl's a fighter, and we're doing everything we can." Alarms sounded in different parts of the unit. Unnerving, to say the least. "You must have questions," the neonatologist continued.

Paul's eyes glistened over. He caught his breath. Everything he had envisioned saying did not fit. Bella meant beautiful yet watching Baby Romano was flat out frightening.

Steroids they had given Vicki should have helped to toughen the child's lungs, one of the last organs to mature. The team looked ready to transport what should have been his bundle of healthy joy into an incubator, warm and soundproof, designed with portholes for hands. This would be baby's world for who knew how long as it maintained temperature for the tiny child who struggled to live, to hopefully see her mom.

"What can I say to my wife when I see her?" For a brief moment, he clutched Pam. *If I see her.* Paul blinked. That thought sent a chill up his spine though this environment was much warmer than surgical suites he was accustomed to.

"The baby weighs what I'd expect. She did a great job on that count," the doctor told Paul. The man orchestrating the child's care laid a hand on Paul's shoulder.

The neonatal nurse cocked her eyebrows above her own mask. "You're Catholic? We can note that on her chart."

Paul's nod affirmed. It saddened him. His knees felt like Jell-O.

Pam's soothing hand stilled as she reached for her vibrating phone. "Paul, a message from Steve: Vicki's out of surgery. Stable, still on oxygen, awaiting new labs. Fifteen minutes and you can see her in recovery."

Paul's eyes surveyed the NICU, its staff. His little darling needed prayers, hope, and him. Vicki, the love of his life, needed him also.

"Take a breather." Pam sensed his dilemma. "I can stay a while. Take this." She handed him the Polaroid that the nurse took since Vicki would be too weak to see her baby in the NICU.

"Thanks." He kissed her cheek, mask to mask.

Paul stepped out and cast off the protective gown and gloves. He brushed a hand through his hair as he walked the hall closer to a window. Norman Rockwell couldn't have depicted the snow-laden tree branches with any more of an eerie stillness. Paul leaned his head into the window frame until *The Godfather* jolted him. He peeked at the screen. "Liz," he answered.

"I thought I'd get voice mail. You have your cell on. How's Vicki?"

"Better coverage by a window," Paul replied. "Headed to recovery in a minute to see her."

"Steve told Maren you had a little girl. Congratulations! I know she's so tiny though."

Paul cleared his throat during Liz's pause. He choked back tears but eked out, "I couldn't do neonatology. How did you work on that unit?"

"It wasn't the only unit I served on," Liz admitted. She innately perceived his torment. The surgery to deliver Vicki would have taxed both mother and child. "Talk to me...unless you have to run."

Paul twisted his neck to the clock. "I have a few seconds." He sniffled. "I don't know what to tell her. She's the childbirth educator, Liz. She knows too much. How can I help if I'm a mess?"

Liz sat on the guest room floor, her back straight against the wall. Knees bent, she leaned into them, phone in one hand. "Breathe in, hold it a few, then let it go." She paused patiently.

Paul heaved his burdens through the receiver.

"Focus on what's positive. Vicki will know that girls don't have the profound impairments boys sometimes face. I remember that fact."

"The status of cases like these change quickly."

"Yes, but you might be summoning an automatic negative thought and discounting the positive." Liz bit her lip. The phone masked a worry-etched face. "Her condition could improve also, correct?"

"You're right. This helps." Paul bent his elbow to the ceiling to massage strain in his neck.

"Did you and Vicki select a name?"

Paul managed a slight grin. "We thought about calling her Carina, Italian for little darling."

"That's beautiful," Liz replied, softly. "Use that name with Vicki."

"Liz, tell me…when is it time to alert the priest or clergy?" Anguish corded in Paul's throat as if he could hardly get that out.

"Whenever it would be appropriate…or a sense of comfort to you."

"I'll get on that…if the priest is still here." Where else would he go? Even the Popemobile would have trouble escaping this weekend. "This is so raw, so very real."

"If I could be there for moral support, I would," Liz told Paul.

"The governor banned all but emergency vehicles," Paul said. "Liz thanks. I feel like I won't fall apart with my five minutes of free therapy, but I need to meet Steve in recovery."

"You go," Liz said. "You sound more centered. We're here for you."

"It helps. I'll keep Steve posted." He clicked off. Paul made his way to the opposite wing and hurriedly swiped his badge to access recovery.

Seeing him approach, a nurse guided him to the curtained area in a corner where Steve leaned over Vicki's bed, his arms on the rails.

"How is she?" Paul asked Steve, gaining data from a new set of monitors. A nasal cannula was the first thing he saw on her delicate face. "Why is she still on oxygen?" Paul scrubbed at the sink.

"Not moving air well; weaker than we need her to be," he said. "Brought in a portable for a chest x-ray. Radiologist standing by to read it."

Paul squeezed Vicki's hand, but felt no tactile movement. He brushed her forehead with the back of his hand. "Carina's here, honey. She wants to meet her mommy." He kissed Vicki's brow. Looked to Steve. Waited. Watched his wife's labored breathing.

"You all right?" Steve asked. "A pretty name."

Paul inhaled, closed his eyes and gently felt his body relinquish air. "I have to be," he muttered. "I can't make either of them well."

"Just being with them helps." Steve registered the agony. His sideways headshake indicated that Vicki shouldn't hear their collective concern.

"Did Pam text more from the NICU?"

"Not yet," Steve said. "Take a few minutes while I update your mom."

By any textbook, Vicki should have improved after delivery, yet she had entered already compromised. Her body fought off infection, another complication that altered her breathing.

Paul's knees wouldn't hold him any longer. With his foot, he nudged a stool closer, sat down and took Vicki's hand to kiss it. He never let it go as he fought back tears and pleaded with God.

Chapter 5

The news Steve had to deliver diminished any comfort his office couch provided as he threw his head back into the leather.

"They're both struggling, Mair. Christ, calling Isabella was hard." Steve banded a jittery hand through his dark hair and gripped his Blackberry with another. "You'd think I'd be better at this."

"He's your best friend and this went south fast. What if…"

Steve stared at the ceiling. Asked what Maren couldn't. "What if she doesn't make it?"

"Yeah." Thick worry clogged Maren's throat. "Liz said Paul's upbeat, but sounded besieged."

"This would jack anyone up," Steve acknowledged. "And Mair, I've wondered what if's myself. I'm sorry I got on you about that."

"It's all right. Anything we can do to help?"

"Just pray," Steve suggested. "Tell me, what's happening there?"

"Kids have watched *The Lion King*, used sofa cushions to build the Pride Lands…and the cliff. Hannah gets to be Nala by default, and the boys take turns being Pumba, practicing fart noises. At which point, Hannah gets disgusted and curls up on the couch with Liz or me," Maren reported. "And we toasted marshmallows in the fireplace."

Steve threw his head back laughing. "Outside of talking to Paul, what's Liz doing?"

"She finally reached Tim last night. He was altogether too snarky. Pretty sure she holed up in the powder room drying her eyes."

"Damn," Steve muttered. "Let me talk to her."

Maren called for Liz and handed the phone "Karma this weekend sucks," Liz hushed. That she knew to lower her voice made Steve chuckle.

"Tell me 'bout it." He sat up now. "Take the phone to another room if you can." He waited. "I'm sorry Tim's being such a prick." Steve cast a long audible sigh for their collective benefit. "Listen, things could go either way with Vicki; the baby's barely holding. They're looking into transport now that the weather's cleared." Steve paused. "If this falls apart, Mair may fall apart."

"Steve, I know she's had her challenges, but she's stronger than you think."

"I hear 'ya. A certain level of composure even attracted me when we first met, but still…"

"What if…" Liz said, "the King of Calm and Composure, worried about us what-if women, becomes unglued himself?"

"Mea culpa. I apologized to Maren." Steve let silence fill the phone connection and glanced at his watch. "Look, I needed to decompress after calling Paul's mother. She's understandably worried sick and on her way here. Your plans went awry Liz, but I'm glad you ended up with Maren and bolstered Paul. I do appreciate what you bring to this. You're OK, you know that?"

"My *going all therapist* comes in handy?"

"Take the compliment," Steve said, "from your big brother. I used to get secretly jealous. Paul had Vicki while I was still searching for the right woman. I can be such an ass."

"I'm supposed to disagree with that?" Liz laughed. "You're long-term friends. Jealousy is normal. Don't I know," Liz sniffed. "You're helping him think, calling family. Validate how this all…sucks." Liz snickered after adding one of Maren's least favorite words that Steve used more frequently than soap and water.

Steve allowed levity. "Been there, done that."

"Forgot to ask. How's Pam and her family?"

"She's running between Chloé and Jerry. Pam's years speaking with expectant fathers paid off for Paul. She helped him out, even functioning at 65%."

"Glad they're improving." Liz quieted before adding, "I mean that."

Steve suddenly realized Liz had changed tune, but if she knew what lingered in his mind—though it fell to the back of his brain in the fast-paced effort to rally around Paul and Vicki—Liz would surely become prickly again about Pam.

"I wish I could do more for Paul," Liz said. "So like a third brother. He really helped me get through Friday." She waited. "Steve, you there?"

"Zoned, sorry. I really do have to run, Liz."

"I understand. Send Paul my great big hug."

In Vicki's newly freshened ICU room, Paul stopped pacing to stare out the window. He'd just come from the neonatal nursery spending time with his little darling. Before Vicki came from recovery, Paul had insisted that housekeeping disinfect her room and check the air quality.

He was being hyper-vigilant, he told himself, given the heavy-duty antibiotics dripping into her intravenous line. Unlike with Carina, Paul could see Vicki's face when her gurney entered the room. Tubes, lines, and attached leads obliterated so much with a tiny baby.

Paul stepped aside while the attendants settled Vicki. He waited as the nurse recorded vitals. Then they were alone. "Bellissima." Paul leaned into Vicki's ear. *Most beautiful.*

"Cara."

His eyes watered. "Carina's sleeping, honey. They're taking care of her. How are you?"

She remained silent. Paul thought her voice had all but collapsed. Until she uttered, "No you."

He smiled. Cara meant dear in Italian. When he kissed her forehead, Vicki closed those dark eyes he had always loved.

"You're out of recovery, getting stronger. We have a beautiful little girl, and you did a great job all those months. You really did," Paul whispered, having to stop. He knew Carina wasn't the picture of health, and he knew Vicki would hold herself responsible, unable to carry their child to term, or even close to it. "I have photos."

Vicki opened her eyes as Paul held up two Polaroid snapshots. Just as he expected, those stunning eyes washed over with tears. "So tiny." She turned her head. "Tell me…"

"She's a fighter. Remember girls do a little better out of the gate. You win on that one."

Vicki's tear-laden cheeks protruded. She and Paul had often teased about which gender was stronger. "But remember. We decided." Four words had the struggle of a major speech.

"Sshh, she'll get better. Every prayer in the Western Hemisphere and in Rome is with her…and you." *To get stronger.*

"Promise me. My parents know."

"Your parents are trying to get here. They send their love, Vicki." Paul brushed dark hair off her forehead. Tears flooded his eyes. He knew that she must have spoken to her mother and father about what might happen if she lost this baby as she had other pregnancies. "What can I do for you? I'd switch places if I could."

"I love you," she managed. "First time, at football. *You* won."

His tears dropped onto Vicki's pillow. "I love challenge. Too proud to admit it," he whispered. "You didn't have to convert to my loyalties."

"Passionate. I want Carina…that way."

"She will be, she will." She needs her mommy. I need her mommy.

Paul stayed with Vicki most of Monday, through dinner until Pam came to remind him the cafeteria would soon close. His hospital yet Pam had schedules memorized and emotions pulled together, helping him piece his own today.

As a nurse entered the ICU room, she acknowledged that Vicki's parents had arrived. Visitors were limited to no more than two at a time. Paul could have pulled some rank, but he needed a minute to dry his eyes so he stepped out, hugged his in-laws, and let them have that time.

He used the restroom, took several long gulps from the fountain. Turned his nose up at the vending machine. A half-hour later, he glanced at the wall clock. The glowing numerals 11:24 confirmed it had been a day.

Paul spotted his mother-in-law pulling tissues from her purse. Wanting to catch her, he was too late. The elevator door closed to take them and another person that he couldn't quite see to where they'd get their first peek at their grandchild through the nursery window, the closest they'd be able to get to little Carina.

A nurse pulled Paul aside. Recent labs had come back. The infection Vicki fought had moved to her blood. Sepsis. Serious.

"They requested he stop by, and the chart indicated religion," the nurse justified. The figure Paul saw leave had been a priest.

"That's fine. We're Catholic," Paul said.

With the weight of his shoulder, Paul pushed the hospital room door open. He'd scrubbed what felt like a layer of skin, a small price to keep Vicki from catching something else.

"I'm back," he whispered as he took her hand to squeeze it. "Ti amo, bella."

A nasal cannula now brought oxygen. Vicki tried to move her lips, but it took too much energy. So when her dry lips pursed together as if to pucker, Paul nuzzled his mask close. Held her. Heard every labored breath. He crooned sweet nothings, in not one but two languages.

When the monitor sounded, he looked in disbelief. Paul didn't think he had any tears left, but his cheeks felt moist. A nurse dashed in as Paul positioned himself to start chest compressions. Not that he had to since the team with its cart to revive patients burst through the door.

An attendant nudged Paul aside. "No, please," Paul said. He tried to pull from a nurse's hand.

"It's best Dr. Romano," she uttered. "Come with me." She guided him to the desk, but he refused to take a seat and instead leaned against the hallway wall. He caught tormented glimpses of the activity through the glass window.

"You paged," Steve said. He had run down the hall, having known there was a code. "Oh my God." Steve saw the intensity Paul now had to turn away from. "How long has she been down?"

"Ten minutes." The next ten would make all else in this miserable day seem trivial. "Steve…"

"Don't say it." Steve could do nothing but pull Paul's shoulders for a sideways embrace.

Paul's head spun. If Steve didn't help shore Paul's weight standing next to him he would have fallen. Paul closed his eyes and prayed more earnestly than he could ever remember. When he opened them, Paul saw the code team, their bodies stilled, with their collective eyes on the round clock in his wife's room. "No. No."

Time of death: 12:26 AM.

Steve pulled Paul tighter as he felt him sink into despair against him. Paul had lost his bella, his wife, and his world.

The staff left Paul in Vicki's room as he held her and cried in the wee hours of Tuesday morning. Somewhere around 2:30 AM, Paul stepped out and into a hug from Vicki's nurse who had been on duty since shift change last night.

Steve looked up from a terminal at the ICU nursing station.

"Still here?" Paul asked, brushing his eyes and forehead with the rolled up sleeves of his shirt.

"Where else would I be?" Steve affirmed. "I got some work done. Let's go downstairs." He scraped back the chair that was his home for the last two hours as he feigned attention, more distracted by the loss of a good friend.

Steve walked with an arm draped over Paul's shoulder for the short ride to second floor offices, including theirs. On the way, Steve reported that he had called the NICU informing the staff there, and he gave him an update on Carina.

Paul stretched back on his office sofa around the corner from Steve's larger one. He thought he was all right until he saw a photo of Vicki on his desk. Emotion flooded him as he cried out in Italian the equivalent of "God help me!"

"Here." Steve tossed Paul a blanket and pillow from a closet. "I'm getting you an Ambien."

"It's a little late to start that. I'm gonna have to call Ma and Vinny in two hours before they head down here. I haven't even thought of plans yet. Christ, Vicki's parents had just left."

"Listen, you'll get at least five, six hours. I alerted your answering service, cancelled your patients." Paul sometimes used Steve's secretary for scheduling. "Suzanna will figure out the rest. I can call your mother again." It wouldn't be the first time either one of them had delivered news of death to family members, just never this close.

"They'll be up at five. Vinny lives at home these days. His girlfriend kicked him out."

Steve heaved a sigh. "I peeked in Chloé's room. Pam was sound asleep. I'll catch up with her." Steve knew he'd also have to encounter Maren at work. Steve handed Paul a pill and a glass of water, dreading the to-do list at hand yet willingly lending support. "This'll help."

Reluctantly, Paul took it, downed the water, and continued to shake his head as he'd done since resting on the sofa. "I'm gonna wake up and this will be a bad dream."

Paul slept as if he had died. Part of him wished he had when his grim reality resurfaced as his worst nightmare as his eyes met daylight.

Parking lots became depositories for snowplows. Schools closed for the week. Businesses allowed non-essential employees to telework. At West Riverside, hospital shifts had begun hours before. The blizzard wreaked havoc with coworker stamina. Paul felt a twinge of guilt that his absence complicated the workload further.

Paul forced himself under a hot shower and rummaged through his suitcase for clothes. Tonight he would take that suitcase home knowing Vicki would never again walk up their basement steps nor greet him as he sought comfort after a long day. They would never hold one another and never raise a daughter together either.

Little Carina was still attached to a ventilator, and though her vitals were stable, the nurses soon had to focus on nutrition. Tiny preemies best tolerated breast milk and benefited from its immune boost, even through a feeding tube. A human donor bank brought concerns about screening and quality. Whenever Paul's mind rested from one detail, five new decisions demanded answers. He alone had to make each one.

He spent an hour reaching into the incubator, trying to pretend nurses were not casting stares. Paul felt his stomach tumble. Pure nerves. The body needed water more than food, right?

That morning, with no school, Audrey offered to watch Dylan along with Tyler and Hannah. Liz drove in to the hospital with Maren.

They waited outside the neonatal unit where families suited up or down. "Paul," Maren said first when he stepped out. "I'm so, so sorry."

Paul stripped off latex gloves. Maren's arms opened and closed around him. She placed loving strokes on Paul's back as he clung to her. "You and I have more than Steve in common now," he said. "It's so surreal."

"Will be for a while," Maren replied. Indeed they shared a connection neither wanted to have. "We all loved Vicki, and we love you."

Paul spotted Liz, standing aside to allow their mutual comfort. He pulled back from Maren to untie his gown. He balled it with one hand and tossed it into the hamper.

Liz's open arms were simply too inviting. Paul fell into them next.

"I tried to stay positive," he managed, burying his face in her shoulder. Fresh tears fell on her sweater. "You'd have been proud." He sniffled and picked up his head. "Not so sure now."

"I'm very proud of you, Paul." Liz still enveloped him. "This is hard stuff, and I'm here if you need me. We all are."

They stepped into the neonatal waiting room, quiet at this early hour. Liz and Paul sat on the couch. Maren faced them in a side chair.

"I don't know what I'd do without such good friends." Paul granted Maren the most pitiful eyes. "Pam was here all weekend with her own trauma but saw me through mine. Steve was up all night but made me sleep. Liz, if you hadn't checked in, I'd have never stayed as centered. Thank you." Paul squeezed Liz's hand tight.

"Steve says your family should be here soon," Maren reassured.

Paul glanced at the wall clock. "No surprise their flight was delayed." He straightened on the sofa. "I talked with Vicki's folks. Devastated. They have to reach her sister. We're supposed to discuss arrangements. I don't...have a clue."

"If you'd like, I have some phone numbers. Mark's buried not far away. I barely got through a two-hour viewing. All I could tolerate."

"I'd really appreciate that." Paul turned to Liz who picked up the handbag she had set on the floor. "I'm sure you need to get rolling. You've been on this side of the bridge half a week now."

"Stranded like everyone else, but I'm going to get my kids home." Liz stood and Paul rose off the sofa as well. They hugged again. "I'm not going to offer all those clichés. Just know I care, and I really hope you'll let me know if I can help out in any way. Tim and I are so sorry for your loss, and we'll keep Carina in our prayers."

Paul pulled Liz to the side while Maren wrote some numbers from her phone on a small pad of paper from her purse. "I told Vicki about Carina. While she was weak, I saw a flicker when I used her name. I don't think I would have named her so quickly. Brilliant suggestion."

After he kissed her cheek, Liz snagged one last hug. "Be strong. You can do it!"

Paul put up a hand to wave as Liz stepped toward the elevator.

"Bye Liz," Maren said. She stopped writing to focus on Paul. "You know my minister Luke saw me through so much of the aftermath when Mark died. I know you're Catholic."

"Technically. Vicki and I didn't attend mass that often. Holidays," Paul admitted sheepishly. "If it's up to me, I'd go for a funeral service only. I have to work with her parents on this." Tears cascaded out of his eyes, and Maren snatched him a tissue from her sweater pocket.

"I know how that goes. You have a baby now."

"I'm all she's got." Sitting again, Paul looked at the carpet. "I've got to pull it together for her."

"I understand. Luke comes here for parishioners. He's easy to talk to. That you're Catholic won't matter. You both have him, too." She clutched Paul's hand. "My parents send their condolences and love. So do Dolores and Bill."

"I appreciate that." Paul latched on to the empathy in Maren's eyes, brown like Vicki's.

Liz had already boarded an elevator, but when another dinged again, rolling open its set of doors, Maren and Paul both startled.

"Ah, Ma!" Paul pushed himself off the sofa. He walked straight into Isabella Romano's maternal embrace. Maren didn't need a translator to grasp the sentiments she slid into his ear. It looked like she had comforted children all of her life.

Maren gave them some space, time for tears to flow and hugs to matter. She grabbed a quick drink at the fountain and made eye contact with the younger man who stood among them.

"Vinny." Paul embraced his brother. "Maren, my mother Isabella and youngest brother."

Vinny and Maren shook hands. He had a firm grip, belying the chiseled nose and small chin that made Vinny Romano look younger than Steve had described him. The dark-haired shadow against his jawline told he could use a shave even as late morning drew near. He kept his emotions in check speaking his sympathies.

Something in the exchange told Maren that just like winter winds chilled to the bone multiple losses had somehow shaped Vinny.

"The lucky lady." Isabella held Maren's hands. The matriarch assessed the length of her. "Our Steve, now your Steve. Like a son."

"So I've been told," Maren replied. "Pleased to meet you, only I wish under better circumstances. I'm so incredibly sorry for your loss. I got to know Vicki on staff and she was a friend."

"I don't know…what we do without her."

Steve had relayed how Isabella came to this country. Barely out of high school, she devoted herself to husband and family as it was then.

"It is hard to go on, but we do," Maren offered.

"Ma, Maren's a widow. She has a six-year-old," Paul added, attempting to connect them.

"He was young when he lost his PaPa. Like my Vinny," Isabella said. She cupped Vinny's hand. "Paul started junior high…more teachers, not enough nuns." His mother parsed a kiss on Paul's cheek. "Seven kids. How many you have?"

"Just Dylan." Maren instinctively saw the coddling that had occurred and apparently still did.

"Vicki don't see her baby." Hit by that sudden realization, Isabella Romano commanded, "I see my granddaughter."

"Only two at a time, Ma," Paul cautioned. "We have to gown up."

His mother nodded. "Vinny, you keep…ah…."

"Maren," Paul said. Name recall waned, he remembered. Seven children could scatter a mind.

"Think mariner Ma, just shorter," Vinny suggested. "Steve: his boats and beautiful women."

Isabella scowled. Vinny instantly straightened. Maren smiled at the compliment and at how Paul's mother curtailed her Casanova-like son.

Isabella opened her clasp purse, pulled out a bill, and transferred it to Vinny's slender fingers.

"You go get Steve's lady something to eat," she instructed. "Then you meet me back here."

"This way, Ma," Paul said. "We've gotta scrub."

Chapter 6

"Where's Dad?" Tyler asked. "Movies instead of school. We can all watch!" he squealed as he flopped onto the family room sofa. Liz stared out the wide windows looking at the water. Icicles dangled from the roof and intruded upon her view. Mounds of snow covered their yard. Ice packed itself thick beneath the pilings of their dock and gangplank. "Mom?"

"Sure, then it's time to read." Liz heard mild protest but turned from it.

She and the kids had settled at home on Kent Island late Tuesday afternoon. The weekend that was supposed to have them solidly in Southern Maryland had stranded them when the sky dumped a large white blast. Liz found the positive: She helped her brother and Maren grasp the death of their close friend and got to express her own condolences to Paul right away.

Liz surveyed the dishwasher that Tim must have emptied. Not even a stray dish. *Odd.* Hannah padded in. Liz jiggled her up onto her hip. "You're getting heavy little girl. You napped through lunch. You did eat breakfast?"

"Just Cheerios," the three-year-old said. "I asked for more but Almost-Aunt Maren didn't hear me. She's sad."

Liz lightened hearing Hannah's name for Maren. "Honey, sometimes we don't always know why bad things happen. We're all sad."

Frozen snacks—mozzarella sticks—had been invented when motivation to cook was at zero. Liz microwaved some for Hannah.

"You're back." Tim let the door slam from the garage and raced up the steps. "Hannah!"

"Daddy!" she hollered, wiggling. Liz had no choice but to hand her over into another set of arms. "Daddy, something bad happened."

"I know, hammered with snow. You've had a long weekend. Hey, bud!" Tim waved to his son.

"Dad, this is so cool. You gotta see." Tyler kneeled on the sofa to get his father's attention.

"I'll be there. Just a minute."

Tyler plopped back in front of the TV.

Hannah tugged on Tim's shirt. "No Daddy, somebody died."

"Hannah." Liz held her off. She took the food to the coffee table and positioned the ottoman near it. "Eat here with Tyler while I talk with Daddy. Tyler, you can have two or three. No fighting. I need to talk to your father."

Tim set his daughter on her feet and patted her bottom as she made a beeline for her snack.

Liz took Tim by the arm. "Downstairs."

"Liz, what happened?" Tim matched her serious tone as they descended the stairs.

While most people might go up a level, four bedrooms, including the master they shared, made up the first floor with the main living and dining spaces gaining the greater view on the second story. Above, guests enjoyed a suite with a view that made them want to move in.

As they sat on their bed, perfectly made and not a pillow out of place, Liz looked at Tim.

"I've so many emotions about the weekend. Those can wait. You remember Paul and Vicki Romano when Eric's band played last fall?" Liz waited for a nod. "Vicki died yesterday."

"What happened? They were expecting."

Liz drew in a breath. "I don't understand all the medical jargon, but essentially her body shut down. Vicki had a terrible infection that her immune system couldn't fight. Born by cesarean, their little girl is having a rough go of it."

"Steve's best friend," Tim offered, "and best man. No wonder you stayed an extra day."

"The weather didn't exactly cooperate," Liz said. "They're shell-shocked, may postpone the wedding, sensitive to Paul's feelings, especially Maren. I hope she's not traumatized again."

Liz noticed Tim scan the room, not fully paying attention. People could have such varying reactions to bad news, she thought. "I'm sorry to be gone so long. Didn't mean to be."

"That's OK." Tim studied Liz's downturned lips and puffy eyes. He rubbed her shoulders as he asked more questions. "That's pretty extreme, postponing a wedding. What does all this mean?"

"A viewing Friday morning before a full mass at Our Lady of Mercy, not far from West Riverside. Vicki will be interred where Mark, Maren's husband, is buried. I'm cancelling my clients on Friday. I'd really appreciate it if you could pull yourself away. I'll get a sitter if I have to." She clutched Tim's wrist. "As for Maren and Steve, maybe they'll back out of their new house, too."

"Seriously?" His mouth opened like a fish, ready to take more bait, only plastered that way.

Liz stared him down with eyes as chilled as the outdoors. *He took my stretched truth: hook, line, and sinker.* "They'll come to their senses over the wedding," she quickly corrected. "Paul wouldn't approve from what I know of him." *A blasted sale, a listing matters more.*

Liz thought about Paul, how he engaged people with humor, and she wondered how this loss would change him. *My husband barely acknowledged us all weekend. Paul desperately wants a family and his is falling apart.*

"You had me worried," Tim answered.

"I could tell," Liz said coolly. "Thanks for keeping the place clean. You weren't here?"

"Oh, I was in and out. I got a lot of computer work done, especially Sunday and Monday."

"Well, we must have lost power. The clock's flashing. You worked at the office?"

"Did you lose power at Maren's?"

"No, Tim. I meant here."

Tim looked at his watch. "Don't you need to fix dinner? I left notes behind. Still have some work at the office." He pecked her cheek. "I'm really sorry about Paul's wife. I'll look at my schedule. I know I've got meetings and showings late Friday, into the evening."

"Whatever," Liz replied. "I'm glad listings are holding so well."

"Oh, I can always use more," he said. "See ya."

Liz followed Tim out to the garage to retrieve one remaining suitcase. Earlier, she had helped the kids inside and put groceries into the refrigerator when she first entered the house. Good thing, since the milk Liz had left looked curdled. She dumped that down the drain. If Tim was in and out, he'd survived on pasta, days-old salad she also tossed, and an open bottle of wine.

Liz hung her gown in the master closet and hurled the small suitcase onto the bed. Did she have any children's books about death? The place looked so tidy. Odd, she thought, but nice.

Unpacking seemed like a rote chore with so many racing thoughts until she dropped her small jewelry bag on the floor and saw an earring tumble out. Getting down on her hands and knees, Liz scoured the soft tan carpet, plush enough to absorb the earring and its post. Brushing hands along the fibers, she seized it. "What's this?" A red card had slid under the nightstand. Fresh vacuum marks had pushed it out of sight.

Liz stood back up. Read it. The card exterior had hearts of varying sizes and shades of red and pink. *For someone so hot* the outer wording read. Inside she saw a handwritten *L*. The inscription: *Won't you melt me with your heat? Happy Valentine's Day!* Hand scrawled beneath: *Love, Tim.*

Feeling ashamed for being so negative, Liz stashed the card in her nightstand drawer. *Tim didn't forget.* With such meticulous cleaning, the card literally got swept under the table.

Liz sighed and swung her suitcase off the bed, carrying it to a corner of her walk-in closet. "Who's hungry?" she hollered as she went to feed her two starving children.

Thankful that the hospital pharmacy filled a prescription, Paul relied on a sleep aid again. With siblings converging—more like taking over—and spending time with Baby Carina, he ran on pure adrenaline. Finally, the weather cooperated enough to move Carina safely Tuesday to a Baltimore hospital for a higher level of care.

At six o'clock Wednesday, a neonatologist woke Paul. Carina had not tolerated a feeding. He asked Paul what measures he approved of and summoned him to his daughter's side while they X-rayed the infant and did what they could.

Isabella Romano stood with her son in the new sterile setting. "I don't understand the words here," Isabella told him. "I had seven babies. Praise Mother Mary. None of this." Almost on cue, an alarm sounded at the isolette next to Carina's, startling Paul's mother.

"A's and B's. Apnea means a baby stops breathing and bradycardia that the heart rate slows, but the vent forces Carina to breathe a set number of times," Paul explained.

Isabella flustered. "In my day, you got A's and B's in kindergarten."

"Medicine's come a long way, Ma." Yet as Paul praised all that technology could do, he knew that there were no guarantees, especially since Carina experienced a major setback. He looked to see if it was the appointed time for Carina's doctor to appear. A meeting he dreaded.

Vicki would have congratulated couples she'd helped, delighted if a baby overcame milestones, maintained body temperature, and latched on to nurse. Vicki's condition had robbed her, robbed them, of nurturance and normalcy.

His neck corded and stiff, Paul couldn't deal with that. Isabella asked a few questions, none of which Paul answered. In medical lingo, his wife had been a train wreck, a patient with everything wrong that could go wrong.

"Excuse me, Ma. Just keep a hand to her head or feet…reminds preemies of the womb." Paul pinched his lips together. Stepped into the small conference room. When he returned, an alarm had spooked his mother, who looked drained though the nurse assisted.

Skin tone had fled from Dr. Romano as well. "Carina has a perfed intestine. That's why she's not tolerating feedings."

"A what?"

"A perforation. Intestinal contents leaked into her abdominal cavity." Paul drew his head back stiffly, feeling every muscle tighten. Again.

"What did her doctor say? I'm sure there's something they can do." If maternal optimism cured, hospitals wouldn't exist.

"They did a procedure to save as much bowel as they could. The call I got earlier was for my consent. She's on high-dose antibiotics. She'll need surgery." Paul tightened his grip on his mother's hand. The other one reached to gently caress Carina's head. "We wait. And pray."

Anyone could see the perspiration bead above the mask Paul wore. Isabella recognized the words her son muttered in Italian. She hadn't known him to be outwardly religious. With the clasped hand Isabella held some of his agony.

"Here," she said, pulling a cross from her pocket and the sweater tight against her chest, even though this unit was already warm. She wedged it into Paul's free hand. "Your grandmother's. You need it."

"Thanks, Ma." Paul fought back tears. "Another thing they discussed with me…"

"What's that?" Isabella waited. Paul's words didn't slide out easily.

"They asked me about continuing extraordinary measures. If I'm not here, they need to know." Paul looked at his mother. "It is something Vicki and I talked about." He hesitated again. "How can I go back on what she and I agreed together? If the outlook isn't viable, we agreed we'd have to let... I feel a loyalty to her, yet I want…I want Carina so badly to get better."

Tears flowed from both mother and son as this new father rested his firm hand securely on his infant daughter, the only nestling he could do.

"Remember what I framed after Pa-Pa died," Isabella recited from memory. "Love is stronger than death, no matter how hard it tries to separate people from love. It can't take away memories." She paused, allowing it to sink in. "If they tell you she…well, make sure you hold her. Just like you did Vicki. She'll have her Pa-Pa here…"

"And her Mama in Heaven, waiting for her." Paul remembered Liz's be strong backing.

An hour later though he felt frazzled, he uttered, "Dio Aiutami."

Isabella needed no translation. "God is helping. He never stops. Or *we* wouldn't be here."

Paul had gained much from his upbringing, but nothing more so than the strength his mom collected and shared with her children after she lost her own husband and forged forward to make sure they had what they needed in life.

Paul skipped lunch but nibbled on a sandwich Isabella brought after learning her way around this mega-hospital, much larger than the one she navigated with Vinny yesterday. Vicki's parents had paid a quick visit after receiving a call.

By seven o'clock when Isabella joined Paul again, he updated his mother. The priest had come by at her urging before dinner. Each nurse on duty had to flick Carina's foot many times because of the bradycardia or her heart stopping. "They don't expect Carina to make it through the night. Her BP's dropping. They've had to stim her so many times. They infused her with pain meds," Paul said. "I'm taking your advice."

Two hours later, the nurse laid little Carina in Paul's outstretched arms. He overlooked the lines attached, prayed that she would rally, that a miracle would visit his child. Paul told her about her mother and described Vicki's dark eyes, the S-shape curl her hair would naturally form into, and her personality as if descriptions would help Carina recognize the woman he lost...and his daughter would meet.

How long Paul crooned at his little darling wasn't significant to him, nor was the time on the clock when she took her last little assisted breath. Carina left this world in his arms. He continued to hold her, tears streaming now as he pulled his mask away to kiss her.

When he finally laid Carina down, he tucked the swaddled blanket around her tight. Only then, Paul fell straight into the arms of the woman who had always been there for him...and cried.

Friday's mass honored Vicki as the priest eulogized her fun-loving spirit, her commitment to friends, family, and in particular, her husband Paul, whom she would meet again someday.

The remarks highlighted Vicki's dedication to helping patients become parents despite struggles she had in her own pregnancies. "In the end," the priest said, "Vicki achieved what she so very wanted, only not in her way nor in Paul's way. She prayed to have a child." The priest paused. He looked out among the mourners, to Paul completely bereft, and then turned to the casket.

"Though we cry we need to remember. Vicki carried Carina into this world, and today, she carries Carina into eternity. A baby forever cradled in her loving mother's arms."

Sniffles could be heard from most pews. As the service closed, the priest added, "May every candle you as loved ones light keep the memory of Vicki and little Carina close to your hearts, today, and every day, until we all meet again."

Steve, Vinny, and older brothers Giovanni and Emilio served as pallbearers as did a brother-in-law and a close cousin. Though only family and close friends rode to the cemetery, the procession of cars stretched one mile. Baltimore friends, hospital co-workers, even many parents that Vicki had helped in her short tenure working at West Riverside had filled the pews. The crowd thinned but some joined Vicki's family at their home, south of Baltimore, where they catered lunch to celebrate her life.

"How does he seem to you?" Pam asked Steve. She sipped wine, holding her goblet with her available hand. "If I need a glass to calm frayed nerves, Paul may need a wine cellar."

"One foot in front of the other. It hasn't set in," he answered her. "Honestly, I've never seen alcohol as his preferred coping method."

"It takes weeks to set in," Maren interjected. "Then: really rough. Dylan kept me going."

Absorbing that somber assessment, Steve brushed his lips on Maren's forehead. It spooked him since Paul had no child to wake up to each morning. He turned to his sister nearby. "Here's where the big brother asks advice. Have any?"

"Just be there. We all should be," Liz stated. "Maren said it: little gestures show we care."

Liz and Tim had made the service, but Tim split after the mass, telling her he would pick up the kids. Liz rode in the funeral processional with her brother and Maren.

"There's really no substitute for time," Maren offered. "Some days are excruciating."

"Today had to be one of those for you," Pam acknowledged. "Your going to that cemetery."

"I woke up thinking about all the coffee klatches Paul and I had since Steve introduced us," Maren said. "Those happened for a reason. I'll make them happen over this next year."

"I hope he doesn't make any sudden, snap decisions," Liz added. "I heard him whisper to Tim that he wants to talk to him. Tomorrow."

She rolled her eyes as she finished delivering the timeframe.

"That means real estate. You don't think he's going to sell the house?" Steve asked.

"Steve, he's been on Ambien all week," Pam interjected. "Paul told me that he couldn't even look at the nursery they decorated. His sisters Ava and Rosa spent yesterday packing baby purchases. Her sister went through her closet."

"If it wasn't for maintaining stability for Dylan, I might have sold my house. My grief group said no sudden changes, but sometimes you can't bear it. The pain is too real."

Steve shuddered. "The expression he taught me: Raw and real."

"This is every bit of that," Liz said.

"Only knowing Paul…" Pam raised her eyebrows and downed the last of her wine. "Means something else." She leaned over to Steve. "Isn't that woman talking to Vinny…ah, Vanessa?"

Steve looked baffled. "I think some of his Pittsburgh friends drove down. So?"

"At our apartment one night. There were others. Plural," Pam whispered. "Don't be dense."

"Paul had a party, kept you up?" Liz assumed.

"You could call it that." Steve answered tersely. "Pam, pain meds and wine don't mix."

"My parents are driving. Don't lecture."

"Mea culpa. Grade point average ahead," he predicted.

"Look, you two," Liz chided. "I don't know what your history with Paul is here. Obviously a lot happened sharing two apartments."

"Three," Pam corrected. "The first one needed to be condemned in the '60s. Two in New York; one we all picked in Pittsburgh."

"My point is—Maren back me up—we must pull together, like last weekend. Even with a herd of Romano siblings, Paul will need us."

"I'm at the tail end of that herd, as you called it," Vinny interjected. "Speaking for all, we'd be happy to have your *lovely* support."

"Vinny, my sister Liz Kramer Phillips." Steve emphasized her married name.

Vinny ignored him to take Liz's hands. He studied the gold band and diamond on her left. "I recall Paul saying you had a younger sister." Vinny shot his eyes straight at Liz. He hesitated. "Steve, what a pleasure meeting Maren."

Vinny smiled. "Pamela, it's been years." Eyes cocked, he reached for Pam's empty glass. "Let me take that. Lend a hand to an old friend." Vinny Romano set it on a table to kiss Pam's now available fingers. "Flipping channels, I saw a TV report. A doctor. Looked just like you."

"It probably was, Vinny." Pam hid her amusement, and after Liz had lit into them, bit her tongue. "Paul says you sell insurance."

"Among other things," Vinny said. "I'm an entrepreneur, in the jewelry business, too."

"Really?" Pam replied. She looked at Steve quizzically, and fingered the necklace she wore since Vinny's eyes had zoned there. "How long have you been doing that?"

"The last few years," Vinny answered. "I acquire stunning pieces and appraise beauty...of all kinds." Vinny's grin encompassed more than the gold on Pam's chest. "The resale market is tremendous." He scanned Maren. "That diamond, almost two carats in a Tiffany setting. That's probably worth..."

"Don't even think of it, Vinny," Steve interrupted. "Already on my insurance policy."

"Steve: still a killjoy. Pamela, we should talk auto insurance," Vinny suggested. "If you get dropped after this accident, you call me." Vinny latched onto Liz's elbow even as his eyes made the point with Pam. "Liz, I'll introduce you to my sisters. You see that brooch on Margherita..." Vinny led Liz to meet another woman whose facial features cast her as a Romano.

When there was enough distance, Pam coughed audibly. Her eyes suggested she needed no Heimlich maneuver. "Is he for real?"

"Quite the entrepreneur," Steve replied. "Making moves on my married sister." Steve snickered. "And you, Pam."

"Funerals bring out the best and worst," Maren said. "I remember my former in-laws."

"Vinny's pretty harmless. He's been spoiled," Pam posited. "Hence everyone else functions *for* Vinny...but he tries." She smiled. "Steve never liked Vinny's wandering eye." Pam laughed.

"At the tail end all right," Steve tossed out. "Guess what: when his eyes wander your way, you're on your own now." He borrowed Maren's wine glass and took a sip out of it. "But then, he could start a fan club now that you're on TV."

"Steve has issues with my media presence apparently," Pam said.

"He's evolving to appreciate PR and promotion." Maren shifted her eyes to Steve since he was taller, then to Pam. "Good for you."

69

Steve changed his demeanor. He straightened with Isabella Romano approaching. "How are you holding up?" he asked, kissing her cheek.

"I dunno, Steve. I thought my Paul was settled with the perfect Italian girl...and a baby." She snagged a handkerchief from her pocket. Paul's mother wore a jacket over her black dress. "Well, Vicki only part Italian. Scottish and Irish. We call that a Heinz 57 in Pittsburgh."

"They were definitely well matched." Maren flexed a smile. "Scottish people appreciate humor. Vicki was always so positive, and Paul so caring beyond his sharp wit."

"My Paul...the nuns used to get after him, but he was the best altar boy, wouldn't you know." The Italian matriarch bobbed her head. "Too small for the football team in Catholic high school, but he kept out of trouble." Isabella Romano paused, turning to the vocal sounds. "Pamela, you all right? Drink water."

"No, Mrs. Romano, I'm...I'm fine." Pam removed a balled up fist covering her cough. Pam's eyes seared into Steve, who tried not to look at her for fear he, too, might chuckle.

"Maren and I will help wherever we can. You returning to Pittsburgh soon?" Steve asked.

"No, I stay as long as Paul needs me. The girls and I pack things." She dabbed her eyes with an embroidered handkerchief. "Then, I think he should be back home, get away for awhile." Isabella pondered. "Steve, you his boss, right?"

"He works on my service, and from that standpoint we've got him covered. He's entitled to personal leave per hospital policy."

"Buono," Isabella said. She clutched Steve's hand and squeezed it. "You like a son to me. And, Mary...Mar...Maren, that right?"

When Maren nodded, Mrs. Romano continued. "Germans don't know sauce. But this one...I taught him. You have Steve cook for you."

"He already has, and you certainly taught him well," Maren offered. "With good cookware."

"The best," Isabella added. "Got it on sale. I bought for Vinny, too. He uses coupons. Good pots and pans...no coupons. Now, Pamela?"

"We eat out a lot," Pam said rather than face admonishment if Isabella Romano ever knew Chloé feasted on Chef Boyardee. "I'll tell you what: if the offer still stands and you're visiting Paul, I'd love to watch you cook sometime."

"That's a girl," Isabella said. "Where's Vinny? You need insurance, Steve? Wedding rings?"

"No, we're set with all that." Steve smiled. No one usually called

Pam Morgan a girl and got away with it. "Vinny's over there with my sister. Maybe you can talk to her about good cooking."

As Paul's mother parted their company, Maren elbowed Steve. "That wasn't nice."

"Like hell we'll buy rings out of Crazy Vinny's Pawn Shop."

"I meant the crack about Liz," Maren clarified. "She can bake."

"Pawn shop?" Pam asked. "Really?"

"I swear it's called Crazy Vinny's Pawn Shop," Steve replied.

Pam laughed. "Well, Paul has certainly proven himself. Giovanni owns the restaurant Vinny couldn't get off the ground, and Emilio's wife and kids look normal...settled." Pam sighed. "By the way, I never congratulated you on your engagement. You both look happy."

"We are. Thanks," Maren said.

Steve nuzzled Maren. "*So* glad you approve," he added. He could lob a look just as well as any Kramer female could and he did. At Pam.

"I'm going to say goodbye. Jerry is resting with Chloé at my parents' condo. They both got released yesterday," Pam explained. "Good luck with your wedding. And Steve..." She looked at him solemnly. "Thanks again for Friday. Keep in touch about Paul. I'm worried about him."

"You're welcome," Steve answered. "Mair and I will keep an eye on him. I'll call you."

As Steve nudged Maren toward some others at the luncheon, he turned to look at Pam over his shoulder. Hoped his eyes conveyed what he couldn't add with words. They had a discussion to continue, and he wasn't about to let it drop.

Most of the Romano family left in shifts to BWI if they had not driven. Vinny drove with one sister. Only Isabella remained with Paul, who had packed possessions in two suitcases for a flight they would catch to Pittsburgh mid-week.

"Sorry to inflict Vinny," Paul told Steve. Paul slouched on his sofa in a much quieter house. "He's best tolerated in small doses, then titrated."

Steve grinned. He sat facing Paul in a chair. "My life is a train wreck," Paul said softly so that his mother couldn't hear. Upstairs she emptied closets and filled cardboard boxes.

"If I could change any of this, I'd do it in a heartbeat. You know that," Steve affirmed.

71

"I do, and I know what all this hovering is about." Paul straightened his spine and scrubbed hands over his face, only to fall thoroughly into a worse slouch. Posture was overstated. "You're all afraid I'm heading off some deep end. I'm not." His eyes watered. "But I don't have a clue how to feel better right now."

"Maybe going back home, back to the 'burgh is the best idea," Steve said. He hesitated, leaning onto his knees, steepling his fingers as he gathered his thoughts.

"What?"

"Last weekend…it had to be early on, but after the gala, I visited Vicki. Chatted. OK, we gossiped about Vinny, too. I'll be honest."

Paul chuckled. "When Vicki met Vinny, it was at full strength. Made a definite impression."

"Must have," Steve stammered. "Vicki wrote Valentines. She'd given Maren and me one, and made a point of handing me something, for you." Eyes filled with sorrow, he knuckled away some of that wet evidence before he reached into his shirt pocket for a small envelope.

Very slowly he handed it to Paul. "She said to keep it, and I told her it wouldn't be necessary." Steve rubbed between his brows. "When you were still with her…before they took her away, I went back to my office. There were actually two envelopes. When I opened the outer one, it was a note to me with instructions to wait a few days, if anything happened. So I did. That day is now."

Paul clasped it, smaller than business-sized. He didn't speak, just stared, and grabbed a handful of tissues from a box on the coffee table. It was new, replenished from providing soft comfort for days on end. "I wrote my own note. Slipped it into her hands in the casket."

"Do you want me to hang around? Whatever you need." Steve dabbed his eyes with a tissue.

"I can't read this now. I have to focus on getting out of here tomorrow. I'll put it upstairs. Thanks," Paul said. His words fell out almost as a whisper. "You've been such a good friend, all these years between you and me, and when Vicki came on the scene…no need to titrate. You just became fast friends with her, too."

"I already miss her," Steve said. He got up and headed to the door. "I wanted to come after depositing Vinny at BWI, but I've got to run."

"Especially since now you're making up for my absence," Paul said.

"It's fine. Isabella!" Steve met her at the railing for parting words and a kiss goodbye. Then with a bear hug to his friend, Steve left to put in the rest of the day at West Riverside even though it was Sunday.

Chapter 7

Isabella Romano left town with Paul the day after he signed the listing papers with Tim as his realtor. Paul wanted it done. The memories and future dreams in that house seemed unbearable.

"Liz, you're on me about my time across the bridge," Tim complained. "You do want Paul's place to sell, don't you? He can close on a condo near Steve by the time he returns if I get this done. I sold Audrey and Jack one in the next building." Tim justified all of this as they cleaned up dinner one night in early March. "With these listings it's not a dead winter."

Liz shelved a large casserole and clutched the cotton dishtowel closer. "Careful how you toss the phrase dead winter, Tim." Liz sighed. Last week, Tyler learned from NBC News that Fred Rogers, everyone's favorite TV neighbor, had suddenly passed. Small comfort that Vicki and Carina rested with another good soul. It also reminded Liz of how somber winter really was.

"I didn't mean it quite like that," Tim replied. "God, you're touchy. This doesn't help my stress. Besides, spring should increase listings."

There he goes again. Liz picked up goblets. Dried them. They had enjoyed wine the night prior after getting Hannah and Tyler to bed. Liz had made sure Tyler printed his spelling homework and that stories caused Hannah to sleep. The rest of the night she had devoted to Tim.

"Why don't you read to Hannah tonight," Liz whispered warmly in Tim's ear, "while I check on Tyler. I'll meet you downstairs. Maybe a hot bath." She tugged Tim closer. When she went for the kiss, he pulled back.

"This is what I mean, Liz. Demands. Expectations. My life isn't my own anymore."

Liz froze. "I don't get it, Tim. I thought we might finish what we started last night."

"I'm sorry I disappointed you. It happens, Liz," Tim said, hardly above a murmur. "Why do you think TV commercials advertise drugs for men?"

"It could be stress. Maybe if you'd unwind."

Tim put his hands on Liz's shoulders and looked squarely into her brown eyes. "I don't need to unwind. I just need a little space...to think, work, be. I had a hard time. Bad word choice, since I wasn't. I couldn't fall asleep. I really need a good eight hours tonight."

"Whatever you say," Liz answered. "It's only been four weeks since we've made love."

"No, it hasn't been."

"Yes, in this cycle, I know. Since you aren't ready for another baby, I went back on the pill."

"Speaking of pressures. We have two children. A full plate I'd say." Tim tamped down a stack of bills and other assorted mail strewn on their kitchen counter. "Think about that, Liz. I'm getting ready for bed. To sleep."

Tim started to walk downstairs but stopped. "If you're looking for something to do, why not go through that stack of social work journals. Fold some laundry. Clear some clutter."

"Goodnight, Tim." It was 8:30 as she looked at the microwave clock. Liz leaned against the cabinet. Was the house really such a mess? Even with closets to organize and end tables to tidy, she loved this place. The house brought comfort, peace, and normally a lot of love. She did have two children, and they brought her boundless joy.

Two healthy children and a spouse; some people crave what I have, she thought.

Liz hung the dishtowel on the crab hook and spotted her favorite Post-It pad that read "Why Do It Today, There's Always Tomorrow."

Running that philosophy through her mind, she surveyed her books. *Twelve Months to Your Ideal Private Practice* won over *Mompreneurs*. She'd read it next. Liz couldn't turn Tim around tonight. Or last, but who was counting?

Working for herself someday was her dream. She could make *this* happen. With the practice primer in hand, she lay on the couch, snuggled with an afghan, and settled in for a long read.

In the days ahead, Liz continued sessions with the Maloney family, gradually getting Ricky to behave at school and educating his parents on proper problem solving. They remained unhappy, even apart. Mrs. Maloney had moved across the bridge. At least they weren't cursing loudly enough that clients cringed in the waiting room.

Liz was pretty sure her boss Hal had never worked a day in mental health before owning this practice. But Hal knew marketing and the slogan: *We bring calm and positivity into your world.* Two years into her tenure, Liz thought it brought confusion and negativity into hers.

Hal could solicit clients, only he doled new prospects to those who agreed with him and didn't make waves. He stocked the supply cabinet from the dollar shop. Anyone who asked for something you couldn't buy for more than a few bucks—like a white noise machine to protect privacy between offices—Hal considered a nonstarter, a troublemaker. Hence, those people earned a paltry paycheck that month.

I love my job; I love my job!

Liz grabbed a book off her shelf and jotted things she wanted to bring up the next time she saw either Mr. or Mrs. Maloney, who were well on their way to filing separate tax returns next spring. The nature of her work required her to guide, mentor, or coach clients as a mediator, a lifeline, and most importantly, a listener. Too often people had endured life-changing circumstances—like Paul who had lost loved ones and had to move forward each day. Some clients were anxious or disgruntled. Liz would teach them to work with their thoughts and challenge them to implement new behaviors.

Liz saw her cell light up. She un-silenced it since she was no longer in sessions. "Liz Kramer," she answered before the automated recording. "Hey, how's the unpacking?"

"Terrible. I promised Mair we'd get the kitchen assembled tonight, but I just booked an OR for Paul's patient brought in by ambo," Steve said. "Another night's plans gone awry."

"Sorry. Any word from Paul?"

"Yes, actually. He's been quiet in Pittsburgh but asked a favor…but now, I need one," Steve said, eating a sandwich while talking to Liz.

"OK, I said I'd help. What do you need? Can you chew any louder?"

"Yes." Steve smacked his lips for her benefit. "I missed lunch. I'm in a hurry. If I ask Maren, it'll stress her out even more." Steve leaned in his desk chair during the only break this afternoon. "Mom says you're meeting over here after school." Liz knew that meant on the Western Shore of the Chesapeake Bay. "Could you stop at Paul's and pick up his passport? Desk drawer is in the den. Downstairs. I mean the main floor. I'll give you the garage passcode."

"Sure, Tim's working. Where's Paul headed?"

"Italy, with his mother." Steve crumpled the wax paper and tossed it in the trash. "He'd saved up time to take in May." Steve stopped. "When birth and bonding were to occur."

"Yeah," Liz said. "I hear you. So sad."

"Write this address down and get it to FedEx by six. I really appreciate it. Put it on my tab."

"Your tab, my butt. Took you three months to pay me for Mom's birthday gift."

"I paid, didn't I? Add interest," Steve said. "Gotta run. Liz, this trip is therapeutic."

"You don't need to convince me," she replied. "Stick to the OR. Glad Paul's taking a mental health break. I really am happy to help."

Liz had another appointment and a psychiatrist teleconference about client medication non-compliance. By 2:30, she shut off her computer and looked at Hal's memo delivered to all clinicians. Scanning the first line, it chastised them for faxing during the day when the rates were more expensive. *Seriously! Stay 'til six to send a freaking fax! This really is Worst Days Therapy.*

She tossed the memo on her desk. She locked her files, grabbed her bag, and headed to pick up Hannah, then Tyler before dismissal.

By 4:15, she pulled into Paul's driveway. "OK guys. I have to go inside to grab something real quick. I don't need you two running through Paul's place even though Daddy says there's a contract on it. Sit back and enjoy." The soundtrack from *Lion King* usually bought 20 minutes of "Hukuna Matata." Today, she only needed five. Liz turned to each of them strapped into the back seat. "Do *not* kill each other. You hear me?"

"Yes, Mom," Tyler droned. He looked to his sister, who by family rules, had to confirm she heard the edict as well.

"I'm always good," Hannah said.

"Suck-up," Tyler jeered.

"Tyler Phillips. Not an expression for a six-year-old." Liz cast the look. "I won't be long."

Liz punched the numbers into the keypad and walked past Paul's Corvette. He likely took their SUV to long-term parking at BWI. No longer Vicki's, now Paul's SUV. Liz climbed the stairs and spotted a wooden desk in the den. A desk drawer, she remembered. Which of the four? Was her brother this precise in his day job?

She pulled out one drawer, seeing only pencils, pens, and prayer cards. She recognized extra mass programs from Vicki's service in the longer drawer. Moving her hand beneath, sure enough she fingered heavy, navy blue cardboard. Two passports. Double-checking that she pocketed Paul's, Liz quickly shut the drawer. She startled at something. Movement came from upstairs.

No one is home. The house is under contract. Liz shook her head.

She stepped into the foyer to go back downstairs. As she turned the corner, she caught a glimpse at the banister above.

"Who's there?" a woman shouted down.

Liz looked, flustered to see a twenty-something blonde wrapping a large towel on her body. By instinct, Liz ascended a few steps. "I, I'm sorry. I'm a friend of Paul's." Liz stopped. "Are you his niece? I didn't realize anyone was here."

"Ah, no." A flush crept across the woman's cheeks, as she fisted the cloth. "I'm selling your friend's house. I had to change and showered."

Liz stretched her neck to the sound of further movement. Saw the same color towel. If Liz hadn't hung on to the banister, she'd have lost her foothold. Instead, she lunged up the remaining steps until she could see the master bedroom.

"You're not selling any house," Liz shouted. "You're screwing my husband!" Liz turned to Tim. Jabbed a finger at his muscled, naked chest. "You son of a bitch. How long has this gone on?" she hollered. If windows weren't sealed shut the neighbors could have answered her question.

"Liz, I can explain." Tim's face raced with the woman's to see which flushed faster. "Lucena works for me, and I…we go running. We're under a lot of stress, and so I knew…"

"Shut up," Liz spit at him. "Loose Hena, huh?" She tightened her handbag toward her, looked around the room, then squarely at Tim. "Pathetic. You distance yourself for months while I'm at home, figuring out how to reach you, buying every one of your damn lies." Her jab this time pushed Tim against the bedroom wall. "Rumpled, wet sheets, and you were *running*?"

"Liz please," Tim pleaded until he jerked his head. "What was that?"

Metal crunched and a horn blared through the townhome community. Liz ran to the bedroom window. "Jesus, the kids are in the car!"

Instinctively Liz ran down the stairs, flew open Paul's front door, and tore across the lawn. Her SUV had ended up across the street, after flattening the passenger side of another vehicle. Liz looked. Hannah was strapped into her car seat crying her lungs out, with Tyler behind the wheel, lodged between the airbag and the seat. "Mom, help me!"

Liz ran to his side. She yanked the door open and punched at the airbag to get at her son.

"Move aside," Tim said, running up behind her, his hands having just fastened his pants. He had loafers on his feet but no shirt. Tim reached between the airbag and scooped one hand under Tyler's body pulling him out in one fell swoop.

"Dad!"

"Are you all right?" Tim set his son's feet on the ground and crouched onto his knees.

Liz ran to the other side and unbuckled Hannah. The child still bawled as she clutched onto Liz's neck and wouldn't let go.

"Make it stop," Hannah hollered. Little hands slapped to both ears didn't dim the noise.

"Oh God, my Prius!" Lucena screamed from Paul's front porch as she ran toward them and the deafening sound. She had hustled on jeans and a sweater without a coat.

"Lucena, not now." Tim said, voice shaking. "Liz, how the hell did this happen?"

The quick skid of a police car halted explanations. Liz noticed that Tyler's eyes had grown saucer-sized at the flashing lights. With the cool March weather, she could also see goose bumps form on Tim's skin—flesh she loved to be near until she found it with another woman.

"Ma'am, what's going on?" the officer asked.

"My son and daughter were in our SUV. I ran inside to get something. They were both buckled into the back seat, told to stay there. Officer, I know I engaged the emergency brake."

The officer listened, called in a brief report on his walkie-talkie. He looked at Tim without a shirt, turned to the woman and asked, "This your father, young lady?" Lucena stepped toward Tim.

"We're co-workers," Tim inserted fast.

By the looks of it, the cop wasn't convinced. He spoke a brief update into his walkie-talkie. "This your vehicle, miss?"

"Yes. Look at it. I bet she did this on purpose." Lucena's face overextended with the accusation.

The cop did a double take. "At the very least, these youngsters need to go to the emergency room after being in a motor vehicle accident. You two are the parents of these minors?"

Nods gave the officer a quick answer.

"Miss, do you intend to press charges on the driver of this SUV?" he asked.

"I should," Lucena huffed.

"Officer, I wasn't at the wheel," Liz interjected. "I don't know what happened exactly. I…I got delayed. I was only inside to grab something out of a drawer." Tears welled in her eyes, and Liz clutched her chest as she could feel her heart pound its way out of her skin.

"We'll take statements at the hospital. Another officer can get her report. Now, the owner of this home?" As he asked, another trooper car pulled behind up. An ambulance eased into the middle of the street.

"My client's, officer. He's out of town. I'm his realtor; she's my assistant." Tim shifted his finger between Lucena and himself. He brushed his arms with his hands to keep warm. The air held nothing to Liz's frosty stare.

"Really?" the cop replied. It didn't help Tim that tears streamed down Liz's face. "Ma'am, under the circumstances, your vehicle has to stay here until we photograph the damage on both cars. We'll give you a ride to the local hospital. Let me see your registration, license, and insurance card while the EMTs get these kids."

"I'll get my shirt and jacket. We'll lock up," Tim told the officer. He left Liz to hand over the requested documents, calm two upset children, and deal with emotion as raw as any arctic chill.

"I came as soon as I could." Maren closed the door to the treatment room Hannah had been assigned to at West Riverside Hospital Center. "Where's Tyler? What on earth happened?"

"He's with his father in another room," Liz answered. "The SUV backed into a car because obviously Tyler couldn't stay in the back seat as instructed, even a few minutes. I think they're fine, honestly. Scared at first; fine now."

"Mommy and Daddy yelled at each other." Hannah sat cross-legged on a gurney, bars closing her in. "The nurse gave me this." She held a coloring book and crayons falling out of a box.

"We designed that." Maren ran her hand over Hannah's hair, in pigtails. "Liz, you don't look like they're fine. You've been crying."

Liz nudged Maren to the farthest corner of the room. "I know. That's all I need is for them to think I'm high with bloodshot eyes," she whispered. "Steve asked me to go over to Paul's to get his passport. When I walked in…" Liz swallowed hard. She temporarily stomached her tears. "Tim was upstairs. With someone."

Maren shifted so Hannah couldn't read her lips. "With…a woman?"

"His assistant." Liz spit it out with disgust. "Works under him…on top probably, too."

Maren's hand to her lips couldn't hide her gasp. "Oh my, oh Liz."

Maren looked over at Hannah happily coloring. "You said you had an urgent favor. What can I do?"

Liz pulled the passport out of her handbag. "Steve said this needs to be overnighted by 6 PM. I'm held captive here by the Maryland Five-O. Would you believe the officer asked little Hoochie if she wanted to press charges because my car—our car—hit hers?"

"I'll send it out." Maren glanced at the clock. "I've got 15 minutes. I'll run back to my office."

"Thanks. Here's the address." Liz handed the crinkled paper she'd stuffed into her purse. "Steve got called into a case. He doesn't know any of this. My license has Kramer as my middle and professional name so he will soon. The police want statements. It's spiraling."

"Take a deep breath. This place looks packed…could be a while and I've got to go," Maren said. "Bye honey, I hope you feel better."

"Bye, Almost-Aunt Maren."

Maren hugged Liz before she headed out. Not that it lightened Liz's mood. If she didn't draw a few clear breaths, Tim might end up on a gurney and she behind locked bars. Liz sat on the end of Hannah's hospital bed. Clutched her stomach.

"Mrs. Phillips," the woman said as she entered the room extending her hand. "I'm Dr. Jade Chen. I've seen your son and spoken with your husband." Dr. Chen scrubbed under the faucet.

Husband? The word didn't tingle her spine so much as stab it. "How's Tyler?" Liz asked.

"Your son has no apparent injuries from the airbag deploying. He's lucky. I spoke to him privately. I'll do the same with your daughter."

"That's fine. Would you like me to step out?"

"In a moment," Dr. Chen acknowledged as she listened to Hannah's chest and ran her hands over her body. "Does this hurt?" she asked.

"Tickles." Hannah broke out in giggles.

When Dr. Chen nodded that Liz could leave, Liz stepped into the hallway where she saw her brother standing at the ED desk. By his leaning upon it, it appeared that he had been waiting.

"Liz," Steve said. "I got a page that my niece and nephew were here. The charge nurse told me the parents needed to be separated for cursing at one another." Liz walked closer. Steve spotted the red eyes and motioned her into a small conference room that only staff could enter.

"The kids are fine. We're not." Liz looked to the linoleum floor, her lip trembling. "Maren has the passport, and I figured out the missing puzzle piece." Tears dumped down her face. "Tim is having an affair. I found him with his assistant at Paul's when I got the passport."

Steve stood back. Sighed. "Shit! I'm sorry." He pulled Liz into his chest and arms. "I was afraid of that." He thought a minute while she puddled his scrubs. "Maybe it's not as you think."

"Naked in towels. Rumpled sheets." Liz pulled back. "I think he's been at this, her—don't get me started—for months. I could kill him."

"Well, makes two of us," Steve said, stroking her back. "Ah, Dr. Chen's done with Hannah." He opened the door and motioned her into the conference room. "How does she check out?"

"No internal injuries. She said she bumped her head on her car seat but there was padding there," Dr. Chen reported. "Now that I've spoken with both children, I think I have the story."

The doctor looked squarely at Liz, then Steve. "Though left unattended, it appears that Tyler admits he crawled to the driver's seat to change the music. He went to stand up and accidentally pressed on the release to the emergency brake."

"I shouldn't have left them. I told them to stay put with a CD to occupy them," Liz said, sniffling. "I was longer than I thought."

"Jade, I had asked Liz to run over to Paul Romano's house," Steve explained. "He needs his passport, and I got called into the OR."

"On one of many cases today," she replied. "I'll give my report to the police. I know you didn't intend harm, Mrs. Phillips. I have to advise you to be careful obviously in the future."

"Thank you," Liz offered. "I will be. I'm sorry to be a mess. I'm just glad the kids are fine. There's more to this. I can't get into it now."

"There always is," Jade Chen said. Her eyes slanted to Steve.

"Jade, Liz is a social worker. She used to work in Baltimore so she's seen her share of domestic incidents, and I know she saw patients in many units including the ED."

"I didn't realize," Dr. Chen acknowledged. "As you can see, it's a full house here today. We seem to be perpetually understaffed. I apologize if you had to wait after triage."

"I understand," Liz said. "I assume we're cleared to leave."

"You are," Dr. Chen told her. Recognizing a quiver still and seeing Liz rub her arms past her elbows, she asked, "Will you be all right?"

Liz nodded. She claimed to be calm when clearly she wasn't. "My husband and I obviously have some things to work out. I apologize if we caused any commotion. That wasn't our intent."

"It happens," the doctor said. "If these two develop any further symptoms, follow up with their pediatrician." She stopped. "By the way, how is Dr. Romano?"

"As well as can be expected, but taking more leave for a trip to Italy," Steve told her. "We're all just trying to help him out."

"He's such a nice man," Dr. Chen said. "I'll check in with him myself when he returns. Mrs. Phillips, have a good evening."

Liz faked a smile. When Jade Chen exited the room, Liz cast sad eyes at her brother. Good wasn't an adjective existing in her vocabulary. It might not be for quite a while.

Since the police rode Tim and Liz to the hospital, the two took the most miserable cab ride to Paul's place. The police said Liz could drive her vehicle, even with a dent in the back bumper. Gladly, she dropped Tim off at his car, parked at a local restaurant where he likely had lunch with Lucena earlier. Liz blanked that part out as she drove east across the Bay Bridge to get home.

She managed her emotions enough to give Hannah a bath after which she cuddled with stuffed animals. Tyler crawled into bed with books. Sipping Tension Tamer tea, Liz mustered the courage to join Tim on the screened-in porch. He ran the space heater this chilly March night.

"Thanks for settling Tyler." Liz spread a blanket she'd brought atop her legs as she pulled her knees to her chest. Subconscious protection, she thought as she pressed her back into the plush cushion on the wicker sofa. Tim sat in a matching easy chair partly facing her, but allowed his blank stare to focus upon water in the distance.

"I'm sorry you had to find out this way," Tim acknowledged.

"Why?" Liz asked. She sipped more. The steam felt good since the room still had a definite chill, and the tension between her and Tim felt like ice. "How could you do this?"

"I haven't been happy for a while, Liz," Tim said. "Things are always so busy around here."

"What exactly is that supposed to mean? We have two young children. We both have careers, though how do you think I feel since I gave up a large part of my time and income to support yours in recent years?" Liz launched the look at him. Only this one carried hurt, disgust, and confusion. "It's as if you're blaming me for going off and screwing Loose Hena."

"Lucena. You really don't know her."

"I don't *fucking* need to know her, Tim." Liz slammed her mug onto the wicker end table splashing tea over the top. "Dammit, Tim! She's mixed up with her married boss, whose two children could have easily stumbled upon their father much like I did. I'm not sure which would have been worse…their bodies slammed into her precious Prius or their minds seared with the image of their *cheating* father."

"I had no idea you'd be at Paul's. At least I wasn't charging hotel rooms on our credit card."

"Oh, I'm supposed to be grateful!" Liz leapt to her feet, casting the blanket aside with a swoop. She sat on the wicker ottoman shoving Tim's legs off of it. *The Valentine card: Tim had written a large L on top. It wasn't mine after all.*

She cornered him now. "Speaking of particulars, I deserve to know when this started. And where have the two of you managed to rendez-vous? It better not have been in this house!"

"Do you think I'm stupid?" Tim held up his hand but realized he'd invited another barrage. "It started before Christmas. All you cared about was shopping and decorating. Where did I fit in?"

"Are you out of your mind?" Liz asked. "We went away for our November anniversary. January, I tried to surprise you with the kids away. I see. You saved yourself for that hussy. Please tell me you had protected sex. God knows where she's been!" *Hooking up with half a dozen guys.*

"We did mostly, but you needn't worry. She's not sleeping with anyone else."

"That you know of! How irresponsible! And where? Answer me! Where?"

"That's not your concern, Liz," Tim answered.

"It is if you had her in our house. Valentine's Day, weekend of the storm, was she here? Huh?"

"Of course not," Tim defended.

"Yet the place was immaculate, tub polished, carpet vacuumed?" Liz waited while Tim evaded that. "I found a card. She was here, wasn't she?"

Tim's complexion lost the color it had before they had started, confirming the card wasn't hers.

"You just lied. Again!" Liz's mouth fell open. It stayed agape until she muttered, "Pathetic."

"You just hound me. Is this being married? Same thing: day in, day out. As good as it gets?"

"You are delusional. We are a couple with two active, young children, a lifestyle and family some would die for." Liz cringed. "Someone recently did die trying to have half of what we have."

"There you go, diagnosing me and dragging someone else into this," Tim argued. "Next thing, you'll cite some theory. This is what I mean."

"I'm hurt. No Tim, devastated. You've put everything at risk with this tawdry entanglement with Loose Hena. Sorry, she is loose, in my opinion. And you blame me for *your* actions."

"Look, I care about what we have here." Tim opened his hands to the surroundings. "Hell, I found us this house. We had a good thing."

"Stellar way of showing concern." Liz's hands pressed into the ottoman. She was in his face. Didn't care. "What do you want?" Liz paused. "Tell me what on earth...do...you...want?"

Quiet ensued until Tim gave up. "Space, Liz. I'll sleep in the guest room. Tomorrow, I'll talk to the kids. I think we should be apart."

"What? That's it? You don't want to fix this? Talk to someone?" *No apology. Nothing.*

"You heard me," Tim said. "I live with a shrink. I don't need another one."

Too stunned by the disrespect, Liz stared.

"It's been a long day. Tomorrow doesn't promise to be any better. Goodnight Liz."

Tim pushed past her and turned off the space heater. Liz looked at the cold, empty room. A metaphor, she thought, as she got the blanket, sat back, and buried her face for a long, hard cry.

Chapter 8

"Vicki was funny last spring," Paul told Maren. For two weeks since his return that April their coffee time started most days. "Steve's catalogs hyped his *previously owned* boat. Vicki fixed the interior to look like those photos."

"Sounds like his request," Maren answered. "Vicki did a great job."

"She was all I thought about fishing with Steve. In Italy, too."

"You haven't talked much about your trip."

Paul stopped studying his cup. "Glad I went. It gave me time with Ma. Vicki and I had honeymooned in Rome and Naples, where Ma's from. This trip: Abruzzo, where Dad lived. Memories." He patted his stomach. "One usually leaves with sweets in the suitcase. Extra pounds carried onto the plane, but my appetite's still off."

"The sugar-coated almonds sustained me unpacking," Maren said. "Is your condo set up? Can't believe we're all at Shore Landings."

"Confetti, Italian for coated almonds," Paul corrected. "I stored stuff. Took what was mine; movers unpacked the rest. Did you try Torrone?"

"Half of the one Dylan declined. Kids!" The child humor made Maren recoil. "I'm sorry. Of all people, I should know better."

"I'm over the denial, the isolation phases," Paul said. "I don't expect people to hide their children because I lost mine. Like Steve, I love kids. Pam felt guilty on the phone complaining about Chloé's behavior. Just like the notion of postponing your wedding. Stupido!"

"Seven weeks and the wedding will be in an album. What about Chloé? So sweet at Disney."

"Mouthy, irritable," Paul said. "Has bad headaches. Pam took her to a Baltimore specialist."

"Sorry to hear that." Maren prodded his elbow. "Look who is in line?" She waved to be noticed.

Liz walked over and set her tray on their table. "Welcome back, world traveller."

Paul stood to peck Liz's cheek. "Have a seat. What brings you across the bridge?"

"Careful what you ask for." Liz scanned the table. "Where's the cream and sugar?"

"Over along that ledge. What do you need?" Paul stole her cup.

"Half a Splenda, skim, no cream." As Paul stepped away, Liz whispered. "Does he know?"

"The guys went fishing. Steve said Paul wanted to demand his commission back and offer Tim a three-day colon prep." Maren broke off. "How's that for an answer?"

Laughing, Liz looked much more put together than the last few times Maren had seen her.

Paul handed Liz her coffee, and she took a sip. "Perfect." She squeezed Paul's hand before she stabbed her scrambled eggs and mouthed a bite. "Tell me about Italy."

"Impressive. When I get prints, we can do pizza. Margherita style," Paul said. "My EAP counselor tells me to be among people."

"Steve said you have a good employee assistance program here," Liz replied. "My colleagues tell me not to hole up in my house." She faked a smile. "I take it you heard?"

"I did." Paul frowned. "Should've taken that damn passport but my mind wasn't working." He paused. "I'm sorry, Liz."

"Don't blame yourself. I've come to realize running into the floozy and philanderer was a blessing in disguise."

Maren and Paul slanted glances at one another.

"If I hadn't found him with Hoochie—better name—I'd be in the dark, putting my health at risk, too." Liz took a deep breath. "No STDs or HIV found. Thank God! Dr. Clements switched me from Xanax to Celexa. Other copays were steep under loser husband's plan."

Paul shifted eyes to Maren who acknowledged the mutual concern over Liz's use of pejoratives.

"How do you like Dr. Clements?" Maren asked. She had given Liz the referral.

"I like her. Helped me save face in case someone saw me falling apart close to home," she replied. "Besides, I have an interview. In 15 minutes. Hope I don't leave with eggs on me."

"Interview?" Paul asked. "You look very professional."

"Casework job. Yippy," Liz said. "But part of the time, they need someone to do psych assessments in the ED. That helps. Part-time, with bennies, which my attorney tells me I'll need."

From Liz's tone and glare, Paul knew she had to be cycling through a few Kubler-Ross grief stages herself—anger evident today.

"Tim is paying support isn't he?" Maren asked.

"In dribs and drabs. Balks at paying expenses. Suddenly he can't afford benefits. We have a scheduling conference soon. Marital bliss will spare you and Steve when I have a hearing in June. You'll be away by then."

"You know we care, Liz," Maren said.

"I'm sorry, too," Paul added. "Steve and I could put him in as bait." Paul cast a sly grin. If misery wanted company, Liz's presence offered it. "We tossed around ideas, but we're in public."

"Your thoughts can't be any worse than mine." Liz clamped her lip and ran fingers as if to zip them. "I see clients who want to destroy each other. I have to rise above that. I'm trying."

"Not always easy!" Maren slid her chair. Gabe grabbing coffee reminded her that they had a staff meeting, and Liz had her interview.

"Exercise does it for me. I'm up to five miles on the Cross Island Trail, and I swim. Lost four pounds." Liz's fists landed firmly on slender hips. "I plan to be slim for my final gown fitting."

Any man would scan Liz's curves with the intensity of an MRI, Paul thought. Did she really need to lose an ounce?

Gabe strolled to the table. "Maren, don't forget Alicia's meeting," he reminded. "Hello Paul, and…" Gabe's fingers pressed to his temple, his lips parting into an appreciative smile.

"Name's Liz," Paul supplemented the lapse, narrowing his eyes. "Wearing purple, huh?"

"Nice to have you back, Paul." Gabe diverted eye contact, his gaze landing only on Liz.

"We met at the fundraiser," Liz said. "Wearing that tie to impress your boss? Alicia is a Ravens fan." She flustered at her watch. "Damn, my interview. I must go. How do I look?"

"Stunning," Gabe curled his lips to the fluorescents. "Good luck," he shouted when Liz paced hurriedly out of the cafeteria. "Did she say she has an interview? Here?" Gabe asked Maren.

"Appears so," Maren said. She rested a hand on Paul's shoulder. "I'm available any time."

Paul squeezed her hand. "Thanks."

Maren tossed her disposable cup into the trash and walked out with Gabe for their meeting.

Paul tapped his fingers. Why was he annoyed?

This takes time. Stick with what works: family, friends, morning coffee with Maren. Even still, Paul dreaded the long day ahead.

Days later, Liz brought her lunch to do paperwork and type prog–ress notes during her only free hour, thanks to Hal being frugal at Better Days Therapy. Hal definitely made it one of Betty's worst days, handing their reliable admin person a pink slip and her workload to the staff. Betty had obtained pre-authorizations, submitted insurance claims, followed reimbursement, and freed clinicians to do what they do—therapy.

Better get to it. Liz picked up the desk phone and punched a toll-free number.

"Welcome to Benefits Plan Provider Services. You can find information on our website at www.benefitsplanproviderservices.com."

Listening to Spanish, Liz noshed on peanut butter and jelly. Not until she got to the office did she realize she had grabbed Tyler's lunch by mistake. The school lunch account shot up now and her tuna on wheat was relegated surely to the school's round trash bin.

"Please know, for quality and training purposes, this call may be monitored or recorded. For your convenience, use your alphanumeric keypad. Note: Information given by this voice-activated system is not a guarantee of payment."

Nothing today is for my convenience.

"Now, say I'm a member or press 1, I'm a dependent or press 2, I'm an in-network healthcare provider or press 3, I'm an out-of-network provider or press 4, I'm interested in enrollment or press 5, I need frequently requested information or press 6, or I don't know or press 7."

Merely 12:05, Liz needed more coffee to decipher that menu. She pushed three.

"In-network provider. Which type of plan are you calling about? Medical, press 1, dental, press 2, pharmacy, press 3, employee assistance, press 4, inpatient pre-certification, press 5, healthy babies and moms, press 6, or mental health/substance abuse, press 7."

Mental health would be at the end of the list.

"You're calling about: claim status, press 1, benefits and eligibility, press 2, deductibles and maximums, press 3, prior authorization, press 4, credentialing, press 5, or appeals, press 6."

Distracted by hallway voices, Liz hesitated. The recording started over. She refocused and pressed two.

"Benefits and eligibility: I need additional information to continue this automated service. Don't have it? Please hang up and call us later."

Liz heaved a sigh. *If I didn't care to continue, trust me, I'd have hung up by now.*

"I'll need the member ID, group number and date of birth, the patient's name and date of birth, and the type of coverage you're calling about. Also, key in your 9-digit tax ID or NPI number."

Liz circled her eyes.

"To hear that again, say repeat that or press 1. If you need to start over, say start over or press 2. If you need to speak with someone, say representative or press 3. If you're finished, hang up."

"Come on Chickie," Liz mumbled. "I don't have all freakin' day."

"I'm sorry, I didn't recognize that selection."

Chickie has sensitive ears. Liz cycled through the prompts. Again.

"Now, does the member ID number begin with the prefix DTY, HNR, or WXZ? Yes or press 1; no or press 2."

Liz would have hung up if this phone queue didn't pave a partial path to her paycheck. She punched a number but missed the numeral as she jabbed the keypad with too much angst.

"I'm sorry I didn't understand. Main menu. Welcome to Benefits Plan Provider Services."

Liz looked at the sign on her wall: Take It Easy, Life Is Short. *My life is short!* She had to be more careful navigating prompts now.

"I understand you'd like to speak with a representative. Please enter your 9-digit tax ID or your billing NPI number."

I already keyed that! With simmering attitude, Liz pushed her National Provider Identification number. Again.

"The number you entered is not a valid provider number. Thank you for calling. Good-bye."

Liz closed her eyes, imagined the bay—in Steve's boat, not Loser's—and breathed deeply. She lowered her head onto the desk. Albert Ellis, a founder of cognitive therapy himself, could fly from New York to talk her out of her irrational beliefs. Freud could be resurrected to decipher where Dolores or Bill went wrong.

Liz didn't care. She simply needed a good cry.

Allowing only the amount of tears two tissues would dry as someone had earlier emptied her entire box, one tissue per tear, Liz sniffed the remainder deep into her sinuses. She would *not* spend her only free hour doing Hal's extra tasks.

She saw her cell phone flash. This week she had entered Paul's number into her contacts, thinking she'd check in with him next week.

"Hi, Paul. How are you?" Liz asked idiot-like. *His wife and child just died. Good going!*

"Day's been busy. That helps," Paul replied. "You have a cold, Liz?"

"No, it's nothing." Sniffling won out over wearing snot on her blouse that afternoon. "All in a day's work. Good to hear from you."

"I talked to Maren earlier. If it wasn't for our coffees, well…it's nice," he said. "Look, she told me about a shower you're throwing. It made me think about my duties as best man."

"You hold the rings because if Steve got them at Tiffany's like that rock she wears, he will *not* entrust them to a six-year-old." Dylan got to be the ring bearer. Steve's little sweetheart grabbed the flower girl spot the minute she was born.

Paul let a chuckle escape. "I meant other stuff."

"What stuff?" How could she let him know her lunch hour was ticking here?

"Guy stuff." Paul waited for Liz only she hadn't caught on. "Normally, we'd pound down some Yuengling—not my favorite but his—and watch a few hot little honeys take it all off."

"A strip club?" Liz drew a hefty breath. *He's a recent widower and he lost his child. Go easy.*

"If my future sister-in-law can't stand the word *sucks* in everyday conversation," Liz continued. "News Flash: your coffees stop if you take my brother to a seedy club with naked *honeys* on a pole."

"The place I had in mind isn't seedy, and I've actually heard those two joke about poles. But Liz, the operative word—past tense—was. It's not in the cards. Not now."

"So Paul, I'm glad to talk to you, but my lunch hour is almost up. I'm just not sure how I can help plan a bachelor party—pole or no pole?"

"My PA, my physician assistant…"

"I know what a PA is but go ahead. Sorry."

"My PA, your gender, said couples today have joint parties. Italian bridal showers could fill a coliseum. Large-scale. Rented hall, dozens of women, slurping wedding soup."

"I am not renting a hall; the Kramer bayside house doesn't accommodate dozens of guests." Notwithstanding playing mom and dad and my small-scale budget, Liz thought. "Really…that big?"

"Italians could have 48 first cousins, hundreds of second cousins."

"We're German. Maren, I don't know what she is, except easy to please. That suits me right now," Liz told him. "If you're asking to combine events, you're in luck. I didn't get invitations yet. To hell with Emily Post, I might just do emails."

"You rock," Paul said. "I'll help cover the costs. Let's find a time to talk. Since the movers didn't put my bike in storage, we could ride that trail you talked about. This weekend good?"

"The Cross Island Trail runs from Stevensville to Kent Narrows. Sure." Liz gave Paul her address and they set a time.

"I'll see you Saturday, Liz," Paul hesitated. "And Liz, please don't tell Maren about the strip club. Fleeting idea that it *was*."

Laughter flooded the receiver. "I've heard them joke about poles, too. I don't get it."

"Hm, wedding gift." Paul snickered.

"Bye Paul." That he could chuckle even a bit made up for her wasted lunch hour and sounded incredibly good to Liz.

That night, Liz combed tangles from Hannah's hair while calling to Tyler to hop into the shower. Without bath battles that prolonged evenings, Liz had time to decompress.

"Can I call Uncle Steve?" Hannah grinned. She clutched the panda bear Steve bought her at the National Zoo and wiggled it back and forth.

"Absolutely not," Liz replied. She gave her little girl a smooch. "Uncle Steve is extra busy."

"Story?" Hannah held up a book. "Short."

Hannah had adjusted to never having as many hours as needed in the day, their new normal. With huge pictures and 20-point type, Liz read a few pages. She kissed Hannah once more and pulled the covers over her tight.

"I love you little girl. You are *my* sweetheart."

"Unh uh…Uncle Steve's!"

Liz wasn't about to argue her feelings. Tim had blown off his last mid-week pick up. Liz held her breath that he'd take the kids tomorrow.

She closed Hannah's door. When Liz passed the bathroom, the sprinkling water sound sparked Liz's relief. Tyler had even left his backpack by the door, ready to grab in the morning. This night though, it looked unusually bulky. Their pediatrician warned against young children carrying a heavy load of school supplies. How many books could a first grader pack?

Liz lifted the top loop. It didn't feel like books. Curious, she unzipped the largest compartment. One of the bulbs in the hallway needed to be replaced so she lowered herself to her knees to peek inside and pull out an M&T Bank envelope. It was addressed to her. Liz rummaged further. Her quarterly Fidelity statement for her retirement account was in Tyler's backpack.

"What the hell?" Liz dug further and found dozens of envelopes plus mail Tyler must have collected over past weeks. Beneath the assorted items, Liz found an 8x10 photo, now ruined with wrinkles from being stuffed into the bottom. It had been taken of him and his sister when a photographer visited a school event last year.

Gathering the evidence, Liz marched into Tyler's room, which had a door from the bathroom as well as the hallway.

"I'm nakie." Tyler clutched his Ravens towel.

"I've seen it before," she fumed. "What are you doing with almost two week's worth of *my* mail in your backpack?" Tim had filled out a forwarding card for his mail already. Deliveries had been sparse, but not this light. "I wondered why I didn't get some of these things."

Tyler blanched. He pulled his fist holding the towel higher to his face to hide his expression.

"I'm waiting for an answer," Liz demanded.

"Mom, I…I need to go pee." Tyler ran back into the bathroom and locked both doors.

Liz knocked. "Open this door. You did that before your shower." She hammered louder. Gently bumping her head against the wood, she yelled through it, "If you don't open this, I take your Game Boy." *Parenting by threat. Just great!*

"Mom, no." Tyler thrust the door, almost causing Liz to fall into the steamy room as she leaned so tiredly upon it. "Not my Game Boy."

"I'll be back in two minutes to talk about this." She stormed out, deposited the mail under her covers. *No one else is home and I'm hiding my own mail. Seriously!* Liz drew in a deep breath and traipsed right back into Tyler's room. She closed the door and took a seat at the bottom of his bed. "Was this your idea?" she asked.

Liz knew how to use silence productively. Harder on home base feeling betrayed. "Tyler?"

"I thought it belonged to Daddy."

Tyler's eyes misted at his mother's firm tone. He had dropped several hints to Dolores and Bill for the Game Boy last Christmas. "Take a game. Please, Mommy. Just one."

"First, you never bother the mail, even on your birthday. Second, those were addressed to Elizabeth Kramer Phillips. No one else." Liz stopped. Her son flooded with emotion.

Liz handed him two tissues out of a nearby box. Tyler blew his nose, got up to discard them in the bathroom trash and clambered back into bed. "Do you have to tell Dad?"

"Yes, Tyler, I do," Liz said calmly. She scooted him over to put her arm around him. "There have been a lot of changes. Just like your father and I explained, these are grown up matters. We don't want to involve you and Hannah."

"That's what *you* said," Tyler leaned into Liz. "Daddy said you made him lonely. Why'd you do that Mom? Now he's gone."

Liz withdrew her arm so that she could face him. The day Tim left, she had insisted on being there so that they could both talk to the children. How did *we're working out problems* become *Mommy made me lonely?* "Your father said that's why he left? Because he was lonely?"

Tyler bobbed his head, afraid to say more.

"I'll handle this." Liz tucked in his covers. "Even if he was lonely, that's not something he should speak about with you. His grown-up feelings aren't your concern. OK?" Tyler nodded. Liz kissed him and shut out his light.

She closed and locked her bedroom door. Knowing how too many kids on her caseload listened in on parent conversations, she took her phone into the bathroom to dial Tim.

Damn him! Voice mail.

"Tim, it's Liz. Tonight I found mail in Tyler's backpack, not to mention the professional photo he must have snatched out of a frame, now crinkled so that neither of us will enjoy it. How dare you put him up to this! His job is to be a six-year-old little boy, Tim—not to play Columbo the Detective for you!"

Liz lowered the phone. She bit her tongue and merely clicked off the call. Anything more he'd take as lecture, his favorite reason to ignore her and stonewall discussions, as oppositional as a teenager in juvie. Why did she leave a message? This wasn't what she bargained for this year.

Liz brushed her teeth, put on pajamas and did yoga stretches before tossing back the bedspread where she found the mail. She stashed the envelopes in her nightstand to claim comfort under the covers. While the stash had rested on her bed 14 minutes tops, Liz wished she could hole up maybe 14 months.

Saturday, Paul crunched gravel in Liz's driveway. "I'm late," he said out his SUV window. He slammed the driver's door and started to remove the bungee cords that secured his Trek onto the bike rack. "I can't haul bikes on my Corvette. Did the kids get off OK this morning?"

"Yes. Get this: Hoochie, auditioning for Victoria Secret, shorts cut up to her butt, got out of Tim's BMW, all open armed with 'Hannah, my sweetheart. Tyler!' But *my* girl set her straight."

Paul leered. Most men could spot a bitter woman miles away. He didn't mind the sarcasm. He knew it helped process hard emotions sometimes. "Hannah is a cutie. What'd she do?"

"Hannah went straight for the opened car door. Said, 'I'm Uncle Steve's sweetheart. Not yours!' I loved it," Liz recounted as she motioned Paul inside. "I can't talk about him anymore. Bring your duffle. I'll show you where to shower later and we'll get going."

"Nice place," Paul said as Liz led him up the stairs to the very top floor. He dropped his small bag on the queen sized nautical comforter. "This is a guest room? More like a Marriott suite."

"We like guests to relax," Liz said. "We," she sniffed. "You know what I mean. Normally, I don't let your type through the door. I made an exception for you and this." She scraped her hand along the black and gold duffle. "Coupons downstairs for the outlets, for a new bag."

"Vinny does coupons." Paul walked out the sliding glass to the deck that overlooked the property. "Today, you lose that attitude."

"I have a good attitude though I work at Worst Days Therapy." Liz stretched an arm to the dock. "Loser's boat. Technically the State of Maryland considers it half mine. There's the pool."

"If snarky is an attitude, yours is grand. There's medication for that, Liz." Paul turned his head to the pool. "With a water slide and basketball hoop, I'll bet your kids love it here."

"They do. I take 20 milligrams. And you?" Liz crossed her arms, and leaned her lower back into the railing to face Paul.

"Ten. It does help." Paul said, turning serious. "I had a bad day, too, this week. Saw her sister's birthday on the calendar. Just lost it."

"I'm sorry." Liz regarded him. Liz veered her gaze, momentarily embarrassed. "I'm not titrating. I have some nausea. It could be pure nerves. Don't need side effects, if I eventually date. I can see it:

'Pardon me, Mr. Rebound. I can't feel anything with my way high happy dose."

Paul removed his sunglasses, slanting his eyes. "Is that what you tell your clients at Worst Days, Liz?" He fixed them atop his head. "Come on, show me the rest of this fabulous place. Besides, you won't have a problem dating."

"I already had *that* offer...haven't decided."

On the main floor, Paul faced her. "Someone's hitting on you?" He braced on the kitchen island.

"Is that so strange? Though Tim thought I was sprayed with sex repellent," Liz spit out. "Here, want a glass of water?"

"Sure," Paul said. "Liz, you are too much." He took the clear glass imprinted with blue anchors and quenched his thirst. "Who is the guy?"

"Maren's friend...Gabe."

"From planet purple?" Paul scrunched his face in opposing angles. "Eew!"

"Encouraging!" Liz thrust out a hip. "Spoken like a big brother though. It's dinner cracking crabs at the Inner Harbor. You have a problem pulling crabs apart?"

"I'm a surgeon. This isn't about cracking crabs, removing gills," Paul said. "He wants more than dinner, like a crack at you. No Old Bay added." Paul let the remark settle. "A little hasty. You sure about this?"

"My lawyer said to play it safe. Tim gets to do whatever he pleases apparently." Liz led Paul down other stairs. "Bedrooms at ground level. The main floor looks out over the water. Hannah's room." Her body pushed the door open.

"Don't let Mr. Purple see or he'll offer to lease it," Paul joked. "Ravens' girls like lavender." He smirked. "Guessing Gabe guy's a little lavender, too."

"*That's* snarky." Liz shook her head. "Hannah loves it in here."

"Someone had better," Paul quipped. "Cute room for a little girl." He quieted suddenly.

Liz recognized the reflective moment. "Hey." She placed a hand on his shoulder and walked him toward Tyler's room.

"Take a deep breath, then enter." A purple accent wall stood out with fully framed photos of Ray Lewis, Ed Reed, and Jonathan Ogden. A small decorative jersey, clearly too small to wear, was nailed to the wall as if it was art.

"*I'm* heading to 20 mg after this," Paul said. "Bunk beds, for two little Ravens' fans. Next…"

"Dylan slept over once last month. He claimed all the stuff would give him nightmares."

"Ah, your brother and I groomed him well!" Paul said it with pride.

Liz showed Paul two spare rooms. One had a trundle bed, a desk and chair while the other housed plastic toy tubs, an obvious playroom. She paused before gentle pressure steered him around the corner. Liz announced, "My room."

Liz walked past the king bed, covered up by a plush comforter blasting all sizes of seashells. Darker navy accents and lighter green and pastel tones contrasted the muted beige color scheme. "Out that sliding glass door, we…I mean, I… have morning coffee. Nice view."

"Nice everything," Paul announced as he sprung the lock and stepped to the patio.

Liz went back to the nightstand, grabbing something before she followed Paul and plopped herself onto the padded cushions of the chaise. Instinctively, she drew her knees to her chest.

Paul lounged on the opposite one, and set his water on the matching table between them. He stretched his legs the length of the chaise.

"This is the life." Paul hesitated putting on his Armani specs, drew in fresh air, and settled his head into a cushion. "Didn't you have a hearing this week?"

"Days after I stopped Tyler from sneaking my mail to Tim." Liz saw his double take. "Exactly. Sets a great tone." She shrugged. "Set a schedule to supposedly settle, as if we can after that."

"I'll say."

"The lawyers talked by phone." Liz clammed up. When Paul faced her, she continued. "We'll try mediation. No counseling. He's not the guy I married and coming back, Paul." Liz's voice faltered as she peered at the paver stones.

Paul looked at Liz. Shifted his legs onto the stones and positioned his specs to be eye to eye. "I'm sorry. You of all people would want to work it out. Even with…" Paul stopped. "Does this Hoochie person have an actual name?"

Liz sniffed. "Lucena. Like loose. Yes, I'd have tried." She blew on a wisp of short hair that cascaded down her brow. "It'd be hard to forgive, not that he's sorry. Blames, rationalizes. If he was *so* unhappy, he didn't say anything. Can't fix what I don't know is broken."

Seeing Liz knuckle away tears, Paul shot up, went inside and returned with a fist full of tissues. "Here." He sat back down. "As you and I know from what we do, people make choices. He'll regret this. To walk away from being with the kids, from you, from this place... I'm sorry."

"The kids he says he cares about. Putting them in the middle really shows that." Liz spat the last word. "He wants a week on/off. This is home, not a cramped apartment shared with a stranger."

"Hopefully it will all work out. Is he reasonable on anything?"

"According to my lawyer, he crabs about the benefits and insists I work more so he can pay less. He's in real estate. He'll find a great place. We, on the other hand, will have to sell." Liz shrugged. "Maybe it's too big to manage."

Too big or too expensive? Paul silenced that since Liz wet a second tissue. She felt comfortable and at peace here. Who wouldn't? "Heard anything about the interview at West Riverside?"

"Not yet. I had to meet with HR, then with Dr. Chen in the ED. She'll get back to me. She had another interview." Liz sniffled remaining tears before stuffing a tissue in a pocket. "I hate to come off as desperate, but if I ever want my own business. I mean a private practice." Liz trailed off. "Never mind. Stuck with cheapskate boss."

"Is it really that bad?" Paul asked.

Liz gave him the short version of cheap supplies, increased work and caseloads built upon whether Hal liked you that day. "When you called, I'd jettisoned my only free hour to call an insurance company, which shouldn't be my job."

"Hal sounds a few sandwiches short of a picnic," Paul assessed. "Stupid to pay professionals for admin. ED work is perfect for an extrovert."

Liz pulled something from another pocket. "Regarding ED. Are these what I think?"

Paul took the small orange bottle, with its label removed. He untwisted the safety top. The Pfizer impression on each was evident. "Ah, Mr. Tim was using Mr. Blue."

Liz's wrinkled nose framed her puzzlement.

"The street name for Viagra." He studied her. "Surprised?"

"Hell yeah," Liz shot back. She leapt to her feet. "He never needed a boost before."

"Thanks to the ads, patients plead for it when they don't need it *diagnostically,* even in one relationship, let alone…" Paul stopped. Visibly cringed. "I'm sorry, I didn't mean to rub that in."

"You'd think if Tim was *trying* to satisfy two women, he might need it. I wasn't joking about sex repellant. He clearly doesn't want me." Liz scooted the chaise and reached for Paul's cool water to temper her mood's heat. "I don't want him. I do want a bike ride. Then joint party talk."

"Exercise helps." Paul took the glass back.

"Let me ask, internists obviously see both genders." She shifted her voice. "For women, just how many nerve endings are *down there?*"

Paul coughed moisture onto his wrist. "Am I a GYN journal here?"

"More than eight *thousand,*" she announced. Her tone matched the cubes surrounding Paul's water. "That idiot could barely find a few."

Paul catapulted to stand. "Mr. Blue buys a guy time, not talent."

Though a waterman could scrape Liz's self-esteem from the oyster beds in the Chesapeake Bay, Paul didn't offer much, particularly on an intimate topic. He had learned that boundary long ago. A few too many positives and women might take them the wrong way. "Let's get out of here," he said. "After you."

They walked back inside, and Liz locked the sliding door. Paul felt her pain as she tossed the prescription bottle on the bed and led them out. He pulled his phone from his pocket to email himself a mere subject header: *Call Jade Chen.*

Chapter 9

Steve peered out of the Boeing 757 as it approached LaGuardia. The skyline had tragically changed since medical school. His three-day meeting would earn him several continuing medical education credits and connect him with Columbia friends. Looking at Ground Zero reminded him that a member of his graduating class, as well as one of his beloved professors, lost loved ones in the terrorist attacks. A dinner would observe that professor's achievements.

After one day, Steve ordered room service while glued to his laptop. Shown pictures of the hotel at Central Park West, Dylan had wanted to stow away in Steve's suitcase. No hotel pool for Steve with hospital reports to review. He powered down his MacBook to grab his jacket and get down to the lobby. Besides, the sightseeing he had planned with a friend would have been too much for Dylan.

"Glad I spotted you last night," Chad said, pacing toward the subway near Columbus Circle. "Haven't seen you since the funeral."

"Glad we caught up. Which stop do we need?"

"Canal Street, then we'll walk." Chad was a thoracic surgeon Steve hadn't seen in years until Vicki's services. Residency took him to Boston, family back to Delaware, just outside Philly.

"We don't live far apart," Steve said. "We should get together more." The two men quickly found their seats on the train to Lower Manhattan.

"Weddings and funerals," Chad acknowledged. "How's your promotion? How's Paul?"

"Job good, difficult few months. Paul struggles to put up a good front. Everyone's devastated," Steve shared. "My fiancée knew Vicki through West Riverside." Subway snoozers woke from the screeching train. "I covered a month for him. Glad to help, but catching up."

"He'll be your best man since you were his?" Chad asked. Steve nodded. "Paul was thrilled to go to Pittsburgh when we all graduated." Chad regarded Steve. "Another chapter in your lives."

Steve shrugged. He knew Chad meant a closed chapter what with Pam breaking off their nine-year relationship when most classmates assumed Pam and Steve had been a sure thing.

"You see Pam much in Philly?" Steve asked.

Chad pushed up his shoulders. "We talk at the hospital. I saw her husband after the accident. He healed well." Chad's smile lessened with the possibly sore topic. "I hear your fiancée is quite amazing. Custom-made." Both men laughed though jolting forward for another subway stop.

"Both." It was Steve's first light moment, untimely tragedy the theme as they headed to pay tribute to victims of the September 11th attacks. "Maren's fantastic. A great support to Paul, having lost her own husband two years ago." Steve brightened. "Seven weeks: I gain a wife and a stepson. Dylan's a really cute kid."

"I'm happy for you, Steve. Mandy and I have three to keep us young," Chad said. "We wanted them out of diapers before hitting another decade."

"Don't remind me. I just turned 40. My wise cracking sister gave me something out of the *Archives of General Psychiatry* about advancing paternal age," Steve lamented. "Possible genetic mutations and risks for psychiatric disorders." Steve shook his head sideways.

"Really?"

"Paul spotted it on my desk. Tried to latch onto it," Steve added. "Since he has enough stress, I took it back. We thought women's biological clocks ticked."

"Paul's got the same pressure," Chad replied. His subdued expression edged into a smile. "Seven weeks. Then you'll start on *that* goal."

Steve laughed. "Oh yeah. This is our stop."

Chad and Steve walked. Chatted until they couldn't hear above the din of constant construction. Jack hammers. Vehicles beeping. Trucks backed into a large pit. Ground Zero.

Like most onlookers, the two men ambled solemnly along the scaffolding. Scuffed along wooden planks, a far cry from when they would ride to the Trade Center and stroll Battery Park as a breeze blew through Lower Manhattan.

Now, following the massacre, machinery exhaust stung their nasal passages. Memorial notes plastered along wooden planking riveted their attention. Loved ones left behind stuck flowers high into the metal fence that separated the living from those now gone. They navigated the maze of concrete construction barriers and had not said a word until Chad elbowed Steve.

"Isn't that...yeah," Chad asked and answered synchronously. "You didn't tell me you were coming to New York, let alone here."

"I'm on the Listserv. I wouldn't miss the dinner," Pam Morgan said as she hugged Chad and kissed his cheek. "And, I think this is New York's obligatory stop. Morbid, yet meaningful."

Right then, she noticed Steve and instinctively snaked an arm around him, pecking his cheek, only refusing eye contact. "Speaking of surprises. I got the impression you were crawling out from under paperwork and wedding plans."

"Between Maren and our mothers, the wedding has its own pulse," Steve whispered so that they didn't disturb those offering moments of silence. "I needed a break."

"How's Paul doing?" Pam lowered her voice enough that Steve and Chad strained to hear it. "Keeping a close eye on him?" Pam summoned them away from other observers.

"Paul does one day at a time. Maren, even Liz, helped him with thank you notes," Steve answered. "Some days an emotional sucker punch. He cut back surgeries to concentrate on primary care."

"He got certified in two fields?" Chad asked.

"Paul's gift of indecisiveness. We teased him through residency," Pam offered. "When I asked him about his Pittsburgh trip, he said he'd been in touch with private practices and a hospital."

Steve raised a brow. "Suzanna, our secretary, took some messages. One from UPMC."

"University of Pittsburgh. Starzl. Jonas Salk." Chad bobbed his head. "Why not? You all couldn't wait to go there."

"Without Vicki, I sense Paul's lost." Pam tiptoed to sniff a bouquet that looked recently picked and twined into the fence as a tribute. "He has your wedding. Probably waiting it out."

"Or vacillating," Steve said. "I'll talk to him."

"If you two have seen enough, let's move along. Happy hour, for old time's sake?" Chad suggested. "Feed the soul after mourning."

Pam nodded. "Suits me." She looked at Steve. The last time they had seen one another they had done just that. The three walked past the Church of St. Peter, miraculously spared by the collapse of the towers 19 months ago. They paused.

"There's a pub a few blocks away," Chad said.

"Trumps hospital emails," Steve admitted.

Pam had reached into her handbag, slung over her shoulder and chest, New York style. She pocketed her Blackberry, and walking between the two of them, let out a sigh. "I'll make my drink a double. I don't ever escape drama these days."

"Your answering service?" Chad asked Pam.

"No, my daughter. Mastering the art of text messaging when she snags Jerry's phone."

"A preteen," Chad said. "Life will never be the same. Ask Mandy."

"Touché. I need a crash course," Pam said. "Poor word choice." She looked to the sky. "Our crash definitely started this misery."

The three slowed their pace as Chad looked to the awnings and signs. Steve thought back to the misery just mentioned—the accident, the chaos as well as an unfinished conversation—about Pam's daughter. Perhaps his. Steve's muscles tensed over Chloé's care he had orchestrated—at Pam's urging. Had something gone awry?

"Here, this is it," Chad said, opening the door. The hostess laid menus on the wooden table of their booth. Pam slid across the wood, followed by Chad. Steve sat across from them.

"Lucky Steve. You get deli fare. Still your favorite?" Pam asked.

"With tomorrow's huge dinner, this is fine," he replied. "No place does deli like New York." Steve gave the waiter his order after Pam and Chad put in theirs.

"So Pam, what's going on?" Chad asked after handing back his menu. "I read in the hospital newsletter you've assumed new duties. This all can't be because of preteen angst."

Pam Morgan remained unusually silent as Steve studied her. Clearly, Pam and Chad had established a solid collegial relationship in Philadelphia and a supportive friendship.

As the bar waiter delivered their drinks, Pam sipped a good two ounces of her double Manhattan on the rocks before the two men could even grab hold of their beers. "My life's a mess."

Steve picked up on Pam's hesitancy. Maybe this accounted for her not returning two voice messages and at least one email. Steve didn't press that in front of Chad. Pam averted direct eye contact, yet Steve wouldn't allow the sudden appearance of salads to let the topic drop.

"Paul says you've been a solid phone friend." Steve put it out there that she could obviously pick up a receiver two and a half hours away. "You had appointments in Baltimore?"

Pam dug into her salad. Took and swallowed a bite. "Chloé's seeing a specialist," she answered. "She freaked out with the neurologist at home, who forwarded my office manager—former manager—a

Kennedy Krieger referral." Pam heaved a heavy sigh. "Of course, Chloé likes *that* doctor, and my husband does also."

"That's got to be two hours away," Chad said. "More with traffic."

"Tell me about it," Pam lamented. "I can't make this about me, my schedule, my newfound driving anxiety. Never mind. My practice has gone by the wayside." Pam stabbed at lettuce.

"You sold your practice?" Steve asked.

At the straight up question, Pam met his eyes, with sadness in hers. "Yes," she managed, bowing her head. "To hell with my timeline."

When Pam asked for ground pepper—even though she had already used it—Steve could tell her focus was off, emotion flowing. Remembering their nine years together, Steve knew the stoic Pam would have a root canal without anesthesia before becoming a sniveling stereotype.

"That explains it," Chad said. "Flexibility."

"I'm a contract employee, a temporary consultant," Pam said. "When this gig's up, I'm toast."

"You couldn't have maintained OR privileges for certain procedures?" Steve asked.

"Steve, the world doesn't revolve around surgery." Pam scowled.

Chad pushed his plate back first, and when his wife called, Pam and Steve continued to quietly debate as he spoke to Mandy. "Love you, too," he said into his cell before disconnecting.

"A happy home front," Pam said. "What I need. A supportive wife."

"Pam, Jerry has supported you from what I've seen," Chad acknowledged. "You'll get through this with Chloé —whatever it is. But look, I promised algebra help by phone, so I'm heading out."

Chad laid $25 on the table, stood up and shook Steve's hand. "If I don't see you, best of luck with your plans. Give my regards to Paul."

"I will," Steve promised. "Great seeing you."

"Have fun solving for x...and y," Pam said.

"Chromosomes easier," he kidded. "See you."

Steve noticed Pam fidget as she sat back down. "Speaking of chromosomes..."

"We should head out," Pam interrupted. She summoned the waiter and pulled money out.

Steve reached into his billfold. "We need to talk, Pam."

"Walk and talk," Pam said as she gathered the dinner funds together into the black folder and left a generous tip. "You're staying at Central Park West, too?" Seeing his nod, Pam followed.

In Maryland, Tim and Liz sat.

"Our goal is to discuss your shared parenting," the mediator said. "We'll take up the finances of your separation and divorce next time."

"Doesn't one affect the other?" Tim asked.

"In what way?" The mediator swiveled her chair to Tim. She was a woman in her early sixties, around long enough Liz hoped, to curtail Tim's habit of sidetracking discussions.

"I've told Liz I want a week on, a week off. She wants them to stay mostly at our home."

"The marital residence, you mean?"

"Yes," Liz spoke up. "We have a waterfront property along the Bay. The children's friends are in the neighborhood. They love their schools."

"Our son's in first grade." Tim shifted. "Our daughter is in daycare. Preschool," he corrected. "I'm the one who found the property, by the way." Tim puffed his shoulders.

"I see," the mediator noted. "Have the two of you considered nesting—an arrangement whereby the children remain in the residence, and the two of you move in and out to care for them?"

Liz looked at her painted toenails. She'd worn sandals as April temperatures began to warm afternoons on the Eastern Shore. "I don't see how that would work." Liz's voice was crisp with concern. "I work nearby and don't have any place else to live." She crossed her ankles, but tried to keep an open posture with her arms. "Besides, privacy has been breached."

"Tell me more about your concerns." Before the mediator gave the total green light, she nodded to Tim. "You can give your thoughts also."

Tim charged right in. "She accused me of having my son steal mail. I don't know what she's talking about."

"Did you talk this over with Mr. Phillips?" the mediator asked Liz.

"I called Tim the night I found more than two dozen pieces of mail and sentimental items stuffed into my son's backpack," Liz explained. She knew her tone and body language was being studied, thus she concealed any look that would have shouted at Tim that his boundaries were so far crossed he was in New Jersey by now.

"Our son has no reason to pilfer my bank and mutual fund statements," Liz continued. "I found brochures for CEU presentations, my catalogs and bills. Mr. Phillips changed his address as of March when he took up residence. Elsewhere."

"All right, so I see the children will have to be the ones to shift between their parents."

"If their mother wants them to remain in their own surroundings so much, I could just move back in, and she can get another place," Tim added. "Remember, I found the property."

"That's really immaterial," the mediator suggested. "You work in real estate, correct?"

"I do." Tim smiled. Shoulders wiggled a notch higher, Liz noticed, until the mediator closed the session and handed them financial sheets. "I have to disclose all of this," Tim chaffed.

"By now, you would have filed your taxes. This is typical information," the mediator said.

"I filed for an extension. You know she took both kids as deductions," Tim complained.

When the mediator turned, Liz spoke. "I filed separately on April 12, after waiting more than a month for his answer about filing jointly."

"I have so much to do," Tim replied.

The mediator let the comment sit in the tense air, but Liz's mind wandered. With hoochie, junior detective training, polishing a BMW, why bother with federal taxes?

"As the disclosure papers indicate, you get out of this process what you put in, honest information so that the two of you can determine how you will share raising your children and divide assets as well as liabilities. There are no shortcuts." The woman took no prisoners. She was a straight shooter down to the details.

"Otherwise, you head to trial. That costs a lot of money. Decisions will then fall into someone else's hands." The mediator rose from her chair, subtly announcing that it was the end of their session and likely the end of her business day. "I will see you at our next scheduled appointment."

Having had her fill of Tim in the first quarter of the mediation, Liz locked her car door and backed out of her parking spot. She drove a few streets and pulled into a fast-food drive-thru. She asked for only a large cup of iced water.

When she veered her SUV away from the restaurant, she parked under a nearby tree, hoping to shade her rising temper, and worry.

Sipping through a straw, Liz flipped through papers that would be her homework over the next weeks.

House Value? Vehicles? Boats? Inheritances? The paperwork was nothing but thorough.

Inheritance, Liz thought. Grandfather Kramer had left her the same stash as he had Steve, who purchased his boat, and Eric, who hopefully banked his. Her funds had paid down the mortgage, at Tim's suggestion and her acquiescence.

Liz bristled, wondering if that made private funds morph into marital property. She wasn't sure, but knew if insurance paperwork weighed her down, these next few weeks might bury her.

In New York, Steve hailed a cab to Upper Manhattan. This kept Pam in proximity so that he could ask questions, though she monopolized the conversation their entire cab ride.

Steve learned that Jerry had put his foot down about Chloé's treatment. Their brush with serious injuries had made him aware of how many decisions he turned over to Pam. The new normal got a rough start, Steve surmised listening to Pam vent and crumple tissues.

As they entered the hotel, Steve readied himself for the exit she'd try. Pam paid a sleepless penance with a resentful husband and responsibilities in a job she possibly hated. Steve steered Pam into the bar. "Let's have dessert. My treat."

"My waistline doesn't need it," Pam insisted.

"Order sorbet." Steve found a quiet corner.

They took turns deliberating dessert choices from a huge paperclip. Their waitress brought water. Pam got the sorbet, Steve cheesecake. They decided to share a carafe of wine.

"I've listened patiently 25 minutes," Steve said. "I'm sorry it's been hectic. I get that you're busy with new job and advice column. Whatever *that's* about?" Steve sat back. "Bottom line on Chloé? What did each neurologist say?"

Pam yanked a tissue from her handbag nestled between her chair and the wall. She dabbed an eye. "One hardly got a history: dizziness, headaches, two seizures. Atypical mood," she said. "No more rule outs. It's a traumatic brain injury."

Steve gaped and blinked. "I had neurology take a look at her at West Riverside. Suzanna told me you asked for her records and operative report. How did we miss a TBI?"

106

"This isn't your fault. TBI symptoms can surface later, and they have. Remember, I was behind the wheel that night. My schedule, my work put us behind in bad traffic and weather," Pam offered. "I'm paying mightily for *those choices*." The carafe delivered, Pam quickly poured wine for them both.

"My sweet little girl with the 'you rock Mom' mentality has now been replaced by an unruly TBI teenager, years ahead of that curve." Staring at Cabernet Sauvignon she rolled in her glass, Pam promptly took a swig. "Decisions. I'm not very good with them, it appears."

"Chloé was born in '93," Steve said. "We were together over New Year's. You said you weren't sleeping with Jerry, started to that fall." Steve steadied a hand on the table, reached the other to Pam's chin. "Who is Chloé's father?" He felt her jaw quiver, a tear land on his wrist.

"I don't know," Pam let out with a muted sob.

"What the hell?" Steve withdrew his hand. "No abortion?" He lodged his elbows onto the table and pressed fingertips into his temples.

"In my panic, I invented an explanation. Jerry doesn't know about that day, that episode."

An afternoon actually that had run into one long sex-filled night. Steve pressed his shoulders into the booth. He glared at Pam, but he listened.

"I fudged dates to cover my tracks." Pam's dampened tissue became sodden. "Pathetic, yes."

"Lies atop lies, even to your mother," Steve spit out. "Beyond falsifying your own medical record and planting it so that I'd see it." *This was Summa Cum Laude?* Steve downed his wine.

"Last year, after you saved Dad's life, Mom peppered me with questions. Why I left the position I'd taken in Pittsburgh to move across state. What happened to you and me?"

"You never ran tests?" Steve asked. "Jerry believes Chloé is his, yet she could be mine." Thick disgust clogged Steve's throat. "You let me live with this, without knowing, ten years?"

"I didn't run tests. I told Jerry I got pregnant after I really did. He knew it was my specialty. He lived across the state as I made plans to join him. It was easy to hide," she admitted.

"From both of us," Steve said. "I'll be damned. What the hell happened to you? Do you have no sense of decency and respect?"

Pam took one last bite of sorbet and tossed her napkin by the bowl. "I'll save you more wrath." She inched out of her chair, shouldered her handbag, and grabbed her wine glass. "I'll get the fuck out of here before you tell me to. Like years ago." Pam Morgan turned and bolted.

Steve reached into his pocket, threw a generous $40 onto the table and followed her.

He reached the elevator bank, and with his outstretched arm halted the two doors from gliding. "You aren't running away from this," Steve warned. His voice was firm and leveled a quiet hurt as the elevator closed. Pam had already punched the button for her floor.

If Pam feared he would lash out, he did not. When the door opened, Steve pursued. "For all I know, I have a daughter, a little girl I only met last fall thanks to coincidence, and I'm supposed to simply accept that. Well, no Pam. I can't."

Pam paced faster down the hall and fumbled with her key opening her hotel room door.

Steve shouldered it open with his weight to ensure Pam wouldn't close him out and their discussion. "Why? How could you?"

Pam gulped the wine she had carried and set the glass on a small table. As she flung her handbag next to it, contents spilled out, but she paid no attention. Turning to Steve, she saw his stricken face. Pam slicked a hand through her hair before she placed it on Steve's shoulder for support.

"I wanted both of you," she confessed. "You and I ran our course. What we had surpassed intense. I wanted to keep it. And move on. You know how many times I've thought of Chloé as your child? How I held onto that possibility?"

"Jesus Christ, Pam." Steve clutched both of her arms. "I could shake you about now!" Murder wouldn't grant the answers he deserved.

"Go ahead," she cried, unleashing her own ten-year burden. "I wasn't worthy of you or him. I was messed up. Still am. I had to go through with the pregnancy. That part I don't regret."

"I want DNA tests." Steve held onto her with a viselike grip. "You owe me that much."

"And then what? Tell Jerry, tell Chloé?" Pam stared at Steve. "I'm her primary parent. She's not mature enough. You don't want to be a part of the problems, Steve, now with her struggles."

"Stop! You've made way too many decisions for me, Pam. It ends now." Steve's fingers pressed more firmly into her arm. His dark eyes left hers to glimpse a pill bottle rolling out of Pam's bag. Keeping one hand on her, Steve reached for the Xanax. "This is how you get by each day?"

"To relax. I don't need lectures or complications. Neither do you." Her voice quivered. "I've been selfish. Then. Now. The accident: my fault. I put my career first. I'm paying the price."

"Pills aren't the answer." Steve put enough distance between them but didn't let go. He knew she might not listen if he did. "Since we're revealing things, you probably didn't know this, but the police questioned me the week after the accident, the day before Vicki's services."

"Questioned you about what?" Pam asked.

Steve could feel her muscles clench beneath his grasp. "They asked me about the extent of her injuries. Chloé wasn't wearing her seatbelt. They're cracking down on negligent parents."

Pam's pupils enlarged. Her chin dropped, and she bit her lip.

"If you're worried that I ratted you out, I didn't. I said you were a good mother, always looking out for Chloé's wellbeing. Zigler, her attending, backed me that there was no evidence to investigate. The police haven't contacted you?"

Her head shook. "Thanks for saving my ass. Good mother?" Pam sniffled back tears. "Not withstanding Chloé's emotions and the mess I've created in so many lives."

"It is certifiably a mess."

She looked at Steve. "I hate what I did, but I was confused, scared, starting my career. I never intended to hurt you." Pam broke one arm free to touch Steve's hair. "You have to believe me," she whispered. "I really did love you. Chloé was possibly a part of you I could keep."

Steve loosened his grip and stared into pitiful eyes. He reached for her chin, but found her lips instead, fingering, thanking them. "I spent a decade thinking you hated me to walk away like that," he said softly.

"I didn't hate you. Please believe me," Pam begged. "Far from it."

Steve's shoulders loosened at Pam's admission. Locked in a stare, he reached down and kissed her forehead. Thrust his shoulders back.

Her fingers dug through his shirt, into his back muscles, plying the load she had saddled him with over the years and in these weeks of her ignoring him yet again.

Steve heaved a heavy sigh. His eyes watered seeing hers dump tears down her face.

The firm pressure replaced the considerable burden. So good that, without realizing it, his mouth glided over Pam's guilty lips. Steve's hands ran the length of her, down her torso and back up until he clutched her head with both hands. Should he shake her? Curse her out?

He had trained those hands to heal, hadn't he? Steve tightened his grip, with desperation. Maybe desire. The slow burn of outrage melted. Every emotion he'd ever felt for Pam Morgan suddenly flooded him. Resentment. Affection. Ire. Ecstasy. Misery. And they had made plenty.

Hours later and squinting his eyes, Steve was painfully aware of something else. They had just made love.

He squirmed from the sheets encasing him, and scrubbed a hand over his face. The hotel clock flashed 4 AM. He reached his pants from the floor. Wriggled them on and stepped into the bathroom to the sound that woke him.

"Leave me alone." Pam nestled against the bathtub. Ashen, having just flushed the contents of last night's pub menu down the commode.

No woman had ever had the urge to heave after a night between the sheets, he thought. Seeing Pam in a loosely wrapped hotel robe—more evidence that they had carried things too far—he wanted to heave, too.

"Something you ate?"

"Stress has messed with everything. My stomach. My cycle," she said. "Do you mind?"

When Steve snagged his shirt from the end of the bed, he spotted a small tote on the nightstand. Vendors gifted meeting bags per specialty that bestowed Pam all kinds and colors of protection. Steve eyeballed the broken Trojan wrapper.

"Pam." Steve tucked shirttails into his trousers. "When was your last period?"

"Ugh." She splashed water on her face, reached for the hand towel, and patted the droplets. "I don't know...five weeks ago. Maybe."

"Help me out here." Steve leaned against the doorjamb. "You're an OB. Don't know when your last period was, and you're puking into the toilet at four in the morning." He silenced his observation of the voluptuous breasts that spilled out of her robe and had taunted him last night.

Steve waited. "Could you be pregnant?"

"We were trying to conceive, but then the accident and well...I told you things are just so fouled up." Pam patted her face one last time and hung the towel on its silver rod. "I'll get tested as soon as I get back."

"Like hell you will. Like now," Steve insisted. "Two drugstores are down the street."

"Oh screw you, Steve."

He recoiled at the too familiar rebuke. "What a Freudian slip?"

"Stores aren't even open." She faced him, pushing into the vanity. Her crossed arms ended the cleavage display. "You don't trust me, do you?"

"Now there's an interesting supposition." He ran a hand over his morning stubble. "Do not leave this room, do you understand me? One of them has to be open 24 hours." He stepped away.

Steve came back, stuffing his wallet into his pants and fastening his watch; Pam reluctantly moved past. "I need to lie down." She threw a pillow into position and stretched out.

"Do you need anything for your stomach?" he asked.

"No. It could just be the effects of the wine."

Steve sighed. "Certainly didn't help either of us think clearly." He ran a hand through his brown hair. "Drinking, if you're pregnant?"

The tension they had released in one another had crept back.

"First time in three weeks." Pam propped up. "Trust me, I didn't see any of this coming."

"That makes two of us." He stuck out his neck. "On the trust issue, it has to be earned."

"I'm married...struggling, but still. And you walk down the aisle in a matter of weeks."

"Tell me about it!" Steve leaned against the wall. His breath hitched raggedly. "I just screwed another man's pregnant wife."

Pam lobbed her head into a mound of pillows. "Maybe. You can't breathe a word of this."

Their minds synced, pensive as they pondered the two they had both just betrayed.

"So I lie about it?" Steve shot back. "Lies of omission or commission. Which are worse?"

"Equal." She clutched her queasy stomach. "I'm acutely aware, but I'm serious, Steve. I deal with women every day when they find out these things. You tell Maren and she will hold up your wedding or not marry you at all."

Tense muscles made Steve's knees nearly buckle. "Why?" His head abutted the wall. "Why did we do this?"

"Emotion. Raw and real."

"Oh, for the love of God, you got that straight from Paul." *Keep a safe distance, she's not meant for you*—Paul's other advice—swirled in Steve's head. "How do we explain this?"

"We don't," Pam said. "This never happened."

If Pam Morgan had not sworn off car crash metaphors, she would have told Steve that he looked like a deer startled by on-coming headlights. Only he was in the middle of her room.

"Steve, if I am pregnant, you and I both know this is Jerry's baby. No one will ever find out what happened here because only two people know. You and me," she said. "My marriage is already fucked up, pardon the expression."

Did she have to keep reminding him? Steve's eyes lingered longer. "I care about you. I always will, but I *don't* love you. What a mess. What a choice we live with."

"Pain with both options, but people do live with pain," Pam said.

Steve rocked his head sideways before he pulled the knob and let the door slam behind him.

Chapter 10

"Dr. Kramer just got out of surgery," Suzanna told Paul as he passed Steve's office. "He's still catching up after his New York trip."

"Thanks." Paul pivoted before Steve's slightly ajar door. "If Jade Chen calls, put her on hold please. We're playing phone tag."

"Sure, Dr. Romano," Suzanna replied. "Go right in."

"Tough morning?" Paul stepped to Steve's desk and stacked charts. "You asked to see me?"

"A lot on my mind." Steve swiveled to face Paul who sat across from him. "You OK?"

"Yeah. Covering for your honeymoon will have its benefits."

"A distraction, I'm sure." Steve fidgeted with a pen. "Pretend I'm not chief of surgery, though I just added follow-ups to your June schedule. You sold your house, you're renting in Shore Landings, and well, I know you're quite collegial with some top brass in Pittsburgh."

"I've had discussions regarding a private practice, plus a hospital job. How'd you know?"

"Three Rivers Primary Care on one message," Steve admitted. "Your name came up in New York. Chad, thoracic surgeon who came down in February, says hello. We all kind of wondered."

"I'll be straight with you." Paul relaxed. "I'm sorting out options."

"What else is new?" Steve emitted a chuckle over that indecision.

"I know I can't spend as much time at West Riverside, whatever I do. I've thought about private practice, expanding it off site."

"Memories here." Steve granted them pensive stillness before mentioning, "I know you're careful what surgical cases you take, especially now. Is there more to that?"

"I never had the zeal you did," Paul admitted. "Hell, you devoted your entire career to surgery. You have something to show for it." Paul opened his palms surveying the trappings of the nicer office and his head motioned to Suzanna's area. "Suzanna's really *your* secretary."

"Feel you missed making your mark?" Steve asked. "You never needed rock star status—what Liz would say of my career."

They each laughed. Paul rubbed his chin.

"Agreed," Paul admitted. "Talked about it with my EAP person."

"Well, everyone needs a goal," Steve said. "This was mine. Liz always wanted her own practice. She had money from our grandfather. Tim convinced her to sock it into the house."

"I'm no lawyer, but the house is joint property," Paul said. "Liz's inheritance wasn't. Now it could be partially his." A frown formed on his face. "He's a loser to cheat on her as he did."

"Pond scum." *I am, too!* Steve repositioned himself staring uncomfortably into the unfinished notes, then re-established eye contact. "Back to surgery vs. primary care...here, anywhere."

"Another decision: I got a large check, the kind most would quickly deposit." Paul slouched. "Life insurance and other funds. Maren says I hang on to it because it symbolizes something."

"She told me Mark's policy helped to fund a trust for Dylan."

"Exactly. What do I do? Fund it to the dog I want to get? I'm OK financially," Paul admitted. "Easy rent. No mortgage. Corvette's paid off, plus I kept Vicki's SUV."

"Did Vicki give thoughts? Ever read her note?"

Paul considered his friend. "I did. Bawled my eyes out a paragraph into it," he admitted. "Instructions on other things. Not that."

"So?"

"Scholarship maybe, research, maternal health grant. I don't know. Probably ought to just bank the funds and then decide." Paul turned his head to the knock on Steve's door.

"Excuse me, Dr. Romano. The call you asked about is holding," Suzanna announced. After Paul nodded, she closed the door.

Paul stood. "I'll keep you posted on Pittsburgh. Our secret."

Steve reclined at *secret.* "Think twice about it."

"Me, make a snap decision?"

Paul stepped quickly out of Steve's and into his own office, grabbing the receiver. "Jade, how are you?" He listened to how busy it was in what docs called The Pit. "Well, speaking of short staffed...Liz Phillips. Goes by Kramer. I heard you gave her a second interview."

"I'm weighing her credentials and two other candidates," Jade offered since Paul was a colleague and she was new. "Any particular reason you ask?"

"She'd be an asset here. I've known her for 15 years, and our paths have crossed obviously with Steve," Paul said. "Gotten to know her since... well, people reach out." Paul's voice shifted, uneasy about needing sympathy or support.

"That's understandable. Her CV looks good, but you know these are sometimes 10-12-hour shifts. All things considered." Jade hesitated.

"Jade, you recognize determination, ability no matter what station in life. Liz Kramer can manage whatever comes her way," Paul added. He wondered if the younger, childless Dr. Chen feared Liz had to balance every commitment with single parenting. He sensed how humiliated Liz felt in the ER after fetching his passport.

"Appreciate the referral. I'll decide soon. How are…I mean, I hope you're getting along." Jade paused. "I…I feel so badly about your loss."

Hearing people's hesitation, their not knowing what to say, drove Paul crazy some days. Those who diverted into another hospital hallway to avoid him cast even more of a pall.

"Thank you. Some days are better than others." *Most aren't.*

"Let's get together. Lunch: my treat," Dr. Chen explained. "I'm a good listener. Comes with the territory in emergency medicine."

"Thanks and for considering my opinions."

They disconnected. Was that a pick-up line for the bereaved? If Paul counted lonely days—and nights—like some people counted loose change, he'd be rich. If he deposited the life insurance check, his bank account would be also. He'd give anything to be poor Paul if it reflected a lack of finances. It didn't. Come Friday, however, his condo wouldn't be so empty. He would create a family come hell or high tides, even if a kennel replaced a crib.

Steve got through post-op appointments. Late afternoon, he powered his MacBook. Music. Energy. He needed both to finish paperwork.

Details raced through Steve's mind. His caseload, chief of surgery demands, unpacking at the new house, honeymoon plans. *Maren will love it.* Thinking of clandestine, his mind sunk to secrets. The DNA tests Pam agreed to. Why the stall? At least two sets of eyes had seen the test strip. The result would literally start showing soon.

Internet music bolstered Steve's focus. His fingers tapped away typing patient notes into the electronic file until he lifted his fingers.

I haven't heard that since… Steve angled his neck to his MacBook screen. "Separate Ways," the 80s hit by Journey. This video wasn't a standout except for the white high heels and tight black skirt on the dirty blonde walking beyond men. Away. Worlds apart, hearts broken.

A decade ago, he and Pam had gone separate ways. Steve survived the tides, in the lyrics, and in reality. Pam was an ebb and flow, like a chain binding him. *God this song still fit.* One night broke those chains. Pam confessed she'd loved him. And kept what could be his child.

Steve planted elbows on his desk and massaged his scalp. A cymbal clash ended the song. A knock on his door, left ajar, equally jolted him.

"Honey, what is it? You look as if you saw a ghost." Maren stepped in and rolled her handbag down her arm. "I've got time before I pick up Dylan." Maren eased into a chair. "Steve…"

He closed the laptop like a kid caught violating parental controls. "It's been a hellish day." *The day busy, my life hell.* "How was yours?"

"Walter Mitchell called. Still trying to convince me to work for his agency." Maren's mouth twisted in disgruntlement. "They're ticked that I sold *Mark's* house, as if I never contributed a dime. It's been mine solely for two years." She shrugged. "Are you almost done?"

"Yeah, we all have difficult fixtures in life. I give you credit for putting up with them. Come here," he said, summoning her to his lap as he pushed away from the desk.

Maren ran a hand through his brown hair and looked into pained blue eyes. Not the calm azure she remembered. "I do it for Dylan. It's just the right thing for kids to know their heritage, their family." She continued stroking Steve's hair. "You work too hard, you know that."

"I love you." Steve tightened his grip on her.

"I'm sorry. I know you can't talk about it."

His baby blues stretched saucer wide, certain Maren felt his stiff muscles and racing heart.

"It's bound to happen. You don't have to worry about my reaction. Maybe Paul's anxiety," she said. "Not after nine months…"

"What?" Steve felt himself turn crimson.

"Nine months. Working here. I know patients pass away, Steve. I can see your damp eyes. Whatever you did, I'm sure you followed your best instincts. You'd always do the right thing."

Steve swallowed hard. "Let's get out of here. Let me turn this off."

Maren stepped to the window. "Did you hear?" She hiked her handbag on her shoulder.

Steve traded his white coat for a suit jacket on the coat tree. Would he feel his blood pressure spike every time Maren got close to the truth? He stretched an arm into a sleeve. "Hear what?"

"Liz says they've moved the shower to her house. Paul's helping." Maren launched into a broad smile adding, "And, he's getting a puppy!"

116

Maren's bag bumped Steve as she reached with both hands to smooth his collar in line with his jacket. "Different species but…" She took her time to canoodle and smooch. "Makes me think about the project, naming it before launch."

"With marketing, you're always good at your job." Steve grabbed his briefcase hurriedly.

"Steve, our project." Maren pressed her tongue to her cheek. "PBK: Project Baby Kramer."

Steve moved one hand along the wall switch plate and his other gently against Maren's back. He brightened. "I like that. Does the project allow testing prior to official launch?"

"Lots of trial runs." She slanted a saucy grin, snuggled into his arms, and walked to their cars.

After picking up his children, Tim headed westbound on the Bay Bridge, exiting at Annapolis Mall. Hannah clamored for frozen yogurt. Tyler wanted a handheld game. Tim only heard the petition Lucena presented: a stop for lingerie.

"Eew underwear." Tyler scrunched his face. Tim handed over cash, ground Lucena against him, and patted her bottom. "How come she gets something and we don't?" Tyler demanded.

Tim steered them to the closest mall bench. "I'll tell you why," Tim spout off. "She listens. You can't even follow simple instructions."

"What do you mean?" Tyler asked. "I just got good marks for listening on my report card."

"Listening to me!" Tim lowered his voice. "You couldn't even get those things I asked for without your Mom finding them."

"But Dad, I got the jewelry you said belonged to Grandma Phillips. That pin and the watch." Tyler fidgeted. "In Mom's room."

"And he got Mommy's money," Hannah piped up. At the time, Tyler had been so entranced by a bill bigger than a twenty that he had to show his sister evidence of $50 and $100 bills.

"Hannah, don't be in the triangle." A hard line formed along Tim's mouth. "It's my money."

"In Mommy's dresser." Miffed, Hannah crossed her arms. "You steal Mommy's words, too."

"Mom said that about her mail," Tyler continued. "That I stole it."

"I'm not stealing anything," Tim persuaded. "I'm borrowing."

Tyler looked wistfully at Tim, who hadn't been a daily fixture in their lives since he moved in with Lucena nearly three months ago.

"I know you miss me. It's hard being kicked out of my home," Tim said. "Don't you want to help me?" Tim scooted on the bench so that he faced his son. "You love me and Mom, right?"

Tyler nodded affirmatively. When Tim pulled Hannah's arms out of her angry posture, she bobbed her head also.

"I know you don't want to upset Mommy. Keep this between us." Before Tim could launch his next sentence, Lucena strutted over. "Hey sugar, buy out the store?" He kissed her greedily on the lips. "Do me a favor. Take Hannah for frozen yogurt. Any money left?" Lucena wiggled her head sideways. Tim pulled out a bill.

"What about what I want?" Tyler asked as Tim jumped off the bench. "Sit back down. I'll make you a deal." He waited until the girls strode down the corridor. "Help me and I'll get games for your Game Boy and video system." Tim swallowed satisfaction when Tyler acknowledged agreement. He unfolded a list. "Now, as soon as you can, here's what I need."

Paul left work that week with a lighter step. If co-workers didn't hit happy hour, thanking God for Friday, then they had family outings planned this first weekend after Memorial Day. Picnics. Good food. Children. Laughter.

He had beer and blankets to spread out, just not the last two ingredients. Though Paul Romano could prepare a meal better than a chef, he had lost six pounds. Fewer mugs of Rolling Rock and a little more exercise he told himself. But his appetite had suffered since Vicki died.

Paul slammed his car door. A smile played on his lips seeing another couple with his very idea. Looking for love in the same spot. They were young—twenty-something. Their new companion had just hiked his leg and watered the West Riverside Animal Shelter sign.

He could hear the other occupants from the parking lot, but as he opened the door, the din echoed off the concrete walls.

"You must be Dr. Romano." The matronly woman lifted her massive figure from the chair behind a sparse desk.

Several dog walks every half-hour might lower her risk factors, Paul thought, but he wasn't there as a healer as much as to be healed. He acknowledged the desk sitter with a nod.

"Come with me." She pulled a metal door handle. "I'm Abigail. Mrs. Phillips gave you an excellent reference as did Mrs. Mitchell." The woman lodged her glasses next to the bun on her head. "You checked out just fine. We never know with…medical doctors."

Paul's stomach seemed to text his brain: Not hungry. The cavernous room reminded him of hospital morgues or the cadaver room. Only these living specimens greeted him in unison.

"That's nice." Paul raised his voice above the howls. "I'm interested in a pet." *Dinner companion. Someone to talk to late at night.* For decades Paul had never had a problem finding either and was known to meow over companions that stood out. Tonight he was sure he could walk away with a true meow, but barking suited just fine.

"Right here we have a Chessie," Abigail told Paul. "I'll bet you work long hours, don't you?"

Paul crouched down and let the puppy sniff his hand before reaching through the cage to rub its tiny head. "Well, yes, but I plan to hire a dog walker, if that's your concern."

"You duck hunt?" Abigail asked.

"Ah, you mean with a shotgun?" Paul could tell his lack of understanding didn't impress.

"You're not from around here. Not a native?"

Paul acknowledged he was not. Western Pennsylvanians might hunt deer or go after Punxsutawney Phil if he called for six more weeks of winter. Not Paul.

"Chesapeake retrievers are bred for waterfowl, popular on the Eastern Shore," Abigail explained. She motioned him to the kennels pre-selected for him. "Chessies are indifferent. Protective, loyal, but don't want to hear your problems."

Plenty of those. Paul cast a goodbye glance to the first little guy. "This one's cute. What breed?" Paul scratched under its ear and the puppy nuzzled him back.

"Basically a black lab mutt with Bernese Mountain markings," Abigail guesstimated.

"I don't know much about either actually."

"Berners, as they're called, are bred to work in the German/Swiss Alps. Labs love water, attention. Read either a kid's book or a scary Stephen King. They'd just lie there wanting more."

While the baby books were packed away and Paul had enough worries to keep him up at night, he certainly craved the company. "What's his history? Pretty playful."

"Pure puppy. Found him running along the riverbanks. Mangy at first, but he cleaned up well. Tough name: Bruno." Abigail motioned Paul along as if she wanted to enjoy another chapter in her novel this evening. "No identification. Sad, no one's claimed him."

Paul felt a little clutch. "He does look adorable but tough." *Bruno Sammartino. Born in Abruzzo, Italy, residing in the 'Burgh.* Paul smiled, yet dutifully followed along the row of kennels.

Abigail stopped at the poodle and shook her head sideways. They kept walking. "This one's a lab, only yellow. He's six months...we think. Owner took ill. Couldn't care for him."

Paul felt that familiar clutch again. He stooped down. As his hand landed on the dog's fur, the dog licked Paul's fingers. "Friendly. Labrador Retrievers are pretty social, aren't they?"

"Absolutely, but you will need to walk them. Otherwise you're looking at vet bills if they gain weight and develop arthritis. If you keep 'em clean, you won't have to bathe them that often." Abigail stood back, watching Paul stroke the animal. "So we've got two more but they will stay small. Down at the end," she said, her arm out-stretched. "What do you think?"

"Tough choice," Paul admitted. "What happens to these animals... if no one claims them?"

As soon as the question left his lips, Paul regretted asking. When she explained their fate due to overcrowding, he felt the worst gut wrench that evening. "Labs are social. The black puppy, the Alps dog?"

"Bernese Mountain lab mix," she corrected.

"Sorry. They're both social. Both healthy?"

"Vet checked them out, and neutered them. It's our policy."

Paul looked wistfully at the yellow lab he crouched close to, then at Bruno. His mother never missed Bob Barker's popular game show, with the send off about spaying and neutering. While these dogs wouldn't make babies, Paul pictured his niece swaddling Bruno in a blanket next time his sister brought her slew of kids.

When they heard the dogs howl a little louder Abigail peeked out the glass of the metal door. "I don't mean to rush you sir, but I have someone out there. I'm not supposed to leave you unattended, but if you want to take one on a little walk, I'll get a collar and a leash."

"Yeah, that will give me some time to think."

Abigail told the people she'd be right there and led Paul outside. Ten minutes later, Paul still hadn't come back in. Bruno rolled in the grass showing off his belly. He took well to tickling.

Paul thought if he had walked one, he owed the same courtesy to the yellow lab. This one watered the sign in exactly the same spot as the dog Paul saw. What else did they have to live for?

Abigail called this one yellow but honestly he looked more golden to Paul. It figures: One black with a touch of gold on its brows and paws, the other all one color. Black and gold.

"Ah, jeez," Paul said out loud to no one in particular. "I'd have to give you an Italian name," Paul told the lab at the other end of the leash. As soon as Paul reached to scratch his head, the dog instantly lapped at his hand again.

I can't decide. "You're so affectionate." He'd almost forgotten what affection felt like.

"But your pal. I can't leave him…just a baby." *He's a dog, dammit.*

"If I don't take him or you, they'll put…" Paul shook the notion.

Abigail turned her book over as Paul entered.

"What happens if I want to adopt both dogs?"

"Can't say that's happened. Sure you can handle two young dogs?"

"There's no law that says I can't have both?"

Indecision: A decision in itself.

"I'll take them. Bruno and…" Paul pondered before announcing, "Franco. There's a jersey with a 32 on it in your future," he muttered. Franco panted and drooled on the linoleum.

Abigail looked at Paul squarely as if he had two heads. He explained, "My niece pushes stuffed animals in a baby buggy. Dresses them. I'll name him after a famous Pittsburgh running back. Franco Harris."

Abigail managed a fake smile, handed him a clipboard, and motioned to the bulletin board. Thumbtacks secured the Ravens schedule.

"Hometown loyalty," Paul added to salve the poor impression he might have just made with her. "You'll bring Bruno out."

"Oh brother! One black, one gold," Abigail managed as soon as she realized the symbolism. "I'll get him. I'll be back in a jiffy."

Paul set the clipboard on the desk. He reached into his wallet and pulled out a credit card since donations helped keep these doors open. When Abigail returned he instructed her to run his VISA for $800.

The look on her face could have converted her to his team's fan base. Paul signed the receipt and thanked her for her patience. He scooped a wiggling Bruno into one arm and held the leash Abigail gave him for Franco.

Franco lived up to his name as he pushed forward through the parking lot to the SUV Paul had fortunately driven that evening. With both Bruno and Franco, the Corvette's days might be numbered. As he started his engine, Paul didn't care. Tonight he wouldn't be lonely.

Chapter 11

"Mom, it's so loud," Tyler complained stomping from his room. "I can't get to the next level."

"Concentrating on your game seems hard." Liz reflected Tyler's frustration as she snapped lids on plastic containers. The clock read 5 PM. She and Paul had finished hosting their Sunday party. The guests of honor had already left.

Liz turned to Paul. "Why don't you go let them out, within the fence," she suggested. "I'll finish with the food. Could you please take this bag of trash? The can is by the garage."

"Sure. Sorry the boys are bothering you, Tyler," Paul said. "Liz, keep the leftovers. I'm hardly at my condo. Puppy Chow has taken over my small kitchen anyway."

"Between the kids and Eric," she said, "This will get eaten."

When Paul helped set up Saturday, Liz was certain he had noticed the gleaming glass refrigerator shelves. Empty. She assured him grocery shopping was on her to-do list. The budget only stretched so far with Tim's check and her slowly growing one from Hal.

They had established temporary financial support, to go into effect after the end of the month. Thanks to Paul, the pulled pork, beef barbeque and various salads would feed them this week. Eric accepted food—more like vacuumed it—for occasional babysitting.

Paul scooted down Liz's stairs to the dogs crated under shady trees. Sprung free, Bruno and Franco pawed, pounced, and played all over the yard. Paul returned to the kitchen cleanup.

"Everything went really well. You so saved me on this. I didn't have a raucous bachelor party in me." Paul regarded Liz with gratitude in his eyes and a smirk on his face.

"Perfect day. Nautical theme. I'm glad her cousin Courtney and Josh could come." Relatives had flown from Florida a week before the nuptials.

"Eric came," Paul said. "Where's Shelly?"

"That's mellowed a bit," Liz said. She looked out at her younger brother with her kids.

"He was mellow," Paul recollected. "You know a lot of bands... experiment on the side."

Liz crinkled her face. "I don't think Eric's into that scene." She regarded Paul. "Better not be."

Paul let that topic drop. "The *I Do BBQ* sign was clever. Vicki was always good at those things too," he admitted.

Planning to reach for a dishtowel to dry wine glasses, Liz reached for Paul's shoulder instead. "Was it hard seeing Courtney six months pregnant? That's why Maren asked me to be her honor attendant. Courtney was…cautious."

"A little. Glad her pregnancy's going well," Paul replied. *Unlike Vicki's.* Liz regarded him.

"Steve was right. You have a good heart." Liz thought Paul represented so much she admired. "Sweet sentiments you wrote as your message."

Liz had gathered beige river rocks and fine-point markers instructing guests to write on them. Paul had penned: Navigate with few storms and lots of sunny skies. Happy sailing through your married life! Love you both so much…Paul.

"Well, you had the ideas. I just covered some costs. OK, I provided the tongue depressors. Another ingenious idea." Paul saw that the glass jar containing them had been left behind."

"I didn't read these." Liz snatched a stick labeled *Date Night Ideas.* "Two entrées, a bottle of wine and a Shore Landings sidewalk café."

"Bruno, Franco and I have found many of those. We walk the opposite sidewalk when there's food," he said. "Look at them, lounging under your trees." Paul waved goodbye to Eric.

Liz set the jar aside. "Hannah's still out there."

"She's bigger than they are… for now," Paul replied. "But let's grab some iced tea and go outside. The dogs do love it here."

"I can tell. One of them snatched a towel from my oven door," Liz said. "I'm missing sandals, too. You don't think they chewed those?"

As Liz and Paul claimed two Adirondacks, Paul shrugged. "Where did you see them last?"

"In a Birkenstock shoebox. My Christmas gift from Tim," she said. "Oh, I'll find them. What are you reading to the puppies?" Liz asked Hannah who sat cross-legged with a story.

Hannah held up the children's book. *Walter the Farting Dog: Trouble at the Yard Sale.* "Almost-Aunt Maren gave it to Tyler. She got two copies by axi…accident." At three, Hannah still stumbled over certain words.

"Maren is working on a children's book. She's collected some to study." Liz sipped tea. "Steve taught Tyler and Dylan that farts are normal, nothing that can't be talked about. Charming."

The corner of Paul's mouth twitched in amusement. He swallowed a mouthful of the cold liquid and jiggled the ice cubes. "It's peaceful yet active here; polar opposite of my place."

"You're welcome any time. Consider this another dog park for the boys," she offered before turning serious. "I thought Bruno and Franco kept you company."

"They do," Paul said. "They're great."

"Pet therapy can lower your BP, heart rate and anxiety levels."

Paul nodded. "You know the song on the radio. Matchbox Twenty sings it." He reached into his pocket. "Take a listen. My existence."

"You have an iPod? Man," Liz took ear buds Paul offered with the fairly new contraption for music lovers. Liz sat back, reached for another sip, and bobbed her head with the beat.

"I'm not crazy...a little unwell." He accentuated the song title.

"Describes my life." Liz coiled the ear buds handing them to Paul. "Dodging glances. Feeling impaired. I hate that, too." Liz relaxed into the chair's slant. "How much sleep do you get?"

"Enough to function," Paul answered. "Six if I'm lucky. Forget eight. Not since..." The last time Paul woke refreshed he lived in a single family home with a wife and baby on the way.

"Paul, you're not. I mean the song says headed for a breakdown. Now that I work in..."

"Emergency psych," Paul interrupted. "No, not to worry."

Liz breathed more easily. "Next weekend's going to be really hard. We have to stand beside them as they take vows—vows my husband trashed. Sorry, we were talking about you."

"It's OK, Liz. The Tim-ectomy has excised him from the property but not your mind. Hearing other people talk—about anything—beats staring at my ceiling. Tell me about the job."

"I was thrilled when Jade called. Last week, I shadowed another social worker in the hospital. With the schedule we have, on weekends Tim has Hannah and Tyler, I can go over there and work. The almost newlyweds said I could stay at their house after my late shifts."

"If I'm away, stay at my condo. You don't mind a little dog fur? If you saw Bruno attack the vacuum, you'd commit him."

"We all have our limits." Liz laughed. "How's your job? Steve says you don't do much surgery."

"Curtailed that. Pam and Steve used to get on me about not pinning down a specialty. I saw two skill sets," Paul recollected. "Since Vicki's problems, I'm pulled more to primary care."

"Who cares what those two think?"

"They are both friends, Pam included." Chagrin etched Paul's face. Maren seemed proximal to Liz's heart within nine weeks of Steve dating her. Pam remained ever distal to Liz with nearly nine years spent in Steve's life, he thought.

"A practice on Kent Island could use an internist," Paul shared. "I'll look at that in July."

"Bruno and Franco could stay here, as free entertainment. The kids complain that I cut back on our cable service," Liz added. "Guest room on the third floor. You called it a hotel suite."

"How would Tim see my staying over?"

Paul narrowed his eyes. "Just hired dog walks twice a day. I do early morning and evenings."

"I don't give a rat's butt what he thinks, running around with that loose woman," Liz chimed.

"A little puttana. Translated: Loose woman or prostitute who eats that pasta salad so that…"

"Excuse me? The pasta you left with me?"

"Lose the look. Pasta Puttanesca got its name because it's quick and easy. Just like…"

A grin broke across Liz's face. She hadn't heard Paul crack a joke in the longest time.

"You have perfect teeth when you smile," Paul noticed.

"Thank you. Trying to get back into my good graces?" Liz took another swig of iced tea. "You must have gotten to another level," she said as Tyler came up to them both. She brushed his hair back. "You need a trim before the wedding."

"It's *my* hair, Mom. And Hannah, that's *my* book." Tyler ran over to her by the dogs. "You don't even like the word *farting*. I'm gonna sell *you* at the neighborhood yard sale," he raged.

Franco let out a tiny growl while Bruno was up for play. "I'm *not* in the mood. Who invited these dumb dogs anyway?"

"Young man, watch it." Liz leapt off the Adirondack. "Hannah, did you ask to borrow that?"

"Yes." Hannah stood up and slammed her hands to her hips.

"I didn't say you could get drool all over it."

When Tyler went to shove his sister, Liz put both hands out holding him back. "Enough. This is where you move away from the situation. DEBUG. Do ignore. Exit or move away."

"He's not friendly either, Mommy." Hannah remembered step three and had mastered the fourth using firm language. "He's just mad Dylan and me are in the wedding and he's not."

"Dylan and I, please," Liz corrected. "Tyler will hand out programs while Uncle Eric escorts people to their seats."

"Maybe I should get my things…" Paul stopped when Liz held up her index finger.

"No, you are our guest. We do not raise our voices when we have guests."

"You and dad raised voices," Tyler avowed. "You kicked him out."

"That incident was weeks ago. I did not force your father to leave. Right now, I'm the mom. You can stew in your room until your attitude improves." Liz crossed her arms. "One…two…"

Tyler managed to move past her before she came close to three.

"I'm sorry," Liz told Paul. "Sit down. Finish your iced tea."

"This has to be hard on them," Paul offered. "Maren said Dylan acted out after Mark died." Paul quenched his thirst with a large swallow. "School's over soon. Maybe he's just antsy."

"His teacher sent a note home. Tyler can't stay seated, tormented a classmate during seatwork. Yeah, I have one angry child. I've become my caseload," Liz said. "Pathetic."

"So? Sometimes I feel as if I've become mine. We're all human, Liz." Paul raised his glass one last time and set it down on the wide arm of his chair. "As the great Michelangelo once said, 'I am still learning.' We all are. Tyler will be OK."

"Teacher agreed he's angry and wants me to have him tested over the summer for ADHD. She didn't know Tim and I separated," Liz reported. "Not a good idea to rush an ADHD evaluation with such uncertainty and anxiety. Tim moved us to the cheapest plan, which won't cover testing. He wanted to drop the insurance."

Paul stood up. Shook his head. "There are preschool age children present so I'm not going there. Figlio di puttana."

Liz mouthed, "Son of a prostitute?"

Paul leaned in close. Liz could feel his breath. "Son of a bitch. We Italians get a lot of mileage out of that puttana word."

She nodded. "Ice cream? I sent Smith Island cake with Maren."

"I'm fine. Busy week ahead," he replied. "Let me collapse those crates and get going."

"I wish they could stay," Hannah said. Bruno had fallen onto her after Franco tackled him. All three rolled in the grass.

"Franco makes his namesake proud. See you at the rehearsal, Hannah. Be good for your mom."

Liz smiled and walked with Paul to lend a hand. Even if only one child took that admonition to heart, Liz's week would start well.

Temperatures that didn't even climb into the 80s made June 14th, Maren's and Steve's wedding day, perfect for outdoor portraits before and after the hour-long ceremony.

"OK, bride and groom." The photographer sounded like a wedding director, one professional they had not hired even with a guest list that climbed to 200 but later landed at 150.

A few guests, knowing the tragedy that had overtaken the bride's life two years prior, dabbed their eyes as Maren took steady strides to meet Steve. She had walked alone to the altar, symbolic of how strong she had become.

Her ivory dress draped her shoulders as it plunged lower with a cowl neckline. From a distance, it made a soft, simple silhouette. Up close, it clung to her, slim to the floor.

"Think of that first kiss," the photographer joked aligning Steve, arms around his bride, who, at the photographer's suggestion, raised the skirt of her wedding dress to show a leg in high heels.

"What's with men and high heels?" Liz mumbled to Paul as they stood awaiting further direction. Liz crossed her arms. "For 24 hours, guys could get over it already."

"You *don't* really want me to respond to that," Paul hushed. Slanted furtive eyes. "The love well hasn't run dry for them, that's for sure."

Maren and Steve locked lips as the shutter snapped away.

"Where's he taking her on their honeymoon?"

"Sworn to secrecy," Paul told Liz. "She'll know soon enough."

"Come on, someplace warm? Wet?"

"Liz, there was a time I'd have welcomed you talking dirty in my ear." Paul sized her up with an appreciative smirk. Standing next to Steve before the ceremony, Paul forced a smile. Not nearly as difficult when Liz Phillips began a slow saunter down the aisle of the church.

A dark, navy sheath outlined her hips and skimmed the floor when she moved. Anyone with an ounce of testosterone would focus on the gown's bodice brought into a V and tied at the back of Liz's delicate neck. Backless, showing off her tan, a golden one already in mid-June, and boasting more than a hint of cleavage.

Shouldn't Liz, with a slit on one side, showcase a leg and spiked heels? Navy peep toe pumps forced her to latch on for stability as they traipsed uneven ground for requisite photos. Paul enjoyed the feel as she clutched him through his jacket, sometimes lacing arms.

"OK, best man and our honor attendant." The photographer snapped fingers and motioned. "Let's get the two of you, then flanking the bride and groom. Here, hands on her hips. And you…" The seasoned shutterbug stood back to assess Liz. Noticing the same attributes, Paul figured, watching their photographer smack his lips and slap back sunglasses.

As photo man pondered his next candid, the more Paul's palms and fingers relaxed against the satiny fabric covering Liz's curves. Paul hadn't laid hands on a woman in months; wearing a white lab coat didn't count. Today proved to be more fun than he'd imagined.

"You two know each other?" the man asked.

"Almost two decades," Paul assured him.

"Like a brother." Liz gripped the lapels of Paul's tuxedo the way she had been instructed.

"Move your cheek to his…closer but cheat it toward me," he directed them. "Angle your chin sir…not so stiff you two. Let me check the light."

"He keeps moving us closer and it will be."

"Paul!" Liz giggled. "Your humor is back."

"A defense mechanism…in your extra brother's brain."

If Liz only knew the 15-year fantasies that ping-ponged Paul's mind, she'd be ethically obligated, as a mandated reporter, to turn him in for such incestuous thoughts. Yet he wasn't Liz's brother, and he'd earned a reputation lobbing libidinous remarks when least expected.

"A little closer. Liz, turn. Say…sexy."

The pair didn't dare move when the photographer's sidekick whispered suggestions.

"Cartwheel?" the best man muttered. "No, save the swinging chandeliers for your *bio* brother."

Liz elbowed him. "Quiet or he'll keep us frozen in this pose."

"Let's get our bride and groom in here," the photographer directed. Nudged. Tilted chins. Encouraged closeness. "Ladies, both of you show some leg. Gentlemen, go for the grins."

Steve smirked. The shudder snapped Maren Kramer's family-inspired scowl: Her first official Kramer woman look.

When they broke the pose, Liz held Maren's flowers as she fiddled with her dress. Steve whispered to Paul, "Years ago you would have donated one hand to science just to have the other one on my sister. Your lucky day."

They both laughed. Paul halted Steve's step.

"Luckier than being put against our apartment wall. Your finger in my face, forbidding me."

"Raw but real image, as you'd say?" Steve groaned at the memory. "Liz can use a little ego boost and ah…just don't do it within sight of Jade. She's got a thing for you."

As they walked into the reception, Paul held Steve back, "She does? I didn't see her here."

"She was too new for the guest list. When I consulted on a case, you were all she could ask about," Steve confessed. Grinned. "I'm out ten days. Your ticket to find out."

Guy code got exchanged with darting eyes and nods. Paul soon forgot as the bridal party was announced before the guests. A dashing Dylan thrust his arm out as Paul had taught him at the rehearsal. The flower girl latched on, beaming. The full lining underneath navy netting gave Hannah the volume she needed to appear quite the princess at almost four years old.

Waiters placed hors d'oeuvres for the bridal party on their round table, but duty called.

"Good evening everyone," Paul started, standing with his champagne glass. "I'm Paul, often confused as the fourth Kramer kid. Yeah, tonight my mother learns she really could have given me away those times she might have wanted to." A few giggled. Some tapped their glasses, but Paul's hands held them off.

"I've known Steve since we started med school in 1984, sharing so much of our lives: Football, fishing, much fun. He convinced me to move here, and anointed me his right-hand man over the six months leading up to this moment. Tonight, he's on his own…with the best catch he's ever reeled in."

The guests chuckled. Maren cast a glance.

"It's OK Mair, it won't get any worse," Paul assured her. "Seriously folks, the months I've gotten to know our bride have been a privilege. Maren is talented, an enthusiastic supporter to everyone in her life. The perfect first mate, with a built-in crew," Paul added as he glimpsed at Dylan. "We've waited a long time for you! So to Maren and Steve, may the knots you tied today navigate you well through the tides of married life. God Bless you both!"

Liz wiped a tear as Paul sat down beside her.

"Jeez Liz…wasn't exactly my A game," Paul whispered. "Your brother got choked up during the ceremony. Forsaking all others, having and holding…didn't hear him promise to obey."

"Men should," Liz replied. Her grin was unrestrained. "This day has been perfectly themed right down to Luke's scriptural take on a cord of three strands that shouldn't be easily broken." Maren incorporated that into her design with a nautical cord tying each invitation.

Paul shoulder bumped Liz, rubbing that navy blue against him. The gesture spared mascara from trickling down her face.

"If you cry, I'm stuck with Frankenstein tonight. Besides, we promised we'd have fun." Paul took his glass, held it for her to do the same. "To lighter hearts tonight. You and me both."

Paul and Liz ate their meals, mingled separately with guests and friends. Eric took the microphone to sing a song he wrote. A hard act to follow, the band went straight for the sentimental songs. Once again, the photographer dutifully summoned Liz and Paul to dance. More candid shots until the photographer took his cue.

Liz recognized "Let Me Call You Sweetheart." Steve walked toward Maren, kissed her and promptly paced away. "What's he doing?" Liz whispered as Paul's hand pressed on her back. Liz stopped their stride. "I should have known."

Steve grasped both of Hannah's hands and sashayed the little girl—always his sweetheart—around the dance floor. If smiles could reach the stars, Hannah's was in another galaxy. At the end of their dance, Steve scooped his niece into his arms for a final waltz, parading her to people's claps. When the song ended he kissed Hannah's cheek and whispered into her ear.

Resting her head on Paul, Liz instinctively knew that Steve had just reassured Hannah that *she* would always be his first sweetheart.

"*You* better hang on to *me*." Paul faltered. He rested his head upon Liz for comfort. In case a tear, or 20 of them, spilled from his eyes. Even Jack Cole, gliding Maren across the dance floor, hadn't hit the raw nerve that watching such love for a child had struck.

"We promised we'd stay strong." Liz's next resolute murmur: "Let's get some air."

Paul willingly took that offer. They escaped onto the terrace overlooking the Chesapeake. Where else would a couple like Maren and Steve choose as the backdrop to their celebration?

Liz had noticed at the ballroom entrance the six-foot sign she had given them: In High Tide or Low Tide, I'll Be By Your Side. Maren & Steve, June 14, 2003.

"This whole day has been beautiful," Liz said.

"Sure has," he replied. They drew in the crisp, clean, Chesapeake air until Paul suggested Liz return to their table. The cake would be cut very soon. "I'll be right in," he told her.

Liz pushed through the country club doors, chatted with another guest, and glanced at her watch as she nibbled on some wedding cake.

"Not needed for this picture?" Gabe asked. He stole Paul's seat, never asking if he could have it. "I've wanted to tell you how stunning you look all night." Gabe's hand enveloped Liz's as she rested it on the table, while his arm snaked around her snugly.

"Gabe, you having fun?" she asked.

"Bouncing between the art school table and work crowd. I get around," he said. "I'm not leaving until you dance with me." Gabe grinned.

"Really? How long will you draw out tonight?"

"You decide," Gabe replied.

When the beat quickened, Liz shifted. Gabe let go of the hand he had hijacked, steered her with his arm encasing her body, and shimmied up close as they enjoyed the music.

"That dress was made for you," he told her.

"It actually was." Liz laughed. Exercise always helped her to cope, even when dressed up.

When the song broke, the bandleader seized the microphone. "Ladies and gentlemen, our bridal couple is about to depart."

Gabe couldn't ignore the little fuss made over removing Maren's garter. Single women got called to the dance floor. Liz squirmed.

Fueled by the sudden swell of available women, Gabe pressed into Liz. "When's our date?"

"Gabe!" A whiskey scent caught her off guard.

"Let's make it next weekend. In Baltimore."

"Tell me you're not driving home."

"I won't be, but if you're offering..." Arching his blonde brows, Gabe volunteered to be more than her dance partner this evening.

"I'll agree to dinner," she relented. "My kids will be with their dad."

"Fantastic. We'll stroll the Baltimore harbor."

If Liz hadn't dieted on two TV dramas for every Lean Cuisine, she might not have recognized the lust Gabe lobbed into that so-alone posture of his. Turned off like a switch when someone plopped into the chair next to Gabe.

"Tyler, you're rubbing your eyes," Liz said. "Can you say hello to Mr. Furtinski?"

"Hi," Tyler managed bashfully. "Mom, here comes Uncle Steve. Is it time to go yet?"

Steve Kramer swaggered a smug nod to Gabe. Just like her brother to pull rank having just hitched himself to Gabe's good friend.

"I've got a hot date tonight," Steve boasted. "We're taking off." He tugged Liz closer. "Thanks for helping Jack and Audrey with Dylan next week. You're the best."

"Where are you going? Does Maren know?"

Steve stole Liz's ear so that neither Tyler nor Gabe could hear him. He jutted his chin high.

Liz jerked her head back. "Color me jealous."

Maren embraced Liz. "This had to be hard. Thanks for everything you've done, Liz."

Outside, Paul fell into the hug-fest, enfolding Maren in his arms. He gave Steve a back slap. "Have a great trip and turn off your Blackberry."

"I will." His phone wouldn't be in range.

Steve eased next to his bride. "You have an appointment with me." Now off the recent restriction Maren had instituted, they locked eyes. She had relegated Steve to the guest room whenever he wasn't on his boat. "These two are relieved of their duties. Just us now."

Steve swept an arm under Maren's knees and cradled another to her back, stopping only for one last photo. Guests opened the club's doors and cheered as he set her down before their waiting limousine. Liz and Paul walked outside, past Gabe, to wave goodbye.

"It's a wrap," Paul said. "We made it."

"We did," Liz offered as they stepped back inside the country club. "I had my moments." She leaned against ornate wallpaper as Paul faced her. "You OK?"

"I'm fine. It's been a long day. Better go rescue the boys. Hired three dog walks for them."

Hannah ambled over, and Liz scooped her up. "Have fun dancing with Uncle Steve, sleepy?"

Done at this hour, Hannah nodded affirmatively. She made one bright-eyed exception. "Paul, where do your puppies sleep?"

"Hm, they're supposed to sleep in their crates." Paul's lips curled. "They do mostly."

"They sleep with you, don't they?" Liz asked.

"On cushions next to my bed. Whimper for breakfast if I sleep late."

"Ah, I wish we could have a puppy sleepover!" Hannah commandeered Liz's ear whispering, "Can we have a presents party for the puppies?"

"We'll talk about that. Destined to become a vet," Liz predicted to Paul. "She named Billy the Blue Heron on our shore, Eddy the Bald Eagle, and a hermit crab Tim brought from the beach."

"Hermy, get it?" she squealed. "Bambi comes in the winter." Hannah thrust her arms out to Paul. "The daddy deer has horns."

"Antlers." Paul picked Hannah out of Liz's grasp. Squeezed her, then set her down onto her little navy shoes.

"Liz, thanks again," he said. "Covering for your brother, I'll need *my* sleep." He tugged Liz tight. Unsure when he'd see her again, Paul flattened his palms against her shoulder. He felt grateful the seamstress had not been too generous with the chiffon. Inhaling her might ward off loneliness that invariably provoked good sleep.

Paul had ditched his tux jacket two hours ago. Liz smoothed his white dress shirt, felt the navy cummerbund that perfectly matched her evening gown. No wonder the photographer spent such time perfecting their poses. They really seemed meant for one another, in so many ways today.

"I'll give you a call next week maybe…to check on the boys," Liz teased. "Goodnight Paul." Her lips landed softly on his cheek, spending sweet time there before she stepped back, holding his hands in hers. As Liz spotted Gabe staring at her, she let Paul's hand fall away.

"Great. Good night Hannah." Paul took hold of the car keys Eric handed over. Eric had promptly parked the vehicle for Paul once the bridal party arrived at the reception. With his other hand Paul tousled the thick hair on Tyler, another sleep-deprived wedding trooper.

"Hey Eric, since when do you smoke weed?" Paul asked out of earshot. "I sent Liz inside before she could recognize the scent."

"Occasionally." Eric punched up his shoulders. "Drummer offered a joint. Gonna rat me out?"

"Not unless you're getting high while watching your niece and nephew." Paul narrowed his brow. "Your brother-in-law could make a federal case out of that. Liz doesn't need trouble."

"I'm good," Eric assured. "Nice toast." He excused himself to help strap kids into the car.

Paul turned and walked to his Corvette, glad that his discovery hadn't tarnished the evening. The day he and Liz had both dreaded was now history. So why did he feel pangs of regret?

Chapter 12

Liz invited Maren and Dylan over July 4th to Kent Island. Before Steve began a long stint on call, he stayed on the Western Shore to organize the garage. Tim switched the schedule, probably to ignite fireworks with his hussy, Liz mulled.

Entertaining three kids provided Liz an excuse to avoid Gabe's third date invitation. The Inner Harbor was pleasant and public enough as they walked following dinner. Gabe had escorted Liz to her car, encasing her in a two-minute hug and a chaste brush against her lips. Days ago after work, he had suggested dinner at Hemingway's, very convenient to the bay bridge, but too close to her house. Liz decided this only after she tried unsuccessfully to dodge the deeper kiss Gabe went for that night.

"You didn't invite him in?" Maren sipped the daiquiri Liz had blended. She sat on a barstool. Liz stood across the counter.

"No. Has he said anything?" Liz took a sip of her own before-dinner cocktail. She moved to the window to check on the kids. They ganged up splashing Uncle Eric, who had watched them the other night. "Eric will escape when they get done with him." Liz let another gulp slide down her throat. "No comparison to drinks in the BVI. I want to hear about your trip. First, about Gabe."

"He asked how things were for you," Maren answered. "It's not my place to tell him Tim's squabbling over lamps and chairs." Maren wiped white foam from her lips. "Besides, Steve walked over, at lunch. Gabe quickly disappeared."

"Why? Gabe's a friend from art school. He came to your wedding. What's Steve's beef?"

"Gabe flirts, harmlessly. Annoys Steve, who changed Gabe's last name to *Fartinski*."

"So educated, yet immature," Liz said. "Paul's the same. Tomorrow, don't bring up Gabe."

"The puppy present party." Maren chuckled. "We spent 45 minutes at PetSmart until Dylan decided on the ceramic bowls."

"Hannah came up with the idea, but wanted Dylan to be here." Liz pointed to the huge dog beds pillowed on her floor with a large ribbon tied around each. "I worked an extra shift but it's worth it to make Paul happy. Paul gets sarcastic over Gabe, too."

"Confines it to team discrimination, doesn't he?" Maren asked.

"Not always. It masks deeper feelings." The tacit agreement in Maren's smile confused Liz, who made hand circles encouraging her to finish. When Maren merely arched her brow, Liz grew impatient. "Say it, will you."

"Liz, Paul cares about you. He always has, according to Steve."

Liz set her drink on the kitchen island. Roared with laughter. "Paul Romano's like a brother. That's ridiculous." Liz picked up her glass and swigged a large amount. Kids shouted Marco Polo out at the pool. Liz chuckled twice when she spotted them terrorizing Eric.

"Paul had dinner with Jade Chen, and he showed off dog photos to my colleague last week. I'm the least likely contender. Just watch tomorrow," Liz affirmed.

The puppy party—Hannah would not call it a shower—had a guest list that extended to Dr. Chen, Liz's boss at West Riverside, Paul's hospital friends, along with Shelly and Eric.

"Paul sees Dr. Chen as a colleague. Any attraction is one-sided," Maren offered. "When we have coffee, he doesn't bring her into the conversation. He does ask about Hannah and Tyler in a roundabout way to ask about you."

"Maybe," Liz acquiesced, focusing on a puddle now forming on her hardwood. The beach towel Hannah clutched absorbed little. "Drip off outside. Ribs go on the grill in…what time is it?"

"It's 5:30." Maren twisted her wrist to answer.

"I'm missing my good watch." Liz scratched her head. "And my Grandmother's brooch. Can't find anything, I swear. I lost a pair of sandals, too." Maren gave her an it-happens shrug.

"Tomorrow, we're having burgers and hot dogs." Liz reached in the cupboard for plates then counted out forks and knives, setting them with napkins to carry outside. "After the fireworks, you and I can look at honeymoon photos."

"The sailboat was just a little larger than the one Steve chartered when he proposed," Maren launched, excited to share. "Three nights on St. John were fantastic, too."

Liz wondered if her twinge of envy would make her smile seem fake. Maren and Steve deserved their relaxing honeymoon, she mused. *Ocean City Daytrip* caught Liz's eye as the blue crab magnet held the idea to the fridge on her summer fun list. *Daytrip.*

Sleepover and fireworks got crossed off that summer wish list tonight. They'd draw a marker through puppy party tomorrow. The budget allowed little. As she took plates outside, Liz focused on what she had rather than lacked.

The next day what Liz had was a house of people and two crazed puppies tearing their way through mounds of discarded wrapping.

Paul could have opened a small pet shop with the loot the boys raked in from gifts. Bruno by best guess was six months and Franco about eight months old. Hannah sat right beside Paul as he opened each accessory and treat. Pam sent gifts through Shelly granting the boys a new squeak toy every month.

Jade gave Paul a large decorative bin that would work in his compact condo kitchen, one she determined to see when she asked twice to help Paul take his loot home. Having one of his better days, Paul actually warmed to that offer.

Two weeks passed. Liz moseyed over to Paul and Maren in their cafeteria booth and clutched Monday morning coffee in one fist.

Seeing Liz's head tipped down, Paul scooted to the wall, and he made a gesture for Liz to sit. "Didn't expect to see you today."

Liz dumped sugar into her cup and stirred it. Silently.

"Care for some cream?" Maren asked. She fixed eyes with Paul. Something seemed off.

"I need it bold. Badly," Liz replied. "I took a colleague's shift on my day off from Hal." To hell with manners, Liz planted an elbow on the table to cradle her head. "I've been Irsayed."

Maren gasped. "I'm so sorry."

"What?" Paul's stare searched them both.

"Remember: he's not from around here," Maren reminded.

Liz drew in a deep breath. "This past weekend, I spent here, earning money that seems to just slip out the door." Liz took a sip and another cleansing breath. "Tyler must have mentioned that I wouldn't be home. Tim hired movers." She rubbed her neck. "At least not the company with ships on their trucks."

"That's who moved me. They did a good job," Paul added. Two sets of eyes pounced on him. "I'm lost," he admitted. "What's wrong?"

"Irsayed as a verb means moving things out in a clandestine way." Did this man really follow football, Liz wondered? "As in the Baltimore Colts were Irsayed in the middle of the night."

"In *those* trucks," Maren explained. "Even the sight of one can raise blood pressure."

"Sorry," Paul relented. "Vinny gave me a coupon. What did Tim haul out?"

"The chest of drawers Tyler kept clothes in. Past tense. Now trampled on the floor. The set including chaise lounges by my bedroom. My one spot for morning calm and coffee," Liz spit out. She held up her cup. "That empty terrace is the *first* thing I see every morning."

"Anything else?" Maren asked, cautiously.

"Lots of personal belongings, some things off the walls, a desk, file cabinets, pots and pans." Liz paused before starting again. "Chairs and book shelves, the trundle bed in the guest room downstairs and a large dollhouse. After I read him the riot act, reminding him that my parents bought Hannah most of that furniture, I found it on my doorstep this morning. Furniture mostly. Strewn, with the playhouse people—naked no less—spilling out of a trash bag. No doll house."

"That's passive-aggressive," Paul noted. Mumbled something offensive in Italian.

"Totally." Liz scratched her scalp. "Should've seen this coming. *War of the Roses.*"

"We have extra things in our newly organized garage. Duplicate gifts I can't return, even All-Clad," Maren added. "Stop by." Maren rose and slid in her chair for her meeting in minutes. "Liz, you're welcome to anything you need."

Maren waved as she left. Liz switched seats to face Paul, caffeine already activated.

"Outside of sneak attacks, what else is new?" Paul asked. He slid his mug on the table. Met Liz's eyes where tears formed.

"I can't talk to you about this. Embarrassing."

Paul cupped Liz's hand in his. "Liz?" When she averted his eyes, Paul rubbed his thumb across her knuckles. "What is it?" His voice smoothed the way and totally disarmed her.

"I'm so tired of expecting better behavior and getting Tim's crap. School doesn't start for a month yet I got a notice about reduced lunches. Never did before." Liz raised her head and tried to blink the moisture away. "Is needy imprinted on my forehead? I want to be independent. Free of him and all his shenanigans."

"You're getting there," Paul said. "I understand needy." Paul's encouragement failed to erase her frown. "There's more, I can tell."

"You'll never guess what Tim accused me of?"

Liz looked away then back at Paul. "Tyler—I seriously doubt it was Hannah—told Tim that at the wedding, we were all over each other."

Paul cracked up. "Hm, that photographer did push us together. Can't say I didn't enjoy it."

Liz reclaimed her hand. She jostled his wrist hoping it would shake some sense into him. "In an *entirely* different context, Paul."

Paul lost the smirk. "Just havin' a little fun with you, Liz." He straightened. "Tim will be Tim, it seems, and Tyler misread a kiss to your cheek…what with glasses dinging and your brother playing Twister with *his* tongue."

Liz dropped her shoulders at the image. "It's not like me to be paranoid, but intercepted mail, missing money, threats to leave me homeless." She blinked. "I wish I could crawl into a hole."

"I know that feeling, too," Paul said. "Look: You're a hard worker. Since we're having this talk, I have a patient release. Suzanna will give it to you." Paul lowered his voice. "I'm Mrs. Maloney's internist. She said she and Mr. Maloney saw you. Said you've taught her how to relax and stay centered through their messy divorce."

Paul paused, allowing the compliment to sink in.

"Besides, you got hired here. You're succeeding at two jobs, and you look great, by the way." Paul smiled. "Must be all that exercise."

Liz straightened her spine then realized she had jut forward her chest. "Stop examining me."

Paul tucked his chin. "I'm your cheerleader." His dimples flickered.

"Something tells me you had a hand in getting me this job." Liz cast exasperation his way. "You weren't on my reference list. Dr. Chen's secretary said someone on staff vouched for me."

"Could have been our chief of surgery?"

"No," Liz said. "It wasn't my brother. That would be too obvious."

"Ti voglio bene." In English Paul expressed, "I care for you. That's all." He reached across and cupped her hand. "It's not as if our losses compete, but I do think I have the easier burden."

Liz swallowed the last of her wake-up brew. "Death and divorce have similarities, but I have three times the dissention to every sweet memory of Vicki." Liz hung her head. "I shouldn't have said that. I really don't mean to…"

"Stop!" Paul demanded. "Just like you're tired of feeling needy, I could do without people tip-toeing through every conversation." He turned his wrist to tell the time. "I've got to run and your shift starts soon. I called Jade Chen to put in a good word. I can assure you, as I've gotten to know her, she makes her own decisions. No one tells her what to do."

Paul resisted telling Liz how she wanted to rearrange both his kitchen and living/dining space when she helped him get settled after the party. "I know the kids are your top priority. They'll get through this. It won't be forever."

"Perhaps you're why my new ER boss has been in an exceptionally good mood lately." Liz slid back her chair and rose from the table. They started to leave. "Maren said you had dinner."

How and what did Liz know? "After happy hour on a Friday," Paul confirmed. "I'm not exactly prime dating material." He sniffed. "Never had any problem back in the day."

"So I've heard." Liz let a hearty laugh escape.

Paul was pleased he could cause her to lighten. "The priest would have stayed after hours listening to me." He leaned closer as they walked. "My mother thinks I still go to confession."

"Secret's safe with me. Ah, walk on this side." Liz suddenly shifted to his right where a tray cart obliterated the sight of her as they exited.

"Planet Purple alert." Paul mocked Gabe, who entered the cafeteria. "Thought you were dating."

"Only twice. He wants a third date," Liz replied. "I'm not sure I'm up for it yet."

At the elevator, Paul pressed the button, content to have Liz wait with him. He leaned closer. "A third date means the distinct possibility of sex. Unless you've already..." He stood back.

When the shiny steel doors welcomed him, Liz thrust her arm to hold them apart. "I haven't."

"Bet he plans to change that," Paul quipped. Her arm moved free and the door closed as Paul saw Liz frown. The elevator lifted him up two floors. Liz's admission boosted him even higher.

Her desk in emergency placed Liz farther from Gabe, whom Paul would gladly Irsay out of West Riverside. Any warm-blooded male would hunt Liz down for one date or a dozen.

As Paul headed to his office, he wondered what Liz would decide on date three with Gabe, and why he didn't ask Liz Phillips out himself, for date number one.

Bruno and Franco had a two-month supply of puppy food. Human groceries ran sparse so Paul leashed up Franco, who knew his way around Shore Landings well enough. The community, best described as a live/work concept, had been conceived as an antidote to urban sprawl.

Residents lived on small streets and alleys in single-family homes, townhome walkups, or in the condo building from which Paul emerged that August morning.

He and others shopped on Main Street with storefronts at street level and could use any number of professionals in second story offices. No big box retailers need apply albeit community planners gave the nod to grocers, a home and garden center, and a bank.

Paul noticed Maren and Steve at a sidewalk cafe. Steve had one arm around her and *The Washington Post* on the table in front of them.

"Where's Bruno?" Maren asked as Paul crossed and stepped onto the curb.

"In doggie time out," Paul answered. He reined in Franco's leash. "He toppled a display inside PetSmart. Brings new meaning to clean up in aisle six. Broadcast twice."

"So where are you and Franco headed today?"

"Whole Foods. I tie him to a post."

"You tie your dog outside the grocery store?" Steve contorted his face in disapproval.

"Not *right* next to the store."

"Whatever," Steve replied. Franco sniffed him, having missed the human treats by mere minutes. After Franco sneezed, Steve looked down. "Ah, your dog snotted on my jeans."

"It's hardly noticeable," Maren chided.

"Mair, it's Paul. I have to give him a hard time about something."

"Well, we're off anyway." Paul nudged Franco with a taut tether grasp. "Let's leave these lovebirds alone."

Minutes later, Maren heard commotion across the street and set down the Style section. A lady picked up her toddler, who whimpered because a small beast greedily gobbled what was left of a large cookie now on the pavement. Maren did a double take. "Honey, Franco's off his leash."

"I don't see Paul," Steve said unphased, scanning the Saturday morning crowd. Then, he bolted looking both ways to cross the street.

"Hey," Paul said. He idled by Maren to catch his breath after sprinting from the grocery store. "Never mind. Franco!"

Just then Jade Chen stepped out of the dry cleaners, recognizing alarm in Paul's shout.

"I'll grab him," she yelled across the street. With a soothing voice she approached Franco, who for once didn't play running back, but sat as commanded licking his jowls.

By the time Steve thwarted passing cars, Jade captured Franco. Paul approached with the leash and collar Franco had slipped from, securing the collar around him, safe in Jade's arms.

"I'm so sorry." Paul profusely apologized to the boy's mother and slipped her a $10 bill to ensure several more sweets for her son. Appreciating the gesture, they continued their errands.

Fussing over Franco, Jade sat on her haunches.

"Franco trampled your dry cleaning." Steve retrieved the clear plastic bag from the sidewalk.

"Looks fine to me," Jade said. She was dressed for the warm weather in a sleeveless T-shirt, the plunging V of which flashed flesh. Given the smirk Paul and Steve exchanged, things appeared mighty darn fine to them also. "Such a sweet little boy, aren't you Franco?" Jade scratched him absently between the ears.

Steve looked relieved—happy Franco had not bolted into traffic. He rested his Ray-Bans on his forehead reacting more to Jade's baby talk, but never losing sight of cleavage.

"Spoiling my dog," Paul said. "Little bad-ass that he is." Paul drew his wallet out from his back pocket again. Reached for a twenty this time noticing the clearly ripped cleaning bag.

Jade hadn't noticed paw prints. "You're a cutie. Yes, you are, you really are." Jade stroked Franco's head, neck. She got him to sit and shook his paw before Franco stood on all fours.

"Lots of tail wagging today." Steve's tongue pushed his cheek out. Franco's lolled out the side of his mouth.

"Ah, your coffee's getting cold over there, you know that?" Paul head pointed to the opposite side of the street. "Thanks for the assist."

"You need a better leash, pal." Steve took the hint and tapped Paul on the shoulder.

Paul slipped fingers between the collar and Franco to test snugness, exchanged small talk with Jade, and insisted when she refused the money. He evaded questions about his day. His Blackberry calendar could have easily confirmed that he remained free. He kept it pocketed.

Once he walked back to Steve and Maren, Paul said, "Lose the Kramer-man look."

"I'm just saying, she's fallen for you," Steve justified. "Go for it."

"As in…romance?" Maren asked. She hurriedly twitched her neck sideways. "No, I don't think so." Maren wiped crumbs off their table, stood, and crumbled her napkin into the nearby trash. "Let's walk to the park with Franco."

"Yeah, the café manager cast me dirty glances," Paul said. "Anything in the paper?"

They walked the sidewalk, Maren next to Paul tethering Franco. Steve was on the other side.

"Teen boys suspected of petty crimes, causing mischief over the bridge," Maren reported. "Ought to call Liz in case she hasn't heard."

Paul furrowed his brow. Faced Maren as he kept walking. "What kind of petty crimes?"

"Yard damage, harassing phone calls, swimming uninvited in people's pools."

Paul thought about the missing money Liz mentioned. He pivoted to Steve. "When was the last time you talked to your sister?"

"Days ago, about family stuff. Eric, specifically." Not the least bit bothered, Steve supplied, "Kids are with Tim this weekend."

"She's probably enjoying time to herself," Maren added. They found a bench and she took a seat, patting Franco's fur. "Paul, aren't you supposed to have groceries after shopping?"

"Ah, jeez." Paul palmed his forehead. "Can you stay with Franco? I left them in the cart."

"Sure. Dylan's with Mom and Dad. We have time." Maren perched her sunglasses on her hair. Paul jogged away. She met Steve's displeasure with her own. "He needs us. What's with you?"

Steve sat down. "Dylan's away. I say we play. PBK way." Steve nuzzled Maren under her ear. Nipped. Even meowed. "Early afternoon delight."

As a couple strolled past them with a double baby carriage, Maren pulled the dog leash in tighter and let a saucy smile raise her lips. "I seem to recall our project work last night. Are you insatiable?"

"Increases our odds." Steve held his amusement and snaked an arm around her waist.

Maren deposited her head on his shoulder content that Project Baby Kramer would recommence, very soon.

Another rescue had occurred, this time by the cart attendant who had placed Paul's groceries at customer service. Having just refrigerated them in his condo, Paul turned to the playful barking that would surely summon another letter from the building manager.

"OK boys, enough." Paul plied fingers through Bruno's summer coat—black and plush because he was a mutt. The tiny brown tufts that resembled eyebrows wiggled when anything piqued this pup's curiosity. "You two are tied for misbehavior. Always need to play."

Ears perked on Franco. New vocab word: Play. Paul brushed a hand over his coarse gold fur and looked at the time. One o'clock.

Jade had mentioned a movie at Shore Landings. Walking to the theater was another perk afforded by this community, only if Paul turned her down, he couldn't exactly exercise the pups along Shore Landings sidewalks.

He thumbed a text into his Blackberry, politely declining the movie. Something came up. Wasn't that the convenient excuse physicians implemented when needed?

Vicki's cell phone sat on a shelf underneath the latest Victoria's Secret catalog that had amazingly caught up with him thanks to mail forwarding. Paul fingered the flip phone. He hadn't dialed into her voice greeting in weeks, which he'd done every other day, months ago when loneliness burned through his stomach.

"We need to get out of here," he told the boys. "You think Liz is OK? Her yard would be a treat," he mumbled. When Bruno barked Paul realized he had adopted intelligent creatures. Another well-understood word: Treat.

He brushed aside the week's mail, including the AT&T bill for Vicki's phone service—small price to pay for occasional comfort. A UPMC Pittsburgh envelope had just bestowed a job offer. Anyone else, Paul thought, would have picked up the phone yesterday to accept it.

"Let's call Liz," Paul told his companions. He dialed from his Blackberry and headed to the biscuit jar, another gift from Jade. Paul felt a twinge of guilt since he'd fabricated his excuse.

He listened for Liz to answer, calling first on her cell. Voice messages both times.

"Guys, want a ride in the car?" He laughed. Another word Bruno and Franco knew. Seeing Paul with biscuits, they ran in circles. He collected two leashes, his Armani sunglasses, and his Steelers gym bag. Spare clothes never hurt. "If she's not home, I guess we'll walk the Cross Island Trail."

Chapter 13

Most of the beach traffic had cleared. Heading east on the Bay Bridge, Paul saw the steady westbound stream of vacationers who had likely checked out of rentals Saturday morning. Returning to normalcy with late August routines.

Paul heaved a sigh. He wondered if he'd get to a new normal and if Planet Purple was with Liz? He focused on the exit after the bridge.

Paul could blame his impromptu visit on the dogs. Liz had said they were welcome any time. What if he had turned down companionship when Liz already had some? Worse: was getting some. Third-date sex? Fourth? Or fifth?

Paul blinked away the thoughts and navigated suburban streets. As he slowed, Paul saw three, no four, teenage males down the road. A bicycle turned on its side. Harmless enough except for what Maren had mentioned. Paul pulled over, far enough not to startle them. He got out, unlatched the hatch, and grasped two leashes.

"Come on boys," he said. "Let's check it out." Bruno and Franco pulled him in their quest to inspect. Paul tried to dissect the idle chatter.

"Look, right there," one exclaimed. Paul saw him perched on the second boy's shoulders with a baseball cap that advertised the Orioles.

"Let me see." The second kid, needing acne treatment badly, Paul thought, bent so that his friend jumped down, handing him something as they strained looks through the fence that might be Liz's or her neighbor's. Paul wasn't sure.

The third lad, sporting a Ravens cap, turned to the sun. He startled at an unfamiliar man with approaching dogs and scrambled swiftly.

"Boys," Paul said. Bruno and Franco perked, and he held them tight. Studying human eyes beneath the caps, Paul sensed mischief as they peered through the shrubbery; certainly poor fashion sense. "What's happening?" he asked.

"Sir…ah, nothing," suggested the O's fan.

"We were…just going." His friend dropped something in marsh grass, left tall and beneficial for the Bay. The fourth boy, sufficiently spooked, hopped on a bike. The others dashed.

Paul trailed the teens then looked at Bruno and Franco. "Not so close," he said with disgust as Bruno hiked his leg upon the fence. Not to be outdone, Franco let loose a hefty stream.

Paul stooped to see what had dropped—binoculars that fortunately neither dog had sprinkled. Paul peered through the lenses. "Marone!"

Becoming bilingual by the day, Bruno and Franco tilted their heads. Paul remained as fixated as the would-be delinquents. "Mamma Mia," he mumbled, lowering the binoculars.

He hoisted them again. No sign of anyone else.

Paul opened the SUV. The dogs jumped up, and he slammed the lid. His tires kicked up gravel until he braked in her driveway. He knew from taking things in and out of the gates that the paver stones led to a handle he could open and let Bruno and Franco run right through.

"Liz," he shouted to announce himself.

"Paul?"

"I'm here with the boys." *And half the high school locker room.*

"Let them in," she shouted back. Paul did.

They beat him to poolside where he heard a splash and a shriek.

"Bruno just jumped in with me!"

Very astute hound. Though black and gold paws paddled the water, they only captured Paul's peripheral vision. "Ah Liz…"

She stopped mid-way through laps, out of breath. Bruno kicked up splashes. Paul grabbed hold of Franco lest he join in hot pursuit. Not that he'd blame him.

"Forgot, labs like water." Liz treaded the aqua depths well. What else could she do? Amused by Bruno, Liz turned to Paul's pained expression. "Can you hand me my towel please?" Her feet gingerly tread the cement steps.

"Here," Paul said. "Jeez, Liz." He turned his head, ostensibly to keep a firm grip on Franco, but slanted her an eye as he tethered him to a fence post in order to coax Bruno from the water.

"I didn't expect to see you." Liz banded the towel across her and slicked a hand on wet hair.

"Pleasure's all mine," Paul replied. "Along with four hormonally-charged teen boys, staring at your naked body, sweaty palms on a pair of binoculars." Paul ripped away the Armani that shielded his eyes. The sunglasses hadn't spared much. "Bruno, come here. Now!"

Liz moved to the side table and lifted her plastic stemware. Until she took a swig, it had sat next to an opened bottle of Ecco Domani Pinot Grigio, a third of the way full.

"Want some?" she offered. Liz reached for the bottle, pouring more.

Paul blinked, completely flummoxed. A bottle couldn't quench the thirst stirred by the sight of her. Liz Phillips could certainly tie a nautical knot but Paul's mind willed the flimsy one keeping that towel in place to unravel. His thoughts dampened when Bruno shook and sprayed him.

Liz sauntered closer, glass in hand. "Have a taste. It's Italian." Her brown eyes sparkled more than the glistening pool.

Paul took the wine glass but held it at his side. Grinned. "So I noticed." What would his hands do without a glass to occupy them?

Savoring a sip bought time.

Liz untied Franco and called Bruno with snapped fingers into the shaded screened-in porch. She positioned a chair in case they charged the flimsy door to barge out. "No humping furniture."

Paul pretended not to hear that command. "You always make a point of swimming nude?"

"Don't be silly." Liz doubled over. "With my children normally careening down the waterslide? I'd be with a paperback or my laptop." She moved closer, took back the glass and tilted the contents into her mouth. It eased down her throat.

After swallowing, she smiled. "With all I have going on, I'm taking the day for me." As she carefully set the wine down, she inched toward Paul. "Ever go skinny dipping?"

Paul nodded his head slightly.

"Then you know how freeing it feels."

A smile built again on Paul's lips, which parted easily at the frisson of that suggestion. "I came over here because I couldn't reach you by phone. I was worried," he said. "Fence jumpers and assorted mischief happening nearby."

"Well, you *walked* freely inside my gate. Feeling mischievous?" Liz leaned in to toy with his gold chain. "Nice collar you're wearing, against a little sunburn." Her damp fingers stroked pink skin. "Unless you're just always this hot?"

Dio mio! "Is this your first bottle?" he asked. "It's three o'clock in the afternoon. And, you're swimming. Alone. Jesus, woman."

"What language for an altar boy?" She didn't expect a response.

Liz's hand ran up his polo shirt's sleeve. "First bottle, not half-way consumed. A liquid calorie lunch. I've been told I've lost weight."

She quieted and then blushed. "Are your eyes examining me, Dr. Romano?" She inched again so close Paul could feel her breath.

"Liz, look at me." Paul brushed his hand under her chin. "When we first met at your family's summer place, there was one thing on my mind. You were what, 19 or 20 years old?"

"And you were...?"

A phallic-focused one-track mind, he wanted to say but chose instead, "Old enough to know I better not take advantage of my friend's sister." Paul thumbed her smooth, sculpted face.

"And now?" Liz waited. She watched Paul's mouth slacken. Her heart quickened before it began a slow tumble. Then, as if someone had literally shocked her, she went off on him.

"Let me get this straight. You didn't make moves on me then. My husband's been immune to me since last year's anniversary sex: A tawdry obligation, given his girlfriend. And now, you can't decide if you want me either?"

Paul saw tears cloud her eyes. "Christ, Liz." He seized her towel against his khaki shorts. The breasts held beneath the knot pushed into his polo shirt. One hand slid lower, pulling Liz against evidence that he wasn't immune to her. The tighter he held her, the stronger that confirmation grew. Another hand held her damp hair. Droplets that hadn't dried soaked Paul's shirt.

Their mouths set off moisture. Molten steam. The kiss was needy, hungry. Paul tasted the fruity wine, smelled the coconut sunblock adding to the sweetness of her neck where he began to inhale and suck.

"Mm," Liz moaned, nipping on his earlobe. She panted into it. Liz's hands roamed under Paul's shirt, skimmed chest hair and stroked nipples. They broke apart, long enough for him to assess her with hooded and darkened eyes.

"Maybe I misspoke." Restraint took leave of Paul when he plunged his tongue along those pearly white teeth, making Liz weak once again. The white-hot rush of desire competed with the sunlight sparkling off the pool.

"The cabana...over there," she whispered. Giddily, she stepped and steered him to it. Her hands started to fiddle with his waistband.

"Are you sure?" Paul framed her face as he darted one eye to the wide-cushioned wicker lounge, site of an unexpected afternoon bonus.

"It closes," Liz assured him. She took hold of his hands and sensed hesitation. "What?"

"Just surprised. I didn't expect this." Paul heard Liz giggle. "Wait: your third date?"

"With the small country called the marketing department? Alicia's birthday." Liz went on, "Ask Maren. Make Gabe the jealous one." She let go of Paul. Her towel started to slide, but she caught it and then pulled the cord on the cabana panel forcing it to the concrete pool deck.

"Private indeed," Paul said. "I wasn't jealous."

"Oh, please," she said. "That's why you warned me. It worked."

"How so?" he asked, eyes blazing even in the shade. He hoisted his polo shirt over his head.

She snuggled against Paul's chest, positioning a hand behind his head before she dragged it in for a kiss. "You heat me up inside." Liz let the towel puddle around her feet. "Also, I'm choosy when picking my playmates."

Christ, was there anything sexier than a woman volunteering herself? Paul buried his fingers in her hair. "And you totally unhinge me."

Lips landed on hers, greedy this time. Hands softly caressed their way lower to where he cupped her bottom and let them idle. Liz opened the button on his shorts, pushing the fabric apart.

"Mom! Mom, where are you?" It was Tyler's voice, and apparently his slam of the gate.

"Oh my God," Liz mouthed. She retrieved the towel and grasped it around her.

Paul secured his shorts. He peeked out of the cabana and saw no one. "Run inside," he hushed. "I'm tanning." Could the excuse be any lamer?

Fisting the towel, Liz scooted and damned herself for blocking the screen door. "Good thing you two mutts can't talk," she muttered as she brushed past the whimpering dogs.

Paul raised the cabana panel. Stood as if he was fixing it. "Hey buddy, I thought you were with your dad this weekend."

"I am," Tyler answered, distracted by dogs. "Where's my Mom? Why are *they* here?"

Paul ignored the tone, the second question. "She's changing inside."

"I need my game console." Tyler scowled.

"I'll grab the dogs. They won't hurt you," he assured walking to assist. "Liz, Tyler's here."

Bedrooms at ground level, his voice carried. Liz faked astonishment. Tyler was none the wiser as she enveloped him into a quick hug.

"Dad's outside with Hannah and…"

Paul recognized Tyler's hesitancy, akin to sneaking girls past a sleeping Isabella Romano. Only this was broad daylight, and Tyler stopped short of describing the other woman.

"Really." Liz cast suspicion as they stepped out to find Hannah, her lips pressed to the screen door making kissy faces at the puppies. "My little girl's here, too."

"Come say hi," Paul offered. "Brought the boys to play this afternoon."

"They're bigger," Hannah recognized as Paul opened the door and she ran to hug Bruno first. "Was he swimming?" She turned her head to shout. "Daddy, come meet Paul's puppies."

Paul looked at Liz since Tim must have let himself in the gate. Without asking.

Liz opened the door, and the dogs charged. A subconscious move, she wondered, as Bruno ran alongside Tim's ankles and Franco made Lucena jump back two feet. Another few inches would have created the perfect splash.

"I'm allergic," she squealed. "Tyler, I'll carry those things to the car." Lucena unburdened Tyler's arms, grabbing the console, leaving him with the remotes and games.

Tyler remained singularly focused and scooted the puppies out of his way with one foot.

"Hello, Paul." Tim extended a hand, which Paul reluctantly shook. "How's the condo?" A hard line formed along Tim's mouth. He lowered his glasses. "I'm certain it has its own pool."

Liz cast Tim a bone-breaking glare.

"It does. Love the condo," Paul lied. Damned if he'd admit that two crazy dogs might get him evicted. Paul caught Lucena clicking her sandal heels along the concrete. Her hips fanned her skimpy yellow sundress. "I'll corral the dogs." Liz and Tim, he thought, might need a word making this 87-degree day even warmer.

Hannah yelled to Franco, "Chase me." He complied in fast pursuit through the yard.

"We wanted video games," Tim told Liz.

"We?" Liz spit out. "I'm surprised you didn't cart them out weeks ago." She walked next to him, and out of Hannah's earshot, seethed. "Do not you bring your little puttana to my house. You can flaunt her on your own time, but not here. Not in front of the children."

"Liz," Tim started. "I haven't signed those papers your attorney sent over. I can and will do whatever I damn well please." Tim grab-

152

bed Liz by an arm and pulled her. "This is still my house. You don't look too lonely in it, entertaining. You didn't weeks ago either in downtown Baltimore, out with a different guy. What a *model* you set for our children, all over town."

"How dare you question my behavior? Paul is practically family. I won't justify what I do on my time with friends," Liz hissed. Tim pressed a thumb into her until Liz snarled, "Let go of me."

He did, with a not-so-subtle push. "You can *try* to impress me with foreign words, but you better clean up your act unless you want to decide all of this in court. It'll cost you." Tim squared his shoulders to intimidate her. "These are *my* kids. I'm *letting* you live in *my* house."

Paul tossed a ball to Franco and leashed Bruno, glancing out the fence to the driveway. He wanted to keep an eye on the argument, which had grown quieter but not friendlier as Liz, braless in T-shirt, shorts and flip-flops, accentuated with hands fisted to her hips. At one point, she poked a finger right back at Tim.

"Hannah, come on," Tim shouted from the gate where Liz had maneuvered him before walking away, arms crossed over her chest.

"I want to stay here," Hannah whined. "Mommy, can I? Please."

Liz, irate by now, did a 180 toward Tim. "We agreed in mediation the kids get some choice," Liz leveled in slightly top-that tone. "If she wants to stay here, it's fine by me."

"Lose the superior social work stance." Tim bent his index finger toward Hannah. She dutifully ran over to him. He squatted to her height, whispered something in her ear, and hugged her.

When he stood up, Hannah ran back to the puppies and to Liz, who tousled her curls. They all heard the gate slam once more.

"Well," she said, breathing freely. "I ought to go start dinner."

Paul watched over Hannah and the dogs zig-zagging her. Overheated, she went to change into her bathing suit, then readied to plunge into liquid relief. "Where'd they go?" Hannah asked.

"If their tongues hang, they need a drink and rest," Paul explained as Hannah crawled from the pool. He screwed metal stakes into the soil and chained them with supplies from his SUV.

"They need a lot of stuff. Like babies," Hannah announced. She held her nose and splashed into the pool, not waiting for an answer.

Liz compressed her lips into a cringe at the word babies. "She didn't mean it that way."

"Liz," Paul whispered into her ear. "They're young, even Tyler. Only he's at that age."

"And under an influence." She studied him. "I'm getting to recognize your wary eyes."

"I spotted Lucena peek into your mailbox, that's all. I'd have said something, but she walked back down the driveway empty handed."

Liz smirked. "All forwarded to a P.O. Box."

"You never cease to amaze me." Paul couldn't rein in a chuckle. "Good for you."

A pout played gradually on Liz's lips. "She must have bought the same sandals I had."

Since Liz had spoken in normal tones now, Hannah said, "Daddy gave Lucena $150, but she bought girly underwear."

Paul sensed Liz might blow a few neurons at that comment if he didn't redirect. "Could you bring the dogs some more water?" When Hannah skipped away, he said, "What is it Liz?"

"My angry face is *that* recognizable?" Liz closed and reopened her eyes. "Just the exact amount of money I was looking for and the same style of sandals, same color that I couldn't find."

"And you probably can't prove it, right?"

Liz nodded. "Something positive. Let's finish the Pinot Grigio."

Paul poured. "Might as well finish something." He winked at Liz as he scooted his Adirondack closer to hers. Rubbed her knuckles soothingly. "That was awkward earlier."

"Which part?" She hoisted her glass for a swig.

"Oh, let's see, walking in on you in the buff," he hushed. "Almost being caught by your son and husband. Whole family. Watching that argument. Now, how it unravels you."

Liz regarded him. "Kids and argument aside, you regret what we did or were about to?"

"Not completely," Paul replied. "Liz, technically, you're still married." When he sensed a storm brewing inside her, he continued. "You two are divorcing. I don't blame you. I had half a mind to haul off and slug him the way he talked to you and grabbed your arm."

"Ever since that loose woman, he's been curt. I so want this over and have to wait." Liz counted the months out on one hand then extended two fingers from another. "Crap. Seven months. You have to live apart one year in Maryland."

"That's my point," Paul admitted. "I heard him threaten you and make comments about us. What did he say about Gabe?"

"He can't say anything. We walked along the Inner Harbor after dinner. Held hands. Had some fun. I've no idea if he saw me, or one of his friends did." She heaved a sigh. "He projects his burgeoning rap sheet of all *he's* done with *her*."

"You attracted to Gabe?" Paul asked flat out.

Liz sipped from her glass. "A little. A man's attention feels rather good, Paul."

He grinned. He appreciated her honesty. Hell, it had been so long since he'd been with a woman that even Lucena didn't look near as bad as he'd pictured her. That observation he'd keep to himself or Liz might push him, literally, to explore the ten-foot pool depth.

"I understand that, and you're one hell of a woman Liz."

"Nice kisser?" she asked, flirting now with one full glass and only a few crackers with cheese to mitigate the effects.

"Nice everything." Paul raised his brow. Allowed those images to tempt his brain.

"I'm thirsty." Hannah dripped a trail of water from her last pool jump. "What's for dinner?"

"Pasta and sauce, which ought to be up Dr. Italian's alley." Liz looked back at Paul. "I pulled it from the freezer. With all that was going on, I didn't get to the store."

"I can help with dinner since you're inviting me to stay, it appears."

"Then Bruno and Franco stay, too." Hannah clapped her hands.

"They're a package deal. Aren't we all?" Liz laughed. "I'll start your shower little girl. Don't be long. Bathing suit in the laundry room."

"She loves those pups. When does she turn four?" Paul gathered things to take inside.

"In another month," Liz said. "I'll have to put her to bed before you leave with those dogs."

After her shower, Hannah brought one of her doll brushes out. She tormented Franco with it until Bruno rolled onto his back, paws in the air as she tickled him with it on his tummy.

"Too cute," Paul said as he turned away from the affection. Paul stirred contents in the saucepan. He adjusted the flame beneath it. Tapped the spoon then leaned over to taste a smidge. "Liz, you defrosted spaghetti sauce?"

"The batch I made last month…some spices, tomatoes, and two cans of tomato soup. A good dash of ketchup." Liz adjusted Hannah's hair ties when she stood up. "I'm putting in a second load of laundry. I'll be back."

Paul looked skeptically at Hannah. "Soup?"

"Mommy buys store brand."

Too many Italian adjectives raced to the finish line on Paul's tongue. Instead he asked, "Hannah, where are the cans of tomatoes?"

She padded over to the tall pantry cabinet and pointed. "In here."

Looking in, Paul practically made the sign of the cross. "OK, I need to feed Bruno and Franco. But I didn't bring much food." Paul played pitiful. "We don't want them to go hungry, do we?"

"No." Pigtails flopped side to side with Hannah's answer. "So they can eat this?"

Paul held one finger to his lips. "Only a taste." Any more, and he would be scrubbing carpets.

"You'll make us dinner?"

"Yes." Paul raised his brow. Hannah was on to him. "I need your mom to stay in the laundry room. Can you help fold clothes? Slowly?"

She beamed and scampered off.

Paul opened 16 oz. tomato cans, rummaged through Liz's spice rack, added red wine, a dash of red pepper, and chopped fresh garlic he found with a lettuce wedge in the vegetable drawer.

"Smells good in here," Liz said. "See, I can cook. My brother used to compare me to Pam."

Which woman cooked worse? Paul had been nursing his Ecco Domani. His glass shielded an emerging smirk. "Does that garden out there yield cherry tomatoes for our salad?"

"Can I pick them?" Hannah asked. She used all her weight to slide open the door. Bruno, who had pestered to be out, ran through it. Franco, for once, wasn't interested.

"I better help her," Liz said.

Paul continued fixing dinner. He pulled out plates and silverware.

When Liz returned, hand on hip, disgust flashed fast.

"Your dog inhaled my tomatoes. Only five left, hidden by another plant." Liz held them with hands under a running faucet.

"Mommy, don't be mad at Bruno," Hannah said crawling up onto a bar stool across from her. "Daddy will *never* have a dog with Lucena."

"Hannah, go wash up! I cannot take any more."

Hannah jumped down and ran at the rebuke.

"Easy, you know she's in the middle," Paul uttered behind Liz.

"Caught in the triangle with Tim and me." Liz's eyes misted. "I should know better. I can't do anything quite right." She turned to him. "I know you started the sauce over from scratch."

"Guilty as charged." Paul put the spoon down and tugged her waist while Hannah wasn't there. "Do you really use ketchup in your sauce?"

Liz let out a weak, "Sometimes." She paused. "If I used the kind that your stadium is named after would that be any better?"

Paul broke up. Clutched his side. "Liz, true, you don't feed a Pittsburgher anything other than Heinz ketchup, but please…not for sauce." He settled. "Though we Italians call it gravy."

"Huh? That's straight-up crazy."

Paul took her hands, led her to a stool. "Did you wake up edgy this morning?"

"With PMS," she admitted. "Damn, I knew there was another reason I needed to run out."

"To the store?" Paul asked. Liz nodded an immediate yes.

He sniffed. "This *is* crazy, but I actually miss shopping in the feminine aisle." He looked at the clock. "I can run out after dinner."

"You definitely need help." Liz's smile turned serious. "I do understand things you take for granted. Even mediocre sex from jack-ass."

"Liz, you set the bar too high." Paul amused himself with that. "I thought he lacked talent."

"He did." Her eyes rolled. "It's been so long."

Paul leaned closer. "Tell me about it!" He brushed her cheek with the back of his hand. "Someday, maybe we'll finish what we started earlier. Tonight, let's talk. I need wise counsel."

"It'll cost you." Liz grinned.

At dinner, Hannah ate seconds after Paul boiled the macaroni, explaining to them that it's not really called pasta in a true Italian household. Liz about threw up her hands at that mystery.

When Paul ran to the store, Liz settled Hannah with a bedtime story. Bruno and Franco listened, sprawled on her comforter.

Bag in his arms, Paul passed that lavender bedroom on his way to the kitchen. He stopped.

Family. A decade ago, he would have found a way to make the raw afternoon temptation tonight's windfall. Why rush? This was very real.

Liz, showered and in lightweight sweats and T-shirt, nestled with a cup of tea Paul made her. "How is it you know just what I need?" Liz asked. "This definitely takes the edge off."

"Among several known remedies for premenstrual tension." He sat down beside her. "Not that you're getting those other cures. This time."

"Rub that in," Liz replied. Sipping the calm. "What's on your mind as you sit on my couch? Pretend you're in my office." She laughed.

"Labor Day weekend approaches," he started. "I need to make a quick trip to Pittsburgh."

"OK..."

"Have you gotten away at all this summer?"

"No," Liz admitted. She couldn't hide the pout forming. "Fall-out from the Liz-Tim financial free-for-all. I have to watch my spending."

"You're allowed to take the kids out of state?"

"For a quick trip, of course. Are you asking us to go with you?" Liz cocked her head.

"Amusement parks are still open. You might enjoy that while I...take a tour."

"You grew up in Pittsburgh. What's to tour?"

"The internal medicine department at a hospital. I have a job offer."

Liz studied Paul. Restlessly, she shuffled a hand along her neck. If he needed wise counsel now it would come from a drooped head and voice that stuttered. "You had to have applied? Was...was that why you sold your house?"

"Not originally. Being there alone, with all we'd planned, just stabbed me." Paul permitted himself to disclose only so much. "Back home, I reconnected with colleagues, had an interview, a second by phone. Offer came this week."

Liz bit at her lip. "You can't decide, thus this discussion? Is ambivalence a lifelong issue?"

Paul held a finger to his temple and triggered his thumb, tilting his head onto his shoulder.

"Stop," Liz chided. "Your mom would love your moving there."

"Italian mothers build nests better than Osprey, Liz. They feed their young and push nice Italian girls at them so that they can also feed them," he paused. "And make nice Italian babies that come home every Sunday to do, what else, but eat."

"There's more to this." Liz nestled into the leather sofa, pulling away from Paul. She stretched out and rooted her feet next to him.

Almost by instinct, Paul picked up her shins and straddled them over his lap. "Tons more," he admitted. "There's a girl I dated in my 20s, during residency. More like a fling." Paul's voice dropped. "She does hair and nails. Always has."

"I hope you got free haircuts."

Paul grinned. *Much more than free haircuts.* "She does my mother's hair. Came to Vicki's service. We had coffee in Pittsburgh, more to get Isabella to stop asking if I saw her because, of course, she's Italian."

"Isabella? Tell me more." Liz chuckled.

"Seems like a magic couch or something. I don't usually call Ma, by her first name."

"Mothers and sons. Look at Tyler and me."

"OK, if I go home, my mother will mention her. Name's Vanessa."

"Bet Steve and Pam know her?" Liz kidded.

Bruno sprung from his hind legs and settled in Liz's lap. Envy shot through Paul.

"Steve and I have an understanding about such matters, and well…don't go there. Besides, last I checked you were pretty snarky about Pam. I doubt the two of you will ever do lunch."

"Probably not." Liz fiddled with the cup brim. It was nearly empty or Bruno's leap would have showered her with Darjeeling. "Shelly told me that Pam needs resources for Chloé. My problem with Pam was her superior attitude. Always pretended to know not just *an* answer but *the only* answer to *everything*," Liz vented. "Critical if I didn't know something, pointing out how she did."

"Pam's not so subtle way of putting herself above others," Paul agreed. "She's not all bad."

"Well, she had Steve wrapped. Sex must have been awfully good in your shared apartment."

"We have…an understanding," Paul repeated, hardly suppressing his amusement.

"You're chortling," Liz stated. "Confirmation enough. I know they took a sex seminar together. Don't know details. She hurt him too bad."

"They had their ups and downs. I mean, bad moments. Every couple does. You know that."

"Freudian slip." Liz veered. "I don't act as if I know it all, do I? Tim accused me of that."

"Tim, va' all'inferno."

"What?" Liz sat up. "Like hell?"

"Tim can go to hell." Paul shifted her legs so that he could stand. "I stopped at the little bakery. Do you want more tea, a cannoli?"

"Cannoli," Liz said. She propped even straighter. "Has such a sexual sound. Yummy!"

Paul turned around on his way to her kitchen. "You could pass as a Freudian therapist." He rattled plates and forks, untied the cardboard box, and served Liz a little tasty tube stuffed with creamy ricotta, drizzled with chocolate glaze.

Liz licked filling out with her tongue, ran a finger on what fell on her plate. Tasted it.

"What did Steve call you when around me?"

"A vamp." Laughter cascaded over Liz as she threw her head back. "Still am, I guess. Back to Pittsburgh: does my brother know you might leave West Riverside?"

"It's come up," he said. "Nothing's definite. I visited a practice here, too; full partnership and new offices. I could work on both shores."

"Wish I had my own office instead of working for Hal, close-minded and closefisted as ever."

"Faith in oneself is the best and safest course," Paul told Liz. "Michelangelo."

"It's easier when you have the means to make a switch. I don't. Shouldn't have worked for Hal. I bought all of his promises," Liz lamented.

"Sophia Loren says something akin to mistakes are part of the dues we pay for a full life."

"Do you quote anyone who isn't Italian?"

"A Heinz 57: Liz Kramer Phillips: I'm choosy picking my play-mates." Paul leaned in to brush his lips against hers. "It's getting late. You've got Hannah here. I've got two dogs to keep out of trouble at my place, and some serious thinking to keep me up. Do I get a rain check?"

"Maybe." Liz leaned back. "Throw in cannoli, and we have a deliciously satisfying evening."

Once Liz sprung from the sofa, they nestled their hands as they meandered to the door.

Paul brushed hair out of her eyes. "Who said worry doesn't pay off? I'm glad I drove over. You're a good listener, among other things."

After a nose tap, Paul kissed her. He squelched the urge to back Liz through the foyer and consummate what they had initiated earlier.

Liz stepped onto the landing, petting the dogs before they scurried into Paul's car. As he drove away, she planted her head against the door.

She thought about his instructions to be careful and swim with clothes on, unless he was there. She wasn't even bothered that he remade dinner. Paul took her talents, or lack of them, in stride. They would talk about going to his hometown.

Liz turned out the lights, brushed her teeth and climbed into bed. Would she like Pittsburgh? Only if Paul liked it, or loved it, where did that leave her?

Chapter 14

Liz busied herself the next week with back to school, working for Hal, and an extra hospital shift so that a colleague could cover hers. Much to Tyler's chagrin, she decided that she and the kids would accompany Paul to Pittsburgh and return on Labor Day as summer's last hurrah.

"I'm starving." Paul looked to knuckles tapping. "Finished patient notes, 30 minutes behind."

"Not bad for doctor's hours." Liz closed his office door, deli bag in hand. "Chicken salad for me and Italian cold cuts as requested."

"You look nice." Paul slapped a $20 bill on the desk. "Put this toward the tab."

What was it about Liz's navy dress blues? This time a tailored pants suit and ivory blouse, with tiny sleeves for the sweltering temperatures, made Paul practically salute.

"I can afford sandwiches. You insist on treating for the weekend."

"We're staying at Ma's. Park admissions are on me. Mutual amusement." He unwrapped his dinner. "Payment for all you'll put up with."

"Ha, not once you hear my son's Pittsburgh potty language." Her eye circles rebuked herself. "Sorry, we're eating."

Paul motioned Liz to his side of the desk. She leaned against it as he swiveled facing her.

"What's Tyler's take now?" Paul asked. "Homework? No, must be wanting to watch another preseason Ravens loss."

"Watch it," Liz cautioned. "The Steelers are no better." When a smile broke on Paul's face, she had scored her point. "His boycott backfired: teacher's giving a homework pass."

"Is Tim pushing for them to stay?"

"What? And interfere with three days to show houses and frolic with loose woman?" Liz bit off more chicken salad. "Tyler said, and I quote, 'There's nothing fun in Shitsburgh,' end quote."

"He got that insult from Tim or Ratbird fans."

Liz kicked his foot only half playfully. "I'll give you Ratbirds, but spot-on with Tim. Tyler's discipline: I made him write feeling words. Dr. Chen will chastise me if I don't get back."

"You're allowed a dinner break. Tyler *will* come around." Paul leaned closer. Smoothed his hands along the backside of her leg.

"There's something on your slacks." He peeled off a strip of plastic and read from it. "Size 10, slender."

"A tag from the store." Liz remarked. "I've worn it for how long?"

"Nobody noticed if you were sitting." Paul doubled over. "Advertises your figure well." He twitched his thick Italian brows. "My mother will see that you gain a pound or two."

A heavier knock broke off their banter.

Liz flushed. "Are you expecting someone? What if it's Dr. Chen, and she sees me here?"

"Relax. Suzanna's gone. Quick: under here just in case." He motioned beneath his desk.

Liz cupped a hand in front of her mouth as she crawled out of sight. "I feel like a kid."

"Come in," Paul hollered, back straight as if distracted from work.

"Hey, favor to ask." Steve peeked inside. "You know that wellness inquiry we all got?"

"The one you take to employee health, due last month?" Paul answered with glee.

"That one," Steve confessed. "Only the nurse isn't in, and I got two late notices. Can you fill it out for me tomorrow, around 8 AM?"

"Sure." Paul noticed red invade Steve's cheeks. "What's wrong?"

"Ah..." Steve backed away. "Sorry to bother."

The door shut with a tight thud.

"That's weird," Paul muttered. "He's been preoccupied lately."

"He's weird," Liz hushed. "Charmed his way through high school turning in late papers. You don't think he noticed me?"

"Of course not, there's a panel there." He pointed to it. "Where were we? Pack for casual."

"Got it. Better get back to my shift." As Liz turned, Paul grabbed her hand. Twirled her back.

"I'm glad you're going with me. I dreaded this drive up there alone."

Liz touched Paul's face. "Glad I can help, but with the packaged deal, these may be two car rides you may soon regret."

That same day entering Care Aid, a pharmacy in Shore Landings, Maren scowled skirting past the infant aisle. The T-shirt on display had *Count down to big brother* emblazoned on it.

She pulled ibuprofen for cramps off the shelf instead of the cute shirt for Dylan. Wouldn't Steve's face drop if that announced PBK success? Maren sulked slipping the unopened home pregnancy test out of the Care Aid plastic bag. Maybe she would miss her next cycle.

"Ma'am, when did you purchase this?" the clerk asked.

"Just a few days ago." Maren dug deep into her bag for the receipt. "Here's my Care Aid card if that helps." Maren pondered if she should keep the test kit, an impulsive purchase, she convinced herself. She could get tested right at work.

The clerk scanned the box and nodded at the screen. "The August purchase or April one?"

Another errand to run, Maren tapped the counter. Steve picked up Dylan at after-care, so rare that she hated wasting time. "It's the only one I bought."

"At this store. The other was purchased in New York. As long as it's within expiration." The cashier tore off the register receipt. "It'll go back on your credit card. Have a nice day."

Maren stuffed the slip and walked to her car. After she clicked her seat belt, she thought about the exchange then livened up like a crew-member when the captain hollers come about. *New York?*

Her mind moved back. Real estate papers shuffled. Moving boxes. Joint bank account and customer courtesy cards. The large card rele-gated to a drawer; two keychain cards, one for her and one for Steve. *Steve went to New York.*

Having completely forgotten the dry cleaning, Maren plopped her workbag on the counter. Her long auburn hair pulled back into a pony-tail, she unfastened it. Fixed it again. Adjusted the thermostat to allow more cool air from the vents.

"Mom, guess what grade I got on my spelling?" Dylan yelled as he ran in from the Jag Steve had pulled into their garage minutes ago.

Maren refocused. "Tell me."

"A+. Steve quizzed me." Dylan proceeded to the pantry. "Got the bonus word, too."

Maren headed him off reaching first for his snack bag of crackers. "Dinner will be awhile so change and play outside for an hour."

"OK, thanks!" he said, snatching the bag and running to his room. The community they had settled into suited Dylan just fine.

With an index finger, Steve held his suit jacket over a shoulder as he walked in. Planted a quick kiss to Maren's cheek and offered a beaming smile. "You will *never* guess what I saw today!"

His hushing would have ordinarily enticed her, but Maren's concentration was blown.

Steve lowered his voice more. "I had a quick question for Paul, knocked on his door and saw a high heel sticking out. Underneath his desk." Steve parted his lips. "Back to the old Paul."

Maren didn't miss the true meaning of the little sigh Steve let slip. It usually had to do with sex. Still, she remained short of words.

"Mair, confirmation: Paul and Jade. She wears shoes like that. He deserves some fun." Steve retrieved a Sam Adams Summer Ale from the fridge and popped the top. "What's for dinner?"

Maren waited until she heard Dylan run out.

"I haven't thought that far. I'm a little flustered," she admitted. "Paul's sex life the least of my concerns. Besides, he's taking Liz and kids to his mother's this weekend. You're joking."

"Liz thinks of Paul like a brother. Pittsburgh has great parks that close on Labor Day." Steve lowered his beer. "Better not steal my little sweetheart." Swig met mouth. "What's wrong?"

When he reached to brush her cheek, Maren caught his arm and forced it lower. "Sorry, I meant to help," he said while regarding her.

"You can help with an explanation," Maren started. "I woke up queasy all week. I thought maybe, obviously wasn't." Her eyes took in the hardwood but didn't linger staring back at Steve. "I bought but returned a pregnancy test. Clerk asked if I purchased it in April? In New York?"

He set his beer on the island and felt as if he was on isolated land. He dipped his chin, scanned the fridge, the floor. "I don't understand."

"Well, I sure don't. The clerk checked twice. Our Care Aid account shows two tests, and I only purchased one. We each have cards to the account," she continued. "You've used yours. Earned rewards back already." She watched Steve sit on the sofa, the arm holding his jacket.

"Mair, come sit." Steve hunched, elbows resting on spread knees. He made a steeple with his fingers, breathing through them, then turned to Maren. "I...I did buy one, as a favor."

Maren sat, but as Steve scooted closer on the sofa, she eased away. "That sounds so 16 with a friend's unplanned pregnancy?" She stood, crossed her arms and regarded Steve's damp eyes. "There's something you're struggling to tell me."

"There are elements I don't fully understand. *That's* an even bigger problem. I didn't want to burden you. New York…got complicated," he admitted. Patting the sofa, he urged her to sit.

"You hardly said a word about it. I take it Pam was there? I heard about Chloé's injuries." Maren sat when Steve mouthed *please.*

"She was. Chad, another classmate, Pam and I all went to dinner where she unloaded about Chloé's diagnosis, the effect on her career, their lives. It's a lot, and she's not doing well with it."

"Shelly's been driving up there to watch Chloé," Maren said. "In case you weren't aware, they're expecting." For a split second, Maren didn't inhale. Her eyes flashed more than the afternoon sun through their family room shades. "You bought it for Pam?"

Steve looked up. Half grateful, half coward, he nodded.

"Pam knows damn well how to run a pregnancy test." Maren burrowed into the couch corner and snatched a pillow. "Why did you get involved?" Patience ticked away. "Steve?"

"That awful weekend Chloé was hospitalized, I brought in specialists. Pam begged me to oversee things." Steve's jaw clenched. "I saw her chart, her date of birth."

"Yeah, DOB. Patient name. Medical record number. Hospital orientation 101," she recited.

"Her *real* birthday." Steve slicked back hair that perspiration had actually cemented in place. "Chloé was born a year before I thought. October 1993. Nine months, roughly two weeks after Pam and I…"

Maren braced Steve's arm. "Oh my God…"

"I don't know definitely, but I wasn't letting Pam out of my sight after she avoided discussion in February. We were all so preoccupied helping Paul. I demanded DNA tests. In July, I think she *finally* had them done. Gave me some excuse that she didn't want to interfere with our wedding." Steve spit that part out, still hotly annoyed at her ability to stall. "It's almost September."

"And you don't know the results?" Maren found her answer in his eyes. She softened hers regarding him, imagining the pain of having had a child he'd never really known.

"You haven't answered why a pregnancy test showed on our account for your former girlfriend." Maren paused cautiously. "There's more to this than Chloé." Maren drew in a breath seeing Steve look down. "Something happened between the two of you, didn't it?"

Steve latched on to Maren's arms and looked at her squarely. "I told you I wasn't letting Pam out of my sight. Pissed me off to press for answers. After ten years, a fabricated abortion, in case I ever questioned her, and wondering what went wrong, it stung, Mair."

Maren could do nothing but listen. Steve's blue eyes unleashed a small storm. "Things got highly emotional. Insane. And inappropriate."

Her mouth quivered. "How inappropriate?"

"I never meant for it…certainly regretted…"

"You slept with her?" Maren jerked out of his grasp but she was trapped in a tiny corner of the sofa as Steve's arms came to either side, resting on the soft cushions. "Answer me dammit!"

A notch of control slipped uncharacteristically from Steve. "One night. One stupid mistake."

"And she's pregnant again? What is it with you two?"

Steve, hearing footsteps near the front door, reluctantly jumped up. He held a silencing finger at his mouth for Maren's benefit, told Dylan to keep playing, and promised to order pizza.

Maren ran to the kitchen, bracing herself with both arms on the island counter. If any dinner prep was to occur, the look in her eyes could be a stand in sharper than anything in the knife block. "We were engaged? Were you drunk out of your mind?" she asked. Oxygen that rushed through her slackened mouth kept her standing.

"Beer plus wine didn't help blood flow where I needed it. Pam is pregnant." His eyes clouded with embarrassment. "I told you it was insane, but *this* baby is *not* mine," Steve assured her. "That's why I insisted on an over-the-counter test, even though like you, Pam argued the necessity. She was pregnant already. Stupid for not knowing herself," Steve sniffed.

"Birds of a feather flock together." Maren flushed. "When were you going to divulge this?" Her tone was cool, direct, and biting.

"Pam and I agreed it would cause pain all over. Take the focus off Paul, put it on us, devastate you," Steve confessed. "Ultimately, I participated in keeping that quiet. I love you. I am so sorry, babe. I wanted to protect you, protect us."

Steve reached out for Maren's hands but she pulled away. He went for the phone book, dialing in a pizza delivery. Hearing a friendly voice helped. It might be the last one he would hear.

"Talk to me, Maren," Steve said. He waited as Maren wielded a knife against lettuce and tomatoes on the cutting board. The wrong word might land him into the salad.

"You have this…this *thing* out there with Pam. This attraction, now possibly a child!" Maren fumed. "Where does that leave me? Did you

168

ever think I should know this possibility *before* we got married?"

When Maren put the knife down, Steve took it, for his safety and her own. "Think back to April," he said. "We had this house. You'd sold yours. I'd found the woman of my dreams. If I had told you then, it would have knifed you. It's not an attraction with Pam. Call it emotional history."

Steve sliced. Rinsed the knife under steaming water, and placed the board in the dishwasher. "It was one regrettable night. And I've hurt you tremendously. Trust me, I know hurt. It sucks."

Maren sighed. She dabbed her eyes with tissues she had fisted from a box. "Having a child, if she's your daughter, is a game changer. I need time to absorb this."

"I get that this came out of the blue." Steve leaned against the counter. "I've no idea where it would place me, if I am her father. You and I put Dylan into our ceremony. I took that commitment willingly as we build our own family here." Steve drew in air. "Chloé's almost ten years old, and I met her when? Last year at Disney." He sighed. "I don't even know her, and now she's got...serious medical problems."

When Steve's voice cracked, Maren looked up. He dragged long fingers through his hair.

"I should've done more after her accident." Steve's eyes welled with tears. He pulled Maren, limp as a ragdoll, to him. "We can work through this if you can forgive me." He squeezed her tight. "I've prided myself on my being able to handle most anything, until this." He banded fingers through his hair. "I fucked up."

Maren ran a hand up the back of his shirt, dumping her own fresh tears onto the front of it. She pulled away. "I know you need me, but I'm not hungry...not feeling well." She breathed out another defeated sigh. "Dylan has homework and school tomorrow. I'm going upstairs."

The leave-me-alone look left Steve cold.

"Go take a warm bath," he finally said. Ordinarily, the hot tub on their patio would have done the trick this August evening. "I'll take care of Dylan tonight. I love you, Maren."

The words lingered as she made her escape. Steve answered the door and tipped the delivery boy. Humid August air rushed in. It would be a hot weekend outside; chilly within these walls.

Paul went to West Riverside Friday. He would meet Liz at noon to beat traffic up Interstate 70 and across the Pennsylvania Turnpike.

Steve arrived at Paul's office form in hand, rolling up his sleeves. "Let's get this over with," he grumbled. "Stupid staff requirements."

"Starting the weekend off on a positive note," Paul replied. He wrapped the blood pressure cuff around Steve's upper arm and pumped it, listening to get a reading. Looking at it again, Paul grabbed another cuff and saw Steve scowl. "A little impatient, are we?" He quieted to listen. "What's the matter?"

"Nothing!" Steve shot back. "I've got a ton on my plate. Appointments. Meetings. Hurry up."

"You can say that," Paul said. "But I'm the one with the numbers here: 170/110 I really ought to recheck this later."

"I don't have time. You've done it twice." Steve fumed and put his wrist out for a pulse. Unbuttoned his shirt for heart and lung sounds.

Paul jotted on the employee health slip and told Steve to slip off his shoes for the weight. He reviewed the labs he'd gotten as part of the required series. "Still going out on the Bay?"

"Might just be Dylan and me. I promised to take him fishing," Steve said. His lips curved down. He was paying a sleepless penance since he and Maren argued well beyond the 11 o'clock news, and again this morning. She was a mess. Nothing he did or said had calmed her. "I don't mean to be short, I just have things on my mind."

"Saw Maren today. She's not usually in on Fridays." Paul didn't mention the spawning tears when he'd asked about weekend fun. Whatever consumed her was the antithesis of pleasure.

"She's focused on a project due next week."

"She looked distracted," Paul said. "Seriously, come back for this. Is everything OK?"

"No," Steve leveled. "It's a fucking mess. I don't want to burden you. Involves other people."

Paul regarded Steve. "Does this have something to do with Pam?"

Steve hopped off the table. "Why do you ask?"

"When I mentioned a place I wanted to take Liz to, how you, me, Pam used to hang out there, Maren's expression fell blank. Ice cold. She's one of the most accepting people I've ever met."

"She is," Steve said. "Everyone has a limit. I'm hoping this isn't hers, but Pam's pulled a fast one, conveniently withholding something. And I've been stupid."

"You finally forgave her last year over the abortion," Paul said. "I kind of like you two on speaking terms. Selfish, but I need my friends."

Steve buttoned his shirt cuffs. "Paul, she never had an abortion."

"What?" Paul scratched his head as if his hand reached his befuddled brain.

"Listen, I get shit for keeping stuff inside. Keep this quiet: Chloé's paternity is at question."

"Christ!" Paul stopped notating. Gaped. "You aren't kidding."

"Oh, it gets better." Steve went on. "I finally confronted her in New York…day before the alumni dinner. She admitted it, said she had loved Jerry and me, but found herself pregnant, and rather than go off totally on her, we both ended up in tears. And in bed."

Paul blinked. In the decades they'd shared plenty of screw-ups professionally and personally. "And Maren just found out which part?"

"Both. Don't ask how. I don't lie well."

"People like you keep priests hearing confession," Paul replied. "What are you going to do?"

"Beg my wife's forgiveness. She's the best thing that's ever happened to me."

"Amen. Fortunately not known for hasty moves. And Pam?"

"Press her for the damn DNA results. I overnighted my sample months ago. Sent her a tersely worded text: RESULTS TODAY."

"Please tell me you have nothing to do with *this* pregnancy," Paul asked. "And if she has gotten results back don't you think she and Jerry have to deal with all that first? Imagine the implications."

"Like I'm real dog shit for sleeping with another man's apparently pregnant wife."

"There are worse things than dog shit. Trust me." Paul quickly reframed. "Just make this work with Maren. Don't end up like me robbed of beauty, comfort, life direction being pulled in *any* direction by cute and fluffy. Then, you can talk about dog shit."

Steve closed his eyes to that. "I have more guilt unloading all this on you," he said. "Oh, another thing. I know you're making the rounds. A little Lothario coming back on board." Steve lightened but wasn't up to a smile. "Just don't break Liz's heart, if she feels more than a friendship. I mean, with Jade in the picture."

"Steve, Jade and I have had dinner, lunch twice, coffee. We worked out at the gym once."

"Just the gym, huh?" Steve tapped his hand on the doorframe. He looked at the form with the empty line for blood pressure. "You're playing hardball on this. I'll be back before you leave."

"Some boy has a crush on me." Hannah unraveled her daycare dilemma from the backseat. "He likes all the girls."

What to do? She liked Dylan, but Dylan was a cousin. Hannah asked Paul if he had cousins. Explaining a mere three-dozen would keep them in conversation the four hours to Pittsburgh and possibly six returning in Monday's traffic.

"Why can't Bruno and Franco come with us," Hannah asked next. Chatterbox: Only a mild descriptor for her during the trip's first hours before they even hit Breezewood.

"Bruno and Franco have a dog sitter," Paul explained. "Besides, Bruno sniffs—Paul silenced *humps*—other dogs." He described their two barks. Bruno's distinct one resonated louder than Pavarotti. Once Hannah played license plate bingo, Paul told Liz he wasn't sure what to do. Had he made a mistake adopting both dogs?

"The homeowner's association can't force you to abide by new rules," she said. "You'd be grandfathered in. I know a few things about real estate." From butthead, she mouthed.

"Bruno can live with us on the shore." Hannah's focus on license plates had ended.

"He can't," Tyler insisted. "Dad complained about the dander. Lucena's allergic."

"Hm," Liz managed. "There's an incentive."

She shot Paul a devilish grin from the passenger seat. Periodically throughout the ride, Liz talked about keeping Bruno until he got out of his pure puppy stage. When Paul promised to pay Tyler for dog walks and pooper scooping, dollar signs flashed. Paul's stature rose, too.

It was 4:30 PM by the time they made it into Oakland, home to Pittsburgh universities, the Romano household, and the meeting Paul had to rush off to in order to take a brief hospital tour.

"Paul works too hard," Isabella fussed at an early dinner at the restaurant her son Giovanni owned. "Vinny, he don't work enough."

Liz agreed that Paul put in long hours. Work plus the dogs helped him grieve, she added. Isabella confirmed that Paul was just a boy when he lost his own father, a few years older than Tyler, and spent that first year grumbling at the nuns.

"Paul doesn't have a dad?" Tyler asked. He assumed most had fathers and two families.

Liz cringed listening to her son answer Mrs. Romano's questions, once with a grunt; otherwise, in one or two inarticulate words. She felt the faintest level of camaraderie with Isabella. Single mom ordeals bonded them, albeit Mrs. Romano had worked for the parochial school, with summers off and a tight rein on her brood.

"Sorry, I got held up on the parkway," Vinny said, excusing his lateness. He sat down to the appetizer and beer Isabella had ordered him. "Liz, welcome to Pittsburgh. Jeet jet? Hi kids."

"Thanks Vinny. What did you say?" Liz puzzled a look. One sip of Rolling Rock brought slurred speech?

"Dinner? Did you eat yet? My brother really knows how to cook." If his substantial order served as a testimonial, then Giovanni's meal would be outstanding.

"With this menu, I'm sure he does. Meet Tyler, almost seven, and Hannah, four very soon."

The kids each mumbled a shy hello. Vinny enthralled them about rides they would love at tomorrow's amusement park. When Tyler spotted the thin chain around Vinny's neck, Paul's brother offered to find the perfect sized one for him to take home.

"How kind of you," Liz told him. "Tyler just started second grade."

"My brother was wearing cologne in third," Vinny added. "Both help attract chicks."

"My dad doesn't have a chain," Tyler said. "Smells good though."

Liz's eyelids fluttered shut. She struggled to follow a thought that had lodged in her brain. "You got held up parking. Are you OK?"

"No, no," Isabella answered for him. "Vinny explain. He shoulda read about detour in the PG."

"You drove the Parkway East to get here, take the Parkway West to the airport," Vinny said. "It could use three lanes but you'd have to knock out Squirrel Hill." He shrugged. "Old: like Ma."

Vinny winked. Isabella elbowed him. Seeing a folded newspaper left on a table, Liz realized the PG stood for the *Post-Gazette*.

Liz got acclimated to more than vernacular, but also to family lore. Paul's hormonal hands may have hidden a *Charlie's Angels* poster, but Isabella had once confiscated Vinny's Madonna music with its themes of unwed mothers, bondage, and burned crosses. Liz hoped her nodding didn't let on that she owned the artist's entire collection.

An hour passed. Liz wiped vodka sauce off Hannah. "It's not really vodka," she explained to Tyler, fearing the Tyler to Tim to Child Protective Services backlash if she didn't clarify.

"Paul cooks better than Mommy," Hannah said. "He doesn't put ketchup and soup in sauce."

Liz caught Mrs. Romano's horror. Acquiescing wasn't going to cut it any longer. "I bake," Liz said, to salvage impressions.

Vinny, who had put forth his best sales pitch, collapsed his shoulders when Liz politely smiled at his suggestion to buy souvenirs from Crazy Vinny's Pawn Shop. Another misstep?

"You owe me," Liz muttered when Paul walked in at 6:46.

"Put it on my I-owe-you tab," he whispered.

When Liz said she had ordered Shrimp Fra Diavolo, he squeezed her hand under the table. He savored bites of linguine with clam sauce she couldn't finish. "Didn't I say you won't go hungry this weekend?"

"Paul." Isabella cupped his face. "You worka hard. Who takes care of you? I come visit."

"Maybe the holidays Ma." Paul filled them in on his tour. All very positive, Liz could tell. She didn't demand details; too afraid that Isabella would push Paul to put down roots in Pittsburgh.

"Can we make cookies like these?" Hannah held up one from the Italian dessert tray. Liz wouldn't get her children to bed until tomorrow with tonight's sugar high.

"Mm," Liz said, " I saved room for cannoli."

A hint of a smile played at Paul's mouth. He took last bites of his meal and leaned into Liz. "Add that to the I-owe-you list."

That they had shared more private jokes made Isabella uneasy. She commented on Liz's simply filed nails. "I take you to Vanessa to polish those. Family friend. Nice Catholic girl."

Paul put down his beer because if he didn't he might choke on it. He exchanged glances with Liz, who understood all too well by 10 PM why Paul insisted on treating this weekend. Real roller coasters at Kennywood Park couldn't dip as low as this conversation had.

They walked Pittsburgh streets to the Romano house. Hannah and Tyler stayed with Liz in one room with a double bed and air mattress. Liz tried to reframe the evening.

When sleep eluded her, Liz remembered a grad school joke she had learned about the essence of families. Each one might resemble fruitcakes—sweet people, fruits, nuts—some liquored more than others.

Paul's family didn't drink to excess. Fuss, fret, and over-function for one another? Oh yeah.

Chapter 15

"I told you, it meant nothing," Steve asserted Sunday morning. He sat on the lounge, facing Maren, in their master bedroom as he slid on his Sperry Top-Siders. "The reasons we could never make a relationship work still lie between us."

"Except for one," Maren argued. "When will she impart this important detail, which of course, puts you in contact once again? If you fell into bed losing your minds, what's to prevent it from happening again? With or without DNA."

"I wish I could convince you I am not interested in Pam." Steve froze in place. "Obviously, the test results weigh in. I was selfish not to have told you." He rubbed a fine line of corded neck muscles. "I am now. It would've cast a pall on our wedding." Hanging his head, he added, "This is all new to me, too."

Maren punched Steve's pillow. She propped straighter in the bed where she still sought refuge. "What was it like, with her?"

"What do you mean?"

"Don't be coy, Steve. When you were together," Maren spit out. "The sex!"

The scrutiny made him shudder. "You're asking me to hurt you. I don't see any point."

"Details!"

He stood, transferred himself to the edge of the bed. "Quick, spontaneous kissing. Ended in straight up sex. Protected, by the way."

"Someone thought of a consequence…this time." Maren seethed. "What kinds of sex?"

"Maren, stop torturing yourself."

He grasped her hand, pulling it from her defiant stance, but she yanked it back, bracing harder as she crossed arms over her chest.

Palms pressed into the comforter, Steve tried harder. "Fresh air would do us all some good. It will be a really nice day on the Bay, in the boat."

"I'd rather work on my book project." Maren tossed the covers aside, straight into Steve.

He had no choice but to stand as she smoothed sheets, plopping pillows back into place. Steve had slept Friday in the guest room after

Maren had deliberately locked their door. Last night she had been too exhausted to kick him out. Her side ached from sleeping on it, turned away from him.

"I understand you're angry, processing all this Liz would say, but your dad is going today and Dylan's wondering. Bring a book. Relax," Steve suggested. "We need to be together."

"Speaking of the boat." Maren moved to the other side of their king-sized bed and jutted her index finger into Steve's gut hard enough to make him flinch. "One night of cheap, stupid hotel sex, really? If you ever had her on that boat, our boat, I swear I'll shipwreck the damn thing."

Eyes wide, Steve reached to her but Maren wrenched away. "It was impulsive. Stupid too. Unplanned," Steve said. "Besides…never mind."

"What? Finish." Maren watched Steve hesitate. Making him squirm replaced drafting a children's book, which had been her top priority just under caring for Dylan, until this had totally jolted her concentration. How could her mind be creative when she practically spit nails?

"It's our boat, though registered in my name."

Maren sniffed. "Think that would stop me?"

"Are you guys coming?" Dylan asked as he rendered a light knock at their door.

How long had he been standing out there?

"Almost ready, Bud," Steve hollered to him, changing to a whisper. "Really Mair, we need to keep some normalcy here. Come with us."

Maren veered to the nightstand clock. "Go get snacks ready. I need a shower." She turned before Steve could open the door. "If I do go out, it's to be with Dylan and Dad. Not with you."

Paul slept restlessly, especially with Liz on the opposite side of his old room in Pittsburgh. A room once filled with prurient, youthful thoughts. The kind he had imagined at 24, when first meeting Liz, tempted him now. Only he was pushing 40 and starting life over.

He imagined Liz stepping out of her pool, wearing only beads of dripping water, and what Steve thought occurred underneath his desk. Both visions shot Paul straight into ecstasy.

He flexed his arms to the ceiling, forcing away what he couldn't do anything about. He moved his mind beyond the maternal pressures he felt also. Wasn't the point of Labor Day not to labor? Isabella Romano hadn't stopped fussing since he arrived Friday. He owed Liz a lot more than a little affection and tasty Italian desserts.

At least he made good on fun for Hannah and Tyler. Hannah's favorite thing thus far had been the Children's Museum; Tyler's the submarine, docked along the riverbank at the Carnegie Science Center. Noticing Heinz Field, Tyler had added that his team would "kick Steelers butt in that stadium next weekend." Paul knew Tyler had embarrassed Liz. Again. He expected as much purple to flow in Tyler's blood, but this wasn't mere banter. Cutting remarks didn't represent how Liz had raised him.

Getting out of bed, Paul hopped into the shower and later helped to cook eggs and sausage. Fast food breakfast sandwiches weren't options with a hovering Italian mother. It would be their last meal here since they planned to stop at Idlewild Park in Ligonier en route home.

Hannah adored the Mister Roger's trolley. Liz appreciated that Paul's mother had packed them a picnic lunch and Smiley cookies. By four, Hannah waved goodbye to Daniel Tiger. Fudge probably made up 25 percent of Hannah's body mass index and even cotton candy wouldn't energize Tyler to climb aboard one more ride.

"I told you it was a true family park." Paul steered his SUV through the turnpike tollbooth. "The whirlwind tour wore them out." He saw drooping heads in the rearview mirror. "Add in all the Italian treats, the pop, and you'll send me their dental bills."

"Took a while to figure that pop meant soda." Liz actually snorted. "The igloo hosts concerts and hockey. An eagle stocks groceries. You drive on a parkway and dine at an Eat 'N Park." She launched the look. "No, I'm not confused."

Paul quirked up his lips. "Pittsburgh, that's all. Vinny taught Tyler that Super Mario means Mario Lemieux, who saved hockey here twice." Paul grinned. "Vinny envy: Tyler likes him."

"Tyler's changing his tune, only he doesn't want to admit it," Liz replied. "He chilled on the water slides." They drove half a mile. "Sorry for the mini meltdowns he had Saturday."

Vinny had walked the kids at Kennywood Park when regrettably they didn't measure up to height requirements. That allowed Paul to ride with Liz on the Jack Rabbit, a childhood favorite.

"He's a boy, Liz. Not always dispensing his energy well. He did like the roller coasters."

"Because his life is one," Liz agreed. "Like your career decisions."

Paul noticed Liz's eyes search him. He had to wear his Armani shades with the sun blazing through the car windows, but he sensed that Liz needed the full assurance of matching body language. Words would have to convince her now.

"Next week, I'll visit the practice again on the shore," he told her. "I have to give an answer to Pittsburgh by the end of October."

"Eight weeks. Why not wait eight months?" Liz studied Paul's profile from the passenger seat. "Let me guess: You're undecided?"

"I'll figure it out." Paul reached and squeezed her hand. "Your thoughts on my hometown?"

"Like driving Mt. Everest only with chairs that save parking spots." She was nothing but honest. "Taking extra highways and two tunnels to drive us into the city: I thought you were nuts."

"Once out of the Fort Pitt Tunnel?" Paul goaded. "Remember, you live on a flat sandbar."

"I get it," Liz admitted. "I know why you're proud of Pittsburgh with that spectacular view. You win. Now, we play the Steelers next weekend. That's another matter entirely."

"May the *best* team prevail."

"Good thing your brother is a Penguins fan. Your mother couldn't care less about either. All in my favor. She doesn't like me though," Liz added. "Tell me more about Vanessa. Does your mom really expect you to limit *future women* to wholesome Italian stock?"

Paul bellowed at that. "First, Ma's a fair-weather fan. Second, she has to get to know you. Shed a little of your stubborn German, Liz."

She gasped. "She only likes me because I'm Steve's sister, and I did say at least one nice thing about Pam." Liz turned to the driver's seat. "She *likes* Pam better. If she only knew..."

"No," Paul interrupted. "We're not tossing Ma's Pam impressions into the rivers. I mean it."

"What's Pam got on you?"

Paul muttered under his breath in Italian.

"She definitely has dirt." Liz shot a one-upping lip curl. "Bet Pam has Vanessa stories."

"Stop!" Paul fiddled with the radio for something else to fill the air, even static. "I had coffee with Vanessa months ago, when I first went home. I felt lonely. Ma got a little hopeful."

"A little?" Liz looked out at the green hills. "Did you date her? I mean back in the day."

"Date loosely describes it." Paul let that comment rest on its own.

"Loose, as in Loose Hena loose? Hm." Liz nodded. "You had quite the parade back then."

178

"Vicki halted that," Paul interjected. "Admittedly, my past haunts me. Your brother thinks I got some under the desk last week." The grin broke into a broad, proud smile. "Your jaw will hurt if it drops any more onto that dashboard."

"Seriously?" Liz checked to ensure she had two incoherent children in the backseat.

"Don't worry: He thought it was Jade. Given the two back there, I think it's best we keep this attraction under wraps."

"Unfortunate and unfair. Loser gets to live it up. Have fun."

"That's why, despite the Isabella inquisition, I wanted to treat you to a getaway."

"I meant other fun." Disappointment leached from Liz's throat. "How much under wraps?"

"You meant cannoli fun." Paul smiled, focusing forward. "Under covers, under wraps. All the same." When he glanced over Liz scratched her head and shook it sideways. "Oh, my family's not the only intrusive one," he added. "Steve told me in no uncertain terms not to break your heart, not that he needed to say that."

If Liz hadn't been harnessed, she would have leaned onto the console between them. "Are you kidding me? That makes me want to mess with you even more."

"Don't I feel special?" Paul's joke didn't stir the kids. "He even said I deserve *Estrogenous Americanas*. You lucky little bambina."

"Hey, that must translate to bimbo."

"Bimbo describes the woman we discussed earlier," Paul scoffed. "Bambina slang for good-looking woman. You, Liz." He drove a few hundred yards. "I am lonely, Vanessa's history. My office, desk, hiding spot, always handy."

"Oh shut up." Liz almost swatted him, but repositioned herself in the passenger seat, lest they veer off the turnpike. "Watch the game with me Sunday. They're with Tim. Bring dessert... to cheer you up after a Ravens win!"

"I'd love to, but I'm on call Saturday night," he said. Paul slowed into the rest stop and gently applied the brakes.

"I'm talking Sunday afternoon."

"Message received," Paul said. He glanced back. His raised arm shielding them between the seats, he leaned over and kissed Liz, full on the mouth. "It's an enticing offer."

After much hype in the media, game day came. Game day went. As a positive, the post-surgical patient Paul had monitored Sunday morning pulled through fine. On his way to Kent Island, the radio broadcast the Ravens-Steelers matchup.

By the time Paul's tires met the intended pebbled driveway, Tim had just pulled out of it depositing two children back with their mother.

"He had homes to show when everyone is glued to the screen?" Liz grumbled as she opened the door to Paul, well into the second quarter. "Tyler really wanted to watch the Ravens with him. Just when I thought Tim couldn't be any more of a jerk." She breathed in deeply.

Paul gave Liz a little squeeze and a heated kiss. "What's the score?"

"You know perfectly well we haven't put points on the board." Bruno and Franco, off leash, lunged past Liz at the whiff of snacks upstairs. "Lose the smirk, Romano."

Paul took steps to the kitchen two at a time, but Liz stopped him mid-staircase. "Tyler's in a snit so no gloating. I'm annoyed enough."

"You disappointed over losing more than football?" He pinched Liz's butt. Her chin drooped. Paul exuded male über-confidence of a game win plus a score in bed if not for the kids.

"I'm put off with Pittsburgh." She managed to mask her longing of another missed opportunity, privately with Paul.

"Ah, I treat you to a weekend. Now national TV blasts that beautiful skyline. Your team's choking, but the stubborn German...."

In the kitchen, Liz shoved a plate of pasta in front of him. "In case you're wondering, it's the leftover sauce you made from the freezer. Now, it's the only sauce Hannah will eat."

Air escaped Paul. How long had she cooked the macaroni? Very likely with a timer than test when it was ready. Paul zipped the thought.

Hannah squealed when the dogs found her, further annoying Tyler. Liz had to send him to time out during the third quarter for shouting about Shitsburgh. The fourth ended: Pittsburgh 34, Baltimore 15. Paul suggested that the kids change into their bathing suits.

"Let him swim off some steam." Paul popped the top on a second beer. "I heard there's a storm brewing in the Atlantic, named Isabel." His cheeks gleamed before he enjoyed his first swig.

"That's too funny. I shouldn't laugh." Liz did.

"Beneath the mama bear, she's sweet Liz. Grieving too this year. Surely you get that."

"I know." Liz looked at the kitchen island where her phone vibrated.

"Great, another one wanting to gloat." She picked up her cell. "Don't start," she said. "No Steve, Dylan cannot talk with Tyler who is headed to the water slide needing a dozen dunks to pull him from a double funk. Tim bailed on him and so did his favorite team."

Liz imparted details of Hannah's birthday party though Steve wouldn't remember them, she felt sure, and they quickly hung up. She headed outside.

Liz set iced tea down beside Paul's beer. He sat in his swim trunks, supervising the kids, the dogs panting away.

"I asked if I could talk with Maren," Liz shared. "Steve said, 'Not now' as if something's up. Maren should be happy their team won. Something seemed off even yesterday." Paul tilted his bottle to his mouth, failing to answer her. "You know something, don't you?"

"Liz, this is where our crossing paths gets sticky." And tempting, Paul thought. Liz had thrust hands onto her hips. Her shorts probably hid skimpy bottoms since her breasts pushed out from the bikini top. Purple, of course. It could have been bright orange or tie-dye. With the glimpse he got of what it covered weeks ago, Paul could tear off black and gold about now.

Liz pulled a chair closer. "Has my brother done something brainless?" Paul finished his beer and tasted her iced tea. She continued. "Come on...on a scale of one to ten?"

"Pretty brainless."

"Scale it!" Liz demanded.

Paul sighed. "Eight, nine...I don't know. Not exactly our business."

"Wait," Liz whispered. "After making party favors, I saw Maren flip through my books."

"She can read. So?"

"*Dinosaurs Divorce,* Paul, and *Surviving Separation and Divorce.* Don't you find that odd for a newlywed?"

"Married couples have their moments. They'll work it out," Paul assured her.

Savoring a Steelers win over their rival, Steve stretched his neck and head higher at work. A boost he needed since Paul shared that he contemplated two job offers—one 300 miles away. If Paul moved to Pittsburgh, Steve would lose a confidante, a co-worker, and a surgeon on his staff.

Suzanna peered into his open office door. "Dr. Kramer, line one. Dr. Morgan. She said you're expecting her call."

"Thank you." Steve waited for the door to close before he picked up. "I texted you from my Blackberry. This is private, not professional."

"Good afternoon to you, too," Pam replied. "I'm sorry, I have to re-enter my phone contacts. Give me your number again."

Steve rattled it off, impatiently, such that he had to repeat every number. "You better have results," he said instead of *cut the bullshit,* which almost leapt off his tongue.

"I do." Pam halted. "Chloé is your daughter. Our daughter."

No amount of training, nothing Dolores and Bill Kramer had taught Steve informed him of how to handle this moment. Sentiment watered his eyes, as he swiveled his chair back and nearly landed on his office carpet. He brought it forward just as quickly. Rage reached his brain that Pam had kept such a secret. Blood pounded through his heart at how his wife might react.

"Steve..."

"I'm here. I want the results."

"I'll overnight them. Which address?"

It wasn't as if he could provide the coordinates and GPS location for his boat.

"Send them here. I know, I just gave you hell for using this number. This is complicated, Pam." Steve repeated the hospital address since she had a pen. "Mark it confidential. What was Jerry's reaction? I presume that accounts for the delay."

"He's reeling. If I wasn't carrying his child now, I'm afraid he might leave."

Steve heard raw guilt cracking Pam's vocal chords. If Jerry walked out, Steve knew he wouldn't step back in. Maren would still worry.

"None of this is Chloé's fault. She's too young to know this, especially with her diagnosis and her treatment."

Steve downed the urge to argue yet another decision she'd made for him. "Does Jerry know about...New York?"

"No. That would be horrible."

"Well Maren knows."

"What? Why? When? How did she find out?"

Steve sniffed into the receiver. Pam's forays into journalism with her advice column showed. "When I bought that pregnancy test, I foolishly used a pharmacy card. Maren bought one—she's not—but returning it, she saw both purchases."

"I told you, didn't I? You're so stubborn."

"You win Pam. Anyway, Maren had 50 questions. I don't lie." *I'm not like you!*

"Great: Maren and Jerry cross paths in marketing. If she tells him." Pam sighed heavily. "I have to discuss this with my shrink I'm seeing."

"A long overdue move."

"Be a sarcastic jackass, Steve." Pam broke off. She was silent a half minute. "Jerry has one request: to talk face to face."

Steve rubbed his eyelids shut. Outside of the New York night, he owed Jerry Carlton no apology. Pam had been his nine-year girlfriend, his live-in lover a decade ago, until Pam found Jerry and played it both ways. Shrapnel from those choices now hit two marriages and several children. "I'm not agreeing to anything until I talk to Maren," he said.

Before Steve could hang up, Pam asked what to tell Jerry. Steve nearly pierced his tongue but held what he could unleash. She toyed with ten years, now she granted him not even that number of minutes?

There were too many things Steve didn't know. One he did: He had to peacefully coexist with both Dr. Pam Morgan and Jerry Carlton. If he didn't, he might never get to really know his daughter.

Paul was glad Steve took his stress out on the treadmill late Friday afternoon. Adjusting the settings on the machine next to his, Paul began jogging. Could a hospital gym foster decision making as much as it improved employee health?

"The kids liked Pittsburgh." Paul worked to a faster pace. Repeated about Pittsburgh when Steve seemed lost in his own world.

Steve used his wrist to wipe sweat from his forehead. "Your sister's kids?"

"*Your* sister's kids. Tyler, Hannah, your little sweetheart." Paul watched Steve's face blanch. When his pace slowed, Paul realized. "Results came back, didn't they?" The hard, impassive line on Steve's face made Paul's scalp prickle. "What now?" he asked.

"Jerry wants to meet. Maren keeps pushing me away. Pam's a thorn. Remove her completely and I'll bleed out. She's my conduit to Chloé." Steve shook his head. "Not where I wanted to be with Mair this year either."

Steve's continual complaining made them each rather pensive.

"That's right, a year ago you operated on Dylan. Maren started working here. So did Vicki." Paul wiped his own beads of sweat.

"There's an Italian proverb about equality: The king and the pawn go into the same box, when the game's all over. Something like that."

"When it's all said and done I might very well end up six feet under in a pine box."

Paul sent off a look he had surely picked up from years spent within the Kramer family.

"Sorry for the death reference," Steve said. "You're friendly with Pam. That I..." Steve wiped sweat again. "That I could toss her ass into Canada right now is my problem, not yours."

"No offense taken," Paul replied. "One cognitive reframe: as we both push 40, at least we know we're not shooting blanks."

Steve angled his eyes to Paul. "Not the family picture either of us imagined," he huffed between treadmill strides. "We both love kids."

"All right, better humor," Paul declared. "You hear the story of the guy who asks the blonde fishing? Launching his boat, he hardly re-members his tackle and pole...well, the one attached reminds him that more than the sun is...hot." Paul chuckled at his own wit. "Sorry, a blonde joke." The irony hadn't escaped Steve's glare.

"Blonde claims 'the water's getting bluer.' Guy's been paying more attention to her bustline than the waterline. Like an idiot, he remem-bers 'drain plug...shit, forgot it' and throws himself Navy-seal style overboard. Plugs the hole. Not the one he counted on plugging."

"Don't tell me stuff like that." Steve quickened pace and watched the panel record his heart rate. "Glad you're cracking jokes but Mair really threatened to sink my boat, thinking I had *the blonde* on it." Steve inhaled sharply. "Pam used to claim sea sickness. Threw up in a hotel room. Maybe it really is me?"

"Maren does know a thing or two about boats." Paul's silliness snapped into concern. "Did you hear my mother is now a cat five hur-ricane, veering to the Carolina coast?"

Steve's demeanor turned ominous. "Crap, if it moves up the coast, I'll need to haul out."

The two remained lockstep side by side. Sweating, for different reasons. "Speaking of the Poseidon Adventuress..."

Maren had just unrolled a yoga mat on the first floor of the hospital's new gym. Those on treadmills and elliptical trainers had a birds-eye view from a second-story lofted over a large space where

Maren contorted herself into several poses, never noticing she had a captive audience.

"She signed up for morning yoga. I don't usually see her here this late. Audrey and Jack take Dylan until Hannah's party tomorrow."

"Gives you two some alone time," Paul said. "It's hard for Liz with the kids. Tim drops them off unexpectedly yet pushes for joint custody." Paul muttered something in Italian.

"I'm sure that wasn't a compliment," Steve assessed.

"Italian for prick."

"Fits." His voice turned even more serious. "Does Liz need a hand with Tyler and Hannah? Mom and Dad are so busy listing the Chevy Chase house. Obviously, we've been distracted."

"Eric helps. Extra hands with two rambunctious kids never hurts," Paul replied. "Unless it's from Planet Purple down there."

Steve looked. "Fartinski at the fountain."

"Fartinski, that's a good one." Paul cracked up. "Too bad he struck out with Liz." The sarcasm dripped with that.

Gabe Furtinski copped a squat on Maren's exercise mat. He chatted with her as she twisted and stretched. "He needs to get his eyes off my wife. Always calling her with work questions, prime Peter Principle specimen. Incompetent."

Maren wore tight black exercise pants and a T-shirt. Steve studied her. Sighed as if he wanted to hug her tight and send their troubles downstream with the tides. Not a minute too soon.

"What the hell," Steve spit out. One hand groped for the treadmill cool down command while his feet stopped so suddenly that Paul reached to catch Steve's wrist. He looked as if he'd sail over the railing to land on Planet Purple.

Gabe had splayed fingers through Maren's hair and pulled her in for a kiss. One hand that had been visible suddenly wasn't. Part of Gabe's arm protruded from Maren's T-shirt.

"So much for conversation," Paul mumbled. "Whoa!"

"He's just... She's just..." Steve's eyes went aflame. He repeated the obscenity Paul muttered.

"You're missing the dialect."

"He's gonna be missing his face." Steve spit the words. "I could take him out right now."

"Clearly, but you won't. Breathe."

185

Steve inhaled frustration, blew fury back out.

Gabe stood up and left. Maren's eyes trailed him. She rose, gathered her mat, and headed to the lockers, leaving no view for Steve to trace.

Steve arrived home after a shower had cooled him down. He parked his Jag outside and walked to the patio, surprised to see his father-in-law, Jack.

"Dylan forgot something at the neighbor's." Jack darted his vision. "Do you have a second?"

"Sure. I have to get back to the hospital, but Mrs. Kramer and I need to have a little talk."

"Dylan seemed upset," Jack informed Steve. The two stood in the September sun at Shore Landings. Maren's parents had sold their Annapolis home for a condo within walking distance. "He said Maren shouts, acts grumpy. His words."

Steve removed his Ray-Ban specs. "We ah, have some things we're dealing with, Jack. It's complicated." Steve looked to the patio stones. "One beyond our control, but...I've upset her."

Jack regarded Steve curiously. A drunk driver had taken out his daughter's first marriage, ending Mark's life. Her happiness had been a top priority ever since. "I'm not prying, but I'm a pretty good listener."

"I know you visit patients for church."

"I like it," Jack said. "Audrey and I met with engaged couples. Years ago. Marriage isn't easy. Harder with demanding careers, outside stress." Jack grew silent. "It was a little mission for us."

Steve brightened at the revelation, but sobered. "That's for sure. Hey, I need a moment with Maren. Could you please keep Dylan outside if he shows up?"

"Sure." Jack lowered himself into the two-seater while Steve opened the screen door.

He walked into the kitchen where Maren fixed a salad, a sign she wasn't very hungry.

"I thought you worked late?" she asked.

"Why? You have a date with someone else?"

"Don't be an ass." Maren only swore when she was very perturbed. A tight face matched her mood. "If anyone would have other plans..."

Steve's right hand reached Maren's arm after she dropped a handful of sprouts into her bowl.

"I saw you at the hospital gym this afternoon."

Maren's eyes widened. "You're spying on me? That takes the cake."

"Rare moment for Paul and me to work out. Imagine catching my wife and art school pal."

"I can talk to whomever I want."

"Sure can, but while you celebrate your one year at West Riverside, just remember I've worked in hospitals for decades. People talk." Steve held Maren with a tight grasp, his body touching hers. Stunned, she didn't move away.

"Let me remind you, I am the chief of surgery; you are my wife. You might not want to be right now, but you are. Your little make-out session, complete with the feel-up, could have been anyone's entertainment. Don't sully your reputation, and mine, because you're incensed with me."

Maren backed up. "You don't own me."

"No, I sure as hell don't." Steve steeled his eyes to hers. "You're not exactly a free agent either. You want to hurt me: Charge a room to our VISA. I'll know it wasn't lunch."

A breeze wafted in a window. Steve inhaled; it centered him as he felt himself going off on her.

"You're consulting attorneys," Maren managed. "So much for making this marriage work!"

Baffled, he inched away, still cornering her. "What do you mean?"

"A call on the voice mail—a lawyer in Annapolis. I looked him up. He does family law."

Steve closed and opened his eyes. "A high school friend who can offer Liz a second opinion. I told her to call me if she ever needed anything. She did." He let go of Maren's arm. "Satisfied?"

"My mistake. If you're truthful...this time."

"I made a mistake, a horrible, regrettable lapse, *before* taking vows. I didn't do it with premeditation. When you asked me, I came out with the truth." Steve took another moment to marshal his thoughts. A tear began to cloud his vision. "I'll consider today an accident, but if you ever pull a stunt like that again, there will be hell to pay. I will shove Gabe Guy in it, for sure."

"You never liked him. Makes no sense."

"Does now."

"I didn't ask him to come on to me."

"You didn't push him off either," Steve fumed. "If this is the game we're playing...I'm in."

"What?" Maren stared at him.

Steve gripped her head with his left hand and pressed her against the full-length cabinet with his body. Lips seized Maren's mouth. His tongue ran along her teeth, ravaging her throat.

As her body melded into his, he loosened the hold he had snagged with his right hand, which crawled fingers underneath her shirt, searching and finding just the spot. He thumbed it, stroked gently the small scar that remained on her breast, a shared memory that rocked her last fall, not nearly with the savage force of Steve's kiss now. He felt Maren's heavy breath against his neck.

"Ball's in your court." He let her go, completely flummoxed. "By the way, *that's* how it's done, complete with the feel-up." Seeing moisture on her lashes, he commanded her ear. "If I never make love to you again—if you don't ever let me—just know you are the hottest woman I have ever been with." He soaked in the sight of her brown eyes as his blue ones misted. "And the absolute love of my life."

Steve bit his lip and stepped away through the screen door. He nodded thanks to Jack and high-fived Dylan.

Maren looked out the window as Steve fastened his seatbelt and backed his Jaguar out of the drive. She sat on a chair and dissolved once again into a ball of abject tears.

Chapter 16

Hannah and a hurricane both turned four on Saturday. While the storm, still at a distance, got downgraded, Hannah's loot upgraded: lavender gown Barbie plus fake muscled Ken, as Tyler called him; *Hello Kitty* books, stickers, hats, mittens. *Hello Kitty* everything.

Tim hosted daycare families in Annapolis days before, essentially beating Liz to her own guests. His upstaging caused some of Hannah's playmates to forgo the party Liz had planned. Liz was spitting mad; Hannah disappointed. They had mediated all of this to take turns with celebrations. Liz's turn came first. A handful of friends and family made up the guest list.

Emergency surgery made Steve miss it. He stopped at hospital televisions for the latest CNN weather after his father-in-law called. A marina crew was pulling Jack's sailboat out of the water. He agreed to give the details when they would crab together the very next day on Steve's boat.

By one o'clock Sunday the two men had hauled in a bushel of blue crabs. Steve grabbed two bottles of Blue Moon while Jack dip-netted a doubler, a male crab carrying a sexually mature female underneath him. When Jack made light of its rarity, Steve raised a beer to his lips. No brown bottle could hide his tension; more than the September sun washed his complexion.

"I try to keep the right distance to acknowledge my daughter has her own life. Enough closeness to show I care," Jack started. "Not treating you any differently than I did Mark." He crossed his ankles facing Steve in the canopied shade. "Open windows don't hide much, however. The honeymoon's over, I take it?"

"Friday?" Steve's fingers pried off the Blue Moon label. "I wasn't quite at my best."

"Hell of a kiss," Jack answered. "Her little squeal made me peek. Heard something about her friend Gabe, Maren's reputation."

"Did Maren say anything after I left?"

"Not a word. Cried like she did when Zane down the street walked another girl home from school." Jack grinned. "My daughter's tears stream like flares signaling for help."

"There goes my nomination for best supporting actor," Steve quipped.

"James Bond gets the woman even if he loses his boat, which you might if you don't focus on this approaching storm," Jack cautioned. A blind man couldn't miss Jack's start-talking scowl.

"Gabe's a worm," Steve estimated. "Comes on to interns, my sister, now my wife."

"Always seemed a player. Not who you want near a daughter."

Was that something in common, Steve wondered, or a half-veiled invitation to confess?

"Maren didn't start our troubles." Steve hung his head. "I was in New York in April while we were engaged. Pam, my ex, was at an alumni function. I confronted her over another omission."

"Go on…" Jack took a swig of his beer.

"For ten years I thought she aborted our child," Steve admitted. "She didn't. She fabricated that to run off with Jerry."

"So there…she had to have…" Jack held back, out of politeness.

Surgery had trained Steve to cut to it. "Chloé Carlton is really Chloé Kramer, biologically." Steve watched Jack's double take.

"How'd you uncover all this?"

"Saw Chloé's chart after the accident. Questioned Pam about her real birthday. Then Vicki and the baby died. April was my chance for the truth…and DNA." Steve emptied his bottle, needing every last drop. "She stalled…to not interfere with our wedding plans."

"I heard you say once how she wields her intelligence," Jack said. "Pretty stupid though."

"She admitted that. Chloé has some medical issues. We argued, cried, comforted one another. It got out of hand." Steve massaged his forehead with thumb and index finger. "As in sexual."

"I see." Jack leaned into the white leather boat upholstery and visibly inhaled. "Status of this?"

"That I'm a damn fool for having a third round of drinks, losing my mind and my wife's trust all in one night." Steve paused. "I kept it inside. Saw no point of ruining things. I love Maren, Jack. Now I'm begging her to forgive me and for us to move forward from this."

"She just found out?"

Steve nodded. "I'd rather not go into those details." More than a cold shoulder had put off Project Baby Kramer. "I truly think we can work through this, only now that we have confirmation, Maren thinks I'll want Pam someday. Can't convince her that ship sailed long ago."

"Catching a glimpse of Pam last December, she's quite the looker."

"She is," Steve agreed. "Add manipulative, controlling, cutting me out of decisions that impact *my* life." Steve wiped drops of perspiration. "Would you put up with that?"

Jack shook his head. "I told Audrey about Dylan and Friday."

Steve's eyes flashed pain. "I lost that fan."

"Not that fast." Jack paused. "Thankfully our daughter does nothing fast or you'd bunk here."

Steve looked to the boat's cabin where he and Maren had first made love. He shut his eyes. Flashed them wide. "Mair's unhappy, but I'm not walking out on a mess I created."

"Then fight for your marriage," Jack advised. "It wasn't always smooth for Audrey and me. We recognized the signs." The revelation riveted Steve. "When Maren was 18 months, we separated. Doubt she remembers. We've never spoken about it. I do grasp vetting details."

"To do no harm," Steve added. "What happened, if you don't mind my asking?"

Jack hesitated. "A six-month affair with my secretary. Appreciate that yours is old enough to be your mother." Too stunned to chuckle, Steve remained silent. "If it would be helpful to hear that marriages do survive—grow from these episodes—Audrey and I could talk to her."

"I'm not asking you to disclose something painful on account of me," Steve said. "I have enough guilt over what I've done."

"I'll talk to Audrey. One time Maren asked about the family photos. I wasn't at her two-year party, and Audrey looked a wreck. Could put some things into context," Jack explained.

When crabbing ended, Steve made arrangements to have his boat hauled out Monday. He felt fortunate to have Jack as his father-in-law, but was ever mindful that if he screwed up again, he would meet more force than the crab trap Jack had hurled to the bottom of the Bay.

Days later, Steve left a message. "Liz: You battened down? I pulled my boat out. Cost a couple hundred, dammit. Checking in. Call me."

After Thursday morning clients, Liz finally got that message. She punched the keypad to delete Steve's concerns. Next message: "Hey, coming to check the boat. Daycare closes early. When's Tyler home? Has a key, right? See ya."

Her own worry percolated. Was Tim getting Hannah? He had no clue Tyler's school cancelled the rest of the week. Of course he didn't have a key, that young. The neighbor had him.

Tim had mentioned the boat as a top priority, before their kids. He'd promised to take care of it yesterday, but would rather spend money on stupid legal motions and nasty-grams. Marinas, busy hauling vessels, wouldn't take his call now.

Liz pocketed her cell, stuffed Tupperware housing her uneaten sandwich into her bag, and checked work messages. The Maloneys cancelled their one o'clock, and her noon client no-showed. With any luck, she'd make it to the house before Tim Irsayed her again, after he had already taken so much. Anything more would mean he pilfered her possessions. Oh, that's right: He's done that, too, Liz thought.

All she wanted was to slip off her shoes, hunker down with Hannah and Tyler, and pray that a tree didn't topple onto the roof. Winds had picked up substantially. Rumor had it that the Bay

Bridge may close if they exceeded 50 mph.

Liz's mind brewed up its own mental storm. Her tires struck home gravel within ten minutes. Pressed by instinct, the remote sent the garage door down. She pushed it again. Tim had parked where Liz normally did. "Ugh." She backed up and pulled in on the opposite side.

Liz slammed the SUV door. She pushed in a drawer left open at the tool chest. Plastic wrap was left strewn on the concrete floor, discarded from fenders Tim probably purchased only today to cushion the boat against the pier. It attached to her shoes. And she was the sloppy one?

"Barbie has a new wind breaker." Hannah thrust the doll at Liz.

"At least someone's ready," she replied, kissing Hannah quickly. "Where's your brother?"

"Helping Daddy. Mommy, guess who is…"

"Hannah, go back inside," Liz interrupted. "Too windy out here."

Liz left her purse and workbag by the door and tore off toward the dock. She crossed her arms over the lightweight sweater she wore. Barbie had better fashion sense today.

Liz came upon the pier. Tyler lay on his stomach, holding the fender to the pylon while Tim pound nails perilously near Tyler's fingers.

"Tyler, where's your life vest?" Liz asked.

"Daddy said it's OK," Tyler grunted as he struggled to hold on. This wasn't work for second graders.

"I'm watching him, Liz," Tim mumbled. He spit nails literally with a silver nail secured between his pursed lips. Tim snatched it and heaved the hammer a few more times.

"You sure as hell aren't. He's barely hanging on." Liz rubbed her arms. Moisture started to settle. "Told you to put those on last summer."

Turning to her son, she said, "Tyler: life jacket. Always."

"Ah, Mom, give it a rest."

"Tyler Phillips!" Liz corrected.

"This'll do." Tim pivoted to fasten one last mooring. "You done nagging? Kids will be with me."

"Oh no, not on weekday nights." Liz stared at Tim. "Your apartment is in a low-lying area. You may definitely have to evacuate." *And you're not coming here.*

"Tyler told me school's closed."

Liz stopped. Tim had just rewritten their agreement. "But…"

"Forget it." Tim shoved past Liz. "Tyler, get your things. We're outta here."

"Just like that. We mediated this," Liz fumed. "You get federal holiday weekends."

"Your lawyer left out the hurricane clause." Tim curled his lips.

"There's no such thing." Liz ignored his haughty tone. "The kids will be safer right here. Where were you going to take them?"

"Last I checked I'm not on your watch." Tim grinned wickedly. "I can clearly take better care of this place. Maybe you're the one who needs an apartment. They can stay with me."

Rain slapped what Liz could have on Tim's face. It started to pelt them both. He took two-foot strides ahead knowing Liz wouldn't catch up in her work shoes. She tried though.

"Where will the kids be?" she shouted. Not that it made a difference. Swaying trees, rustling branches overpowered other sounds. Tim dashed to the garage beyond the soaked hedges.

Liz put up an elbow to shield droplets from her face. Stepping in what at first resembled dog poo but was only mud, she wiped her soles on blades of damp grass. When she looked up, Tim disappeared into the passenger seat of his car. She saw him pull the seat belt harness.

Who drove? Liz strained her neck. Lucena!

That meant Lucena had been here all along… inside. Heavy droplets assaulted her forehead, same as the hand Liz slapped to it. Hadn't Hannah tried to tell her until she foolishly cut her off?

Frazzled by her own impatience, the weather, Tim's nastiness, and determined to catch up to him, Liz quickened her pace until she felt her knee wobble. It met the ground as her ankle gave out. Next thing Liz knew, her bottom hit wet boggy grass, her slacks wearing an appreciable amount of soil. She watched as the taillights vanished from their long gravel driveway.

"Dammit," Liz cursed. Hundreds of yards from her house, she had crawled only a few inches with the wind battering her.

Strong gusts made advancement seem mountainous. The sky grew dark, as predicted. Crying wouldn't get her inside so she planted both palms into the gritty yard and lifted her torso. Few people on the shore had manicured lawns. Most, like theirs, was a mixture of soil, tufts of grass, moss, now sticks and leaves leveled by the gale. Walking backwards on her hands netted her a nicked finger and dirt under her nails.

Her pocket vibrated. Liz had silenced her cell phone at work. She dug it out and heaved relief.

"You answered," Paul said. "Was hoping I'd catch you. Do they ever close the bridge?"

"Not since we've lived here, but I'm not the transportation authority," Liz replied. She pulled her sweater tighter to crawl while she held the phone. "Why? It's nasty outside."

"Patients cancelled. Dog walker called off. Thought about you." Paul pressed the phone to his ear. "Liz, what's that noise?"

"The wind, silly. Right now, I'm outside trying not to land in dog shit, thank you very much. I lost my footing in the grass so I'm crawling my way back inside. Slowly."

"Dio mio! Are the kids inside the house?"

"No. Long story: Tim was here to secure the boat, must have had what's-her-name in *my* house. I'm so angry," Liz fumed, voice croaking from welled-up emotion. "His usual nasty self piled the kids into his car. He wouldn't tell me where they were going. I tried to catch up and fell on my butt. Came down on my ankle."

Liz heard Paul curse in Italian. She made a mental note to add another word to her own vocabulary. "You're alone…injured…outside…with Isabel on the loose?"

"Told you your mother hates me." Liz looked down at her filthy hands. "Neighbors Brenda and Chuck didn't evacuate either. I see lights. Number's in my phone; I think I have it memorized."

"Give it to me." Paul readied a pen to scrawl the digits. After he repeated them back to Liz, he directed her, "Don't bear weight until I look at that ankle. I'll call next door. We're on our way."

"Paul, you don't need to risk coming…" Liz stopped. The connection had gone dead.

In five minutes she had inched possibly five feet. Twenty yards to go; minus a foot by the time Chuck and Brenda came running through the rain.

"You poor thing," Brenda said as they found her. Chuck pulled Liz up, and with their help on each side, Liz hopped the rest of the way on her good leg. She ached all over but made it.

Brenda called Tim a son-of-a-bitch once they were safely in the garage. Chuck handed Liz rags to wipe off mud. The bedrooms were at ground level just inside the one door. Brenda stayed long enough to help Liz get into and out of the shower, which had a bench thankfully.

"With this I'll be OK for a while," Liz said as the plush robe that covered her hit the seat of an office chair on casters. Brenda retrieved it in lieu of crutches. She found ibuprofen in the medicine cabinet. Liz downed two with a glass of water.

Brenda turned to the door knocking. "Chuck must have found the crutches he used after his knee surgery." Brenda went to Liz's garage, opened the door, and took possession of them.

"Thanks Chuck." Liz's voice travelled the hallway as she scooted her good foot in the chair.

Chuck poked his head inside. Smiled having caught a glimpse of Liz in a plush white bathrobe, towel still banded around her neck from tousling her hair.

"You're both a godsend. What would I do without good neighbors?"

"Life's always interesting over here," Chuck razzed. "That friend of yours, the one with the dogs, he's on his way." Chuck arched a perfect eyebrow. Liz saw him moisten his lips and was glad Brenda had turned away. A blush rose on Liz's cheeks.

"Unless the bridge closes," Brenda added. "First time in history."

"Made landfall in North Carolina. Virginia Beach getting a lickin'," Chuck said. "Weather Channel reports it's accelerating up the coast."

"Must be bad then." Liz glided a hand over still damp hair. Reached for the towel. "Listen, thanks so much. I don't want to keep you."

"You call us, if you need us," Brenda said.

"I doubt they will." Chuck notched his lips into a smile. He waved a hand in the air. "I better put this garage door down out here."

"Paul has a remote. Thanks for rescuing me." Liz heard them run for it and the door thud.

She finger fluffed her short hair and scooted the chair over to the clock that read 3:07.

Someone had placed her purse and workbag in the hallway. Brenda? Lucena?

Liz rummaged through her wallet. Could have sworn she had a twenty, a ten and two fives, yet the larger bills were missing. Lucena no doubt.

Nothing she could do about it now. Liz spied the sandwich container. A flight of stairs didn't seem so easy after all. She settled for turkey and cheese, holding the bread with one hand so that she could press the remote for a weather update.

Liz felt her heart, not her sandwich, drop farther into her stomach. The Maryland Transportation Authority had closed the Bay Bridge at approximately 3 PM. Had Paul made it over in time?

The few bites weighed like a brick. Tea might calm her jagged nerves. Liz grabbed the crutches and scooted her chariot to the edge of the steps. Hoisting herself out of the chair she attempted to climb, crutches doing the work. When the edge of one missed the next step, Liz tumbled.

"Ouch." Her head landed on the carpeted steps. What else could make this day any more miserable? Liz would have cried again but for the jolt she heard in the garage a few minutes later.

When the door opened, damp fur shook. Franco careened into her. Bruno sniffed her out. To think wet dog smelled heavenly?

Paul set that black and gold duffle—suddenly not ugly—inside the doorway and jostled a bag of groceries with his knee. "Whoa boys," he said. "I just let them out. It's wicked out there."

Still wearing pressed slacks and a button-down shirt, Paul looked better than an angel at the gates of heaven. Bruno nudged under Liz's robe. Paul leached a jealous pang before he shuddered. "Did they knock you down?"

"No, I've developed a talent for it today." Liz pouted. "I almost fell on my face going for tea."

"I'll get that." Paul slid by with groceries. He deposited them in the kitchen, but returned fast.

Paul slung the arm Liz extended around his neck and picked her up. "Your make-shift wheelchair?" He set her into the office chair.

"I had to improvise." Liz bit her lip. "I'm so glad you're here. I'm worried sick about the kids. Tim's an ass, more interested in his boat or that bimbo. Hannah will freak out in this storm."

Paul maneuvered Liz into her room. "I'm going to look at that ankle, and you're going to relax," he said, helping her up so that she could stretch out on the bed.

He touched her puffy ankle. "Inverted fall."

"Yes, ouch," Liz replied. "I took an anti-inflammatory, but it still hurts and it's hot."

Paul trailed a hand up her leg to her knee. "Not nearly as hot as the rest of you."

Blood flow should have found its way to her knee as Paul's fingers examined it. It landed much higher, with a huge force of need and desire that tingled everything up to her navel.

He ran his hand along her Achilles back to the site. "It's not broken but a ligament sprain likely. Do you have an Ace wrap and ice bag?"

"Under the counter in my bathroom." Liz tossed her head deeper into the pillows. She was so thankful he had made it across the Bay.

"You're in luck," he said, returning. He deposited the wrap on her nightstand. "We're going to ice this first. You still want tea?"

"Actually, can the doctor order wine and cheese?" Liz smiled. "I need to chill."

Paul sat beside her and stroked a hand along her face, soft and slow. "Not even that howling wind will penetrate the heat you put off." He kissed her lips lightly. "I'll have to monitor you." His hand found the double-looped tie on her robe. Fingered it. "Through the night." He brushed her lips again. "Just to make sure."

"I have cannoli from weeks ago," Liz whispered. "Frozen though."

"I've got delicious and fresh right here," Paul murmured back, nuzzling her neck. "They can come to room temp while I take you hot."

Liz pushed on his thigh. "It's throbbing."

"Sure as hell is." Paul took the not-so-subtle hint. Placed a pillow under her foot. "Stay that way. I want the pleasure of untying that knot."

Her belly clutched just watching him leave. Shouldn't it be illegal to look that good? But it was time, Liz thought. Time to feel something other than frustration. Time to toss discretion out with the howling wind, for one night, where she would otherwise be lonely and worry.

Liz reached into her nightstand, feeling for a small pack of matches hidden in the back. Magically, she found them and struck one to light the candle on the bed table nearest her. Switching the lamp off, she scooted across the bed to strike a match and light the other candle.

She tossed most of the blankets aside and nuzzled only her feet under them.

Paul returned with a small tray bearing cheese, some crackers, two glasses and a bottle of wine plus the needed ice pack. Bruno and

Franco followed him and positioned themselves on the floor, eyeing the provisions.

"Power must have gone out," Paul joked, having just shut off the lights in the hallway.

"Must have." She winked. When she felt the chill rush into her bones, Liz winced. "Really?"

"Twenty minutes on." Paul poured the wine, handed her a glass. "Then 30 off...all off," he said, fingering her robe. "Or 35, 40...whatever it takes." He took a sip out of his glass, emitted a delightful sigh, and set it on the nightstand.

Paul unlaced his shoes, pulled off socks, and wriggled out of his slacks. He left the rest for Liz. She toyed with his shirt, unbuttoning it. Liz splayed the fabric and slid her hands along his gym-toned muscles. "You've been working out."

Their mouths met and clung before he answered. "Not like the workout I'm about to get."

He pressed his body into Liz. "I love the way the light flickers off you. I thought you were gorgeous the first time I ever saw your face." Paul thumbed her cheek. "No, you've never been more beautiful than you are right now."

Liz tugged on Paul's shirt. Her hands found a waistband, covering further unexplored territory. "Fifteen minutes and counting."

Liz reached for another sip of wine and tilted her glass for Paul to enjoy some also. The candles flickered, sending glimmers along the wall. As she returned the glass to the tray, on the table next to her, it touched something. Liz lifted the napkin uncovering three, square packets.

"Told you I went back on the Pill." Liz granted Paul the sexy version of a Kramer-woman look. "Three of these?"

"For starters." Paul's lips curled with amusement. "I plan to do so many things to you tonight bella, but you know..." Her sexy look fizzled. "Even the Pill can fail," he finished. "Not chancing my luck any more this year."

Liz put a finger on his lips that she grazed then caressed, sending a delicious current that melded them together.

She arched her back, appreciating deft fingers that massaged her skin under her robe. She ached all right. One extremity had started to numb. The other went weak. Not from pain, but from pure, unbridled pleasure. Paul's hands roamed, finding her breasts. He cupped them, taunted them with his thumbs.

The knot was so his now, to unravel, push open, or toss aside. He traced her nipples with a wine-drenched finger. Tasted, taking his time. He trailed lower along that invisible line that made its way to where it mattered.

His first touch forced her skin to flush, her breath to hitch. Paul stroked. Teased by nuzzling his nose and cast a long stare into her eyes as his hand idled lower.

"Please…" Her breath hitched. Heat pooled inside of her.

Paul inhaled her hair. Lavender never smelled so sensual. After trailing feather-light kisses down her body, he made slow, deliberate circles. His mouth met with hers greedily, ravenous as his tongue taunted her teeth and plunged deep.

Liz crooned. Paul admired what he held in his hands. Felt Liz's trembled breath. Listened to her urgent demand: "Don't stop. It feels so good."

"Lie back. You're to rest, remember," he settled into her ear. Nuzzled her neck. Seized a nipple again. Teased her belly button.

Caught in her own web of pleasure, Liz felt nothing…and everything. It was a slow, deliberate climb. An ache that spread through every inch of her that had never been explored. All him. All her.

When Liz's pleasure tipped toward explosion, she cried out. Tightened and tore the sheets away. She couldn't breathe, until she moaned out a satisfying sigh.

Paul eased his grip on Liz, and his hands worked their way to her waist. He burrowed his face back into her neck. "How many thousand did I find?" His eyes lit with confidence.

Lying still, sated by amazing pleasure, Liz slowly focused. Her hands began their own wild journey of caressing him. "What?"

"Nerve endings." He chuckled warm breath onto her neck. "Six, seven thousand out of eight?"

Liz lost it in a cascade of chuckles and rolled over Paul. "My ice pack landed in another county. How's that?"

She kneeled on the bed to give him the full force of illumination flickering off her body.

"Christ, he was a fool to leave you," Paul uttered. His mouth overtook Liz's, and when they came up for air, he added, "But thank God, because you're all mine tonight."

"If that's the case," Liz replied, reaching to the nightstand, "then you've got another few thousand give or take to discover yet."

Never removing eyes from him, she ripped a packet, unrolled it, and built his arousal. It grew more urgent as skin met skin. Want met need.

Tempestuous winds tore up outside while another gale force raged inside. Thrashing with passion that had been pent up, now unleashed after months, call it years, of longing. Unhurried. Possessive.

When they found that pinnacle together, the waves of what they created made Liz forget where she was until Paul lost that last bit of control, falling limp with her nestled around him.

A hand brushed against skin. A breath created even more warmth. A name landed from whispers into one ear. Whatever was hers became his in one glorious blur.

"How did you get this damn sexy?" he asked, draping his arm cozily around Liz and spooning as they sought refuge through the night.

When Franco decided he needed to go out hours later, Paul booted Bruno through the door without a vote. Liz stirred. Paul slipped back in bed, and looked at how the pups plopped down.

"I think they're jealous, Liz," he quipped.

"The stories they could tell," Liz finished. "How'd you dry them off so quick? I can hear the downpour out there."

"A man can do anything fast when the payoff awaits him, Liz."

Paul reached for his abandoned wine, downing its contents. He went next for the silky, sizzling warm body next to him. "Round two?"

By daylight, the line between water and land seemed difficult to distinguish. Much of the shore had flooded, along with parts of Baltimore and Washington suburbs. Only the head on the Alex Haley statue in Annapolis managed to stay dry. Water submerged several areas that had been given evacuation orders.

Some homes had been swallowed into the sea. Tree limbs collapsed causing power outages for more than a million residents. Paul opened the shades. The little bit of light left Liz squinting.

"What time is it?" she yawned, glancing at her nightstand. "Power flickered but we still have it."

"Satisfied in sleep." Paul brushed a bit of beard over her for a morning kiss.

He sat, showered and dressed already. "Time for you to retrieve messages." He handed over her cell that flashed 8:05 AM. "It's blown up the last half hour with them."

Liz shot up in bed. Looked out to the water.

"I see two boats—we only own one—and no dock. Holy cripe!"

She punched into her voice mail. Hearing one message begin, she hit speaker. Backed it up: "Mommy, there's water *everywhere*. Tyler went swimming in it. Daddy went to find him."

Panic coursed through Liz much like acid revisits after a bad meal.

Second message: "Liz, how are you? Call us…Maren."

Third message: "Lucena just yelled at me. I *hate* her. Can I come home?"

Fourth message: "Liz, Tim. Disregard Hannah's message. I told her Tyler would be OK. How's my boat? Check on it and call me."

Liz hit call back. "Tim: What's going on with Tyler?" she asked. Listened. "Your boat's still in the water." *Where else would it be?*

"Yes, Tim. Surrounded. Hannah said Tyler went swimming in floodwater. Did he?"

"Stupidly," Tim replied. "I'm taking those games of his away until Christmas 2013. Ten years, I tell ya. Fire and rescue got him. Clothes stunk up this entire hotel. We had to evacuate."

Dah! With so much to process, Liz aimed her attention at the details. She repeated many for Paul's benefit, partly to keep from going off on Tim as she said back questions Paul mouthed.

"Any injuries? Did he ingest the water? Get totally washed off? There could have been bacteria, all kinds of filth."

"Jeez Liz, I'm no Doug Ross on *ER*. You sound like Steve."

Close enough, Liz thought. "Tim, do you have any idea the health risks he was exposed to? Where are you? Where are Tyler and Hannah right now?"

"With me. Bridge just reopened. We're going to Baltimore City. They got hit, but not as bad.

"But Tim, it's important to…"

"Lectures by Liz, Segment: Twelve hundred and four. They're fine. I'll see you Monday. Maybe." Tim clicked off the call.

Paul muttered out loud. Took Liz into his embrace.

She breathed deeply. Could have passed an Italian exam, if insults counted as vocabulary.

Her bare shoulders, chilled by Tim's callousness, felt warm next to Paul. "The nerve of him."

"He left you injured; acts this way about Tyler. Doesn't grant any details. Where is his head?"

"That's how he maintains his passive-aggressive control. Limit the information to throw me off," Liz said. "My life's a mess as well as my yard, but my ankle feels better. Can I walk on it?"

Paul took a look since she thrust a leg out from the covers.

"To get into the bathroom," he answered. "A warm bath with Epsom salts will help the rest of the swelling." He flicked the remote several stations. Isabel's aftermath was everywhere, but they settled on their local WBOC-TV, on the Eastern Shore.

"Once you get in the tub, the boys and I will take a little walk outside to assess any damage."

"You're too good to me," Liz replied. She squeezed his hand.

They listened more. One news report talked about power outages, safety tips, and warned to watch out for looting after the huge storm.

"Why would people do that?" Liz frowned. She looked at the clock again and started to get up. "Don't you have to get back over the bridge for work?"

"I checked messages, too." He held his phone. "Your brother cancelled all elective procedures."

Amid the chaos, Liz smiled.

"You're stuck with me. For the weekend," Paul announced. "You know what else?"

"I'm afraid to ask?"

"Bruno's loud bark just found a new home. No one will bother you with him." Paul patted Bruno, wagging his tail. "Consider it an all-expenses paid-by-me vacation for him. A kind of permanent loan until he wears out his welcome."

"He won't," Liz said softly. "And neither will you."

Chapter 17

Maren had confided to Liz the full extent of her marital woes when they had taken in art exhibits at November's Waterfowl Festival, in Easton. Today, a week before Thanksgiving, they met for a late lunch over Chinese. More for a bitch session confined to their corner booth.

"How's the clean up coming?" Maren asked Liz, now nearly two months after the hurricane. "Steve refused to re-launch his boat. I guess he really thought I would sink it."

"Given his actions, would serve him right." Liz speared her sweet and sour pork. "Tim's convinced I did something to partially sink ours. Meanwhile, our son ran off. Tim lapsed paying our mortgage, and I'm hearing about the boat." She ran a shaky hand through her short hair. "Talk about messed up priorities."

"Tyler's all right. That's what really matters," Maren said. "When did the boat take on water?"

"The morning after Isabel, a boat rammed ours." Liz sipped tea. Among many topics oolong helped to soothe. "In his mind, that was my fault. It was insured…more funds to divvy up."

"With a sprained ankle, how did Tim expect you to handle a damaged propeller and hull, too?"

"No one in his right mind would have attempted boat salvage," Liz answered. "This was four times the two feet of flood water Tyler was in. As the tide went out, we noticed problems."

Isabel's record-breaking storm surge slammed parts of Maryland at high tide wiping out piers, closing businesses. Authorities estimated cleanup would cost millions of dollars across the state.

"Seriously, given a littered yard, downed branches, and the boat… we're still fairly lucky," Liz said. "Trying to see the positives."

"Speaking of upbeat. Glad Tyler's birthday worked out better." Maren's grin acknowledged that it made up for the disappointment Liz felt over Hannah's party. "Tyler seemed happy at the aquarium, but Paul didn't join us. What's up with that?" Maren's face washed with humor. "Won't step foot in Baltimore?"

Liz stopped short of smiling back.

"Ask Dr. Undecided." She leaned across her plate. "He had an emergency at the hospital, but get this…he asked for an extension in

Pittsburgh, and they gave it to him." She tossed her napkin on top of Maren's magazine on the doublewide table. "Do you believe it?"

"Frustrating, but nothing shocks me anymore." Maren's earlier happiness faded. "You and Tim would have had an anniversary, right?" She considered. "Yep, Steve watched the kids last year."

Liz nodded. "Explains my funk. Anniversary reaction. Literally."

"Dah! Explains mine, too," Maren admitted. "My anniversary with Mark would be November 29th. Last year was so different. My parents met yours, on Thanksgiving. We were so happy then."

"Steve gets second place for Dim Wit of 2003. Sorry, you can imagine who gets first place." Liz regarded Maren. "But I interrupted."

Maren leaned back. "After my parents got back from Florida, my mother stayed with Dylan after school. She saw that I dumped Steve's things into an angry mess in the guest room."

"I so know," Liz replied. "But go on..."

"One night, Steve took Dylan to watch him play racquetball with Paul. He's never done that before. My parents invited just me to have dinner." Maren looked out the window. "They told me something upsetting." Her gaze shifted to Liz. "When I was maybe... not even two years old... my father cheated on my mother. He'd been having an affair for six months, actually moved out." Maren snapped her mouth shut into stony silence before adding, "Imagine that!"

"Obviously they kept it from you since they reconciled," Liz replied. "Why divulge it now?"

"My mulling whether to toss your brother's butt out." Maren criss-crossed her arms. "If I could keep you as a sister-in-law but dump him."

"Marry the family, get the husband." Liz laughed. "What do you make of the revelation?"

"Right now, I'm disillusioned with both adult males in my life. The two biggest role models for Dylan." Maren downed the remaining tea in her cup. "When Dylan catches me crying, all I say is how disappointed I am with Steve or Grampy, but he knows it's more. He has to."

"Kids are perceptive. Don't I know!"

"Yeah, when you're seven, and you're a worrier, it gets worse," Maren admitted. "Dylan hid a huge LEGO set under his bed and all of his Muppets. Said he's afraid I'll throw his stuff away when he disappoints me. Not if, but when."

Their waitress stopped by with a black tray, containing their check and two fortune cookies.

"I've got this Liz." Maren grabbed the bill and pushed the tray with the cookies at Liz.

"Thanks. Every spare penny goes to saving my inheritance that I think is now considered marital property. Money I socked into a joint asset." Liz eyeballed the ceiling and let her gaze fall again. "Steve told you I had to shell out another retainer for my new lawyer, his friend?"

"He did," Maren replied. "I yelled at Steve when he spoke to a lawyer before I found out it was for you." Maren slid her magazine toward Liz. "I'm so done with that. Check out page 48."

Liz picked up the glossy women's magazine and thumbed to a page. *"Too Personal & Private to Pose.* Is that what you want me to see?"

"Catch the byline."

Slanting her eyes down the page, Liz gasped. "You've got to be kidding!"

"Rich, huh?"

Liz tried to read two things at once: Maren's face and the advice column by Dr. Pamela Morgan, expert in women's health and sexuality.

"This is good." Liz voiced out loud. "Health benefits to having a loving, active sex life."

Two Kramer women, only one look ping ponged from one side of the table to the other.

"Have you totally…I mean, ah cut Steve off?" Liz scrunched her lip, a tad embarrassed now to have asked. "Sorry, it's not my business."

"That's all right. Our sex life sucks," Maren admitted. "That's a good word, after all."

Liz chuckled. "You're newlyweds, but given what happened…"

Maren nodded. "Steve's left me notes, sent flowers to work, pulls me in against him at night." She frowned. "I've given in a few times, ending up in tears. Thought about *her* with *him* the entire time, and now, I can't even pick up a magazine for escape. I see *her* advice!"

"For as smart as Pam is, she's no expert…far from a saint," Liz said. "Though Paul's mother canonizes her. Pam can't cook worth crap. I at least bake. You think Isabella Romano likes me?"

"She just has to get to know you."

"Everyone tells me that." Liz rolled her eyes.

"Sorry. You could have Mildred Mitchell. At least I haven't heard from them in a while." Maren knuckled the wooden table. "Back to… the columnist. Will these reminders ever stop?"

"Did your parents give you any good advice?" Liz asked. "Since they survived infidelity."

"They said there's no real timetable for this stuff. Marriages can grow from it." Maren sighed again. "My mom said the hurt is bound to linger. Well of course, Steve just wants me to be over it and go back to the way it was before. I don't know how to do that."

Maren didn't disclose to Liz that Pam's daughter had turned ten last month. No one outside of Paul, Jack and Audrey knew about Chloé. Not yet. Steve felt strongly that they should send a small birthday gift, as a family. A sweater was supposed to start a relationship with a daughter he never knew he had?

"You know what we need?" Liz announced. "A girl's night. Tim has the kids for Thanksgiving weekend. No more anniversary reactions. Why don't you—just you—come out to the shore and spend the week-end with me? We'll go to St. Michaels and take Bruno if he behaves. It's a dog-friendly town." Liz took her last sip of oolong. "And, we'll bake Christmas cookies."

"Sounds good," Maren managed. "Warning: I'm no elf this year. I don't have to tell you that women make holidays happen. *Always*." The tea didn't foster the same calm for Maren. "I'm not into it. Steve can put up his own big, fat tree, make himself cookies and stuff his face."

"That's the spirit!" Liz laughed. "We make 'em, we take 'em."

"You're right. We'll stuff our faces."

"And open a bottle of wine. We deserve it."

At West Riverside, Liz headed straight to social work where she clocked a few hours doing casework. Maren had a brochure mock-up to complete. Before she left she had to obtain signatures in the executive offices, on the top floor. On her way out of them, she spotted Paul.

"What are you doing up here?" Maren asked.

"You remember that check, the one I procrastinated on depositing?" Paul replied. "I have a meeting about how to best spend the funds. Plus all the contributions, in Vicki's memory."

"Ah, Paul." Maren reached out, clutched his wrist. "What are you leaning toward?"

"Write this moment down." He laughed. "I decided to split it, between maternal health and pediatrics. It's in Carina's memory, too."

"Beautiful!" Maren pressed her clipboard into Paul while hugging him, but the impalement didn't faze him. "I'll let you go…good luck."

"Thanks." Paul walked backward a few paces to the executive offices. "I *can* make decisions."

Maren had one more signature to secure, but a secretary could obtain this one. Stepping off on the second floor, she walked to an office, to Suzanna's desk, but didn't find her.

She looked at the wall clock. It was 4:35. Suzanna wouldn't have left yet, would she?

Maren rested her rump on the desk, nervously clutching the clipboard in front of her. Just to get it over with, she knocked on Steve's door herself. No answer there, either.

Hearing voices approach, Maren took a seat in the chairs across from the desk. Only it didn't sound like Suzanna down the hallway.

"You never had a problem with me observing one of your surgeries before," the woman said.

"Well, I do now." Steve's tone was curt.

"Our new product is amazing. I left you information months ago, and again last week," the woman asserted. They walked closer, Maren could tell. "Why won't you return my calls?"

"How many times must I tell you: I don't need your new product. Period." Steve had stopped right around the corner. Maren craned her neck but couldn't quite make out the woman.

"No, you need my product," she continued. "You just don't want *me* selling it. But rumor has it married life isn't all it's cracked up to be. Maybe what you *need* and what you *want* are two very, very different things." Silence filled a 10-second gap.

"I need no surgical products, no sales pitches. I need to call the 800 number to fix my computer," Steve said. "I doubt you moonlight as an Apple technician. So if you don't mind..."

When Steve rounded and saw Maren there, he stopped cold at mid-sentence. Maren caught sight of Steve's scrubs, figuring he had just finished surgery. Then her eyes landed on the high heeled, knee high boots. Long hair, all dark and silky. Painted nails. Maren had seen this woman before.

"Mair, I didn't realize you were here." In a nanosecond, Steve approached her.

Maren extended the clipboard. "I need your approval. Suzanna's not here, so I waited."

"Glad you did." Steve scrawled his signature, suddenly oblivious to the woman who trailed him the corridor. "You may know: My laptop freezes. You helped me before." He smiled.

Observing the scene, still refusing to give many inches lest her husband think he was off the bad-behavior hook, Maren leaned against Suzanna's desk. "One of us has to get back to marketing. You'll have to figure it out, Dr. Kramer. Or call the IT department."

"But it's my *personal* laptop," Steve added.

"I just got a Mac," the sales rep said. "I'll be happy to take a look at it, *Steve*."

Completely flummoxed, the chief of surgery turned pink. He stammered, "Samantha, I…"

"You're Samantha," Maren interrupted. A smoldering blaze flashed through her eyes.

She remembered now. A year ago, she had seen Samantha, the ex-girlfriend sidling up to Steve. It had been pathetic then, more so now.

"I am." The woman stood straight, jut her chest out, and extended her hand. "And you are?"

Maren wrist-checked the time on her watch. "Mrs. Kramer…and actually, I don't think your services are needed."

Steve stood back, mildly amused, but very cautious. "Paul's office is…over there." Steve pointed a finger across the way.

"Paul's in a meeting upstairs," Maren said. "A very important one. With all due respect to your saleswoman here, he has no time either." Maren turned to Steve. "Now then, you needed me?"

Steve's nod dismissed Samantha, who summarily swiveled in her boots and left. He hid a chuckle, steered Maren through his office door that he quickly closed behind them. "I always need you, *Mrs.* Kramer." Steve brushed his lips against hers. He rested a hand on her waist.

"Let's keep this professional." Maren went straight to Steve's desk where she found the ailing MacBook. She took over his commanding office chair. "Don't get any ideas either."

Thanksgiving: Another first where planned distractions mitigated the impact on Paul. First Easter, then Vicki's birthday, July 4th, their anniversary, his birthday on December 2. Christmas and New Year's. One year of grieving firsts.

Dolores and Bill Kramer followed tradition, hosting a huge feast at their bayside home in Southern Maryland, which they had renovated to full functionality for retirement. The master bedroom was level with living areas on the second floor. Bill and Dolores had appreciated Liz's layout so much that their contractor gave them space and windows, overlooking the Chesapeake Bay. Maren brought whipped sweet potatoes, Audrey added green beans, and Shelly homemade cranberries. Liz always made desserts.

Steve—and this year Paul—helped with the meal. The three young kids picked the bacon from Steve's brussels sprouts. Cruciferous vegetables, Steve declared, were potent anti-carcinogens. They would all live to be 100, Eric teased, with the amount his brother made.

Steve and Paul gave Dolores a break after the meal, drafting Eric to help with clean up.

"What's with you today?" Steve asked his brother. "It's as if you're somewhere else."

"Chillaxin that's all." Eric grabbed a dishtowel, swatted Steve with it. "I crashed on midterms. Semester grades suck." Eric eyeballed their mom and dad. "Afraid they'll find out."

Paul stood back. Quiet. Did Steve know the extent of his younger brother's extra-curricular activities?

"Apparently you're not chillin' with Shelly," Steve continued. "She's giving you the evil eye."

"How can I when she's always in Philly with that niece of hers?" Eric's tone grew edgy.

That niece, Paul knew, was also Eric's, and not by virtue of dating Shelly Morgan.

"Hold on," Steve said. "You help with Hannah and Tyler. Don't talk about Chloé that way."

"Sor-ree." Eric straightened at being corrected. He turned to Paul. "Did you say something?"

"Not me," Paul replied. "But now you have."

Eric dropped his towel on the counter and made the door thud when he stormed through it.

Steve looked at Paul, who remained silent. Shelly walked over from the family room.

"What's with him?" she asked. "Does he seem high to either of you?" She hushed the question.

"Whoa." Steve tugged Shelly to a corner of the kitchen. Paul stood close by. "I never said anything in January." Steve turned to Paul and explained. "Loaned them my apartment last Christmas and found a joint. Is this more than occasional use?"

"He gets high several times a week. Most of the times we're…ah, together." A pink flush invaded the fair skin of Shelly's cheekbones. "Enough to make it the subject of her next month's column in *Too*

Personal & Private to Pose." Shelly scowled. "I never should have asked Dr. Pam for her opinion."

"What?" Steve asked.

"My sister's advice column. Runs in a national women's magazine," Shelly informed. "She's their women's health and sex expert."

Shelly granted Steve a moment. Paul smirked.

"Digesting that will take longer than this meal, Shelly." Steve drew in a heavy breath. Turned to Paul. "Did you know about this?"

"Pam's sexpertise or Eric's smoking weed?"

"My brother! First things first," Steve spit out, annoyed by each, unable to focus on but one.

"Caught him smoking a joint outside your wedding reception." Paul shrugged. Eric had already blown his own cover. "Supposedly offered by a band member."

"It's not just when it's offered." Shelly hushed her voice to them. "He buys it, resold it to a buddy. He wasn't like this when we started dating."

"Sells it?" Steve sealed his eyes for a second. "Otherwise, he treats you all right?"

"If you call blowing off dates, complaining and not caring about anything, then yes," Shelly replied. "I'm just fed up. I need a break from this...from him."

"When was his last physical?" Paul put out there. "Labs, all that?"

Shelly wiggled up her shoulders.

"How would I know?" Steve turned the topic with no apology. "How's Chloé doing?"

"She has her moments...sees a pediatric neuropsychologist for behavioral regulation. You knew about her TBI, right?"

"Yes," Steve admitted. "How severe is it?"

"Moderate. Hopefully short term with the treatment she's getting, but it's hard to see her struggle with school. She tires easily."

Paul understood the inquiries. Shelly provided a quick link to Chloé. "Your degree program gave you experience with special-needs kids, didn't it?" he asked.

"Yeah, I did a placement in an elementary school," Shelly admitted. "Chloé gets preferential seating, accommodations in her school for having a short attention span. Her social skills are a little off these days," Shelly shared. "But she loved the sweater you and Maren sent.

You guys met her last year, right?" Shelly's smiled faded fast. "And in the hospital, I guess."

"We rode rides at Disney." Steve immediately busied himself drying dishes. A roasting pan hid eye contact that might convey how much he actually ruminated about Shelly's niece. His daughter.

"Looks like you're getting ready to leave, Shelly?" Paul covered, catching on.

"I am," she answered. "I'll go say good-bye to Dolores and Bill. Find Mr. Moody."

Paul waited until the air cleared and Shelly disappeared. "She doesn't have a clue, does she?"

"No." Steve refocused. "So that's what this column is about? Sex!" Steve rolled his eyes.

"Apparently." Paul thought a moment. "You get royalties with that?"

"Smart ass." Steve's elbow poked him.

"That's my cue to catch up on the NFL." Paul joined the rest of his adopted family that day. Steve left his mother's kitchen sparkling.

Maren had driven to the shore mid-Saturday, straight from planting flowers on Mark's grave for what would have been an anniversary. "I thought maybe I'd forget," she told Liz after dinner. "Not this year."

"I totally get that." Empathy filled Liz's reply.

"Didn't you tell me that Tim drops the kids off unexpectedly?" Maren asked. "Think he'll park them here tonight?"

"I told Tim I was staying at your house, purposely." Liz cupped a hand over her mouth. "Steve might get a surprise knock on the door. What's he up to tonight?"

"He's jealous I'm here, but doing a great Mr. Mom impersonation," Maren shared. "I mean… he genuinely loves Dylan. Don't get me wrong. They're spending *guy time*."

"Speaking of guys," Liz said. She threw her head back from her perch on the family room sofa, spotting Paul in the kitchen. "What kind of wine does the maître d' recommend?"

"That's why she kept me here, Maren." Paul approached. "Dinner and wine service."

Paul had offered Liz a lot more than wine, spending two nights. They continued to keep their love life quiet, but Maren was a trusted friend. She had advocated their coupling from the start, and since

September, Steve realized how their support of one another had blossomed.

Paul approached with a bottle of Moscato and two wine glasses. "Tending two beautiful women. *Such* work!" He poured them each a glass. "Franco and I need to get going soon. Looks as if Bruno has settled into his new home."

"Bruno loves it here," Liz said. "Envious?"

Paul brushed her forehead with his lips. Patted Bruno, who snuggled his head on Liz's lap. "Completely!" he agreed. "You ladies behave. Bruno's in charge."

"Bye Paul. Thanks for dinner," Maren said.

He left them alone to gossip and watch *Stella Got Her Groove Back.* The DVD sat on the coffee table next to Hannah's *Hello Kitty* stickers. Bruno leapt off the sofa. His snout pushed open the blinds and he put forth a pitiful whimper as his fur brother Franco jumped into Paul's Corvette, back in service with only one dog to haul.

Maren crunched on an Italian cookie. "When did you make these?"

"I made the pignoli cookies yesterday…did the amaretto ones this morning." Liz grabbed a rum ball off the plate. "Thanks to baking the bar's stocked too. Courtesy Paul. Since his mother's visiting, he wants a traditional Italian Christmas this year."

"Hence the two large tins," Maren noticed. "Better drink more than we eat." She considered Liz. "We're bad…but we deserve it."

"We do." Liz shifted her legs. Bruno hopped back up with her and settled on Liz's blanket. "Since Paul's gone, tell me about Gabe. He actually made a pass at you?"

"You heard," Maren managed. She covered her face with the blanket that had warmed her. "Awkward. I'm sorry."

"Don't be," Liz replied. "I'm done with him. Not that he's all bad. There just wasn't that spark with him. Apparently a few flew when Steve spotted you."

"I had extra time that day. All I wanted was some yoga to relax," Maren admitted. "Gabe knew I'd left the office. Tracked me down. He's been…extra friendly, let's say."

"I'd call kissing extra friendly." Liz laughed. "Bet my brother flipped. What's Gabe's MO?"

"Gabe never realized that Mark had passed away until last fall when Alicia hired him and we crossed paths again." Maren stopped. "You know Samantha, that bar chick *last* year?"

"The ex in leather and high heels?" Liz scowled. "Looked like a dominatrix only missing her chains and cuffs." Liz's chin shuddered sideways. "No wonder he never brought *her* home."

Maren winced. "Her," she confirmed in a huff. "Dominatrix still calls on Steve...and Paul."

"Does she know Paul's single?" Liz asked.

"Probably. Everyone does." Maren shifted her weight into the blanket. "Shoe therapy has lost all appeal after spotting *her* near Steve."

"I'll bet." Liz pondered. "We'll do Nordstrom's. Exposure therapy, with shoes."

Maren crinkled her bottom lip. "Sounds like a plan...and like the door just opened again."

"It does." Liz startled. "Don't tell me Tim..."

When a gold tail fanned across the family room, they knew it wasn't Tim.

"I'm back," Paul announced. "Tire's flat. My spare doesn't look so healthy either."

"Well," Liz smiled. "I guess you're stuck with us. You can call a garage in the morning."

"Good wine, Paul. Join us."

"No offense, ladies, but I'll leave you to the Moscato." Paul snitched a cookie and walked back to the fridge. "I'll grab a beer and read a journal. Just pretend I'm not here."

Maren waited until she heard no more feet slapping the hardwood floor. Paul had gone downstairs. "Looks like you'll have company in your room tonight, since I'm in the guest room."

"If the kids are around, he stays up there...but it's nice." Liz blushed. "Back to Gabe."

"Gabe told me he would have wanted a chance with me." Maren leveled her eyes at Liz. "If Steve knew that, he'd definitely want to re-arrange Gabe's skeletal system."

"Paul said Steve almost did. I've seen his temper a time or two." Liz bit her lip. "So what did you tell Gabe?"

"What could I say?" Maren poured more wine. Got up, poured more for Liz and hit play on the DVD remote. "I might have dated Gabe, but I'm hitched now. Maybe Stella will give us answers."

They both laughed and snuggled under two respective blankets while the dogs kept watchful eyes on the remaining cookie plate.

Downstairs, Paul stretched on Liz's bed, his journal in both hands until he heard his *Godfather* ringtone. "Hey," he answered. "Racquetball's off tomorrow. Flat tire. Stuck at Liz's."

"Likely," Steve chimed back. "Saw you called. What are our girls doing? Tea and gabbing?"

"More like polishing off a bottle between them and comparing notes on Gabe, when I walked back in, but I didn't hear that much."

"Ugh," Steve uttered. "Where are you now?"

"Liz's room...downstairs. It's either that or be poisoned by purple in Tyler's room or *Hello Kitty* Lavender." Paul sniffed. "Ya know, hello Kitty used to fill some of my nights. M-e-o-w."

"Redhead, hot as I remember. Didn't she drop out second year?" Steve sighed. "This is what happens when your wife leaves on a Saturday night. Go find out what they're talking about."

"Just when your dirt-bag titer isn't high enough you want me to eavesdrop on your wife and sister." Paul took a swig of his beer. "Perfectly fine with the *Journal* and beer, right here."

"There's nothing stellar in that issue. Trust me, my nights are relegated to reading again," Steve replied. "Grab another beer." Steve held out the phone when it was Paul's turn to sigh. "Gabe could be after Liz again," Steve reminded.

"I only wanted one beer." Paul put his cell down, muttered the word *manipulate* then something in Italian and traipsed up the stairs. He turned his ear to the women.

"She's gonna have some fun with him," Liz commented during their movie.

"He's got the moves." Maren pointed to the screen. "Young too. See, he wants her."

The dogs scrambling to the fridge announced Paul's presence.

"Just getting another beer." He decided to steal cookies. Walked closer to the ladies and noticed opened bottles and shot glasses. "Don't mind me." He snitched a handful of confections.

Paul made his way back to the kitchen. Captivated by a scene in the movie, he stalled. "Ah Liz, where's the bottle opener?"

"Didn't you just have a beer?" Liz hardly looked up. "Wherever you left it?"

"That's what we need. An island escape when we go out on strike," Liz declared. "We're the ones who shop, wrap, make our houses look festive. I like the idea of a strike."

214

"Your brother can decorate however the hell he wants." Maren poured herself another shot glass and downed it. "Wonder if Mrs. Claus ever told Santa to shove it?"

Liz let out a series of laughs. Paused the movie. "Paul, what's the problem over there?"

"Oh, nothing…" He couldn't stall any longer, so he joined Steve back on the phone.

"'Bout time," Steve scolded. "What now?"

"A movie where middle-aged woman hits the high thread counts with buff young man, who postponed medical school—hell, I'd have taken a gap year for that—cooks, too. Hangin' out in Jamaica mon." Paul chugged his beer.

"Sounds like you…only with a different accent. And you didn't need any extra year," Steve said. "You fit it all in quite well."

Both men hooted at the double-entendre there.

"I did chase a lot of tail in my day," Paul agreed. "Oh, and they're doing Kahlua and Vodka shots. Both decided they're going on strike, Mrs. Claus can tell Santa to stick it…or something like that…and pretty much you can too." Paul cracked up again.

Steve didn't find it the least bit amusing. "I've never known my wife to do shots."

"Well, she is now, buddy."

"You know where you can stick your sarcasm."

"Hey, I'm not the one rolling over tonight into a pile of LEGO people." Paul snickered. "I got a real woman in my bed tonight." He exhaled suggestively to annoy Steve even further. "But then, Bruno gets to sleep with Liz more than I do."

"Maren is staying over there. Hide her keys."

"Now I'm to rummage through her purse?" Paul muttered. "She's fine. They're on to me."

"Tell them you can't find something. Women always complain we men can't find things."

"What I do for a forlorn friend." Paul stood up, still speaking into the phone. "One last time. And don't complain how long I'm gone."

This time, Paul climbed up the stairs slowly. From the top step he heard Maren and Liz commenting about the movie. Paul decided forgetfulness was way too lame an excuse. He hung out on the top step until Franco literally high tailed it his way. Then he was gone.

"I'm back," Paul said to Steve. "You really ought to put this curious energy to getting back into your wife's good graces, ya know that?"

"What's that supposed to mean?" Steve sounded perturbed. "What'd they say now?"

"Let's see, Maren thinks screwing Jerry Carlton would be a fitting Christmas gift, and Liz will probably be fast asleep by midnight, waking up with a hangover." Paul sighed. "You owe me."

Steve groaned. "Slip water into the Vodka. At this point, they won't know the difference."

"OK boss," Paul kidded. "I'm signing off now. Have fun building bricks...with Dylan." He clicked off before Steve could comment.

Chapter 18

The second weekend in December had Hannah and Tyler with Tim again. Hospital shifts were easy to trade since holiday events posed work conflicts. Liz would take day shift Saturday and Sunday, earning the differential in her paycheck at West Riverside. She'd also see Paul.

Friday afternoon, Liz drove westbound across the bridge to settle in since her alarm would chime at 5:30 the following morning. In the condo garage, she slid her purse to her shoulder, wheeled her overnight bag, and tightened her grasp on Bruno's leash.

"Excited?" she asked. Anticipation leached into the air as he stood panting in the elevator.

Bruno heard a familiar bark inside Paul's door when Liz entered with a key she now had.

Bruno muscled up droopy ears and wiggled his pointed tail back and forth. Franco greeted Liz on hind legs, pawing her pants. He sniffed Bruno, a non-verbal Tyler would have commented about with a 7-year-old snicker. Couldn't they remember they were both still boys?

"OK, don't knock over the furniture." Liz turned on a lamp. Late afternoon darkness had descended. "I'll take you both outside."

They stopped. Perked ears. Panted eagerly.

Liz lifted the hood on her jacket and kept her head down, walking only behind the condominiums. Sidewalks might lead to stores, restaurants and townhomes, like the one Jade Chen, her boss in the emergency department, had purchased.

Keeping this relationship under the radar weighed Liz down more than Bruno and Franco maneuvering between patches of grass and trees.

Hadn't someone else's needs maneuvered her this entire year: Tim's decisions and Hal's penny-pinching business practices? These days, as Liz worked a second job to make the mortgage payment Tim didn't, she sacrificed being honest because of one more person's reactions. Liz yearned to have some semblance of control, living the way she wanted to go about her life.

When she heard her cell phone vibrate, she jumped. Took a breath, reaching into her pocket.

"THX 4 walking boys. BFD in ED. 121 w Jade. CU@6, TTYL," the text read.

Figuring out texts and deciphering doctor's scrawl! Using a mere three symbols comprising a smile in her reply wouldn't divulge her text-lingo ignorance.

Liz pocketed her phone. She thought about the message and felt like a fugitive, in the dark corners of Shore Landings. Her mind unscrambled the text. Paul was delayed by a big freaking deal needing a private, one-on-one discussion with Jade. He was happy she walked the dogs, would see her at six, and talk to her later.

Liz breathed more easily when she slipped inside the lobby door, rode the elevator back up to Paul's unit and hung her coat on a hanger.

"You were good boys." She gave each pup a treat out of the large jar Jade, of course, had given Paul at the puppy presents party.

Jade Chen was very smitten with Paul. Everyone at West Riverside was fond of this year's most eligible bachelor since Maren had snared last year's prime catch. A practice courted Paul on the shore. One in Pittsburgh bent over backwards to get him hundreds of miles away, as did a hospital there, too.

Liz fingered ornaments on Paul's five-foot tree—a Pittsburgh Steelers helmet, a stethoscope peering from a medical bag, a doctor in scrubs, and another in a lab coat. World's Best Doctor dangled from a branch. Only Puppy First Christmas sat opened in a box, still in its tissue with a tag that read: "Paul, Thought you had to have this! Here if you need me—Jade."

Liz felt a clutch inside. Paul had fully anticipated Baby's First Christmas. Talk about game-changing years! He had lost most of his world while much of Liz's remained intact. Stressed, but with the same key players.

Didn't Paul deserve to make whatever choices best served his goals? Jade Chen had no bitter ex baggage, no ornery son, nor a daughter that had to remind him of losing his own.

Is this going to work, or is this how we both spell r-e-b-o-u-n-d?

She wheeled her case to hang up her clothes. When she checked the time, she spotted a book and magazines on Paul's nightstand. Liz walked closer perusing them. *The Chief—Art Rooney and His Steelers* by Jim O'Brien sat on top of two recent issues of *Pittsburgh Magazine*.

He certainly had ties to his hometown, and family, Liz thought as she thumbed through the glossy evidence. Isabella Romano would soon arrive to stay and worry over her firstborn son.

Paul's mother had pointed out in not so subtle ways that Liz wasn't even free to marry. The black mark of divorce wasn't even hers to claim for four months. A lot could happen in that time.

Liz felt a raw rush of panicked guilt travel her spine, settling in the back of her neck. She stretched arms to the ceiling, flexed her shoulders, and announced, "I need a hot soak. Be good."

Liz moved two candles to the tub deck. Lighting these illuminated the framed proverb above the towel rack: *Count your nights by stars, not shadows; count your life with smiles, not tears.*

She ran that through her mind. Turned on the small CD player to mood music. Stepping into the tepid mix of bath salts and bubbles, she breathed in the lavender and allowed her mind to spin improbable dreams. The water washed away worries and all track of time.

"You look relaxed." Paul leaned upon the doorjamb. Liz's naked legs sprawled over the tub. The probable pleasure ahead consumed him. She startled, ending his appreciative stare.

"I closed my eyes. What time is it?"

Paul sat on the tub edge. "Time to strip down to nothing and have dessert before dinner." Paul picked up a foot. Massaged it, then nibbled. "I'd rather feast on you," he said as Liz put her head back. Paul bent a knee to untie his shoes, which when tossed, almost clobbered Franco.

"What's for dinner?" Liz asked, enjoying the show. She twisted the hot lever and slid over.

"Eggplant parm and veal marsala from the restaurant down the street." Paul unbuttoned, unzipped, and soon Liz had convincing evidence that dinner was indeed his last intention.

How could someone be so outrageously sexy? Even more so when he nestled next to her in warm water, languishing long caresses over her legs, to make her belly clench.

"I'm so glad you came over here tonight," Paul whispered. He brushed fresh bubbles off his lips and ran them freely across her neck. "Eighty erotic thoughts sprang to mind, seeing you lying here so scintillating, so mine."

When his mouth took hers, the hot, hard kiss disarmed Liz. Branded her to him with a force that trembled from her throat, down her chest and through her feet. Feeling a man's full weight on her never felt so light or buoyant, all at once.

Liz arched her back to the touch that slid from her knee to her thigh to just where Paul could seize any control she had left that evening. A battle Liz willingly lost to reach new heights with Paul, as he cradled her in his arms.

When several surges of satisfaction let up, Liz tangled her fingers through Paul's hair. "You spoil me, and I'm getting used to it."

"The pleasure's mutual." Paul angled his head. "I love hearing you want me." He shifted to satisfy both of them.

She tucked her legs around his hips as he took her. Possessed her. Plunged into her, making waves that rippled over both of them.

When the upsurge of swirling pleasure ended, he groaned into her damp skin. They lay still until a wet nose grazed Paul's arm. He turned to a four-legged audience.

"We corrupt the little mutts again." His breath still ragged, Paul asked, "You took them out?"

"Sure did. Incognito, as usual." Liz's tone defied the gratification they had shared. "I wish we were going to the hospital holiday party together." Liz splayed palms. "What's wrong with this picture? Hiding that we date." Liz drooped her chin. "Doesn't it make us seem tawdry?"

Paul scraped her cheek with his seven o'clock shadow. "You little goomara at 36." He chuckled. "I'll go to confession for both of us."

"You told me you don't go to confession," Liz reminded him. "What's a goomara, anyway?

Paul held Liz by the wrists. "Slang for a woman on the side."

"You move aside." Liz wiggled from him. "I'm getting out before I shrivel or smack you." She stood flicking droplets from the long, lean legs he had lavished earlier.

Paul took one long look. "Please, tie me up, too." He arched a perfect brow. "Later?"

"Oh, stop!" Liz wrapped a towel around her and sat on the edge of the tub. "That's a little too raw...and real."

"I'm sorry." Paul silenced his chuckle. "I picked up our favorite dessert...well, my second favorite." The delight Paul projected toward Liz was nothing but outrageous. He sat spine straight, leaned over and lowered the towel to savor a nipple. "Perky and delicious."

"Leave the sex, take the cannoli." Liz clutched her towel, tossed him one. He barely caught it before it would get soaked.

"You can't alter great quotes like that Liz," Paul chided. "We should watch *The Godfather* here since it's a little out there for Hannah and Tyler at your house."

"Just a little," Liz replied.

They ate dinner in robes. Bruno and Franco hoped beyond doggy dreams that a morsel of veal or eggplant would find the floor. None did. Their expectant eyes landed on each other. The pups tumbled on the carpet, and when play exhausted them, they sidled up to their owners.

By the time Liz and Paul shared the war of their weeks and kept from having one over two teams that would face off again on Sunday, they crawled into bed. Still hungry, cannoli remained in the fridge…for breakfast.

Saturday morning, Maren rubbed at her lower back as she bent to empty the dishwasher. She stopped to stretch and grimaced.

"Honey, what's wrong?" Steve lowered *The Washington Post* with both hands.

"Nothing. Just stiff," she replied. "I ought to make time for yoga twice a week."

"Your cousin the massage guy…"

"His name's Josh," Maren abruptly corrected.

"I was getting to his name."

To Maren, Steve's tone sounded hardly curative, but wholly remedial. "Fine…whatever."

"Josh taught me how to work out those knots," Steve continued. "Why don't you let me try?"

"It's two weeks before Christmas with a zillion things to do." Maren straightened her back. "Seriously?"

"It's hard to sit here, Maren, day after day as you punish me with your silence," he answered. "Can we please talk?" He waited. "Please."

Consulting the microwave clock, Maren pulled out a chair and sat down. "Fine. Talk."

"I've been patient. I've sent you love notes. A bouquet of flowers to mark when we first met." Steve stood up, walked the kitchen, resting his arms on their large kitchen table. "I've asked you, when I could, to join me for coffee or lunch. There's always some excuse from you."

"What you did in April still really hurts. I do work. I have Dylan, this house to take care of."

"Another thing: I've spent even more time with Dylan. Like when you ran off to Liz's and left me a list of things." He wagged a finger. "I got most of that list knocked out in two days."

"I appreciate that part, but it's your home, too." She raked a hand through her hair. "Would you like a medal, or let me guess, a newsletter mention of how wonderful you are?" Maren crossed arms. "I don't need a lecture. I need time."

Steve walked closer. Lowered his voice some, but not completely. "Speaking of time, imagine how I feel when I asked you to stop seeing

Gabe outside the office. Then I find him taking yoga with you. That isn't why flex time was designed, so that my wife and her amorous art school pal can lie on the floor listening to an instructor tell them to let their bodies relax. Together."

Steve's ire kicked up. "Oh, *feel* the stretch. Let your thighs *open*," he mocked, with feminine tone. "If you don't think *that* imagery has his blood flowing south, guess again. It's not what any husband wants to hear. And a wife who really wants to work on her marriage should not subject herself to it with her lecherous friend."

"That class helps me to unwind," Maren shot back. "Takes my mind off of our problems."

"It takes your mind off of that, plus Dylan, me, our future," Steve argued. "Whenever I pose an alternative way to de-stress and come together, you ignore me. If not for me, think of Dylan."

"Leave him out of this." She fisted a hand to her hip. "I'm trying, amid reminders, like a Christmas card from Pam's parents, not to mention her sex column in a magazine that lands in our mailbox monthly." Maren felt like she was reluctantly on an angry roll.

"Throw it out or cancel your subscription. I have no control over that," Steve replied. "I should have some say with us."

"I'm done discussing." Maren got up. Poured coffee into a travel mug, pulled her coat from the closet and shrugged it on. "You're trying to guilt me, in my own house, which I helped pay for with the sale of my happy home when you were off adding to the columnist's learning curve."

She grabbed her mug, slung her handbag over her shoulder. "I'm going to the mall. I have errands to run." She turned to Steve. "Did you ever think this was all maybe an impulsive mistake?"

"What?"

"Us? This house? All of this?"

Steve blanched ghost-white. "Never," he finally answered. "But apparently, you do."

Maren popped her trunk in the garage four hours later. She inched her way inside with several large bags, hoping she would steer them past Dylan. So much for the elf strike, she mused, as she rustled plastic bags into corners and onto shelves of their upstairs closet.

"You're back." Steve found her on the bed removing her shoes. "Have you seen Dylan?"

"No, I hope he's off playing. I just stashed gifts out of sight."

Maren carried her shoes to their closet and came out again. "Is he napping?"

"I thought he was in his room, but he isn't. Not in the family room or outside." Steve shouted "Dylan" once again down the stairs.

"Better not be," Maren replied. "It's getting chilly out there." Maren walked across the hallway to the guestroom. Called out his name herself. Checked another spare bedroom. "He's not up here. Steve, where could he be?

"We watched college football, and he said he was tired. I fell asleep shortly after that."

These days, Maren tried in the worst way to avoid looking at her husband. Yet when his eyebrows pulled together tight, and he drew in a calming breath, she regarded him.

Cordless phone in hand, Maren punched numbers on it. She walked with it downstairs.

"Dad, is Dylan at your place?" She listened as Jack shouted out to Audrey asking the same. "Well, I ran some errands. He was here with Steve, supposedly sleeping in his room. I came home, and neither of us can find him. Steve just ran to check at the neighbors."

Maren waited agonizing minutes as Jack rode the elevator of their condo building to see if the secured lobby door had thwarted Dylan. She opened closets and looked under tables at their house while Steve did his own search.

"Maren, he's not here," her father told her, breathless as he picked the receiver up again. "Could he be at Paul's maybe?"

"Dad, he's never been to Paul's condo, but it's anyone's guess. Wait, I hear Steve." Maren turned around as Steve advanced. "Hold on Dad."

Steve extended one arm to her shoulder. "Did you walk through the garage door?"

"Yes, why? What's this?"

"Found it taped to the back of the door," Steve said. He took the receiver from Maren. "Jack, looks like Dylan ran away. He left a note behind. I'm calling my contact at the police station."

Steve paused, listening to Jack. "Yeah, time to worry."

Maren lowered herself to a chair. She read the one paragraph on three-hole punched paper.

Mommy,

You do nut like it. You ar mad at me & Steeve. I mis daddy, my famlee. You nut hapie. 2 much fiteing. ☹

Luv, Dylan

The second grade printing was Dylan's all right as was the sad face she had taught him to draw when he couldn't even print his feelings, back when Mark had died.

Maren knuckled tears from her eyes. She heard him mention light brown hair, brown eyes, bangs that fell across the forehead. He talked to Sarge, the contact she had teased him about, with his police car pick-ups, now a godsend.

She backed her head into the chair and heard the front door. Spine-straight she jolted only to slouch again. It wasn't Dylan but her parents who lived blocks away in Shore Landings.

"Any news?" Audrey dumped her purse onto the floor. Pulled her arms from her winter coat.

Steve had taken the cordless into the kitchen. He clicked off and returned hearing the door.

"They'll alert all units, but it'll be dark soon. They asked places he might go," he explained. "Not many since we moved here. With the shops and restaurants, it's a high traffic area..."

Jack drew in a breath. He started to say something but stopped.

Audrey sat down beside her daughter as Maren twitched her lips nervously. "What were you going to tell us?" she asked. "Say it, Dad."

"I think Steve's trying to say that someone might have found him, or could have taken him?"

Maren clutched her stomach that felt abruptly heavy while the rest of her became light.

"We hope not." Steve kneeled down to look Maren in the eye and cradle her ragdoll body. "We need to stay here in case he comes back. We should check to see if he left with anything they can identify if found. And I'm going to make another call."

Audrey jumped out of her chair. "I'll scour his room. See if I notice anything."

"I'll come, too." Maren struggled to breathe, but managed to stand up. "You'll call where?"

Steve hesitated, but didn't hold back. "I'm calling the hospital."

Maren took one look at her father and fell into his quick embrace. Then, she broke free and bolted to Dylan's bedroom.

It approached 4:45 and hospital staff had technically passed reports along to incoming workers much earlier. Liz stayed on to help her replacement assess and place the five patients locked in the psych unit as well as one patient hooked up to monitors elsewhere in the emergency department. She had just hung up with an insurance company, finally able to attain a pre-cert after she had to put Dr. Chen on the phone. It had been that difficult to obtain.

Glad her boss had left the unit, Liz recognized the incoming caller ID. "Hey, just running a little late. What are you up to?"

"Walking the dogs the past 45 minutes. Liz, Dylan's missing. He ran away, left a note, and they're worried sick," Paul told her. "Street lights just came on."

"Oh my God." Liz drew in air.

"Check the board. Steve put the charge nurse on alert."

Liz clicked the computer screen with the entire list of patients admitted to emergency, even some on the way. "I don't see his name, but I see a psych case coming. An emergency petition." She sat back. "We're slammed. Happens when it's cold out. The holidays stir up so much. I may never get off duty."

"There's nothing you can do here, but I thought you should know."

"Paul, hang on. Charge desk calling." Liz punched the hold button. Two minutes later, she stopped its flashing. "I have a sinking feeling. The police have a peds case. Threat to self."

"You don't think?"

"I don't know what to think," she answered. "We'll know shortly."

"Then stay there," Paul said. "Wait, now my phone's beeping."

Liz looked at her computer screen for any additional names. Paul rejoined the call.

"It was Steve. Definitely stay. It's Dylan."

Since her shift had technically ended two hours ago, Liz left her desk and walked out to where police or ambulances would swirl lights in the parking lot. A minute later, she saw Dylan, sandwiched between one male and one female officer. The male carried a small backpack.

"Aunt Liz!" Dylan's eyes, the size of saucers, landed on her.

"Dylan, thank heavens." As one officer loosened his grasp, Liz folded her arms around Dylan's shoulders.

"This boy a relative?" the male cop asked.

"Yes, he's my nephew. And I work here. His parents are on their way over."

"Well, ma'am...he said he doesn't have a father, and that...well..."
The officer drew Liz to the side. "He said his father's in Heaven, and
that's where he wants to go because it's peaceful there." The officer
scratched his head. "We picked him up walking along the side of a
busy road. He said something about a car could hit him. Hard to make
out, him cryin' and all."

"Put him in room eight," the charge nurse directed.

The female cop started towing Dylan, who looked back at Liz as if
she had magic powers.

"Dylan, it'll be OK," Liz said. She turned to the nurse. "Obviously,
Tanya who came on at three will assess him, but I can sit with him
while he gets triaged."

"In case he runs again." The nurse took the papers from the officer.
Dismissed him back to his vehicle. "Dr. Kramer's stepson?" she asked
Liz. "He called here hours ago."

"Yes, I don't really think Dylan means what he said. His real father
died two and a half years ago." A cringe tugged at Liz's lips. She tried
to mitigate any embarrassment, having had a full deck of her own this
past year. "A lot going on."

"All right. Dr. Chen will be in to check him out. Then Tanya can
talk to him."

Stopped by a doctor who had questions on a prior case, Liz got
delayed. The nurse assigned had charted Dylan's vitals and gotten his
brief story by the time Liz got to his room. She slid the glass door shut,
screeched a chair close to the gurney, and helped him tie his hospital
gown.

"Dylan, what's going on?" Liz asked. "Did you get hurt?"

"My shoulders." Dylan pointed to them. "I packed too many toys."

Liz curved her lips just a little to keep him talking. "You ran off,
away from home, I heard."

"Tyler ran away, and he was OK." Dylan's brown eyes glistened.
"And Aunt Vicki's in heaven with my dad. I know where she's buried.
I know what happens," Dylan said.

Liz handed him a 3x5 box of patient tissues. Thought she'd need
one herself.

"Everybody said my daddy was in a better place, and I heard
somebody tell that to Paul," Dylan continued. "Can't be that bad?
Better than yelling. My mom even cusses now."

Liz ran a hand over Dylan's head. "Ah, Dylan, you've been through
so much."

226

The door slid open. "Young man, I'm Dr. Chen." She extended one hand to shake Dylan's, washed up at the sink, and pulled her stethoscope into position. They had met at the puppy party but Jade kept it professional. "Liz, your brother and Dylan's mom just arrived. I'll be out when I'm finished."

Liz took her cue. When she reached the waiting area, Maren flung arms around her. Steve heaved relief. "Paul said you might still be here," What's happening?" he asked.

"Did you talk with Dylan? What did he say? What's this about harming himself?" Maren managed two other questions, but Liz could only wrap her mind around the first three.

"I talked to him, but I'm not at liberty to disclose anything until Dr. Chen talks to you." Liz eyed Steve, motioned Maren to take a seat along with her. "She's in with him now."

"What are we supposed to do?" Maren's impatience bubbled out with every word.

"We wait," Steve answered. "Jade runs a tight ship. That's why they hired her, as opposed to… years ago." Like the year Mark had been brought in, but Steve stopped himself.

They were called back within 15 minutes. Dr. Chen briefed Maren and Steve in a small conference room, while Liz waited in the hallway. The three went into Dylan's room next. The sliding door separated Liz again. When Jade Chen made her exit, however, Steve stood in the hallway while Maren stayed with Dylan.

"My guess is, he's going inpatient," Steve whispered into Liz's ear.

"I'm not surprised," Liz said. "I can't say more until Dylan talks to Tanya."

"When?" Steve looked around. "Never mind, we were lucky to get a room, right?"

"Welcome to my world," Liz said, slapping a hand to Steve's back. "'Tis the season and it's a cold, long Saturday night. You might want to get Maren a cup of tea." Liz walked to the small staff kitchen and punched the code before he did. "Help yourself."

A cup of tea eased Maren considerably, and by the time Tanya spoke to Dylan, then Maren and Steve, the decision was definitive.

"I'll call around for a bed and pre-cert this with insurance," Tanya told them. "You can sit with Dylan until we know more."

"What do you mean call around?" Maren tried to hush the tone. "Can't he go upstairs?"

By now, Jack and Audrey had locked up at the house and driven over for moral support. When they weren't taking turns being with Dylan, the rest of them occupied one corner of an already crowded waiting room.

Tanya looked at Steve, but this was hers to explain. "West Riverside doesn't admit children or adolescents for psych. Not all hospitals do." Tanya kept her voice low. "This placement could take awhile... hopefully less if you're willing to sign him in."

Looking confused, Maren leaned her head against Steve. "Can't you do anything here?" she asked. "I think he'd be perfectly all right at home. I really do."

Steve wrapped an arm around his wife. "There really isn't anything I can do, Mair," he admitted. "Look at the positive: he's safe. This could have turned out so differently." He looked back at Liz's colleague. "We'll sign the papers. No need for an involuntary."

Tanya nodded and went back to her desk to find a hospital that could accept Dylan.

Liz explained the difference. If the of-age patient or guardians signed for a voluntary admission, there were more choices in hospitals and facilities. If two doctors determined a patient needed to be admitted, against voluntary consent, their signatures sealed the deal. But an involuntary transfer couldn't cross state lines. That would rule out Children's Hospital, just an hour away in the District of Columbia.

"Psych beds overall are hard to come by, particularly on the weekend," Liz continued. "Harder for kids and teens. It's frustrating."

Maren gently shoved her disposable cup at Steve, asking for one more calming round. Liz went with him this time and brought back tea for herself and Audrey. Maren went off to sit with Dylan until Tanya summoned her nearly an hour later. She had more paperwork on a clipboard. By now it approached nine o'clock at night.

"That was quick," Liz said to Tanya. Maren shot a silent, steely gaze at the clock then back at Liz. Liz cupped Maren's hand. Squeezed it. "Honestly, 50 minutes to arrange things is fast."

Tanya explained that the ambulance would arrive to transport Dylan to Towson where a hospital had an open spot and accepted the clinical details Tanya had run past them.

Maren, as Dylan's sole biological parent, would have to sign him into the facility at arrival. Steve technically had no rights to do so unless he had adopted Dylan.

"I see," Maren managed. She scribbled her signature onto the transport papers. Maren thanked Tanya, who, clipboard in hand, went back to process the paperwork. "I've got this, Steve," Maren said. "You can go on home."

"And let you drive on your own through Baltimore at 10 or 11 at night?" Steve asked, the model now of applied patience. "No way."

"Maren, he's right," Jack spoke. "Not wise."

Maren, recently as annoyed with Jack as she had been with Steve, plopped back down onto the sofa. She propped an elbow to hold her head from fatigue. "Fine," she replied.

Liz sat and pondered. She understood the tangle of unclear thoughts and jangled emotions all too well. She knew the personal pain of infidelity, fearing for an angry, distraught child, and the drill here. Legal paperwork cast light on domestic messes most would rather sequester within their own set of walls. Maren and her brother both worked here. It had to be awkward.

Liz said her good-byes, enfolded Maren into a tight squeeze, and grabbed her belongings. In 14 minutes, she would walk into Paul's condo, to a glass of wine and two furry heads to scratch.

For her brother and sister-in-law, the night was far from over.

Chapter 19

Paul heated up dinner while Liz relaxed under a steady shower stream. She came to the table in a red robe, her short hair towel-fluffed.

"Warmer now?" Paul kissed Liz and fingered the robe's neckline. "Christmassy." He set a plate of pasta in front of her. Bruno and Franco plopped themselves onto the floor. Thumping tails told Paul that puppy chow didn't seem quite fair.

"You're so good to me," Liz said. Garlic wafted off the steam. "Spinach, pine nuts, shrimp."

"I had an easy day, was about to start dinner; walked sidewalks instead." Paul placed two glasses of Merlot next to her plate and sat.

"All things considered, a good ending." Liz lifted a goblet, inhaling the aroma before downing some wine. "This all smells, tastes so good."

They lamented the drive Maren and Steve faced. Both backed the decision to send Dylan inpatient. "You really think Dr. Chen has no clue about us?" Liz asked, shifting topic.

"Call me protective. You don't need hassles. I think she's put the pieces together." Paul arched his brows in conjecture. "My telling her I needed time, not always calling back, not making moves on her." His smile was nothing but mischievous. "My habits sure have changed!"

"Did you ever kiss her?" Her curious stare called out for an immediate answer.

"Not on the lips." Paul fingered Liz's red robe tie. Twirled it. "Had you not separated, I might have played the field a little."

Liz softened. "Would you rather?"

Paul brushed a hand over her hair, down her neck. It settled on the red robe. "No." His eyes scanned Liz softly. "Hell, I'm jealous of Bruno. He gets to see you naked more than I do."

Her playful pinch needled Paul. "Keeping us quiet gets old," Liz complained. "People know I live on the other shore. It's hard work."

"Guess who else labored in a hospital most of the day?" When Paul set down his wine, he sensed Liz needed a huge hint, not a quiz.

"Pam sent out a text around seven this evening," he offered.

"The baby?" Liz tilted her head. "Boy or girl?"

"A little boy," Paul answered. "Jerry's thrilled, though they haven't picked a name."

"They have a built-in babysitter with their daughter being…nine?"

"Ten." Paul hurried his reply. "Pam joked it was a tenth anniversary gift, Chloé's October birthday present." When Liz started to clear her plate, Paul took it and motioned her to the sofa. "Let's relax. I'll finish dishes in the morning."

"Don't mind if I do," she said.

Hand cupping her wine glass, Liz lounged on the sofa and patted a spot where Paul soon stretched out beside her. "Wait, if Chloé's ten that means…" Liz counted back on one hand, adding more fingers. She blinked. "Something's literally not adding up."

He buried his face on her to stall. Liz combed fingers through Paul's hair. "Pam couldn't have aborted Steve's baby and had Chloé that close together." She shook his shoulder. "Do the math."

He evaded eye contact, until Liz blew out a very long, perturbed breath that settled on his skin. Would anything short of full disclosure mollify her curiosity?

"I should've been more careful," Paul admitted. "I was excited for them, when I could have been…well, envious." Paul's facial muscles tensed, no longer rejoicing in good news.

Shock stole words from Liz's throat. "She…I mean…Chloé is Steve's daughter? My niece?"

"You really need to talk to your brother, Liz. Pam led us to believe Chloé was younger, until the accident when Pam begged Steve's help, and your eagle-eyed brother saw her true birth date."

"Who knows? My mother teased constantly about grandchildren," Liz shared. "When Hilary told her about the procedure, Mom was horrified. I don't know if she'll smile or cry at this."

"Maren and her parents know. Steve still has to discuss moving on with Pam and Jerry, obvious adjustments for Chloé. Now, a sibling."

"Yeah. Shelly asked me about cognitive delays and behavioral problems," Liz said. "Take tonight with Dylan. Who knows what goes through a child's mind? News like this could rock that girl's fragile sense of security."

"The whole thing's complicated." Paul stroked Liz's hair. "According to Steve, Maren worries that he'll want a future with Pam. Of course, Steve can't totally write Pam out of his life because she's the pathway to his child."

"Oh no! Taking a tumble with Pam is bad enough; we'd take him down if he left Maren for her," Liz uttered. "Dio Mio!"

Paul pulled back. Beamed. "Why Liz Kramer Phillips! You're an Italian wannabe."

"Imperfect one," Liz kidded back. "Enough serious. My best Mrs. Claus act and it's failing, too." She ran a finger under Paul's always-present gold chain. "I need Christmas ideas?"

Paul knew Liz was punning his "I'm Italian, I'm Perfect" plaque. "You'll come up with something. You've many talents." Paul let out a lecherous grunt. "In the kitchen…in the bathtub."

She elbowed him. "My apricot and nut biscotti turned out best. The anise flavor?" Liz teetered a hand. "I brought you almond cookies, too."

"I had some. I cook, you bake." Paul ran his hand under the robe, over Liz's leg, let it settle on her hip. Cupped behind it. "Back to last night: we couple up well. That's a gift."

Paul pressed his body into her. Brushed his lips full on her mouth, Merlot to Merlot. "Besides," he nodded to Bruno and Franco curled on one large cushion. "These two won't even tell Santa if we're naughty."

"Who wants to be nice then?" Liz murmured.

Trailing an ambulance that took Dylan north, Maren sat in the passenger seat racked with worry and miffed at Steve. She shared Liz's assessment from her own run-away weekend: One night with Jerry's wife possibly made up for his stealing Pam years before.

For his part, Steve admitted he felt responsible for Maren's uncertainty and some, not all, of their strife. "It was a mistake," he reiterated. "A horrible lapse after a wine binge." Steve would face the consequences, including a meet-up with Pam and Jerry in the New Year.

As they finally pulled into their garage and slammed car doors, Steve told Maren she was welcome to join them.

The nightstand clock read 3:15 AM. They had yanked the covers and crawled onto cold sheets around two, but sleep evaded them, and it was no warmer despite lying there…thinking.

"Come here," Steve said. He spooned Maren close in spite of her protested grumble. "Be angry with me tomorrow. Tonight, you need me." He kissed her hair softly. "We need each other."

"Dylan needs us," she sniffled. "And where is he? Locked up in a kid psych ward because he said something he surely doesn't mean."

"But he didn't back down," Steve said. "Jade and Liz's colleague had no choice, Mair." Steve rolled her to him in the dim light emitted from the clock. "He'll learn from this. We all will."

"And now we have to go nearly two hours away for family therapy."

"You heard what the unit nurse said," Steve reminded. "If we work out what's ailing us, Dylan will be better for it. That's not new information. Just hard to swallow."

"I've been a real witch, haven't I?

Steve smirked. "Well, since you didn't dress up this Halloween, it's a costume idea."

"Very funny." A bony elbow made him groan.

"Mm." Steve nuzzled kisses onto her neck. "Your costume last Halloween. More like it."

"I didn't dress up then either." Her hand covered her yawn.

"Precisely," Steve reminisced. "Private computer consult: my hardware, your software."

Steve's hands felt warmer already as he pulled off Maren's pajama pants. "This cold war has lasted a little too long." He brushed his fingers higher to unbutton the flannel top. "We're in this together. I want no one but my sexy wife, and I want her back. Now."

Maren rolled on top of Steve. Her initiative alone made more than his breath rise.

"You think Dylan will act out if we bring more changes his way? An older sibling, a baby someday?" Maren smoothed fingers along Steve's face.

"I think he'll be just fine. If we're fine."

They kissed. Slowly, attentively loved one another and slumbered into the morning's light.

Santa granted Dylan his desire for jolly good cheer. He learned some important lessons during his inpatient stay through play, art, and therapy. Family sessions had gone well, and Dylan went home to parents who had called a truce.

Maren and Steve decorated their first tree in their new home, and when Steve lifted Dylan on his shoulders, Dylan put the star on top. He made a wish, assuring them it was a good one.

Mrs. Romano flew south in time to prepare three of the seven fishes, an Italian tradition on Christmas Eve. Liz simmered oyster stew, and

Paul finished the rest of their meal at Liz's house, which was larger than Paul's small condo.

After the holiday, Rudolph ran Santa out of town in the nick of time. A regional football rivalry moved in December 28th at M&T Bank Stadium with both the naughty and the nice.

"Who called?" Isabella asked as she sat in Liz's family room.

"Steve, Ma...said this game's too close, into overtime," Paul replied. Steve actually said *sucks,* but Paul knew his mother hated that word as much as Maren. "He and Dylan are watching."

Liz's one saving grace was being Steve's sister. Nothing else suited the Italian matriarch. With Hannah and Tyler at Tim's, Liz was the sole Ravens fan, outnumbered in her own home.

"Their little boy has a Terrible Towel," Isabella replied. "I sent him one last year." She lowered her voice since Liz busied herself in the kitchen. "Vicki liked our team. Why can't she?"

"Ma, enough," Paul hushed. "Vicki didn't have to like my team. The Ravens were new when we met." He shot his mother a look that could have been forged from Pittsburgh steel.

Isabella moved off her seat and knelt by the Christmas tree. She picked up a half-opened gift from Liz. The apron read: So sexy, so spicy, so Italian. Paul's mother crinkled her face.

She whispered to him, "You two...serious?"

"Maybe," Paul managed, understanding the depth of her question. Liz shut the oven, which meant she was bringing the warm crab dip closer to them. "Now, watch the rest of the game."

Paul stretched an arm securely around Liz as play resumed, and he plied her Ravens sweater, sending a non-verbal message that he had given his mother many times. Very likely: serious.

When Baltimore scored, clinching the game 13-10, Steve phoned Paul again.

"We'll have to face the Baltimorons at work, that's all," Paul muttered. "They can pound their purple next season." Peripheral vision caught a smug Kramer-like sneer. "Ah, I mean, purple. Lovely. Liz is wearing the earrings I got her, Steve. Purple ones."

Paul snagged Liz mid-thigh. Pulled her closer. "Tell Maren and Dylan my mother sends her love." Paul winked at Liz. Uttered "Ciao" to Steve. "Muted misery at their house," Paul said.

"When you move home, I get you and Steve tickets," Isabella offered. "For Heinz Field."

Him and Steve, not him and Liz, Paul noticed.

"Ma, you don't have that kind of money," he declared. "But I appreciate the thought."

"I'm going to take these presents to the kids' rooms." Liz tried to keep things light, turning to Mrs. Romano. "Thank you for bringing Smiley cookies and little gifts for the kids," she said.

Isabella seemed pleased, but quiet. She merely curled her lips.

"I'll leave the two of you... to chat," Liz said, exiting after that thinly veiled request.

Isabella waited until Liz, with stacked boxes under her arm, fled.

"If you ask me," she told her son, "she needs to redd up more than a few boxes around here."

Paul drew in a cleansing breath at the clear jab at Liz's housekeeping. Liz's directive hung in the air as much as crab and seashell ornaments dangled from the tree.

"We say clean up here, Ma. Not redd up." Paul positioned his legs to support his elbows. "Look, I turned down the Pittsburgh position."

"What you say?" Isabella countered.

"Please don't pretend you didn't hear me," Paul added. "Furthermore, you're a guest in Liz's home. Is it as put together as the White House? No, but she's a busy, working, single mom. You of all people should appreciate that."

Paul straightened and glanced at the mantle crèche, wall wreath and candles that made Liz's family room reek Christmas. He overlooked boxes piled in two corners. Stockings had gifts falling out of them as they lay under the tree.

Liz had already framed recently snapped photos of the kids. In one, Hannah held Bruno by his collar. The tag from his doggie stocking read "The Terrible Dog." The humans and pets that made this place a real home, with family images rivaling any Hallmark card.

Isabella Romano crossed arms in front of her generous bosom. She wasn't a tall woman and years of pasta preparation had rounded her torso. "Why you do this to me?"

"I rejected a job, Ma," Paul insisted. "Not you, not my hometown." Hadn't they retired Isabel for hurricanes? This felt like a storm.

"I have a good job and another one offered to me, here on the shore," Paul continued. "Where I have a life with tremendous support and a terrific set of friends. Right here."

Isabella Romano hung her head. Tears flowed the same way her red sauce always had—fresh and hot. "You lose Vicki and gain what?"

She thrust her hands out, open palmed. "She not single. She not even…divorced." Isabella's face proved the bitter aftertaste the word had left.

"Enough," Paul hushed. His elbows drilled into his knees. "Let me tell you something, Ma. I thought I knew what my life looked like. I thought I planned for it." He rubbed his temples. Knuckled away the formation of a tear. "I would not have made it through this year without Liz Kramer Phillips, whose husband…"

Paul shot up from the sofa. How could he defend divorce to a devout Catholic? He'd be here forever justifying why Liz shouldn't remain with Tim. "Liz's husband: Pezzo di merda."

Isabella gasped.

"Yes, he's a piece of shit, Ma," Paul fumed. "He walked out on her, with a little goomara, left two adorable kids." Paul stopped, considered. "OK, one has a little temper, but didn't I? Didn't Giovanni and Vinny when Dad died?"

"I tried my best," Isabella defended.

Paul sat back down, next to her. "Grazie, for all you did, Ma." He regarded her. "Liz made Christmas happen with all those boxes you complain about. Tim probably shopped last minute, and by the looks of it, bought his kids blue light specials, spending the rest on… Hoochie, while he's stiffed Liz on the mortgage."

"Hoochie?" Isabella asked. "That's Italian?"

"Never mind." Paul was only infuriating himself. "I don't know exactly what the future brings, but life is short, and for now, Liz makes me happy." He paused. "I'd appreciate your being happy for me, for us while we figure out the rest." He let that fester.

Isabella took Paul's hand in hers. Years of raising a crew of kids had taught her to mute her worries, until she finally burst forth.

"Whatcha gonna eat, huh?"

"I learned from the best, Ma." Paul smirked, focusing on his skill rather than on Liz's deficit.

"I didn't see you turn down the dessert Liz made, or that oyster stew she prepared Christmas Eve. I cook more. She bakes." Paul rubbed his fingers over his mother's hand. "As for keeping house, it's really not that bad."

Isabella shot a steely glance at tufts of Bruno's fur that had lodged into the tan area rug, obliterating some of the nautical images.

"I brought Bruno here. Cleaning can be hired," he insisted. "Liz sets her priorities: Hannah and Tyler. Appreciate that, per favore."

"You must love her," Isabella remarked. "To give her your dog. I saw your dresser, the one you took from Pittsburgh, in her boy's room."

"That's because his father absconded—ran off with—furniture, too," Paul defended. "Why store furniture when it could help them here?"

"I worry about your soul," Isabella conceded. "You sure her… marriage…wasn't her fault?"

Paul understood that what formal education didn't bless his mother with, hard-won wisdom from an immigrant upbringing had. "Ma, divorce is in the Italian dictionary, ya know. We're even going on a cruise…to Italy this spring. She's never been there."

His mother grumbled something in Italian. She stood up and headed for the kitchen.

After dinner, Isabella devoured another piece of Smith Island cake. Liz explained the origin of the Maryland state dessert with eight layers that took obvious time and talent to create. Liz had made red velvet with cream cheese icing.

Paul's mother retreated into the spare bedroom where Paul had also parked an extra bed he pulled from storage and a dresser. It was too early to hide away in the guest suite. Paul knew better than to sleep in Liz's room with his mom there and the kids returning any moment so he hung out with Liz watching the NFL roundup.

Bruno and Franco charged the window, then down the stairs at the sound of gravel outside.

"I'll go grab them," Paul told Liz. He trotted briskly down to the ground level, and grabbing collars in both hands, saw the garage door had been raised already from the outside code box.

Bruno and Franco sniffed but didn't jump. Paul held back to be unobtrusive and unnoticed.

"Now look young man." The voice belonged to Tim. "If you can't get me those things—in her file drawers probably—I swear I'll return every last Christmas present I bought you this week."

"But Dad," Tyler pleaded from the driveway. "Mom locks her file cabinets."

"Dammit Tyler, find the key!" Paul heard Tim say it harshly. "Hannah, more family pictures, plus the giant coin jar. You can grab those surely, or I'll behead Barbie." Hannah started to cry.

Paul would have thanked God, on his Grandmother's Rosary, that the dogs didn't rustle collar tags and give him away. Though he had been crouched on the other side of the door, Paul decided now to let Bruno out of his grasp, and pretended he'd just walked into the garage. He pulled the knob briskly and slammed the door. "Hey kids, your mom's upstairs watching TV."

"Bruno," Hannah squealed. The dog had become hers, even though he was technically on temporary loan. Paul could see that Bruno found her face salty, probably from tears Tim caused.

Off-kilter, Tyler brushed past, bumping his backpack into Paul and dropping a gift box as he nudged through the doorway. Paul stooped to pick it up. He met Tim's eyes when he closed the door on the dogs behind him and stepped further into the garage.

"You're here." Tim sniffed, smoothing a hand along his Ravens sweatshirt. "I have Hannah's dollhouse. So Liz can stop hassling me."

The name Paul had given Tim earlier fit. The shit-eating grin on Tim's face reflected his team trumping the Steelers. Paul also knew Liz had asked for Hannah's dollhouse months ago when Tim had moved it out on the moving truck. He had withheld it out of spite or stupidity.

"Do you need a hand?" Paul asked. It took every ounce of Catholic education to hide the hard line he felt forming on his face.

"Sure." Tim shrugged. They both grabbed an end and set it down.

"I'll take it from here," Paul offered. He wasn't going to let Tim nor his greedy hands anywhere inside.

"You know, it seems you're spending an awful lot of time here," Tim assessed. The haughty tone could have hit the garage rafters. "You gave Hannah your dog and Tyler furniture."

Paul knew better than to justify that Bruno helped keep them a little safer with his loud howls. "Loaned, would be the word."

"You or any of her other guys better not get too comfy here," Tim warned. "Our settlement isn't final. This house is technically mine, and Liz is my wife. She better prepare to move out or face me in court. Ought to get her on adultery."

If Isabella Romano and the nuns hadn't raised Paul well, he would have had Tim by the collar against the garage wall.

"You know, Tim," Paul started. "I'm only schooled in medical ethics, but I'm pretty damn sure it's against some kind of real estate code to fornicate with another woman in your client's property when you're…a married man."

Paul paused. Deadpanned a look that could flat line Tim. "And in the bed of your client's deceased wife, when your client just buried her."

239

"Are you threatening me?" Tim shifted the focus, playing victim. Paul wasn't buying that.

"Tim." Using his first name was better than what Paul pushed back on his tongue. "I was trained to do no harm, and tell it like it is."

Paul raised his head. "When Liz's attorney needs witnesses to prove that you put your own kids, a seven- and four-year-old no less, up to fleecing their mother, I'll be so ready with what just transpired in this driveway minutes ago."

Tim's cheeks heated into would-be apoplectic shock. "You think you're so smart."

Paul drew in a silent breath. He remembered the problem-solving steps Liz taught to her kids and clients. Tim could do more than bug off, but he watched his tongue. Choosing to ignore, Paul started to walk inside. He stopped, turning his shoulders to Tim.

"You're pitifully dense if you think I would not." Paul spat the words firmly at him. "Now, get the hell out of here, yours or not, before I close this garage door on your lame brain."

Tim flinched, refusing eye contact as he paced out, his boots clomping the concrete floor.

When Paul heard Tim slam his BMW door, he punched the button banning Tim from Liz's garage, and hopefully from making any more misery, at least for tonight.

For Bill and Dolores, a new realtor secured a contract on their Chevy Chase home. Thus in 2004 their lives centered closer to Shore Landings when they threw a Super Bowl party.

Sadness adhered to Eric with Shelly conspicuously absent from his side. His Redskins could not keep him company either. The Super Bowl belonged to the Patriots and Panthers, and to Justin Timberlake and Janet Jackson at halftime.

"Look, he ripped her top off," Tyler shouted. Little boy giggles racked him, quickly moving to Dylan, who asked, "What happened?" Though the same age Tyler had grown more worldly.

"I don't call that entertainment." Dolores reached for the remote, muting the commentary. Cameras had quickly cut to the fireworks finale.

"You think that was scripted?" Liz stretched her legs on Paul as the third quarter commenced.

"No bra." Tyler commanded Dylan's ear and didn't do well hushing something about boobs.

"He was holding it," Eric added. "Nice ones."

"Eric!" Liz scolded. "The boys are seven. You're two decades older. Watch your language."

"Correction: 26." Eric shot an appreciative smirk to the adult males. "Just sayin'."

Paul laughed. Steve, recently on solid footing with his wife, didn't dare remark. Bill intervened. "Come on kids." He steered Tyler, Dylan and Hannah to the kitchen. "There's dessert for you."

The commentators did a fine job discussing the wardrobe malfunction allowing the Kramer household to put the matter to rest.

The Patriots pulled ahead. Not that anyone really cared. It had been a football season, honestly an entire year, to retire. Another two weeks would mark pivotal events that had transformed Paul's world. The ripped bodice they tried to ignore still seemed easier to talk about.

Dolores commented that in another two months Liz would be a free woman. "If you need more money for Blake, your lawyer, the offer stands," she added. Dolores, Liz, Paul and Steve finished dessert while Maren showed the three kids a draft of her children's book downstairs.

"I appreciate it Mom." Liz bit her lip and eyed her brother. "Blake's year starts off well. You and I just funded a semester for his kid's college."

Dolores's eyes widened. "Oh my, I thought things were good with you and Maren."

Steve settled his hand on top of his mother's. "Blake, my family law friend..."

"From high school, I know," Dolores interrupted. Worry lines etched her face.

"Blake is filing papers for me to adopt Dylan."

"I had no idea." Dolores breathed out relief. "That's wonderful. How did this come about?"

"Sorry," Liz spoke. "I spilled the beans."

"It's all right," Steve replied. "Maren's former in-laws are at it again. Before he ran away, Dylan actually grabbed a Christmas card and the stamped envelope, writing about missing them. He drew a sad face with teardrops," Steve added. "The Mitchells penned a nasty reply to Maren. They have a lawyer petitioning for more time."

"Just what Maren needs," Paul said. "I think she's always offered them plenty."

"Exactly," Steve ceded. "Blake suggested I adopt Dylan, who could use Mitchell as a middle name. Mark and Maren never gave him one."

"We weren't giving him the name Walter," Maren added. She had come up behind Steve and massaged a knot forming in his scapula. "They weren't happy and bitch again, now."

"Whoa," Liz said. "Back to swearing."

"Yeah, New Year's resolution to swear less." Maren rushed her tongue to the side of her cheek. "To think I once threw a brush at my cousin when she said so much as dammit to hell."

"Brush words." Steve chuckled. "I think you're holding up well considering. Come have a seat." Steve pushed back his chair and offered Maren his lap.

"Well, I worked with a family this past year that's graduated from cursing to co-parenting," Liz said. "If that's possible, anything is."

Paul knew it was the Maloney family. Mrs. Maloney was also his patient. "If anything's possible, seriously consider keeping the house," Paul suggested. "The kids love it. Bruno barks highly about it, too."

Liz's lip curled but quickly collapsed. "It's a bit much. We still have to decide who gets the rental property, the boat, cars." She heaved a sigh. "Figures, I'm stuck with the gold SUV. Want to trade the one you're driving around for mine? But like everything in my life, it comes with more mileage and a rooftop carrier."

"Leave the car, take the cannoli," Paul teased. Out of earshot of Dolores, refilling the coffee pot, Paul added, "Your sister does cannoli really well." He smacked his lips. "Tasty."

Maren leaned into Steve and grinned. Liz lodged a half-amused smirk.

"She's not a…freakin' Italian pastry." Steve altered words with Dolores carrying coffee.

"Oh yes she is," Paul chimed back. He reached a hand under the table to Liz's leg.

Afraid it might slide higher, Liz held his hand. Paul was back to his old sex-starved ways.

"I'd love to keep the house, but that's another adjustment we'll have to make," she admitted.

"And lose all the inheritance?" Dolores pursed her lips. "I remember telling you at the time…"

"Mom," Liz stopped. The sound of that reminder made her scalp tingle. "This is stressful enough. Maybe Blake can work wonders." Liz wouldn't hold her breath. "With any luck, we'll find a new place big enough for Bruno. If we can keep him a bit longer?"

"I have a better idea," Paul suggested. "Since I'm joining the practice over on the shore, I'll need a place to stay. Why don't I rent out the top floor? You put the money toward the monthly payment. Charge Bruno rent, too."

"What? You already pay for the groceries when you're there. Next you'll have me charging your mother in front of my TV for *The Price Is Right!*" Liz remarked. "That's ridiculous."

"Not any more ridiculous than my best friend quitting," Steve lamented. He purposely changed the topic since he had always hated Dolores-Liz struggles. "Could be 300 miles away. Either way, I'll see less of Paul. Work kept us connected."

"You should give away my office," Paul said. "I'll be there two days, but in the new clinic. Three days on Kent Island in my private practice."

While pouring Paul a steaming mug of decaf, Dolores announced, "The Kramer Foundation matched clinic funds from the gala, in Vicki's memory." Paul smiled.

"I hear Alicia has an office suddenly open," Liz interjected. She shot a wary look at Maren, and then at Steve. "Did Gabe really quit?"

"Praise God." Steve knit his brows, never minding the snarky reply.

"According to Alicia, Gabe found a better job in Virginia." Maren's tone cut to the point.

"Over with the Mitchell brood." Steve sipped decaf his mother had refilled. "Remind me not to drive that side of the Potomac."

"Maren, would you like some regular or decaf?" Dolores asked. "You look a little tired."

"If it's decaf, Dolores," Maren said. "I've decided to give up wine and cut back on regular for 2004. All in the interest of good health."

"Drink less coffee?" Paul was surprised. "Promise me, at least weekly, we keep tradition."

"Wouldn't miss it." Maren leaned on Steve, who slipped an arm around her waist. Giving up wine and caffeine had nothing to do with will power, but with perseverance.

Project Baby Kramer only six weeks along and with the anniversary of Carina's passing, they kept quiet, holding hands and embracing a secret only they shared.

Chapter 20

Paul slammed the door on his Corvette once he parked it beyond the tall iron gates. Today he didn't have to worry about cracking a window for the dogs. He had made this trip alone.

Early morning fog burned off, but a nip remained in the air. Paul traipsed from the bottom of the grassy knoll where he parked, never minding the bit of dew that settled upon the leather of his Italian loafers. Dampness seeped into his trousers when he knelt into the grass.

Uncrinkling the paper in his pocket, Paul studied the note spread out in his hand.

"You didn't have to write this," he said aloud, as if answering the note back. "It's taken me all this time to get through it…without the tears you told me I could have." Paul knuckled one away from his eyes. Part of a grief cycle he didn't fight any longer. He recognized a Sophia Loren Quote: *If you haven't cried, your eyes can't be beautiful.*

When Vicki had let loose tears, Paul had recited that. "Ti amo, bella." Paul muttered idle chatter about changes at work and how the football season had ended. He told literal tales about two real dog tails, in his one-sided conversation, as the sun began to warm him.

He placed a small bouquet at the headstone. Stared at Vicki's birthday engraved and the date she left a huge hole in his world. For a brief moment, he rested his head against the stone, sturdy and fixed into the ground.

Paul reached into his pocket, this time fingering delicate metal. He held the note Vicki had given Steve well over a year ago. He had already dampened it from his eyes, yet struggled to read it a second time out loud:

"I was lucky to have you as a husband and best friend," Vicki had written. "I remember shopping in Italy, the day you told me to grab a table at the café. You think I didn't know what you were up to?"

Paul found amusement in that. His wife had understood his every move, his very essence.

"I thought you'd be in that store forever deciding what to buy me, but you weren't." Vicki's words were handwritten on West Riverside stationery. "For an impulse purchase, you outdid yourself." It continued: "If this whole hospital stay doesn't go well, promise me you'll give my Valentine's gift to our child, when he or she is old enough to appreciate love like we have had."

Paul had to momentarily look across the cemetery. He drew in brisk air and then looked again at the cursive handwriting. "And if that's not possible, then gift this to a special lady in your life. Whoever you find, she'll be as lucky to have Paul Romano as I was. You have my support, my love, with whatever you do."

Paul skimmed Vicki's wishes for their child. Those were still too raw to read 14 months from events that diminished those dreams. "Sei speciale. Sei bello. Buona fortuna! Ti amo, Vicki."

Paul brushed away another tear. "Not bad for a half-Italian, you know that. You were the special, beautiful one, and I was lucky to have you, bella. I miss you so much," Paul said aloud.

He fingered the chain he removed. Kissed and returned it safely, pulling the zipper on his windbreaker. "Message received. Better go start my day. I have to decide what to pack." Paul chuckled. "You know how decisions go."

Paul strode back to his car. The engine thundered to a start, but with his mind spinning through events of the past year, it took him minutes to pull away from the curb. Steve had just turned 41 and Paul 40 last December. One year ago he had returned from Italy with Isabella. In a few hours, he would leave on a flight with Liz, bound for Barcelona where they would board a Mediterranean cruise.

For her, it would celebrate an official divorce decree, granted a week earlier. He and Liz both worked with physically ill, disgruntled or sad people daily, giving of themselves in professions where they were to have all the remedies. Today, maybe he'd found some resolution, certainly an answer for himself.

Loss wasn't something he would forget or totally resolve. Loss, lived daily, he would integrate into the fabric of his life. Uncovering a memento, a keepsake as he did today, gave Paul new meaning after a year of heartbreak.

April through June, Liz's guidebook read, was the absolute best time to visit Italy. Whether *Under the Tuscan Sun*, which had hit theatres months before their departure, or beneath the Roman, Sicilian, or Napolitano rays, Italy's countryside burst with spring flowers.

Temperatures didn't boil the peninsula; the devout didn't stifle the small streets, but with Holy Week, they descended upon St. Peter's.

"You seriously told your mother you didn't need the Pope's permission for this trip?" Liz slicked a hand through a layer of her dark hair. "She's gonna hold this against me."

The muster drill aboard their 900-ft. ship had just ended, and the vessel had set sail. They remained on the upper deck with bon voyage drinks until the breeze kicked up in the Mediterranean Sea. Paul stashed suitcases under their bed while Liz lounged on the stateroom sofa, the guidebook propped open. Unread. The azure currents out the large porthole stole her focus.

Liz leaned her head to better glimpse white caps their cruise ship created, crashing through the water, leaving a wake. Some worries she left on the gangway, but a few failed to disembark.

Clatter falling upon the cabin floor caused her to shift. "Liz, you didn't close this case," Paul groaned. He knelt and stretched along the floor to pick up clothing and rolling cosmetics.

"Mea culpa...Latin, right?" Liz put the pages face down to mark her place. "Represents my life: an open disaster."

Paul poked his head up from under the bed. "It isn't a disaster, and please stop bringing Ma into our discussions." An Italian guy could stare as well as any Kramer woman could. "You need to get over this. You're a therapist, right?"

"I'm sorry." Liz shifted her legs from the sofa to floor position, ready to pounce. "You're trained as a surgeon, same as Steve?" She slid a frown in Paul's direction. "Right?"

"Well, I just gave that up for the new practice."

"If a surgeon needs to be opened up, as you say, would he need anesthesia?" Liz stood. Fingered her hair again. "A knife still cuts. And it hurts."

"What does this have to do with my mother?"

Reasoning with a man had the same success rate as keeping the deer from munching shrubbery in her bayside yard. Property Paul had convinced her to keep in her divorce settlement. That lawn would resemble a disaster after a week of not tending it. Selling it still might have been best.

"I've had so many reflections since this turning point in my life. I've thought about what went wrong with Tim and me, that's all," Liz replied. "My mother-in-law put her work first when she raised her kids. Tim had an insecure attachment. Never learned how to be soothed. He doesn't get closeness. That's my best guess." Liz sat back down. "You listening to me?"

Paul crawled under the bed after reaching Liz's loot. "Uh huh," he mumbled.

"I, on the other hand, like to work things out. When people are stressed, they pick a force. I pick closeness. He picked distance. It explains his keeping me at arm's length."

"Ma just needs to spend more time with you."

"She doesn't act as if she wants to," Liz lobbed. "If one more person says that, I swear. I want this to work with us, but the more I read about your culture, I'm not convinced it will."

"That's ridiculous."

Liz crisscrossed her arms. "You can't disregard the strikes against us. Tyler's still hissy, claiming I divorced him and Hannah."

"Who do you think planted that idea?"

"Doesn't matter. I still have to deal with it," she replied. "You and I have our differences. Heck, Hal even commented once that the Montagues and Capulets had a better chance of making a relationship work than Steelers Nation and a Ravens fan!"

"We're only referring to Italian authors, not Shakespeare on this trip," Paul said smugly. "And that's who I want to take advice from. Right behind my former realtor."

Liz chuckled. "OK, Hal probably has mastered Shakespeare like he's mastered mental health," she admitted. "It made me think about mother issues and family expectations, with good cause."

"Mother issues?"

"Yes," she continued. "And many people face family pressures."

"Well, I don't face either."

Liz remained unconvinced. "Fact is Vicki was half Italian and totally Catholic. You'd have raised your kids Catholic, right?"

"Probably." Paul rose off the floor. "I don't buy into every piece of the doctrine."

"Like?"

"This." Paul held up a plastic case. "It's a diaphragm, right?"

Liz nodded. "I had headaches and stopped the Pill." She sighed. "Spontaneity just got tossed overboard. Hate to tell you."

"Manageable," Paul replied. "I obviously believe in birth control." A smirk tugged at the corners of his lips. "If I didn't, I'd have created a small parish by now."

"Yeah, with a nice Italian girl like Vicki or Vanessa. Did you ever date a Veronica?"

Paul rubbed his chin. Licked his lips. "She had the best set of…"

Liz lobbed a towel creation, molded into a dog by their cabin steward who left it on the bed.

Paul caught it before it lost shape and fell to the floor. "I'm kidding. There was no Veronica. My past isn't exactly fodder for the *National Enquirer*." Paul amused himself with that.

"Speaking of V's." Paul reached a hanger with a V neckline from the closet. "Wear this tonight. I want the pleasure of peeling it off of your toned body. Very chic and totally Italian."

Liz shook her head. "You're not being serious."

"Quite serious." Setting the towel dog and the dress aside, Paul contained his lust. He tossed a stray compact into the now filled cosmetic case.

"You don't need all of this makeup to impress me." Paul sang a bar from "The First Time Ever I Saw Your Face."

"Stick to your day job." Liz smiled at his rendition and held up the dress. "I know how important family is. I come with a lot of baggage. As for major rifts: been there, done that."

"I'll take that all under advisement." Paul pulled Liz closer. "Practice a little mindfulness. You know, all that behavioral stuff, on this trip. We Italians savor the aroma, the smell, the taste of everything." Paul nibbled on her ear lobe.

"What if there's no cannoli on the menu?"

"Then, I ask for whipped cream," he crooned, "and I have you."

In Maryland, Maren headed straight from the Jaguar to the ladies room to steel herself.

She sat on the upholstered vanity bench, running a hand along the gold metal as she looked in the mirror. Rummaging through her purse, she then applied lipstick, finger fluffed her hair, worn long, and treated herself to a handful of scented lotion. Hands massaged together, her inner strength returned. Resolve really kicked in when the lavatory door pushed open.

"Maren." Pam jostled a diaper bag, slung over one shoulder, a bundle held snugly in her arms.

Maren stood. "This must be the little one." A buffer: something to talk about besides the fact that she slept with Steve.

"Four months old next week. Caden Bradley Carlton." Pam turned to showcase the baby, fully alert after having been changed. "He's got Jerry's eyes."

Did she throw that in to prove a point, Maren wondered. She touched the blanket that swaddled the baby in Pam's arms. "He's adorable." Managing a smile, she reached for the door.

Pam stepped forward. "Could I have just a minute…alone?"

"I suppose." Maren sat back down on the vanity cushion while Pam rocked Caden.

"I want you to know directly that I'm very sorry for the pain I've caused." Pam ping ponged her eyes from Caden to the florescent illumination hovering above. "I resurfaced in Steve's life right as he took up with you last year, and I never meant to interfere."

"Though you did." Maren wasn't about to fade into the delicate wallpaper. Her tone was factual, not hasty.

"Yes," Pam admitted. "Unintentionally. I don't expect you to believe that." Pam put Caden up to her shoulder and patted his bottom.

Why was it so difficult to despise a woman who coddled an infant?

"You're far superior, Maren, than I could ever attempt to be in so many respects." Pam's eyes caught Maren's and tried to lock them in a hold. "You mean everything to Steve. I convinced him to keep what happened from you, based upon… working with women. I've seen shock, agony."

Maren darted her focus to the floor. Pam continued. "Please know that I didn't intend to create a stir, and I don't have designs on your husband. I have one of my own that I love, and I'm trying to make amends with."

When another woman came to use the mirror, those comments got relegated to silence. Down the hall, Jerry found Steve at the bar.

"Scotch and soda," Jerry told the bartender. He parked himself on the stool next to Steve.

"I hear congratulations are in order," Steve offered. "I thought Pam was joining us?"

"Thank you," Jerry replied. "She's in the ladies room." When Steve cringed, Jerry asked, "Meeting up with Maren about now, huh?"

"Yeah," Steve breathed out, uneasily.

"While we're putting hard feelings out there, I know what occurred between you and Pam in New York." Jerry nodded thanks to the bartender's delivery of liquid calm. He took a swig.

"It wasn't planned." Steve clamped onto the wooden counter. "A clear mistake."

"Not revenge?"

"Actually…no." It was Steve's turn to down his Seven and Seven.

"Obviously with these new revelations regarding our daughter, your path and my wife's are bound to cross," Jerry said. "I hope you've gotten your fill of her."

"It won't happen again." Steve looked to the doorway as two wives and a baby approached. "I'm a happily married man."

Steve leapt from his stool to kiss Maren's cheek. Pam shifted the baby into Jerry's arms and made introductions for a little one who could only coo and squirm. "Shall we?" Steve asked, turning his palm to where the maître d' showed them to the table, nestled in a quiet corner as Steve had requested in the reservation.

The topic of New York got left with the empty bar glasses. Once they shared about marketing, Steve's job, and Pam's new administrative and publishing roles, their entrées signaled that time was a commodity. Chloé's name got used enough that to someone overhearing, it was as if a fifth chair had been pulled alongside their table.

"So play dates for a few hours when we're in town visiting Mom and Dad," Pam put forth. "Or when Jerry's in DC for business."

Steve nodded. "If later on we do choose a mutual vacation spot, I suggest a theme park again. Grants independence." All four affirmed that they had enjoyed Disney where Pam and Steve had attended a Florida conference and families could tag along. "Of course, DC has a ton of museums, locally."

Jerry turned to Maren. "Your former father-in-law…we've collaborated on a project or two in his Washington office."

"Better you than me," Maren answered. She briefly explained how she had turned down a job with the family firm, an offer that Jerry knew of. Maren shared how it, like all interactions with Walter and Mildred Mitchell, had not set well.

"How close are you to him?" Steve asked.

"Not very," Jerry answered. "Walter invited Pam and me to dinner next time we're both in the area, or if we care to visit Seattle."

"Steve, just say it," Pam interjected. Caden had snoozed quietly in his carrier until he began a slow fuss that earned him a cuddle in Pam's lap. She could still read Steve like a textbook and something didn't sit well, Pam could tell.

"Walter and Mildred Mitchell create nothing but trouble for us." Steve looked to his wife for permission to continue. "Broaching visitation here is far easier than discussing the topic with them." He mentioned the legal hassles and Dylan's adoption. "That said, discretion in what you share would be appreciated."

"Of course." Pam discreetly draped a cloth, unbuttoned her blouse, and snuggled Caden close. "Congrats on gaining a son. I remember Dylan at Disney, how he looked up to you."

Maren saw Pam about to nurse her baby. She cast Steve the tacit look-away command. Yet if Pam was a toxin to her husband, Maren knew that she had become more like a drug in Steve's system. He promptly peered into his plate and reached to clasp Maren's hand under the table. Her other hand rested on a baby bump, not yet evident this evening. "Go ahead, Steve. You're dying to say it."

"Something else about Walter Mitchell we should know?" Jerry inquired.

"That would keep us here past closing," Steve acknowledged. "Maren and I are expecting."

"I wondered," Pam admitted.

Steve rubbed his temples and shook his chin. If he didn't, he might chuckle at Pam.

"You really think I can't tell the signs of a pregnant woman?" Pam asked. "Four months?"

"Three," Maren replied. "Just past 12 weeks so we're telling people now. Dylan is thrilled."

"Congratulations," Jerry offered. "We ah…do agree that we wait until Chloé is older and establishes a satisfactory relationship with… your growing family…until we share."

Steve heard Jerry's voice trail off as if he couldn't bear sharing the daughter he had raised thus far. Steve saved him any further embarrassment stuttering around the topic.

"Agreed. No rush," Steve said. "Dylan already asks questions about siblings, where they come from. Explaining this won't be easy."

"Let's cross that bridge, in time," Jerry insisted. Ordering his third drink, Jerry had already announced to Pam that she was the designated driver since she sipped sparkling water.

Reluctantly, she agreed and admitted it took a year to get used to being behind the wheel again.

"I know a good book about where babies come from," Pam suggested. "From my column."

Maren compressed her lips. She reached into her purse for paper to write on. She hadn't used this dressy handbag since their wedding day. All she could find was a program, noticing a quote: *Therefore what God has joined together, let no one separate.*

She had paused. Quickly flipping it over, Maren explained her concentration lapse. "It's from our reception," she said. "The name of the book again?"

Pam spouted the title and author's last name. "Funny, I've been carrying something around that I got at that restaurant near West Riverside a year and a half ago."

Steve looked puzzled. Pam flashed the memory. "My Chinese fortune, after Dad's surgery. Conquer your fears or they will conquer you."

Having finished their meals, including Baby Caden who ceased his, all doubts about this much-needed negotiation got cleared away.

They exchanged no hugs, only firm handshakes between two families who agreed to be there for one little girl—a preteen who was responsible for nothing but the need to be loved.

The floating hotel for Liz and Paul had moored at Palermo on the island of Sicily as well as Naples, Livorno, outside of Pisa, and at a port town Liz could neither spell nor utter.

"Civitavecchia," Paul rolled off his tongue. He stretched an arm around Liz on the last train out of Rome before they boarded ship. "You look molta bella in those tight slacks and ankle boots."

"Grazie." Liz patted Paul's jacket and his tailored shirt collar. He wore Italian denim so well, she mused. She took postcards from her European-styled bag with its long neck strap. She had worn it around her neck while they visited the Vatican Art Museum and strolled through the boutique shops of Gucci, Armani, and others.

"The Sistine Chapel was amazing," Liz said. "I should have sent that card to your mother."

"That you sent one from Naples, her birthplace, and had it postmarked at the Vatican will score points." Paul flipped through a catalog he had picked up at La Perla with its provocative couture and Black Label Collection. "Mm, must we go to the second seating?"

"The juxtaposition of our two excursions amuses me," Liz snickered. "The Vatican and hot lingerie. You bought out that store."

"Wait 'til the package arrives." Paul nuzzled Liz. "Make sure the kids don't open it."

"Back to your question: Yes. We picked the late seating so that we could enjoy ports of call."

"Counting the hours until I get to enjoy this." He jostled the only La Perla bag they didn't ship. "Some things a man can't live without."

Liz relaxed her head on Paul's shoulder. She closed her eyes and snoozed for 20 minutes until their train screeched to its stop. They embarked the cruise vessel and hurriedly got showers before dressing for the last formal night.

Paul brought along his tux from the wedding. Liz already wore the gown that had matched so well then and again days ago. For tonight, she chose a beaded tulle dress, a silver geometric design with a jewel neckline, long sleeves, and straight miniskirt landing mid-thigh.

Was it any wonder the ship's photographer snapped away, posing Liz alone before dinner?

A bottle of Lambrusco set between them, their waiter brought chilled soup for Liz and lobster bisque for Paul. She chose Veal Scaloppini, though Paul had made it back home just as well, and he selected Prime Rib. He went with Tiramisu; warm chocolate lava cake literally melted in Liz's mouth. Her forkful taunted Paul.

"Talk about a turn on." He pried a knee between her legs, under the table. "Gives me a dozen delectable ideas."

"We're dancing after dinner," Liz announced.

She tightened her thighs and her gaze. "I better fit into this dress again. My cruise calorie reduction plan."

"He who is not impatient," Paul whispered, "is not in love." Liz puzzled him a glance. "Italian proverb." Paul laid his napkin down and scooted his chair. "Come, I want to watch your every move in that tight dress."

The pleasure wasn't Paul's alone as Liz captured the notice of several men in the disco. No man dared to intrude as Paul brushed against Liz. She shimmied to the strobes, the beat pulsating through her feet, up her legs. Paul pressed close to her until Liz was giddy and leaned on the wall once she staggered from the dance floor.

"Had enough?" he asked. Paul steadied Liz by the elbow, unsure if it was the Italian wine, the levity of all that activity or the subtle pitch and roll of the ship as they sailed back to Spain.

"Showing your age, Dr. Romano." Liz bit her lip. Pouted playfully. "Dare you to catch me."

At the challenge, Paul dashed after Liz who hustled through a corridor, taking the stairs down three levels to the deck that housed their stateroom. Paul jogged past one elevator bank, turned around, and jolted his head both ways. Liz clutched her stomach, doubled over in delight. She darted down a different hallway, hanging on to the railing once or twice. She nearly stumbled over an abandoned dinner tray from someone's late night bite.

When Liz reached their cabin, she suddenly realized Paul had the key since she hadn't taken an evening bag. Resigned to wait, she slipped her heels off and held the straps by a finger.

"You little vamp," he lodged in her ear as he came up behind. His weight pinned her against the door and he took his own late night nibble behind her ear. The key card freed the lock.

Liz stepped in. Tossed the shoes next to a pair of stilettos. "Look, more towel dogs." She scurried into the bathroom and latched the door.

Paul kicked off his shoes, stripped pieces of his tux, and picked up the two formations. Their cabin steward had fancied their every wish.

As soon as he had learned about Bruno and Franco, terry cloth became canine art each evening. Paul settled into terry cloth also and tied a knot loosely around his waist, stretching out on the bed.

When Liz opened the bathroom door, she brushed the switch with one hand and stepped into a cabin, darkened save for a dim glow.

Paul let out a low whistle even before Liz slid into stilettos. "Sneaky aren't you?" His elbow protruded as he shifted one hand behind his head and settled into a mound of pillows.

She twirled on her tiptoes in the teddy. "You like?"

Who would have thought baby-doll would beguile so? La Perla was worthy of every Euro Paul had spent on it, he mused, moistening his lips. He stretched his arm and hands to Liz, yearning to fondle the sheer lingerie. It hardly hid the satiny strip clasping black stockings that ran the curve of Liz's legs.

Paul got a better glimpse of those when she kneed her way across the bed. "Like?" Paul fingered the fabric. Massaged through it. "You make my mouth water for you."

Liz looked into the mirrored panel just above the headboard. Yes, he had done well today, she thought admiring the gift for her, and very clearly for him, also.

"You know, you're rather outrageously sexy lying there yourself," she managed. Liz moved a hand slowly along Paul's face while her other hand fingered terry cloth. Then, she yanked the white tie.

The cloth had separated domestic urges from wilder ones.

"A vixen you are." Paul dragged her close. He kissed her hard and kissed her long in a pulse-scrambling twist of mouths and tongues.

When Liz broke for air, she curled the lips he had just tasted. She grazed down the line of masculine hair on his chest. She lifted her face. "I sailed to Italy with a mixed nut."

"Careful what you ask for." Paul's endorphins had already gotten a rush at the disco, through Liz's crazy corridor chase, and now, as her lips feathered his happy trail...sweet Jesus. What she could do to him! She could have asked for the statue of David, and he would have found a way to seize it for Liz.

Paul threw his head back, drowning in her. She stole his breath, his senses, his mind. "Liz." He could hardly get her name out. He needed air. He needed her.

Paul eased fabric over her hips. He unclasped the black garter, leaving stockings to encase those sexy limbs. Then he rolled Liz, tangling sheets and compressing pillows. To hell with the shoes and the La Perla, which had blindsided him. Save for silky legs, the mirror reflected nothing but naked beauty.

She laced stockings around Paul like ivy on a vine. Urgency swamped Liz. She consumed him, called out his name in a throaty moan. Her hands clung, one holding onto him, another fisted into a pillow, as if she required a lifeline to save her from the tremors of pleasure. They had all night. And they used it well.

When the tension depleted them both, Paul pulled back to quell his jagged breath. Liz tightened her grip on his sated muscles. She stroked his suddenly lazy body as she lay on his chest. With a satisfied gleam in her eyes, she announced, "I came, I saw, I conquered."

Belly bouncing, Paul moved them both with his chuckle. "That's my line," he whispered. He stroked Liz's hair, down her shoulders, and clutched her close.

As he stifled a sudden flood of emotion, Liz fingered the Figaro gold chain. "Honey, what?"

"You are so special," he said. "I set out for this to be a reprieve for you. You never get away. You do so much for people, your two kids, now me." Paul cupped her face. "You literally saved me this past year."

"That's the sweetest pillow talk I've heard." Liz brushed lips on his forehead. "You've added so much to my life that I never expected."

Stray hair fell onto Liz's brow, and Paul brushed it back. "Then let me add something else. Close your eyes," he commanded.

Paul nudged her aside, turned her head into the pillows to get up, but quickly returned. "Keep your eyes closed. Just trust me here."

Paul rummaged, slid a drawer open and then closed it. "No peeking." He shifted weight closer to her. "Another thing I'm a little rusty at..."

When Liz felt a sudden chill surge around her throat, her breath hitched. Paul puffed out relief. "All right, open your eyes."

Liz's fingers latched on to a fine metal rope around her neck. She fingered her way to the clasp and slid up to the mirror, for a torso view. She wore nothing, only a necklace that reflected gold. "It's beautiful," she gasped. Liz nestled back into Paul's arms. "When did you buy this?"

"Not recently," Paul confessed. "Let me tell a story. Begins with a different trip to Italy..."

By the end of what he shared, tears streamed out of Liz's eyes. "I don't know what to say. Are you sure you want me to have it?"

"I'm following instructions. I've thought about this." Paul rubbed Liz's left hand, lingering where she once wore jewelry. "It's all I have right now. We'll figure out the rest."

"Paul," Liz breathed. "I love you so much."

"We need to be together," he vowed. "No one gets to judge whether we should be, though the Kramer and the Romano families don't feud. Good history there." Liz nodded.

"Will you have me?" Their eyes caught and held. "And a family that fits into the Colosseum?"

"Yes." Liz stunned herself with a quick reply. "I mean it." She laughed. "And la famiglia!"

Paul pulled her into his arms and launched into a smoldering kiss. They held each other into the night, lavishing more love on one another, again and again, until eventually the Mediterranean Sea lulled them fast asleep.

Chapter 21

Without domestic duties and work, Liz and Paul could be themselves. It was May. With suitcases stashed, Liz returned to being Mom, chief of emptying the dishwasher and cleaning up messes. Dr. Romano met his new partners and set up practice on Maryland's Eastern Shore.

"Remember Tyler, I'm paying you to clean up the back yard," Paul reminded. "Chores first, swimming second."

"Hannah doesn't have chores," Tyler argued. "Besides, you're not my dad. You're a renter."

"Hannah is four. You're seven and a half."

"Almost eight," Tyler proclaimed.

"Even better…now scoot!" The surgeon tone he had left behind at West Riverside came in handy as he stayed half of most weeks at Liz's, relegated to the top guest suite.

It was 6:15 when Paul heard pebbles pushed aside by Liz's tires. Minutes later she slid open the second story sliding glass door.

Franco and Bruno scurried up the stairs of the deck, filling their lungs with Liz. Approving that she belonged there, they both quickly retreated to the grill. Better aroma: Steak.

"How was your day?" Liz asked Paul, who stood in shorts, a polo shirt, and sandals. A tray with pasta salad, plates, forks that sat nearby on the table was a greeting in itself.

"Getting used to the staff, protocols." Paul lowered the flame. "I put four steaks on the grill. Eric is stopping by and the kids can share one."

"OK. What's Eric coming by for, outside of free food?" A crooked smile formed on Liz.

The grub improved significantly when Paul worked on Kent Island. His insistence on paying to stay in the guest room helped her to maintain possession of her house. It had taken her three extra paychecks at West Riverside to finally catch up on the mortgage after Tim's financial disregard, and a fourth to pay off the credit card.

"Eric has a morning interview for an internship. Asked if he could bunk with Tyler." Paul flipped the meat. He craned his neck to see if Tyler was doing as he was told.

He wasn't. "Tyler. What did I ask you to do?"

Tyler strutted quickly to the patio after he heard his mother was home. "I don't have to listen to you. This isn't your house. It's really Dad's. You helped Mom steal it."

"Tyler Phillips, I've had enough." Liz plopped into an Adirondack. "Since we've been back, your mouth is worse. Don't concern yourself with who owns this property. If you must know, your father and I settled that in our divorce. I own it. He got other things. Case closed."

"No, you stole it!"

"To your room," Liz said with jaw-clenching authority. "Right this minute. One...two..."

When Tyler stomped off, she bumped her head against the Adirondack wood. Paul closed the grill and put the tongs aside. "I had to use that tone earlier with him."

Tears welled in Liz's eyes. "I thought after I called him out a few times, he might learn. Why do I get the impression that the extent of Tim's grooming Tyler runs so much deeper?"

"Because it did, Liz." Paul put out his hand as he saw Liz's control slip a notch. "You had so much stress right after the holidays, but I caught, overheard actually, mere feet away, Tim instructing Tyler and Hannah to steal from you."

Liz's face fell. Her lips formed a stiff, impassive line. "This really is something I wish you would have told me, Paul. Stress or no stress."

"I tried to protect you." Paul squeezed her hand. When she blinked and grew disheartened, he changed the subject. "How was your day?"

"Same old." Liz lost her disdain in a glass of iced water she had brought out with her. "Hal sent another edict: All therapists become independent contractors starting July 1st. No more withheld taxes, less flex time, and we have what, 45 days, to find other health insurance?"

"He can't set your schedule and claim that you're all independent," Paul replied. "And that's only one IRS sniff test."

"Hal makes his own rules." Liz slid a refreshing gulp down her throat. It chilled her nicely. "Reminds me of my ex." She cupped her mouth. "Where's Hannah? I should watch what I say."

"No worries," Paul said. He closed the lid on the grill and took a seat nearby. "I should wake her up. She seemed really tired." Paul brushed a hand over Liz's hair. "Like you."

"I've been exhausted all day." Liz leaned her head onto Paul. "What do I do? Ask Dr. Chen to up my hours and commute south of Annapolis most days?" Liz still had on her work attire of casual slacks, a short-sleeved blouse and dressy sandals. "At least this is close."

"Dinner's almost ready," Paul said. "Come with me tonight. Eric can watch these two. He'll be here any minute."

"Why? Where are we going?"

"It'll all become clear when we get there," Paul assured her. At that, he got up. "How 'bout you check on Hannah and change. I need to keep an eye on the grill, and I'll set the table."

An offer too good to refuse, Liz made Tyler apologize. After dinner, the kids got pool time with Uncle Eric. A short swim since they had school and daycare the next day. It gave Paul a chance to chauffeur Liz in his Corvette, which he didn't drive that much with either the boys or Liz's kids needing the extra room of an SUV.

"Why are we visiting offices right next to loser's building? I mean the one Tim got in our settlement. After Hal's news, I'd have been better off getting that instead of the house."

"You're grousing," Paul pointed out, sliding Armani to his head. He slammed the door on his Vet. "Come see." Paul slipped a key for after-hours access. They walked to elevator bank.

Once onto the second floor, Liz stared at Paul, perplexed. "This building is vacant," she said. "Built last year. If you think I can afford to rent here, Italian pirates have captured your brain."

"You could make darker circles form under my eyes, 'ya know that?" He opened the door to a large suite, its door just down the hall from the elevators. Waiting area chairs faced a counter with desks behind it. Paul led her through the door to the left. "My partners and I just leased this for our practice. We move later this summer."

Liz peeked into the shiny exam rooms and the counter space for physicians and assistants. Void of equipment, it wasn't hard to visualize. "Nice. I'm happy for you."

Paul flicked off the light switch and paraded Liz again past the rows of chairs in reception. "Now over on this side…" He opened the door and flicked on more fluorescents. "Offices."

Liz looked around. "Which one is yours?"

"Haven't chosen." He laughed. "Hey, some things don't change."

Paul stopped Liz by the window in one large office where they stood. "We don't need all this space. The entire side of this building."

"So why are we standing in it?" Liz's impatience signaled her fatigue and an unending day.

"Because, the three over here. They're yours."

"What?" Her lips parted in surprise. "I told you I cannot possibly afford a large rent tab. I'd be evicted for late payment."

"Not if the landlord is…kind and patient…and loves you like I do."

"You would be my landlord?" Liz smiled but sighed. "Look, I know you mean well, Paul. But I wanted to take this step, whenever I can manage my own business, independently."

"I'm not just the landlord. Our group bought the building. We need to gain a few tenants." He cupped her chin. "I'll work out very favorable terms. This is your start. I have full faith in you."

Liz surveyed the multi-room suite. "Could I sublet the other offices?" Liz let the thought sink in and returned to the window where Paul waited. "Is that allowed in the lease?"

"Oh, it's allowed." Paul's mischievous smile spread higher.

Liz walked closer. She flashed a wide grin and kissed him sweetly. "What about dual relationships, with my landlord?"

"I'm not your patient, and you're not mine darlin'." Paul smirked. "I think there's a clause encouraging drop-in visits." His lips brushed hers. "To check on the property, of course."

"Yeah…the property."

A week later, Liz signed the lease. The kids were away until Tim would return them the next morning for Mother's Day.

No longer being pulled into surgeries, Paul worked better hours though he saw patients one Saturday each month in his new private practice.

He agreed to meet Maren and Liz in St. Michaels. The women had chosen to eat along the harbor, outdoors on a restaurant deck. Furry family members, meaning well-behaved dogs, were always welcome. The bar attendant even kept a bowl of biscuits under the counter.

Liz spotted Paul and waved. She jumped up to take one leash while Paul tethered Bruno.

"Ciao." Paul pecked Maren's cheek. He gave the down hand signal to his furry companion. "Did you ladies boost the local economy?"

"I found Steve's anniversary gift and things for the baby's room. Plus a name book." It lay face down on the table between Maren and Liz.

Paul looked at Maren's more pregnant profile as she sat under an umbrella, glowing from more than the bright sun. "You both look wonderful," he told Liz, quickly brushing lips against hers.

Liz wore a short-sleeved blouse and slacks. "As do you in your polo and khakis. Working on the shore must suit you," Liz said.

"Sure does," he quipped. "Not finishing that?"

Paul eyed Liz's plate with another crab cake, some vegetables and coleslaw remaining.

"Appetite's off," Liz said. "Since I'm having it out with Hal Monday, a little worried he will have a cow, or my head when he finds out Betty agreed to come back to work, in my practice."

"Didn't he let her go?" Maren asked.

"He did." Liz sipped some iced tea through a straw. "That doesn't mean anything. People can get ugly when you transition to a solo gig."

"He doesn't own you," Paul said. At Liz's invitation he feasted on the rest of her lunch. Bruno and Franco panted with anticipation. "I spotted the forms you created. They look great."

"Maren helped with the graphic design." Liz smiled. "Did you see Tyler's good work?"

"Vacuum marks on the carpet? Yes, I did." Paul took a last bite and pushed the plate aside.

"Bruno may have a little PTSD," Liz admitted. "Tyler terrorized him with the sweeper."

"Poor pup." Maren patted his head. Bruno cushioned himself against Maren for attention. "Dylan's been asking for a dog."

Paul rubbed his chin. "Canine cousins."

He slid his chair back as Franco stirred and he didn't want to risk him levitating the table. "Down," Paul told him.

"Because introducing two siblings..." Maren stopped. "I mean a baby is enough change."

She dabbed her lips with her napkin and took extra seconds to lower the cloth. Maren eyed Liz cautiously. She darted her eyes to Paul, who remained silent regarding her slip.

"Pretend I didn't make that plural," Maren admitted when Liz locked her into a mutual stare.

Liz instantly lunged into explanation. "I sensed something was up. One day, Paul and I..."

"I don't need details," Maren interjected. "Steve wanted to tell your Mom about Chloé first. He's on call and will talk to her since she has a committee meeting at the hospital."

"I was shocked, Paul can tell you," Liz added. She paused.

"I don't know how Mom will take it," Liz raised. "Eric bombed half his classes in grad school, and he's been lying around the bayside house feeling sorry for himself because Shelly dumped him."

"I heard she had her reasons." Maren glanced only at the dogs.

"Since you brought up sibling introductions…" Liz said. Arched eyebrows made the transition that words found difficult to broach.

"We have Chloé for a day next weekend." Maren added the last drop of lemon juice into her iced water, squeezing the lemon dry. "A break-the-ice kind of visit. We're calling it a play date of sorts since the kids had fun together at Disney last year."

"Does Chloé know anything?" Paul asked. "Will you tell Dylan?"

"Negative on Dylan, and not until she's older, we all agreed." Maren fingered the top rim of her water glass. "She is a cute little girl. When everything came out…months ago," Maren admitted, "I unloaded in Luke's office."

"My objectivity was a little shot with my own circumstances." Liz smiled. "What did he say?"

"Yeah." Maren wrinkled her lips. "We talked about Chloé being innocent in all of this, the trauma endured with the accident, and her recovery. She deserves to know Steve, and he to establish a relationship with her." Maren straightened in her chair. "Luke reminded me how Dylan benefited from that after Mark died. The more caring adults in a child's life the better," she said. "I'm willing to be one of those."

The three pondered that. Paul motioned for the bill. Before Liz could respond, Paul preemptively said, "Tyler will get there. We had a heart-to-heart talk before you got home yesterday."

"See, tell her," Maren piped in. "You're a great influence for Tyler."

"Tyler asked me if he could get a therapist like you, Liz." Paul grinned. "I think we'll skip your colleagues in Hal's office." He saw Liz smile but remain silent. "He said he knows the stuff Tim fills his head with isn't true. He actually started crying about it."

"Really?" Liz's eyes blinked away tears.

"I have just the book," Maren said. "Vicki loaned me *The Angry Child* last year." Maren winced. "I've needed it."

"Bequeath it," Paul suggested. "Any nuggets?"

"Yes, in fact." Maren took a last sip of iced water. "When there's light to be seen, children will see it."

She grasped Liz's hand. Shook it. "I know from the times the Mitchells have said things about Steve and me that it's not easy to see the effect on your child. Wasn't it you who told me the closest distance between two points is a straight line? Even in relationships?"

"I did." Liz nodded. "My own therapy words back at me."

Paul tucked his credit card back into his wallet. "Don't forget this book," he reminded Maren. "Any good picks for Baby Kramer?"

"We'd love a nautical name." Maren picked up her place in the book, licked her index finger and turned to the nautical-sounding first names. "For boys: Brendan...the patron saint of sailors, Finn...ah, no, or Noah...hm," Maren turned the page. "Girls have many more options: Brooke, Catalina, Dawn, Serena." She stopped, lowering the book to the table. "Anyway...

Liz, now curious, picked up the tome. "Oh come on...Mother's Day karma." She continued from the list. Liz scrolled her eyes to catch where Maren had left off.

"On second thought." She cringed and eased the book to Paul, pointing to one name: Morgan. "Let's focus on being happy...for Mother's Day!"

On Monday, Liz saw adults in the morning, a couple on their lunch break and two teenagers following school. She locked her files, filled her time sheet, and left it in the bin by Hal's office.

"Liz, I'll take that," Hal said, palm turned for Liz to deposit her income stream into it. "Did you sign the new contract, with my changes?"

Liz turned away to reach the sheet of paper. Hiding her face, she filled her lungs with air, grabbed the document and deposited it into Hal's greedy hand. "Not on Mother's Day, Hal."

"I need it this week," Hal insisted.

"The memo says the return date is next week."

"Well, let's just get it done."

Liz steeled him a look. "No, let's not actually."

Fatigued as if it was four hours later, Liz leaned into the doorjamb. "I had planned to catch you earlier, but you were on the phone. End of June, I'm leaving Better Days Therapy."

Hal sat back. "To do what? You're divorced. Don't you need a job?"

Captain Obvious! "Yes, Hal, on both counts." Liz faked a smile. "I'm working out the details."

Many plans she had committed to her positive thoughts journal for years, and the remainder she had brainstormed with Paul ever since he had shown her the office suite. "My contract states I need to give you at least 30 days notice. I'm giving you slightly more."

"You know you can't take clients?"

"Clients have free choice in their therapy, Hal, but if anyone does follow me, I will honor the pay-back clause for the months it mandates."

"You need to tell me who plans to continue with you, when they schedule, and why they're seeing you." Hal shot back. "You must."

Tired as she was, Liz straightened her spine. "That's not in my contract, just the percentage of earnings, for six months. Period. I'm not obligated to disclose the details of therapy to anyone."

"Yes, you have to."

If Hal wanted to modify federal privacy laws like 12-year-olds changed rules mid-Monopoly, Liz was determined to send him straight back to Go without collecting. "No," she repeated.

"You're fired then."

"What?" Liz replied. "That's baseless."

By the time Liz reached home, she couldn't remember what else she had interjected into that argument. Hal heard none of it. Stunned, Liz only remembered tossing a few frames, her stash of herbal tea, some hand lotion and a tube of lipstick out of her desk into the too-small box Hal had handed her.

"Really, he watched your every move?" Paul asked incredulously when Liz set the box down on the kitchen island. "And didn't answer your questions about health insurance?"

"I'm surprised he didn't follow me into the restroom," she said. "Darn, I left my favorite water bottle. I need a glass. I'm hot suddenly."

"Always hot to me." Paul smirked. "I'll buy you a new one." He turned to retrieve a glass from the cabinet, but his hand never made it to the water dispenser. He turned to the thud.

"Liz…" Paul rushed over to find her sprawled on the hardwood. He listened for her breathing, felt for a pulse, then grabbed a thick dictionary and Hannah's Barbie case to raise Liz's feet.

"What happened?" She came to seconds later. "I'm…on the floor."

"You fainted. Don't get up just yet," Paul told her. "I'll get water."

He brought her a glass and propped her to sip a little at a time, watching her intently. "When was the last time you ate something?"

"Half a sandwich at lunch," Liz answered. "With some iced tea."

"You shouldn't be that dehydrated." Paul studied her. "Maybe I should take you over to the office…run some labs."

"Honey, I'm fine." Liz palmed the floor, attempting to get up.

Paul pulled up a seat next to her and helped her into the chair she had teetered out of minutes before. "I'm sorry…I just…"

Liz clutched him close. Felt his heart racing. "I scared you didn't I?"

"Hell yeah!"

"I didn't mean to." Liz kept up tiny whispers into Paul's ear.

"That's the sweetest thing I've heard in a long time." He cupped Liz's chin.

"Are you OK?" Liz asked. Paul smiled to reassure her, and she leaned her head into him.

"There's been a lot going on. Vacation spoiled us," Paul said. "I think that Ocean City trip we have planned will benefit us as well as Steve and Maren. I'll talk to them. We'll make it special." He rubbed Liz's left hand, idling at one finger.

Words failed Liz. "You're kidding?" Her eyes bugged, flummoxed. "Just like that? We can't hijack their weekend. We're their guests."

"Yes, just like that. Leave the details to me."

Neither Paul's impulsive plan nor Liz's ideas usurped anything Maren or Steve had intended for their joint weekend getaway. When Maren found out how the weekend would play out, she gladly ceded the details to Paul and Liz.

On the outskirts of Ocean City, the beach house for Memorial Day provided plenty of room for the Kramer and Romano clans. Late Friday, the sounds of a rattling muffler announced Vinny and Isabella Romano's arrival.

"Your shop doesn't carry auto parts, I take it?" Steve asked.

Maren nudged him as soon as the words left his lips. "So nice to see you again," Maren greeted as she stood up from the rocker on the front porch. "Under happier circumstances."

"You get bigger," Isabella exclaimed after taking one look at Maren, approaching six months into her pregnancy. She pinched Steve's cheek. "You proud?"

"Oh very," he replied. "Let me take those clothes upstairs for you." Steve snatched the dry cleaning bag as well as Isabella's suitcase.

"That Paul, he told me to bring a dress…for the beach?" Isabella appeared perplexed. A faint ocean breeze warmed everyone's skin. Maren opened the door for Paul's mother.

The dining room table, with a large tray of Italian cookies, immediately captured Mrs. Romano's eye. Isabella feasted her vision next on the purple tapers sticking out of glittering gold candlesticks. Silk floral arrangements lay gathered on another table, including a large bouquet of tumbling lilacs, a few sprays of deep purple, and the scent of fresh oregano blossoms.

Vinny lowered his sunglasses. "Hey bro, so happy for you." He shook Paul's hand as he appeared, Liz at his side. "Giovanni said they checked in at their hotel and Margherita and Rosa are there, too."

"Glad you could bring Ma. Emilio and Ava arrive tomorrow."

Isabella Romano walked around the room, considering the atmosphere, the trappings. She narrowed her eyes to her son. "What you do with all this?" she asked, one hand cupping the air.

Paul walked closer to lay both hands on her shoulders. "Ma, we're celebrating a special day. Two of them," Paul admitted. "Steve's anniversary a few weeks ahead and…our wedding."

"Wedding?" Isabella sat down. Narrowed her eyebrows to her oldest son, who took a seat beside her. "You and Liz?"

"No Ma, me and Sophia Loren!" Paul winked at the others. "Yes, I wanted it to be a surprise."

Isabella was taken aback. She fisted a magazine from the end table and fanned herself. "Vinny, you know about this?" she asked.

Paul spoke. "I tipped him off yesterday to be sure you came."

"I didn't bring you a gift," Isabella muttered.

"I did," Vinny spoke up. "Well, more like a surprise for the bride. Here Liz," he said. Vinny handed her a gift-wrapped box.

Liz tore off some paper. "This isn't for Paul?" She puzzled a look at her future brother-in-law.

"No, but I did ask him about it," Vinny replied. Paul smiled at his brother, resting a hand on his shoulder, as they all watched Liz tear open the gift and lift the lid.

"This…how?" Her mouth parted wide. She fingered the gold watch and lifted the brooch from the velvet box. "Where did you find these? I thought I lost them forever."

"They yours?" Isabella asked. Liz nodded, eyes fixed hopefully on an answer.

"I went to a trade show in Baltimore recently," Vinny explained. "When people sell homes, they often leave stuff behind. I gave out cards...like these." Vinny handed Liz one bearing the descriptor: Crazy Vinny's Pawn Shop, just like the other four he'd given Liz prior to this.

"So I met up with this guy who asked me if I could get him a good price on these things," he continued. "When he gave me his card, I got suspicious. I called Paul."

"It was him," Paul confirmed, a gloating smile taking shape. Hannah and Tyler ran in and out, thus he had to choose his words carefully. "I told Vinny to stall, get a written receipt from...the supposed owner who claimed them, and to take them into possession to research them."

"Wow!" Delight edged Liz's lips higher. "And..." She motioned.

"End of story. Forgeddaboutit!" Paul winked.

"Paul?"

"Liz, I've had a few words with him over the months." Paul took Liz's chin in the palm of his hand. "Emphasis on few, but between those words and a little mention of a well-connected Uncle Guido he doesn't want to mess with... Tim's not messin' with us either." A wicked grin emerged on Paul's face.

"Works all the time," Vinny said. He considered. "Probably got me kicked out of Catholic school, too. Oops," he acknowledged with his mother close by. "Sorry, Ma."

"You're great, Vinny." Liz rose and squeezed him tight. She loosened her grip. "Do you really have a scary Uncle Guido?"

Marry Paul, marry the mobster. Really?

"Hell no," Vinny whispered. "It's like Mr. Robinson's Neighborhood on *Saturday Night Live*. We use it when we need to."

Liz groaned. You really do marry the family, she thought, and hers was now walking in the door as Dolores and Bill arrived. They carried in their bags and a large gift basket. Liz had given them the heads up also just this week. The caterer followed soon after.

Food and conversation distracted Isabella from the shock of her son's sudden announcement, and a nightcap of Amaretto helped ease the idea that no priest would bless this union. Paul half-promised he'd seal the deal a second time in Pittsburgh for their hometown friends.

The following morning Liz and Paul took a walk on the beach before they would meet with their minister one last time.

"This feels so surreal." Liz wore a short lavender sundress and stepped gingerly through the moist sand in her bare feet as the waves lapped in. Paul rolled his pants up to enjoy the ocean currents.

The sun had just minutes ago peeked out of the horizon filling the sky with a mix of purple, yellow, gold, and lavender and part of the ocean appeared black at this hour. "Hey, our favorite colors." Liz directed Paul's attention to the light hitting the water's surface.

"Purple at *my* wedding." He laughed.

"And such a snap decision to just…do this." Liz leaned and Paul entwined her in his arms.

"When it's right, and you know it in your heart, it takes but a second to decide." He kissed her tenderly. "We have a busy day ahead. This may be a rare moment alone."

"I love you," Liz whispered.

"Amoré." He squeezed her. They had that engraved on their rings.

Ocean City was a close enough day trip for guests to join them on the beach at six o'clock, as the sun shone down and started its evening decent. The ceremony began with Hannah scattering purple flower petals from her white basket to where Paul stood.

Tyler, puffing his shoulders when people told him he looked handsome, latched on to Hannah's arm, brushing against her purple satin dress as he escorted her over sheeting placed atop the sand. Maren stood in a sleeveless lavender maternity dress when she walked after the kids. Steve, always Paul's best man, flanked him.

The strains of Pachelbel, Canon in D, played as Liz paced the few feet to Paul, with a gentle waft of air kicking in that evening and fewer than 60 people attending—most family, but a few close friends.

"You're stunning," he whispered to his bride, slanting an approving eye. Liz returned the silent appraisal. Armani always suited Paul well.

She wore a simple white cocktail dress flared at the skirt to show off legs as the hem fell just above her knees. A purple sash hugged Liz's waist. At her neck, Liz wore the glittering gold chain Paul had presented as a promise of their devotion, and she knew this union was blessed on so many levels.

Eric had pulled himself out of his recent moping to sing a rendition of "Love Will Be Our Home." Two of Paul's sisters read Scripture. Ava read from Genesis that the Lord declared it was not good for man to be alone. Rosa cited Ecclesiastes that two are better than one.

Liz handed her bouquet to Maren as she and Paul recited traditional vows and he placed a gold ring enhanced with diamonds on her finger.

They hadn't even had time to shop for a separate engagement ring. She slid a gold band likewise onto Paul's finger.

After the minister pronounced them husband and wife, Liz slid easily into Paul's arms for a 20-second kiss that ended with applause.

Bruno and Franco enjoyed the beach. Bribed by treats to pose for photographs meant that they, too, got hors d'oeuvres before their meal.

Guests dined at the beach house on Maryland crab cakes, beef, or chicken marsala. Champagne had a gold tint while the wine and sparkling grape juice flowed purple. The caterer had been instructed to serve Rolling Rock or Iron City Light for those preferring beer. Jade Chen had been invited, but declined with a note that wished them both well.

"I'm so happy for you," Pam breathed into Paul's ear as she wrapped her arms around him. She and Jerry couldn't stay long, needing to get back to their kids.

"Did you get wedding cake? Take some home." Paul whispered his thanks, for supporting him over the many months. He lingered at Pam's ear. She hugged him again. "Congratulations!"

Pam's embrace was more perfunctory for Liz, but then they had a different history, one Liz knew she would have to put aside.

"Pamela." Dolores Kramer had stepped out of the front door's path as guests exited.

Pam compressed her lips and forced them to curl. "Dolores," she said. "How are you?" Pam looked at the corner of the porch where no one sat or stood. She stepped three feet with Dolores Kramer following.

"Shocked, frankly," Dolores admitted.

"Steve's spoken to you?"

"He did." Dolores repositioned her coffee, the black brew slopping over the cup's rim into the saucer. Two weeks was hardly enough time to adjust to having acquired an older granddaughter.

"I know you must hate me for what I've done to Steve…to your family," Pam admitted. The pain wouldn't easily remit, Pam recognized in Dolores's disdain. "I don't expect you to forgive me. I am sorry how I managed things then."

"I don't hate, Pamela," Dolores acknowledged. "This will take time. I'd best keep my remarks to that. Today."

Of all the memories she had slipped deep into her mind, Pam Morgan instantly recalled the icy stare Steve's mother slid her.

"I'm happy for Liz and Paul," Pam offered, swallowing hard. "As I'm sure you are." Pam darted eyes from the front porch floorboards to the car she saw Jerry drive up. "I must be going."

"Have a safe trip." Dolores said nothing more.

Steve approached and took a seat. He gathered what may have happened and squeezed her hand. Steve immediately set his beer aside to slide a little purple angel onto his lap.

"Uncle Steve, bad news," Hannah started.

"What could possibly be bad news on such a happy day?"

Hannah tugged on Steve's dress shirt, since he had removed his suit jacket and tie hours ago. "I can't be your sweetheart any more."

Hannah held up five widely spread fingers to hold off the gaping mouth ready to resist. "No tears, I still love you, but you have Aunt Maren now, and a baby in her tummy."

She leveled Steve a look—inherited, learned, or both from his side of the family. "I have to be Paul's sweetheart now." Hannah paused. "Cause his little darling went to heaven."

Hearing her rationale, Steve drew Hannah tight. "I'm still your best uncle, right?"

Hannah pursed her lips and put a finger to them while bobbing her head. Steve shook her with his hearty laugh.

"Steve." Maren peeked her head out the door. "You had your toast, now Paul's making one."

Steve stepped inside, faked a pout since Maren had overheard his letdown on the front porch. He slid his arm around her waist and patted her where Baby Kramer hung out.

"Everyone," Paul began. "Thanks for joining us as Liz and I celebrate the start of our lives together. Please enjoy your desserts. There are cookies and a new tray of cannoli we just put out." Paul turned to envelope Liz under one arm.

"You know over a year ago, Bill Kramer. Hey, I really can call you Dad now! OK, Dad gave a toast to Steve and Maren upon their engagement. His recipe for true contentment in life, he called it. With his blessing, I may amend percentages."

Isabella Romano sat on the sofa, a plate of Italian cookies in her lap. Vinny nursed an Iron City Light near his Italian family members and assorted friends who strained to listen.

"The recipe starts with work you love for 15 percent of that true contentment. Liz and I have done that. We have outside interests, another five, represented by different loyalties and colors, but we're working that out." Everyone chuckled.

"Luck accounts for five easily," Paul stated. "Having the right person by your side, another 45 percent, when you know hands-down it's the perfect choice—it's not hard to decide." More laughter sprinkled through the living and dining area of the beach house.

"I hear some murmuring at my math," Paul continued. "There's 30 percent to account for. Tyler gets ten, Hannah ten herself, and well, the gift of new life here for the final ten percent, for true contentment for our Kramer-Romano team."

Paul patted Liz's abdomen and nuzzled a kiss into a thatch of her short brown hair. "Yes, you heard me correctly. Next January: another blessing appears in our lives."

Liz gazed up at her husband. She pulled Tyler, who was standing close, in for a shoulder pat. Hannah sprinted fast for Paul to jiggle her into his arms.

"In time for playoffs," Bill kidded, with a gentle shoulder slap. He captured Hannah and eased his excited granddaughter to the floor.

"We're happy for you." Dolores embraced her third son, officially.

"Your second chance at being a PaPa," Isabella offered. She hugged Paul first then thrust Liz into her arms. "I...Nonna now."

One more shock hadn't done Isabella in. Liz smiled happily.

"The way the two of you have reinvented your lives," Bill added. "You needn't ask my permission to alter the formula. I'd say you nailed it."

"Sure did!" Paul's grin boasted with multiple meaning.

Dolores blushed. Isabella looked thoroughly muddled. Bill laughed. And the bride? She did what she always did best and slanted her new, ever amusing husband a loving Liz look!

The End

If you've enjoyed this, please consider leaving
a star rating and a few remarks on
Amazon.com or BN.com under
the paperback option as this supports
future work and readership of the series!

Acknowledgments

I couldn't continue this series if it weren't for readers I have connected with via signings, social media, happenstance, and pockets of fans. When you recommend this to friends, write a positive review, or purchase as gifts, it's the ultimate compliment!

My test readers, who have read early drafts, told me what I needed and bolstered me when I thought I had already found the last synonym on the planet. Kathy, Mary Lee, Patty, Audrey, Bill, and Sue pushed me to make this better. Special thanks to Bruno, lending his name and helping my Italian; and to Karen, not only for her work on tight shoulders and "mouse arm," but for enlightening me about team purple. Judy edited and challenged; Ariel added helpful research; Andy Brown created fantastic covers; Cheryl at Maryland Transportation Authority and Brent kept history straight.

Given medical and legal elements, I owe Jim, Alyce, Bobbie, Alyssa, Gina, Karen and Lynn gratitude for answering questions and reading for accuracy. You are all why readers tell me my writing comes across as real.

Local retailers have invited me into stores, hosting signings and recommending the novels. Their shops are local treasures that I continue to promote. My husband Bob read, answered questions, and offered feedback. Amoré! Finally, the Eastern Shore Writers Association has introduced me to much talent and many new friends.

About the Author

Lauren Monroe is a novelist residing on Maryland's Eastern Shore. A Pittsburgh native, she grew up around boats and the beautiful scenery of Western Maryland, later moving to the Washington, D.C. suburbs before settling across the Bay Bridge. Various experiences shape her writing including marriage, family, friendships, a graduate degree in the social sciences, and both of her career paths as an author and counselor. She enjoys reading, boating, swimming, biking, good food, and travel. Lauren Monroe is a pen name for her fiction. *Letting Go: Book One of The Maryland Shores* was her first novel and the first book in this series.

Follow series at Goodreads and at: *www.laurenmonroenovels.com*
www.facebook.com/lauren.monroe.novels
www.pinterest.com/novelistlaurenm

www.ingramcontent.com/pod-product-compliance
Lightning Source LLC
Chambersburg PA
CBHW071233250626
47163CB00001B/164